PRAISE FOR ALEXIS HALL'S LONDON CALLING UNIVERSE

"Brilliance on every single page."

—**Christina**

"It's a fun, frothy, quintessentially British rom-com about a certified chaos demon and a stern brunch daddy with a heart of gold faking a relationship."

—**Talia Hibbert**, *New York Times* bestselling author

"Every once in a while you read a book that you want to SCREAM FROM ROOFTOPS about. I'm screaming, people!"

—**Sonali Dev**, award-winning author

"FAKE DATING, REAL FEELINGS, BEST JOKES."

—**Olivia Waite**, award-winning author

"Alexis Hall's *Boyfriend Material* perfectly balances laugh-out-loud-while-reading-alone-in-an-empty-room with those-aren't-tears-in-my-eyes-just-allergies."

—**Kris Ripper**, award-winning author

"Alexis Hall is the undisputed master of romantic comedy."

—**Jenny Holiday**, *USA Today* bestselling author

"I'm in awe of Alexis Hall's talent. I don't want the book to end."

—**Cathy Maxwell**, *New York Times* bestselling author

"*Boyfriend Material* is the joyfully queer British rom-com escape book I didn't know I needed."

—**KJ Charles**, award-winning author

ALSO BY ALEXIS HALL

LONDON CALLING
Boyfriend Material
Husband Material

SPIRES
Glitterland

10 THINGS THAT NEVER HAPPENED

ALEXIS HALL

Cover design and illustration by Elizabeth Turner Stokes
Internal image © Bakai/Getty Images
Internal design by Laura Boren/Sourcebooks

Published by Sourcebooks Casablanca, an imprint of Sourcebooks
P.O. Box 4410, Naperville, Illinois 60567-4410
(630) 961-3900
sourcebooks.com

Cataloging-in-Publication Data is on file with the Library of Congress.

Printed and bound in Canada.
MBP 10 9 8 7 6 5 4 3 2 1

AUTHOR'S NOTE

I'm aware that a lot of my readers are international and, therefore, might not be super familiar with specific UK dialects. The narrator of this book is from Liverpool, and, in my head, his narration has a noticeable Scouse accent. If you want to know what that sounds like check out Wayne Rooney, Cilla Black, Mel C, or The Vivienne.

PART ONE

LOSING MY JOB & LOSING MY MEMORY

CHAPTER 1

IT PROBABLY SAYS GOOD THINGS about modern Britain—or maybe just about modern Liverpool—that when I was growing up, I got way less shit for being gay than I got for being named after a hobbit. And while I'm glad my classmates weren't homophobic, the hobbit thing did hack me off a bit, especially because the hobbit I was named after wasn't even one of the weird ones. If I'd been called Meriadoc or Fatty Bolger that'd have been one thing, but my name was Sam. Still is Sam, really. But my full *legal* name is Samwise Eoin Becker and so every time I started a new class, on the first day, the teacher would be reading the register and they'd call out "Samwise" and I'd have to say, "here, miss" and that'd be it from then on. It didn't help that the first set of movies came out just as I was starting primary school and the second set hit just as I was starting my GCSEs, so I had jokes about second breakfast and hairy feet from the age of five until I was eighteen.

Still, you've got to laugh, don't you? My dad taught me that. And it's probably the most useful thing I've ever learned.

For example:

"Hey, Ban." yells one of my employees. He knows what I'm really called, but this is Amjad, and Amjad is even nerdier than my mam and so once he found out I'd been named after a hobbit he thought it was hilarious to refer to me by Sam's original Westron name from the appendices that he apparently knew off the top of his head. And I let him get away with it because at least it was an original bit. "They're going to need you in bedding."

I love my team. Not *love* love, obviously. More tolerate bemusedly. But the phrase *they're going to need you in bedding* inspires a feeling so far from confidence I might almost call it concern. "Why?" I ask.

The only answer Amjad gives is the only answer I need. "Brian."

I give a small internal *fuck* and head over to the afflicted department. Bedding's half the store which means I've got quite a wide area to search, but Brian has a way of creating a little zone of chaos around himself so I'm not terribly worried about finding him.

And find him I do. He's standing next to the Country Living Hamsterley mattress, which with its double layered calico pocket springs, hand-teased soft natural fibres of lambswool and mohair, and one hundred percent natural Belgian damask, is one of the most luxurious, most expensive, and—importantly—most "don't-trust-Brian-with-this" mattress in the store.

He's looking flustered. He's also holding an extremely ominous mug.

"Please," I tell him as soon as I'm close enough to be heard without shouting, "please for the love of *everything* tell me you did not just spill tea on the Country Living Hamsterley mattress with the double layered calico pocket springs and the hand-teased natural fibres."

"No," he says, "I didn't."

And like a muppet, I let myself feel relieved.

"I spilled coffee on it," he explains.

It's not the detail I should pick up on. It's really not. "I didn't think you drank coffee."

"I don't." He's doing his best to look apologetic. "But I thought Claire might want one so I was bringing a mug through to the office just in case and, well, here we are."

So many details to address. And so little time. "And you picked a path straight past the most expensive mattress in the store because...?"

"Well, I thought I should steer clear of the Flaxby Nature's Finest 9450 Pillow Top on account of what happened last week."

The fact that I hadn't been aware of anything at all happening last week as regarded the Flaxby Nature's Finest 9450 Pillow Top probably said not-entirely-great things about me as a manager. "Should I ask?"

"Well, I was having a jam sandwich—"

"You got jam on the Flaxby Nature's Finest 9450 Pillow Top?"

Brian nods, sheepishly. "It's fine, though. Tiffany helped me flip it over, so it doesn't show."

Once again, I make the mistake of feeling relieved. Then the bits of my brain that are professionally required to know how beds work start talking to each other. "Hang on Brian, you can't flip a pillow top mattress. Because it's got a pillow top. On the top."

"Ooh." Brian winces in a way you ideally never want a man in charge of two grand's worth of mattress to wince.

I decide that the pillow top issue can wait. "Well, I suppose we can at least flip this one. Come on."

Flipping the mattress is hard work but at least it's simple work and, once I've reminded him to put the bloody mug down, Brian can handle it with something approaching competence. We heave the whole kit and caboodle up onto one side, pivot it about the middle, and lay it down nicely on the frame that's being used to display it.

Then I step back and check it looks okay, and I see another large, brown stain spread right across the middle.

"Ah," says Brian, "now that one *is* tea."

I'm heading back from bedding, trying to work out how to replace not one but two display models of high-end mattresses, when Claire, my assistant manager, sticks her head out of the office door and yells "His Royal Dickishness is on the phone" the entire length of the store. Which she follows with, "And don't worry, I've got him muted."

"That just means," I yell back, "that you can't hear him, not that he can't hear you."

"Well, balls."

One of these days I'm going to have to do something about Claire's habit of calling our boss His Royal Dickishness. And also about her habit of shouting swear words across the showroom. And also, for that matter, about Brian just, y'know, in general.

Though I'm guessing that right now His Royal Dickishness is going to care more about the swearing.

I'm guessing right.

"So"—Jonathan Forest's slightly too-polished accent glides down the phone line and into my ears—"this isn't what I was originally calling you about, but why the hell is your assistant manager calling me a His Royal Dickishness in front of what sounded like the whole shop?"

There's no way to cover for this, but I try anyway for Claire's sake. "It's affectionate?"

"How's it affectionate?"

"It's a northern thing. Y'know, like when you've got a mate you call y'bastard."

"I lived in the north for sixteen years," says Jonathan Forest—he likes to bring that up because it makes him sound more working class even though he's a rich fucker who only gives a fuck about other rich fuckers. "And I never had a mate I called *y'bastard*."

Privately, I think he's probably never had a mate. "I'm just saying it's how folk talk."

"Even so, *bastard*"—he says *bastard* with a short *a* like a normal person, even if everything else he says sounds like one of the shittier royals—"has a very different connotation to *dickish*."

"It's the same principle," I try. It sounds weak even to me.

"Okay." I'm pretty sure Jonathan Forest isn't a robot, but I almost hear his brain click as he moves on. "While this isn't what I wanted to talk about, it's very much connected to it."

Oh fuck, he knows I call him a dick as well. We all call him a dick because he's a dick. The way I see it, if you don't want people calling you a dick, you shouldn't be a dick. "Is it?" I ask, trying not to sound too much like he's just caught me wanking.

"Splashes & Snuggles has three branches now and a fourth opening next year. The Croydon branch is performing as I expect it to. The Leeds branch is performing as I expect it to. The Sheffield branch decidedly is not."

Probably not the time to tell him one of my employees just wrecked four grand's worth of mattress with a tea run. "In what way exactly are we not performing as you expect us to?"

"You're over budget and under target. And, frankly, I'm a bit concerned you don't already know that."

Oh why does this dick have to be such a dick? Yes, we are technically a *bit* over budget what with all the stock Brian has trashed, and yes, we are technically a bit under target, but that's because Jonathan's targets are bollocks. "I know what the figures are. But we're a new store, it's a competitive area, and we're getting pretty close."

"I didn't hire you to get *pretty close*." Somehow he manages to sneer just with his voice. "I hired you to meet the goals I give you, and if you can't, I'll find someone who can."

Part of me really wants to say "fine, do that". This job's not worth putting up with this kind of crap. Except it's not just my job we're talking about. If I get the boot, then Jonathan Forest replaces me with somebody who'll give him his precious fucking "targets" and then what'll happen to Claire and Amjad and Brian and the rest of them?

So I don't push back. Instead, I try to walk that line between promising results I won't deliver and giving him an excuse to replace me with someone who will. "I'm sure we can work something out."

"I've already worked something out." He gives the tiniest, tiniest pause and then his tone softens just faintly. "I don't want to let you go, Sam. I think you've got it in you to be a really good manager."

You patronising shit. As far as I'm concerned, I'm already a good manager. Or at least as good a manager as you can expect in a second-rate bed-and-bath showroom in a competitive area with a team full of Brians.

Claire is holding up a piece of paper. It says, *Is he being a dick?*

I mouth *yes obviously* back at her, and she holds up another piece of paper saying *sorry I can't read lips*.

Normally this would be fine, but normally I'm not trying to work out whether I'm at risk of losing my job. I wave at her to get her to stop. She doesn't. And there's no way she was ever going to, but I like to pretend I'm in charge sometimes.

"So that's why," Jonathan's saying when I can focus on him again, "I want you to come to Croydon tomorrow so you can see how I do things."

Tomorrow is Friday. My least favourite day for going to London. My favourite day for going to London is never. "We're quite busy what with the run up to Christmas."

"I'm sure Claire can handle it. She seems to have a lot of time on her hands. Certainly she has enough time to invent 'affectionate' nicknames for me."

Looks like *patronising shit* is still where we are. "Claire is a valued member of the team and..."

Now Claire is brandishing an elaborate and lovingly rendered picture of a giant cock and balls.

"...and...and..."

She adds ball hairs.

"...makes an important contribution to morale."

"Then," Jonathan snaps, "I'm sure she can cope without you for a day. This isn't a request, Samwise."

I just about manage not to make a noise, but I physically cringe. I know it's my name, but nobody's ever used it except my mam, and I don't want to be thinking about her right now. "Please don't call me that."

"The point is, Sam, I'm your boss and you're coming to Croydon tomorrow. The company will reimburse your travel."

He hangs up before I can say anything else. Which, at this point, is probably for the best.

"Are you all right?" Claire has put down the dick pic, which is what you might call a small mercy.

I sink into my chair and sit on my hands to stop them shaking. "Yeah. He's such a...such a..."

"Dick?"

"*Such* a dick."

"Do you want to"—and now she's giving me the sort of uneasy look you should never get from somebody whose paycheques you sign—"talk about it?"

"He just gets to me, and I can never tell if he's evil or if he doesn't know or if he doesn't care, or which would be worst."

She thinks about it for a moment. "He's evil."

"I have to go to Croydon tomorrow."

"Well, that's a relief. I thought he was going to fire you."

"He still might," I point out.

"That's not very likely. To drag someone all the way from Sheffield to Croydon just so you can fire them, you'd have to be a complete—oh."

"Yeah, it's not looking good, is it?"

Another pause. Claire runs a hand through her platinum blonde hair and looks at me like I've got brown sauce on my face and she doesn't know how to tell me. "I'm trying to come up with something comforting here, but you're totally fucked."

"I know. But"—I do my best to pull myself together, to pretend this isn't affecting me—"what can you do? You can't stop a dick from being a dick. Will yez be okay to look after the place tomorrow?"

"Love, it's a bed and bath superstore, not a nuclear submarine."

"Yes, but Brian's opening up."

"Then we're screwed." Now Jonathan's off the phone, Claire's looking more serious. Maybe because she heard enough of my end of the conversation to know we're in a serious situation. "You know," she says, "if Jonathan's getting on your case about numbers, you might really need to look at letting Brian go."

I can't believe she's saying it. I mean I can, because she is, and because she's said it before, but still. "Brian's one of us."

"He's the worst Customer Advisor I've ever worked with, and I worked with Chel."

Them's harsh words. "Chel punched a child."

"A very annoying child. And she didn't cost us money."

"Technically"—nothing good ever follows *technically*—"everybody costs us money."

She's not impressed. "Amjad told me what happened with the Country Living Hamsterley. And it wasn't the first time."

"Oh come on, he's spilled a few things on a few mattresses."

"Five since June. And he ripped the seat off a VitrA Sento rimless while he was trying to show a customer how durable it was."

I've backed myself into a defending Brian corner and now I can't get out. "Toilet seats are easy to replace. Besides, Brian *needs* this job. It's just him and his nan, and he's the only one can cover the bills."

"I know." Claire gives me a sympathetic look, which she doesn't do very often, possibly because she doesn't very often think I deserve sympathy. "But if Jonathan's out for blood, and you can either save Brian or me, honestly Sam I'd rather you saved me."

I want to tell her it won't come to that. But I can't. I can just hope like fuck that Jonathan Forest will be reasonable. Which, thinking about it, means that we are *definitely* screwed.

CHAPTER 2

I MANAGE TO FORGET HOW definitely screwed we are for about ten minutes until I take a walk out to make sure everything is where it's meant to be and I realise we were supposed to have our Christmas displays up already and they are very much not up at all. So I go in to find Tiff, who I usually put in charge of that sort of thing because she's good with design even if she's not necessarily the most reliable person in the world, and she tells me that all the kit was meant to be delivered on Wednesday, but it never arrived and she didn't think to tell me until now because she figured it'd sort itself out.

"I mean," she asks, a lock of blue hair covering one of her eyes in a way I have to admit doesn't radiate professionalism, "does it really matter? Christmas is a pagan festival anyway and—"

"Actually"—Amjad could hear a factual inaccuracy at eight hundred paces in a high wind—"that's a misconception."

"Is not." Tiff is pretty young, and she still goes to the is not/is too school of debate.

Deciding that half past two on the first of December in the middle of a decorating crisis is the exact right time to get into the details of comparative folklorics, Amjad begins counting on his fingers. "The tree is a German protestant tradition, Santa Claus is the same—the early Lutherans pushed him as an alternative to the

Christkind because they thought it was too Catholic—yule logs are eighteenth or nineteenth century, carols are—"

"Amj, is this important?" I ask. I don't quite snap. I try to avoid snapping; there's never any good reason for it.

"It'll stop Tiff spreading misinformation."

Tiff didn't seem like she cared if she spread misinformation or not. "Okay, so Christmas is an *authentically Christian* festival but these days it's just a celebration of consumerism and—"

I give her a look. "I know it's a celebration of consumerism, Tiff. But in case you haven't noticed, you work in a shop. Consumerism is our whole deal."

"That doesn't mean we have to support it," Tiff insists.

"It kind of does." I like my team to think for themselves, but sometimes fucking hell don't I wish they'd do it less. "We're not putting lights up so people will be reminded of the wonders of their salvation, we're doing it so they'll shell out a couple of extra quid for some novelty bedspreads with reindeers on them."

Tiff looks at me with more disappointment than you should be allowed to direct at somebody who's nearly ten years older than you and also your boss. "This is exactly what is wrong with late-stage capitalism."

"Y'know," I say, "you're very Marxist for a trainee hairdresser."

"Hair and beauty consultant," she corrects me, "and isn't the whole point of Marxism that it's a philosophy for ordinary working people?"

She's got me there. "I suppose, but it's odd given the man himself had famously terrible hair."

"You're thinking of Einstein," Amjad tells me.

"I'm not. There can be more than one famous historical person with bad hair."

Tiff already has her phone out.

"What are you doing?" I ask. "Are you googling *did Karl Marx have bad hair*?"

She looks up. "Just finding a picture"—she turns the screen around—"hair looks okay to me."

The picture she's found is of his tomb in Highgate Cemetery. "That's a statue. You can't use statue hair as evidence. Plus, it's on his grave. Nobody's going to put a statue with bad hair on a feller's grave." Against all my better judgement I pull out my own phone, find a photograph of the man himself, and show it to Tiff. "There you go, look, bad hair."

"According to this"—Amjad has joined in the google party, although knowing him he's been searching for something like *Karl Marx Hair People Are Wrong*—"he actually got his hair cut shortly after that picture was taken so it's probably not that representative."

"*And*," Tiff adds—they're ganging up on me, they always gang up on me—"that's not bad hair."

"It looks pretty bad from where I'm standing."

Tiff does the disappointed look again. "Sometimes bad isn't bad."

"That sounds a lot like shite."

She gives a long-suffering sigh, which is a cheek because she's far too young to be long anything. "It's the nineteenth-century equivalent of those guys who spend hours mussing their hair up just right so that it looks good but also like they're too cool to care if it looks good. If you're in the business, you can spot it a mile off."

"You think he worked at looking like that?"

Tiff nods. "I think he was consciously aiming for Big Das Kapital Energy."

Realising that I've let myself get distracted, I slip my phone away. "Right. Well, that's been enlightening as always, but if you'll excuse me, I need to go and find out what's happening with our Christmas displays because if we don't get them up by tomorrow—"

"We'll get them up on Monday?" Tiff suggests.

"We'll miss the first-weekend-in-December sales and that will make His Royal Dickishness even more pissed off than he already is. And since Claire managed to call him His Royal Dickishness to his face, that's a pretty high level of pissed off."

Amjad, who is sometimes useful when he isn't being a gigantic pedant, looks thoughtful for a moment. "I think we've got some stuff from last year kicking around in the back. We could use that in a pinch."

"And it'll be all right after a year in a cold back room?" I ask.

He's thinking again. "Some of it should still be usable."

"Can we at least hold out for new lights?" Tiff picks idly at the collar of her black work-issue shirt. "Last year I had to go through over five hundred of them trying to find which bulb was broken."

"Tree might be an issue too," Amjad points out. "We had a real one last year, which I thought was odd because we *sell* artificial ones."

I cling to the theory that this is all still doable. "Right. Well, I'm going to go check with the supplier. Absolute worst-case-scenario we use last year's decorations until everything gets here."

"And for the tree?" asks Tiff, who I think is enjoying the chaos more than she really should be.

"We're on a retail park in December. There'll be at least three places we can buy one within a twenty minutes' drive." I'm doing my optimistic voice, because in an absolutely ideal world I *wouldn't* be having to drive around looking for a last-minute Christmas tree that I'd probably have to buy with my own fucking money, just so I could tell my prize dick of a boss that I at least got the Christmas display up on time. But in an ideal world Karl Marx would have better hair and Christmas wouldn't be a soulless spectacle of conspicuous consumption. Sometimes you just play the hand you're dealt.

I head back inside and call the distributor. One of the sort-of-advantages of Jonathan Forest's habit of being a massive control freak is that there is only one distributor to talk to. Of course the disadvantage of his habit of being a massive control freak is that the distributor isn't really in the habit of talking to individual branch managers even though that would be much easier for everybody. Every year he has his team in London design the Christmas displays, select our fairly limited range of Christmas stock, and then ship the same combination of fairy lights and Santa pillowcases to all three branches from one central location. And since there are only three stores, you'd think that'd be pretty simple, but if there's one thing I've learned in the past few years managing a bed and bath showroom it's that pretty simple things can be surprisingly easy to fuck up.

"How," I ask the man on the end of the phone, "did you wind up sending everything to the Isle of Sheppey?"

To give the lad his due, he seems embarrassed about it. "I don't know what to say. We do a lot of distribution for homewares. We were sending a load of shipments out to the B&M in Queensborough, and Kev in dispatching has terrible handwriting and so—"

"Hang on hang on hang on." I'm not letting this one slide. "I don't care how bad somebody's handwriting is, *Sheffield* doesn't look anything like *the Isle of Sheppey* on account of how *the Isle of Sheppey* has the words *the Isle of* at the start."

The man at the end of the phone makes a noise that sounds like a shrug. "We just call it Sheppey. Anyway, that's where your stuff went."

"Can we have it back like?"

"It's in Sheppey."

"I know it's in Sheppey. I need it to be here. I need it to be here as soon as possible."

He goes quiet for a moment. It's not a moment I think he's using to decide how best to satisfy my needs as a customer. "We can do Wednesday?"

"That's in a week." I'm really trying not to get angry. I wasn't brought up to be angry. "How is in a week as soon as possible?"

"Well, there's scheduling—"

I wasn't brought up to be angry, but I *was* brought up to stand up for myself. "I don't care about your scheduling. You were meant to get a delivery to us yesterday, and now you're telling me I have to wait until"—I did a quick count in my head, maths was never my best subject—"the eighth. That's a third of the Christmas run-up gone and you must know how important that is for retail."

"Out of my han—"

I'm still not letting it go. "Okay, but level with me, lad to lad, is it *actually* out of your hands, or is it one of those things where you *could* get it sorted but it'll be a lot of aggro at your end?"

"It'll be a lot of aggro at my end," he admits, "and I don't *want* a lot of aggro at my end."

I'm pretty sure I've got him. Apart from the Jonathan Forests of the world, most people won't just tell you to your face that they're making your life harder to make their life easier. "And I understand that, mate," I tell him. "I do. But this was kind of your mistake, and it's going to cost me and my team a lot, so it'd be great if yez could find some way to help me out here."

He's quiet again, but I think this time he's really trying to think of a way to help. "I can probably get something tonight," he tells me at last, "but it'll be late."

"How late?" I ask. I'm pretty sure I don't want to know the answer.

"It'll take at least six hours which'll make it—what, half eight, nine?"

I have to take it. It'd be ungrateful not to.

Although it's not my fault, putting all this crap back together *is* going to be my responsibility. Redecorating the entire store by myself is almost entirely outside both my skill set and my having-to-be-on-a-train-to-fucking-Croydon-at-the-crack-of-dawn-set.

I slope out to the front of the store to have a think, and find Tiff outside taking an unscheduled break. It's something she does sometimes, and the one time I confronted her about it she pointed out that if she smoked, then going outside to have a quick ciggy would be completely socially acceptable so by normalising that and not allowing non-smokers equivalent mental health space, I was reinforcing destructive habits.

"You alright?" she asks.

"Oh, yeah." I'm leaning on a glass-fronted door staring at a grey sky on one of the coldest days we've had this year so I'm not really. I'm glad of my scarf, which is a slightly unfashionable powder blue and used to be my mam's. "Fine. Except I've just got off the phone with the dispatcher and the decorations won't be here until nine and—"

Tiff's already grinning at me. "We're doing decorations?"

"Not really we," I explain, "I can't do overtime and so I'll—"

"I *love* decorations."

"Okay but."

She's already backing through the doors, doing a little dance. "Leave it to me, boss. I'll get everybody in, it'll be great, just, like, order us a pizza or something."

"But," I try again. Only she's already heading into the floor, singing *De-cor-a-tion par-taaay* to a tune I don't really recognise.

And I hope, then pray, then go back to hoping on account of being an atheist, that this doesn't go disastrously wrong.

In the end, it's Tiff, Claire, Amjad, Brian, and this new feller called Chris who's always the first to volunteer for everything and keeps telling me he'll be doing my job in three years. I do get pizza in to say thanks for sticking around so late, and we sit in the returns kiosk eating garlic bread and planning how the display is going to look. Well, in theory we plan how the display is going to look. Mostly we just argue over toppings.

"There's nothing wrong," Brian is saying, "with pineapple on pizza."

"Yes there is." Tiff is holding fast on this one—she's shifted her focus from the inequities of global capitalism to the more relatable question of whether Hawaiian pizza is shit or not. "It's the avocado bathroom of pizzas."

Amjad gives her a nerdy smirk. "You mean it's fashionable to hate on it but it's actually fine?"

"No, I mean it's objectively the worst."

You should never use the word "objectively" around Amjad. I once heard him argue that the sky wasn't objectively blue because of wavelengths. "It's not objectively the worst," he replies, "it's subjectively the worst. Taste is subjective *by definition*. And in fact, if you want to go by *objective* metrics, then both avocado bathrooms and Hawaiian pizzas are objectively amongst the best because they're consistently popular and popularity is something you can actually measure."

"My nan's got an avocado bathroom," offers New Enthusiastic Chris. "It's fine."

New Enthusiastic Chris hasn't fully settled in yet which makes him a bit lacking on the banter front, so whenever he chimes in it's always in a way that kills the conversation. I'm about to launch boldly into a whole new topic when we hear the truck rolling up outside. New Enthusiastic Chris is first on his feet, with Tiff shortly after. The rest of us follow them at a more sensible pace, except for Brian who's spilled pizza on his shirt and is trying to dab it off with a different bit of the shirt.

Outside we meet a lorry driver who seems surprisingly okay with having been sent on a six-hour drive at short notice perhaps he needs the overtime—and the team pile in to help him unload all of the tastefully selected and corporate approved tinsel. New Enthusiastic Chris and Amjad double-team the Christmas tree, while Brian and Claire start a distractingly in-depth conversation about a range of candy-cane duvet covers that we're already selling but which'll now get their own proper display.

"All I'm saying," Brian is saying, "is that I don't hold with them."

"Much as I appreciate the cynicism," Claire is saying back, "why exactly?"

"They just feel very American."

For some reason, Claire thinks this is perfectly reasonable. "Fair."

"Hang on," I say over an armful of festive shower curtains. "That's not fair at all. You can't just say something *feels American*, and even if it *is* American, that's not a reason not to like it."

"It fucking is," replies Claire who, unlike Brian, is at least managing to continue this debate while also moving merchandise.

"I really think it's not," I insist. Then I turn to Amjad. "Hey Amj, you *must* have an opinion on this."

Amjad glances at me from his end of the Christmas tree. "Kind of got my hands full here."

He does. I'd help him but I also have my hands full, and besides, he's working with New Enthusiastic Chris and it's hard to help New Enthusiastic Chris with anything because he's so keen to show he can do two people's jobs at once. So we make our way back into the store, and Amjad manages to get halfway across the car park before he breaks. "But they're actually almost certainly German."

"We're not on Christmas origins again, are we?" asks Tiff, who has armfuls of fairy lights.

"Whether candy canes are American," I explain.

"Super American," Tiff agrees. "They're super American *even if* they technically come from twelfth-century Bavaria or something."

Now fully committed to balancing tree-lugging with Christmas-explaining, Amjad shifts the weight of the fir and launches into his extemporaneous yuletide lecture. "Eighteenth century," he says, "and they were probably white to begin with because you couldn't do the colouring without modern machinery. And it's not Bavaria, it's Cologne."

Brian is carrying exactly one quite small cardboard display stand. "What's aftershave got to do with it?"

"I assume it's Cologne the city," explains Claire, dumping five identical displays onto him.

Overwhelmed by the sudden addition of a medium-sized amount of cardboard, Brian looks down in a panic. "I can't handle this, it'll get all unwieldy."

Claire is very rarely in a mood for people's shit. "No they won't, they're in a stack and it's fine. Get them inside."

It takes three more trips to get everything in. Well, it takes one more trip from most of the staff then two more trips from New Enthusiastic Chris who insists there's "not much left" and he's "totally on it". Around ten thirty Amjad and Brian head home, which is fair because they've done more than enough. Claire fucks off a little while later because she figures I've got it in hand and while she's second in command she's also covering for me tomorrow so I can't complain. Tiff stays until gone midnight getting the displays ready.

She's an odd one is Tiff, because ninety-nine percent of the time she gives so few shits I feel like getting her senna pods for secret Santa, but one percent of the time something catches her imagination and she's a fucking miracle. And honestly, I'm glad she's here because there's no way I could do up a showroom in festive style without her. I'd just whack a bit of crepe paper on a headboard and call it done, but she goes all out with the lights and the little stick-on snowflake things, and when we're heading off—just me, her, and New Enthusiastic Chris who's always last to leave on account of being new and enthusiastic—we look back for a moment and it's kind of magic like. It's probably just me being a sap, but in that moment, standing outside on an industrial estate on the first day of December, staring at a bathroom warehouse that a trainee hairdresser—sorry, trainee hair and beauty consultant—has done up to look like a fairytale kingdom, I'm almost proud of us. Sure, we're a bit over on budget and a bit under on sales, but by the very specific standards of wholesale bed and bath retailers, we've done a good job here. We've got a good team.

Check that. We've got a great team. Even if sometimes Tiff isn't exactly where she's meant to be and even if Brian drops the odd toilet basin and even if New Enthusiastic Chris is currently slightly more enthusiastic than he is useful, we're still…we're still the Sheffield branch. And I'm not going to let Jonathan Forest take that away from me. From us.

CHAPTER 3

HAVE I MENTIONED THAT JONATHAN Forest is a dick? In case I haven't, he's a dick. He's the kind of dick who tells you on a Thursday afternoon to be in London for a bollocking at eight o'clock on a Friday. And don't get me wrong, I'm a morning person. But I'm not a four in the morning person. Which was when I'd had to get up to be on the train for five to be where I am now at seven forty-nine, which is standing outside Jonathan Forest's office in the suit I wore to my nan's funeral, waiting for him to let me in, which—knowing him—won't be until exactly eight.

He lets me in at exactly eight.

His office is on the second floor of the Croydon branch of Splashes & Snuggles, which makes it look like it's trying much too hard to be a penthouse. If I squint, I can almost imagine that I'm in some fancy skyscraper in the city instead of in a retail park between a Nando's and a DFS. There's a little six-seater conference table and a sofa that looks like it gets slept on more than it gets sat on. And it's got a desk—a more cluttered desk than I'd have expected—with a picture frame facing away from me and a well-used coffee mug with *we're Wednesday aren't we* repeated over and over again around the outside in white on blue. Behind the desk, Jonathan Forest is sitting, watching me.

I think he wants me to be intimidated like, but I'm not giving him the satisfaction. For a while he just stares at me with those dark intense eyes of his and when it's clear he'll not make me mess my kecks, he finally asks me to sit down.

"I'm sorry it's come to this, Sam," he says. At least he doesn't call me Samwise this time.

"You can't be that sorry," I tell him, "or you'd've just not done it."

"I'm sorry it's come to this," he repeats, "but Splashes & Snuggles is a business."

When he says it aloud, I find it quite hard not to laugh in his face. There's something very wrong, I reckon, with a man who calls his business Splashes & Snuggles and can't see the funny side of it. "I know it's a business, Jonathan, but it's a business that makes good money and so I don't quite see why you're making a massive drama over a couple of points on a spreadsheet."

Jonathan Forest leans back and gives me another look. In other circumstances—like not being my boss and not having dragged me the length of the country at four a.m. on a Friday—he'd probably have had that sexy-ugly thing going on. There was just something about his craggy, angry face and the unruly white streak in his otherwise carefully groomed hair that made you want him to do things to you. Or maybe for you to do things to him to see if you could get him to chill the fuck out. "I think the fact that you consider your boss asking for a meeting to discuss your performance to be a"—he does actual fucking air quotes—"*massive drama* might be exactly what's wrong with your management style."

We've been talking for less than five minutes and I already want to stick his pencil up his nose. "There's nothing wrong with my management style. Ask anyone on my team."

"If no one on your team has a problem with your management style, that's a problem."

He's not making sense. Being unpopular is not how you get

results. He's evidence of that. "How is that a problem? That's my job."

And now he's pinching the bridge of his nose like he's disappointed I didn't do my geography homework. "Samwise—"

"Don't call me Samwise."

"Don't interrupt me. I took a chance on you..."—he gives a nasty little pause—"...*Sam,* because I thought you had potential. But I'm beginning to suspect that you don't understand what the role requires."

"It sounds like you're saying you want me to treat the staff like crap."

"I want you to prioritise targets."

"I do prioritise targets," I tell him. "I just don't prioritise them over people."

The expression on his face makes me want to shove a lot more than a pencil up a lot more than his nose. It's the expression you get when your new puppy shits on the floor and you can't be angry at it because you know it can't help itself. "People don't pay your salary. I do."

It's really tempting to point out he's just said he isn't a person. But I'm supposed to be saving my job, not scuppering it. "Well, I don't want to teach my granny to suck eggs, but the people run the shop. The shop makes the money, and the money is how you pay me. So in a way they do."

"And at the moment, those people are costing more than any other branch, bringing in less than any other branch, and—" He looks over at his monitor and for just a moment I see something. Something almost like caring. Only it's explicitly about money. "It's concerning, Sam. Genuinely concerning."

Somehow, this is going even worse than I'd expected. I'd done alright at interview but then I'd not had much investment which made it easy to say all the right things. He'd said *what's your biggest weakness* and I'd said some pack of bollocks like *ooh well I'm just too focused on providing quality customer service in the field of bed and bathroom supplies* and somehow that'd worked. Now if I nod or smile at the wrong thing, I'll be having to hike back up to Sheffield and tell the team they're all taking pay cuts because this prick wants to buy himself another. "Look," I tell him, "I can see where yez're coming from, I really can. But do you not think a company has an obligation to its employees? I mean is it really worth making somebody's life crappier than it needs to be just so we can shift a few extra duvets by the end of the quarter?"

It's not what he wants to hear. But that's because what he wants to hear is *you're right about everything, I'll go back home and start firing people.* "Their lives will be even crappier if I have to close the branch entirely."

"But you won't have to, will you?" I'm pushing my luck now. My mam used to say she had the luck of the Irish and I'm really hoping it didn't skip a generation. "You might *choose* to, but if you do, you should at least be honest about it."

And maybe, just maybe, that gets through to him. Just not necessarily in a good way. If he was wearing glasses, he'd have pushed them up his nose, but he isn't, so he just pulls his brows down and glowers at me. "I'm sure you think I'm an extremely selfish man, Sam. I'm sure you think I'm just trying to get you to squeeze more money out of people so that...so that..."

"You can buy an extra Ferrari?" I try, hoping that an adorable Scouse cheekiness will prove my path to salvation.

"Exactly." He lets the *Exactly* hang there for a long time before he continues. "But Splashes & Snuggles"—the serious context makes it even harder not to giggle at the name, and I just about manage—"is a small fish in a big pond. We're trying to compete with Dreams and Wickes at the same time. And Bensons for Beds. And all the local retailers. Even Morrisons are doing soft furnishings these days."

"Morrisons don't sell beds," I remind him.

"They sell cushions and throws." He's not relaxed exactly, but he's not giving off half the boss energy he was a minute ago. "You're not going to go out of business because Morrisons sell a couple of pillows."

"I'm aware. Just like I'm aware that I'm not going to go out of business because the Sheffield branch writes off"—he starts scrolling down what seems to be an ominously long document—"a fourteen-jet double ended LED-lit whirlpool bath worth one thousand, five hundred and ninety-nine pounds over an *uncrating incident*."

That was code for *Brian backed a van over it.*

"Or twenty-two TheraPur memory foam ice pillows, priced eighty-five pounds apiece, over a *stockroom mishap*."

Brian again, and that one he'd never quite been able to explain, and I'd eventually stopped asking.

"Then there's the fact that one of your employees has taken eighteen sick or personal days in the last twelve months."

"She's young and she's on a course."

Now Jonathan's getting that business-owner aura back again and in some way I'm relieved. "And am I *paying* her to be young and on a course, or am I paying her to sell bed and bathroom furniture?"

"You're paying her to sell bed and bathroom furniture," I admit, mildly resenting—no, strongly resenting—Jonathan Forest's ability to make me feel like a naughty schoolboy. "But..."

"But what?"

I don't actually have a but what. "Could you not have told me all this over the phone?"

"I could." He nods. "But I thought this would be better face to face."

Fuck. He's going to fire me, isn't he? "Fuck, you're going to fire me, aren't you?"

"My ideal outcome"—he gets up from the desk and strides over to the window—"is that you keep your job, but you accept that you need to improve the efficiency of your branch." He's not looking at me now, he's standing with his hands behind his back and looking outside like he's some king surveying his domain. Which'd be a lot more impressive if we were in a skyscraper overlooking Manhattan, instead of a bed and bathroom superstore overlooking a car park and one of them yards that sells reclaimed wood by weight.

"I'm not saying that we couldn't be more efficient." I'm beginning to feel like the bastard's pushed me into a corner. I'm just saying that the only way to make it more efficient is to make it a much worse place to work."

He's still doing emperor pose. "Not my concern."

Sigh. "So what is it you actually want me to do? Because all I'm hearing is *be better,* and if you don't mind me saying that's not very effective management."

"Firstly"—he turns back from the window like Medusa turning to face him with the sandals—"I do mind you saying. Secondly, I've checked the numbers, and you need to do exactly this: you need to get your team to sell more protection and service plans, replace your lowest-performing salespeople, stop permitting hourly paid staff to take breaks during their scheduled hours, implement the company policy regarding sick days, and fix whatever is causing you to lose quite so much stock. Once that's in place, we can talk further."

"So be a dick, basically," I say.

To my surprise, Jonathan Forest almost smiles. "A right royal dick, if you want to put it that way. It's how you run a business."

I don't agree, but it's not the time. "My worst-performing salesperson," I tell him instead, "has an elderly nan to look after."

"So do I."

"Yes, but you're a fucking millionaire."

"My personal finances are no concern of yours. We live in uncertain economic times."

I think I might actually scoff. "What, and you're worried that your extremely lucrative bed and bathroom empire is going to disappear overnight, and you'll be out on the street busking to Ed Sheeran?"

And though I don't expect it, that brings him up short again, makes him waver a moment. Like I've breathed too hard on a candle. "Worse things have happened."

"Not to the likes of you they haven't."

Jonathan's eyes narrow. "You should really think about the way you speak to your boss."

"Why? You're already threatening to fire me, and I don't see how minding my Ps and Qs around you will help me sell more CoolTouch cloud elite mattresses."

Having stood up for the drama, he can't really sit back down, so he just hovers. "Perhaps. But if you're this insubordinate with me, that suggests you let your team be insubordinate with you, which would explain...well, quite a lot of your issues, frankly. At the very least it explains why your staff aren't motivated to meet their targets."

When I first got this job, Jonathan sent me on a short training course because I didn't have management experience, and they talked a lot about intrinsic and extrinsic motivation. What I took away from those three days in a conference room in Burnley was that *intrinsically* motivated salespeople are pricks who'd sell their own nan to somebody who already had a nan of their own, just for the buzz, and *extrinsically* motivated salespeople won't be able to feed their kids if they don't make commission. I didn't want to hire the first sort or exploit the second, which is how I wound up with Brian. "How about," I try, "you give me a year to get my numbers up, and if my way doesn't work, we talk about replacing people."

I open with a year because I expect him to come back with three months so we can shake on six.

He doesn't. "It's gone too far for that."

Has it fuck. But I don't say that. It gets to the point where pushing your luck crosses the line into just being a pillock. "I'm sorry you feel that way."

"Here's what's going to happen." He sounds all take-charge like in a way that would probably be a lot more attractive if it wasn't going to fuck up my life. "Today, you're going to shadow me around this branch so you can see how I run things. Tomorrow, you're going back to Sheffield where you will start making immediate changes *including* replacing underperforming staff. Do you understand?"

I do. I don't like that I do, but I do.

I follow Jonathan Forest around until lunch, from his all-business morning briefing (here's the new stock, sell it, fuck off) to his rounds of the store's departments where he sniffs out insufficiently-hustling workers like some kind of predatory animal that feeds on slacking. It's not the only thing about him that's got a werewolf vibe—his thick eyebrows and permanent scowl make him look like any moment he could snap and grow claws and start ripping your skin off. Or maybe just your clothes, if he's more like the ones from those books that Claire says she only reads ironically.

Eventually, we take a break for lunch. He doesn't offer to take me anywhere or show me anything, probably because this is still *technically* a disciplinary meeting and while he's meant to be helping me learn and grow as a manager, he seems to think the best way to do that is to keep subtly reminding me I'm scum.

Because Croydon is the head office, it's in a slightly nicer retail park than our home store up north. It's not quite a proper shopping centre like Meadowhall back in Sheffield or Liverpool ONE back home, and it's certainly not an American-style "mall", but they share a car park with a Vue cinema and there's a PizzaExpress a few doors down, so compared to our branch it's practically on the Champs-Élysées. I'm not really in a pizza mood, though, so I slink next door and grab a cheeky Nando's without the lads. Not that I've got lads in Sheffield either.

I'm shown to my table by a nice lass named Rita who asks if I've been to Nando's before and talks me through the menu even though I say I have. Once I'm settled in, I whip out my phone and use the app to order a Fino Pitta with Smoky Churrasco sauce and a corn on the cob. Because there's something about fast food chicken places that mean you have to have a corn on the cob, just like you have to have candy canes at Christmas.

While I'm waiting for my scran, I ring Claire so I don't look too much like a lonely bastard.

"Everything's fine," she says straightaway. Too straightaway. Way too straightaway.

"It's not, is it?"

"It's mostly fine."

"All right." I curl round my phone so I'm not yelling across Nando's. "What did Brian do this time?"

Claire makes a sound. A sound she keeps special for talking about Brian. "So, you know the alarm?"

"Yeah, I know the alarm."

"You know the code for the alarm?"

"I do. I'm guessing Brian didn't?"

"He did not."

I'm beginning to wish I'd got a starter. "It's 1-2-3-4. How did he forget 1-2-3-4?"

"He says he panicked. Apparently, the timer was too much pressure."

"Tell me the police didn't have to come out."

"The police had to come out."

I should really have got that starter. "Tell me they haven't put us on a freeze."

"They've put us on a freeze. They said it was the third time this month and they couldn't keep answering frivolous callouts from a bed and bathroom warehouse."

"We're not a warehouse, we're a superstore."

"Strangely, they didn't consider that to be an important distinction. Point is they won't be responding to our alarms for another six weeks."

Given how much Claire likes to yell across the shop floor, I have a flash of panic. "Don't say that too loud, we'll get burgled."

"Don't worry, I'm in the office with the door closed."

That worries me worse. Which probably says bad things about my faith in my team. "Are you sure you shouldn't be out supervising?"

"It's fine, Amjad's watching Brian, and I've assigned Tiff and New Enthusiastic Chris to different departments, so she isn't a bad influence on him. How's it going with His Royal Dickishness?"

"He's still not happy you call him that."

She makes a musing noise down the line at me. "I bet he is, you know. Men like that secretly love thinking other people hate them. They confuse it with getting results."

My pitta arrives and I realise I forgot to order a drink with it. "I couldn't ask yez for a coke, could I?" I ask the feller that brings it to me.

"Sorry, you need to use the app or go to the counter."

I look at the queue at the counter. Things are a lot closer to heaving now, so I minimise Claire and order on the app. I'm too young to be saying things like *and they call that progress,* but this does not feel like progress.

"Hello?" Claire is half-shouting from the other end of the phone. "Are you still there?"

"Sorry, my chicken came."

"Oh, are you in Nando's?"

"How'd you know that?"

"KFC doesn't do table service, I remembered there's one next to the Croydon branch, and in another life, I was Sherlock fucking Holmes. Now how'd things go with Forest?"

"Badly."

"Thanks. Very clarificationy."

I take a bite out of my Fino Pitta with Smoky Churrasco sauce. "Well, I don't want to cause any panic, but he might have implied he'd close us down if we didn't step our game up."

"He what?" asks Claire, audibly panicked. "That…that makes no sense."

"I think he's just playing hardball but—"

"I'm pretty sure that man *only* has hard balls."

"Would you not talk about Jonathan Forest's balls when I'm trying to eat?"

Claire slips into denial right on cue. "He's bluffing. He has to be bluffing."

"What, the man you've just pointed out suffers from a rare ball-hardening medical condition?"

"Fuck," she swears down the phone at me. "Fuck fuck fuck fuck fuck. You have to do something."

She's doing well. That was anger straight into bargaining. "I *am* doing something. I'm going to shadow him today and then when I get back I'll—"

"No, I mean, do something big. Something now. Because if our only hope is to get better at doing our jobs, we are mega, mega shafted."

"So what do you want me to do? Ask him to show me the warehouse and then bash him on the head with a Soft Close Tongue & Groove Wood Effect Toilet Seat?"

"Yes."

"No."

"Okay, probably no." I hear the air go out of her. "Shit. Shit fuck shit fuck shit."

Welcome to depression. "I know. It sucks but we'll work through it."

"We really need to revisit firing Brian."

"Brian has his nan to look after. Besides, when we were talking, Jonathan made it pretty clear that just firing Brian wouldn't cut it." I explain the details of the point-by-point screw-your-staff-for-a-few-extra-quid plan.

"Right." Claire's quiet for quite a long time. "Just out of interest, who *is* our second-worst employee, by Jonathan's numbers?"

"Tiff."

She's quiet again. "To be fair, she *does* have a pretty shitty work ethic."

Some weird, probably mildly sexist, instinct makes me want to defend her, like she's my sister or something. "She's not that bad."

From down the line, I hear Claire moving across the office to the window. "She's in the car park right now kicking leaves."

"Better for the staff to be giving one hundred percent eighty percent of the time than seventy percent one hundred percent of the time," I say, not quite sure if the maths checks out.

Even if it does, though, Claire's not having it. "Tiff gives forty percent forty percent of the time and about one percent of the time she gives ten million percent. Which is sweet but not necessarily what we need."

"Claire." I'm not sharp exactly, but I do let my exasperation come through in my voice. "We're meant to be a team. Whose side are you on?"

"Ours, obviously." She sounds resigned. "Guess you'd better grab that toilet seat and smack him one."

"Not helpful."

"Okay, but we need a plan. And if you won't let Brian go, it might have to be drastic."

"Drastic like what?" I ask.

And she's quiet again. "Fake a heart attack? He can't ask you to fire people if you're in hospital."

"You're right, he'd make you fire them."

"Trick him into sexually harassing you?"

I choke on my Fino Pitta with Smoky Churrasco sauce. "Firstly, how? Secondly, no. Thirdly, I think that's disrespectful to actual victims."

"Fair point. How about you very quickly discover evidence of his shady financial dealings and threaten to tell the shareholders?"

There's smoky churrasco sauce on my fingers, so I switch my phone to the other side and wipe them on a napkin. "Good plan. Couple of tiny problems: he hasn't *got* any shady financial dealings, and even if he did S&S is a privately owned company so he doesn't actually have shareholders I could tell on him to."

"Well, if you're going to nitpick."

"Sorry."

"What if we invite him to visit *our* store so he can see us as people and be too sentimental to make you fire any of us?"

"Now you're really reaching. He's met me loads of times and I'm pretty sure he still wouldn't piss on me if I was on fire."

She's silent again.

I'm silent back.

"Shit," she says at last.

"I know. I've got a few months, like, but I think we're basically fucked."

"Well." Claire doesn't sound very helpful, or very hopeful. "Do what you can?"

"I will," I tell her. Not that I have the first fucking clue what that is.

I've lost my appetite for my Fino Pitta with Smoky Churrasco sauce, so I slide the plate across the table, get up, and head back to face Jonathan Forest.

I CARRY ON SHADOWING JONATHAN as he prowls the shop floor looking for staff who aren't being productive enough, and I'm sure if I paid attention I could learn a lot. A lot about being sort of a knobhead, mind, but a lot. Problem is it's hard to concentrate with Claire's voice saying *yez've got to do something, Sam* in my head all the time. We move upstairs from bedding to bathrooms, and I find my eyes straying to the merchandise as if the bash-him-on-the-head-with-a-bog-seat plan is in any way workable. It definitely isn't.

Probably isn't.

"I do really appreciate what you're doing here," I tell him. I don't, but kissing his arse is the only strategy I've got that's not illegal, immoral, or embarrassing to try in front of a pyramidal display of Croydex Flexi-Fit Grosvenor Toilet Brushes. "A lot of bosses wouldn't have given me this chance, like."

"Are you sucking up to me, Sam?"

"Is it working?"

He raises an eyebrow. I'm beginning to think he seriously overuses them. "Do you think I'm the kind of man who likes being sucked up to?"

I do. But I also think he's the kind of man who likes to think he doesn't. "Probably not, sorry. Still, I really am glad you've given us a chance to get things straight before we start with the firings."

I'm hoping he'll go along with that, but you don't get to run a chain of bed and bathroom superstores with three whole outlets by letting stuff slip by you. "To be clear, there *will* still have to be reductions."

So, he was calling them reductions now, was he? "I know, I'm just building my way up to it. Mentally and that."

He gives me a look that would be almost kind if it wasn't so fucking patronising. "I know it can be hard, but you aren't there to be people's friend, you're there to be their boss."

I want to remind him that being a boss doesn't mean being a money-grubbing little shitebag, but for all he says he doesn't like to be sucked up to, it's pretty clear he doesn't like being talked back to either. "True," I say instead.

We're leaving bathroom accessories and moving into showers and wet rooms when Jonathan stops, and his avaricious hawk eyes turn to a team member who seems to be closing a deal on a Nexa by MERLYN 8mm Sliding Door enclosure.

"I know it's top of the price range," the team member is saying—he's a tall lad, very tall, but he handles it well. He's got that skill of being large without looming that big fellers learn quick if they don't want to go through life scaring the shit out of people. "But it's worth it. It's classy, it's luxurious, and because of the shape"—he indicates the width and depth of the unit, mostly for distraction I'm thinking—"it fits really well even if you have a smaller bathroom."

The customers—young women, white collar jobs, probably outfitting a first house if my sales instincts are working—give him a collective not-sure-we-want-to-spend-the-money look. "The thing is," says one of them, "we've just bought our first house"—called it—"and so we're a bit… We want it to be nice but we're also a bit…"

"It was very expensive," says the other lass. "With stamp duty, solicitor's fees, furniture, white goods, a *Dyson*. It's all adding up really quite fast."

The first one elbows her partner and gives her a sharp *Allie* which I'm pretty sure is code for *Allie, why are you talking about our personal finances in front of a man who sells showers.*

"It's alright." The lad nods. I swear he's just got three percent more South London. Sometimes a working-class accent makes people trust you, because it makes them think you're too thick to have an agenda. "This is just me," he says—it's not just him, it's a well-rehearsed bit—"but if you want some free advice, there are things you skimp on, and things you don't skimp on. And something you're going to use every day that will last you ten years, that's something you don't skimp on."

They look at the Nexa by MERLYN 8mm Sliding Door enclosure with a mixture of desire and apprehension. "Do you have one at home?" asks Allie—it sounds like she means it as a gotcha but we get this all the time.

"I got the next model down," he says, "but I'll be honest, I wish I hadn't. It's fine, but I look at this every day and think *if I'd just put down that couple of hundred quid extra*."

They're this close to treating themselves. And the lad's right, this isn't something you cut corners on.

"Delivery?" asks Allie.

"Free. Installation's a bit more but we can work something out."

Work something out is code for *charge exactly what we intended to charge, but be friendly about it*.

The customers exchange glances and squeeze each other's hands in a let's do this kind of way. And the lad is just about to close the deal when Jonathan *fucking* Forest steps in like a smarmy badger. "Sorry to interrupt," he says, "but my colleague here seems to have forgotten to tell you about our protection and service plan."

The sales lad looks at him and then, when he realises that'll do no bloody good he looks at me. And though we've never met, I know exactly what he's thinking, because it's exactly what I'm thinking. Which is that you do not under any circumstances try to upsell a couple of twentysomethings who are a harsh word and a loud noise away from running out the showroom without spending eight hundred and eighty-five pounds plus installation on a walk-in shower.

"Is that...something we'll need?" asks the one who isn't Allie.

"You can find," Jonathan says with a confidence that he most certainly has not earned, "that with this kind of unit—if it's not treated carefully—problems can build up, seals can go. It's all minor things but by buying our protection and service plan now you can save yourself much more in callout fees for small maintenance work."

He is blowing this. He is fucking blowing this. And worse, he's doing one of his own fucking team out of commission on a sale that'll be nearly a grand by the time they get it through the till. The tall lad is looking at me like I don't know what and since he can't say anything on account of not wanting to get fucking fired—

I step forward like a deer stepping in front of another deer in the mistaken belief it's immune to being hit by cars. "Can I let you in on a secret?" I ask. And to my *immense* good fortune Jonathan Forest is too stunned to tell me to shut up immediately.

"Sorry," asks the one who *is* called Allie, "who are you?"

"Oh, don't mind me," I tell her. And like the tall lad I've gone just three percent more regional. "I work at a different branch so it's not my place, but the thing about this extended warranty malarkey"—to be clear, I very seldom say *malarkey* in everyday life—"is that when you think about it, we wouldn't sell it to yez if we thought you'd need it."

Allie and not-Allie hover in confusion just long enough for Jonathan to say, "Sam, I don't think—"

But I ignore him. And fuck does it feel good. "What I mean," I go on, "is that this is a good product. I know he might have made it sound like it's hard to take care of, but it's not. You just give it a bit of a wipe down when you're done, spritz it with some grout cleaner every now and then, and it'll cause you no trouble. If you've got the cash spare, and you want the peace of mind, the protection and service plan can be a load off, but I'm not going to sell you anything you don't need, or anything that won't last you, or anything I wouldn't use myself, and neither would any of my colleagues." I gesture to Jonathan and the tall lad who is looking as relieved as he can given that I'm still only half convinced I've saved this.

Not-Allie still seems a bit unsure, and says she's unsure. I used to be better at this, but I've not been on the sales floor for a while. In some ways I miss it—not in an always-be-closing, thrill-of-the-chase kind of way, but when you do a sales job right you really feel you've helped someone. Management's more like washing up. Any sense of achievement is fleeting.

"Well, tell you what," I say, "how about you have a talk with"—I turn to the tall feller—"sorry, I don't actually know your name."

"Liam," he tells me—his mam must've been an Oasis fan.

"You go have a talk with Liam here, and he can run you through some options, and I bet he can find something that works for you."

A lot of the time, what the customer really wants is for somebody to give them permission to do what they were always going to do. Allie and not-Allie nod gratefully, and Liam takes them aside.

Jonathan doesn't even wait until they're out of earshot to start bollocking me.

"What the *fuck*,"—he isn't keeping it down that much, but

he whispers the word *fuck* like he doesn't mind people seeing him lose his rag as long as they don't hear him say a bad word—"was that all about?"

"You were tanking the sale."

His eyes narrow. He definitely overuses those eyebrows. "I was *not* tanking the sale."

"You were, mate." I shouldn't call him mate, but it just slips out. "They were worried about spending the money, and you made it sound like the product would be hard to live with."

"I was demonstrating to you *and* to Liam how to inform a customer of the advantages of the protection and service plan."

"No." I'm in a hole, I should stop digging, but I'm from a long line of diggers and in some ways, this is the most honest conversation I've had with Jonathan Forest since I've been working for him. "You were making them think that the product wasn't good enough on its own, so they'd need to pay extra or suffer a load of aggro they didn't want. Problem is they were what you might call highly aggro-sensitive people. You nearly put them off the unit completely."

For a while he's very quiet, and when he speaks again his voice is very low and very tense. "Are you trying to tell me how to do my job?"

"No," I say as calm as I can because this is very close to getting out of control, "but selling showers *isn't* your job. It's not even my job really, it's his." I nod in Liam's direction where—it has not escaped my notice—he and Allie and Allie's other half were hovering in a cloud of not-sure-how-to-react-to-this. "And he was doing fine. You don't have to manage every little thing everybody does."

"Are you *trying* to get yourself fired?"

I take a breath. Honestly at this stage I might as well be. "I'm sorry. I know I was out of line. I was just trying to save the sale."

"The sale," he insists, cold like, "was *fine*."

And before I can stop myself, I've said, "No it wasn't. Y'know, for a man who says he doesn't like being sucked up to, you're not very good with constructive criticism."

It's a little dig. Just the teeniest, tiniest digette. But I must have been on thinner ice than I thought what with all the times I've said fuck in front of him today, because just like that, it's as if somebody has flipped a switch. He doesn't lose it exactly—the impression I get of Jonathan Forest is that he's not an emotional man even when he's angry—but he gets very still, and very focused, and somehow seems taller than he actually is.

"How *dare* you." He's not shouting, but his voice carries, and he's got this energy to him that makes it feel like he means really serious business.

"I'm sorry I didn't—"

"Do you think I let *anybody* talk to me that way?"

"Obviously not but—"

"You are *fired*."

"Okay but—"

"Your whole *team* is fired."

"Now hang on—"

He's taking a step towards me. Not threatening, just closing the distance like he's about to hand me an imaginary P45. And that what with the stakes and what with my very much needing cooler heads to prevail here, I decide to give him space.

So, I step back.

And I catch my foot on the lip of the Nexa by MERLYN 8mm Sliding Door enclosure, trip backwards, and bring the whole fucking thing down on top of myself.

CHAPTER 5

I DON'T KNOW WHAT HAPPENS next, but it feels like I'm watching TV and the cat's stood on the skip button. That lad Liam is pulling a sheet of 8mm tempered glass off me and asking, "You all right, bruv?"

And then he's saying, "I don't think he's all right."

And someone else is saying, "Give him some space."

And someone else is saying, "Who's the first aider?"

And someone else is saying, "Who's calling the ambulance?"

And then I hear Jonathan. "Hello, Sara? I've got an urgent liability question—"

Something that's probably a face hovers over me and I've got the worst headache I've had in my whole fucking life. "Look at me," she says, and I think I am but I'm not sure my eyes are getting the message. "What's your name?"

I tell her it's Samwise but that she can call me Sam like, but it doesn't come out that way—I sort of burble at her.

She pinches my ear, and I flinch.

"He's conscious," she tells somebody I can't focus on, "and responsive to pain but can't answer simple questions."

My teachers used to say that in school as well.

"Jamie, tell them we'll definitely need that ambulance."

It's getting fuzzier, and with the throbbing in my head it

feels best to just embrace the fuzzy. Feels best, probably isn't best.

As things start to go black and swimmy, I see Jonathan hang up his phone, and I wonder if he *really* called a lawyer instead of the hospital.

I'm in an ambulance. A good-looking paramedic feller is asking me questions I still can't answer.

I'm in a curtained-off bed in A&E and I'm feeling a bit more with it, but not much. I've had stitches, I think. There's blood on my shirt. At least I'm answering questions okay now. The doctor asks me my name and I tell him. He asks me what happened and I'm less certain.

"That's normal," he says, all reassuring and that. "Some memory loss is to be expected after a severe concussion."

The words "severe concussion" and "memory loss" seem to have triggered Jonathan's Superman hearing, and he pushes his way into my little cubicle full of smiles and sympathy. "Sam," he's saying, "I hope everything is okay. And don't worry, the company will—"

"Who are you?" I begin. I'm about to follow up with "and what have you done with Jonathan Forest?" but I don't get that far because he gets this look on his face like he's just had an unexpected tax bill and turns gravely to the doctor.

"Is the memory loss really that bad?" he asks.

It's not. I didn't mean it like that. "I—"

But they're not listening. "Head injuries are tricky," the doctor is saying. "He's experiencing quite a lot of confusion."

Too bloody right I am. I remember falling, and I *definitely* remember Jonathan Forest firing me and my whole branch and while I'm hoping that was exaggeration, I'm not quite wanting to take the risk.

"But he'll be okay?" asks Jonathan, and either he's faking concern for me really well, or he's concealing his concern for his public liability insurance really badly.

"Probably." The doctor's evasive, and I know how he feels. What I really need now is time. "As I say, it's tricky."

"How are you, Sam?" asks Jonathan, in that slightly too loud, slightly too clear voice that people use with kids and old people when they're not good with either.

"Fuzzy," I tell him. Which is true. "It's all very…" I trail off. In the back of my mind, I can hear Claire telling me I've got to *do something*, and while I still don't really know what that something is, I'm hoping if I keep things vague enough, I might have space to work it out.

"You'll need to keep an eye on him," the doctor is saying. "For at least a fortnight, ideally. He'll probably be okay but if he starts experiencing nausea or dizziness, or he's still showing symptoms in a couple of weeks, you'll need to bring him back in."

"Me?" It's almost funny to hear Jonathan trying to pretend he gives a shit while also trying to wriggle out of actually helping. "Surely there's somebody more suitable?"

For once I agree with him—a live alligator would be more suitable than Jonathan Forest—except also, there sort of isn't. It's just me. And sitting there in that cold A&E wing in Croydon, looking up at a man who I know for a fact cares more about his bottom line than my cracked skull, I can't face the thought of explaining that. Because it's not *for* him, it's none of his business. So instead I just say, "There might be, I just…I don't really remember."

Acting like an actual human being is clearly taking a toll on Jonathan. The white streak has flopped loose across his forehead.

"Ordinarily," he says between his teeth, "I'd be happy to. But it's the start of the Christmas season so I'm going to be very busy."

"I don't want to be any trouble." Acting like I believe Jonathan is an actual human being is taking a toll on me. I can't believe this smarmy fuckhead fired me, knocked me into a shower, called his lawyer before the ambulance, and is now explaining why he thinks his business is more important than making sure I don't have a fucking brain haemorrhage.

"Can't you just keep him in overnight?" Jonathan asks the doctor.

"Haven't got the beds." The doctor's giving us serious *I need to go right now* body language. "And we've already tried his emergency contact. The number's not recognised."

Yeah, because I've not got round to changing it. But I don't want to have to explain about that either.

"I don't believe this," says Jonathan to nobody in particular. "So, you're telling me I've got no choice?"

The doctor doesn't squirm exactly, but he doesn't look comfortable. "Well, if you refused, we'd have to find a way to make sure he was taken care of but"—with perfect dramatic timing, he twitches the curtain aside to reveal an overburdened A&E corridor full of people with things broken, bleeding, or wedged places they shouldn't be wedged—"I'd rather you didn't."

For a moment, just for a moment, I swear Jonathan Forest is considering bailing on me. But either he's not that much of a fuckhead or he's that scared of a lawsuit. "Fine." He sighs. "Come on."

That's the only signal the doctor needs to dash off in search of some other poor bastard. Meanwhile I'm stuck with Jonathan Forest and he's stuck with me and I'm not sure which of us is more fucked off about it.

I am in no way surprised that Jonathan Forest drives a BMW. I'm sure there is, somewhere in the world, a man who drives a BMW and is not a bellend but I've not met him. The thing about a Beamer is that it's the car you get if you really want to be driving a full-on-midlife-crisis-cock-on-wheels but you're too insecure to own it.

I get in the passenger side and he gets in the driver's seat and it's as awkward as fuck before we even make it out the car park.

"Thanks for this," I tell him. If I'm honest I'm not entirely sure what "this" is and I'm pretty sure I've got nothing to thank him for, but I only think that because I know he's an arse and it would be really convenient if we could start from a place where I *don't* know he's an arse, or at least where he doesn't know I know he's an arse.

Jonathan's eyes flick briefly to mine in the rearview mirror. "Think nothing of it. I'd do the same for any employee who'd had an accident."

Any employee who'd had an accident he'd caused maybe.

He clears his throat. "How are you feeling?"

Pretty crap for a whole lot of reasons. "Still a bit confused."

"And"—he's trying very hard to sound gives a crap, and he does, just not about me—"you really don't remember anything about what happened?"

This is why I'm shit at lying. It's way too much effort. "I don't remember much at all."

"Including me?"

Fuck. The right thing to do here is to be honest. To say *actually it's not that bad*. Only then we'd have to talk about what went on at the showroom, including the bit about how fired we all are. And it seems like he's as keen to forget that as I am. I'm not as confident about this sort of thing as Claire, but I get the impression that Jonathan Forest is the kind of man who can't go back on something he's said, even if he knows it was wrong. So maybe this is my chance to give us a fresh start. "I know I know you," I try.

"I'm your boss," he explains.

"Well,"—this might be pushing it, but I can't resist—"you seem like a good one."

To his credit, Jonathan looks the teeniest bit ashamed. Because, when you get right down to it, a truly great boss doesn't chase his employees into shower units and land them up in hospital. "I..." He seems genuinely at a loss. "Thank you."

If a fresh start is what I'm aiming for here, I probably shouldn't be enjoying watching him squirm. And I'm *mostly* not. After all, I've still got a head injury to deal with. But there's something feels very turnabout-is-fair-play about letting this prick pretend everything was hunky-dory this morning. Which means I can't quite resist needling him, just slightly. "So what did happen? Maybe it'll jog my memory."

There's a silence as Jonathan tries to balance covering his arse now with covering his arse later. "Well, I wasn't really—I didn't really see what happened. But I think you fell into a Nexa by MERLYN 8mm Sliding Door Shower enclosure."

"How did I do that?"

He aggressively overtakes a car that's going at a perfectly reasonable speed. "I suppose you must have tripped."

"Oh aye?" I let that hang for a bit. "Here's hoping none of your staff left out the thing I tripped over because then I'd be able to sue yez."

Jonathan goes white. "I think that's very unlikely."

"I'm only messing."

"You probably shouldn't joke about lawsuits, Sam."

I shrug. "Maybe I'm just that sort of person. I'm clumsy and I make inappropriate jokes."

"Or maybe," Jonathan suggests, "you're a model employee who never cheeks his boss."

It's the first time I've heard Jonathan Forest indulge in anything resembling humour. It's annoying because if he was like this for real, I might be able to stand him. "I'm not sure, but I don't think that sounds like me."

He doesn't answer that. Then again, how could he? Either he starts trying to convince me I've got a completely different personality like I'm Goldie Hawn in *Overboard* or he says "actually, you were an insubordinate cock and I'd just fired you" and neither of those are good options for him. Finally he settles on, "Not far now", like he's worried I might think I've been kidnapped. Although since he's driving me into a woodland, I'm not sure that's reassuring.

I've never given much thought to where Jonathan Forest lived. He's like a schoolteacher in that way—you just imagine that he only exists at work and when you go home he stops existing unless he needs to ring you up to be disappointed. If I'd had to make a real guess I'd have assumed he had one of those London apartments the size of a roll of sticky tape that cost as much as a five-bedroom house in a normal city.

He doesn't.

The other thing I'd never given much thought to, on account of how I never come south unless it's a work thing and even then I try not to, is whether there were fancy bits of Croydon. I mean I don't want to sound ignorant and that but just the name makes you think way more of, well, of a bed and bath superstore on a retail park next to a Nando's than it does of cosy detached houses with trees out front and grass all round and little stone walls running along the side of the road. It's not quite cottagecore because it's mostly new builds and half of them are way too big to be cottages, but it's strangely, overwhelmingly *nice*.

It's the kind of place that has good schools, is what I'm saying.

And Jonathan's house is huge. It's not a mansion, it's not even a McMansion. But it's a home. A proper family home—as long as your family had a lot more money than you'd ever make working at Splashes & Snuggles—with a garden so big you could lose sight of the house.

It feels wrong for him, somehow. He parks up and lets me into this big reception room, all plush carpets and open space and leading onto this kitchen-diner that's meant to be full of life and people but just looks sterile. I'm half expecting to find out he's housesitting for somebody who isn't an arsehole, or maybe that he killed the people who really live here and stashed their bodies under the floorboards and now he's going to do the same to me.

"Just sit…anywhere," he says.

I set myself down on a firm two-seater that I'd bet money he didn't pick out for himself while Jonathan stands there like he's not sure what to do in his own house. Which, from the shirts and slept-on sofa in his office, he probably isn't. After a while, he gives a little start like he's got a shock off a nylon jockstrap.

"You're going to need," he says, "things. A toothbrush."

If he hadn't been threatening to sack everybody I know, this'd be almost endearing. "A toothbrush would be nice."

"And clothes. You'll need clothes. You can't wear"—he indicates my outfit—"that for the next…until you're better."

It's my best suit so I'm a bit offended. "Why? What's wrong with it?"

"Well, it's covered in blood for a start."

I look down. Someone had removed my jacket so I'd bled spectacularly all over my shirt. I'd have felt like an action hero if I hadn't known I'd got this way by losing a fight with a shower unit. "Oh," I say. "Right."

"You should probably take it off," he says, "or it'll stain."

For all of three seconds he sounds like a normal person. A person who worries about whether you've got blood on your best top and if the chippy'll still be open if you head off now and put a sprint on like, and I'm so distracted that I'm half out my shirt before I realise that this is exceptionally fucking weird. But by that point it's too late, so I finish up and hand it over and pretend it's the kind of thing that happens all the time.

It's not the kind of thing that happens all the time and we both know it. Jonathan stares at me for too long and then looks somewhere else for too long and the part of me that's still keeping a list of shit I could sue him for notices that from a certain point of view he put me in hospital, took me back to his house, and then told me to take my clothes off.

"I..." I didn't think Jonathan Forest could blush. "Um. I."

"Do you want to call your lawyer?" I ask.

Jonathan's gaze flicks back to me, and I worry I've given the game away. Except, no. He's just flustered. "No. But I didn't mean—that is. You should— Let me do something with this and then I'll find you something to wear."

He strides into the absurdly huge, absurdly expensive kitchen space and opens a discreet wooden door revealing a brushed-steel monster that looks like a spaceship.

"Right," he says to no one in particular and then searches my shirt for a label.

I take pity on him. "Just stick it on at forty."

He's now on his knees in front of washing machine like he's in some dodgy cult obsessed with spin cycles. "I'd worked that much out. It's the interface."

I'm about to say, "what kind of washing machine has an interface?" but the answer is clearly, "the kind of washing machine Jonathan Forest would buy." So I go over and check. The spaceship has one dial and a touch screen.

"Don't crowd me," snaps Jonathan, forgetting he's being nice.

I ignore him. It's a fake amnesia perk. "How can you not know how to use your own washing machine?"

He's still looking at the spaceship like he wants to fire it. "I've got a housekeeper."

"Well, if they have to use that thing you should give them a pay raise."

"She's amply compensated I assure you." Jonathan jabs the touch screen and a row of incomprehensible symbols pop up. "Fuck."

Leaning over him, I take a gander. Up close, it looks a lot less spaceship and lot more slightly complicated microwave. I press some buttons.

"What are you—" Jonathan protests.

And then the door pops open. "That should do it," I tell him. "Now where do you keep your detergent?"

CHAPTER 6

SO MY GOOD SHIRT'S IN the wash and now I'm in a T-shirt that Jonathan gave me. It's got the word *I* and then a picture of a heart and then the word *Blackpool* and then a cartoon seagull. It's probably the least Jonathan thing I could have imagined, other than the house he lives in, but since he's in a snit about not being able to work his own washing machine, he wasn't very keen to give me its backstory. He sorted me out a towel and toothbrush as well, so I'm pretty took care of, all things considered. I mean, I'm still living with my boss and I've somehow backed my way into full-on pretending to have amnesia, and I might still technically be fired, but my dad always used to say you've got to look on the bright side because no one else will look on it for you. He might have been talking out of his arse, but it worked for him.

Jonathan, meanwhile, has fucked off to his study where he's been on the phone for an hour. I don't know who exactly he's talking to, but I'd put money on one of those calls being the lawyer again. As for me, I sneak into the bathroom—well, one of the bathrooms, he's got at least three—and turn on all the taps like I'm in a spy movie. Then I ring Claire.

It doesn't exactly fill me with confidence that her first words are "Are we fired yet?"

"Not exactly," I whisper.

"Why are you whispering?" yells Claire.

"Because I don't want Jonathan to hear me. I'm in his house. In his bathroom."

"Oh my God. Are you actually trying to get him to sexually harass you?"

"No. Firstly, like I said, I wouldn't. Secondly, he thinks I've got amnesia."

Claire's quiet for a moment, then she says: "I'm sorry, you might have to speak up because for a moment it sounded like you said *he thinks I've got amnesia.*"

"He does."

"How?"

If I knew that, I'd probably be in a much better position. "It just sort of happened. He knocked me into a shower, and I got a crack on the head from a Nexa by MERLYN 8mm Sliding Door enclosure, and the next thing I know I'm at A&E and the doctor's saying *there might be some memory loss* and I'm asking Jonathan who he is—as a joke like because he's coming on all fake nice—and he's saying *oh no, he's got amnesia* and I don't want to correct him because if I do then I'm probably fired and if I'm fired then Tiff and Brian are fired—"

"Why would you be fired because *he* knocked *you* into a shower?"

"He was firing me *as* he knocked me into a shower." Okay, he didn't *knock me* exactly, I more sort of *tripped while he was nearby*, but that's a detail for another time. "And while I'm not sure *exactly* what Jonathan's religious beliefs are, *thou shalt not do takesie backsies* is probably on his personal list of commandments."

"So you decided to tell him you had amnesia?"

"To let him think I've got amnesia. I don't think I've actually said the words *I've got amnesia*. I've just said I, y'know, don't remember much. Which at the time I didn't because, I repeat, he knocked me into a fucking shower."

She's quiet again.

"Claire? You still there?"

"What? Oh, yes I'm still here. I'm just running through all the ways that this could go horribly wrong."

"To be fair, it was going horribly wrong already. Did I not mention the he-was-going-to-fire-me part of the story?"

She sighs. "So do you have an actual plan now?"

"I've got an actual concussion now. The plan might have to come later. What I'm hoping is that if I stick around for a few days, I can get better and he can cool down and we can see where it goes from there. Also, I guess...I guess I'm maybe hoping he'll get to like me a bit and that might give me, y'know, influence like."

"What *sort* of influence?" asks Claire. It seems as though she's not quite sold on my brilliance here.

"Just, y'know, general sort of influence. Like if he gets to see me as a human being, gets to see how much yez all mean to me—how important we are to each other—"

"Are we really *important* to each other?" Claire's tone is trending impatient. "I mean I like Tiff and Brian as much as anybody but..."

"Yes, yes." I reckon I'm not doing so well tone-wise myself. "You care more about your job than you do about theirs. I get it. I just mean if he starts to think of us as people instead of boxes on a spreadsheet, he might not want to fire anybody."

For a while, Claire is silent. Then at last she says, "That doesn't sound like very *much* of a plan."

"Well." I try to be lighthearted. "I'm in his house now so in a pinch I can still kill him with a toilet seat if I have to."

"You realise he's going to do way worse than fire you when he figures out you don't have amnesia."

I sit on the edge of the Duravit Starck Two Backrest Slope Rectangular Bath With Combi System—I'll say this for Jonathan Forest, he really doesn't sell a single thing he wouldn't use himself. "I don't think he'll be able to tell. Memory is peculiar. Worst comes to absolute worst, I'll just arrange to get whacked on the head again and say that's brought everything back."

"That's not a thing," says Claire very firmly. "You don't undo brain damage with more brain damage."

"Okay, I'll just say things are coming back slowly."

"Your entire life is coming back slowly?"

"I didn't say I'd forgotten my entire life. Just the bits it was convenient to not remember at the time. Like him being a prick and me being fired and—oh fuck, what about the cat?"

"You mean you actually forgot your cat or you told him you forgot your cat?"

"How could I tell him I forgot my cat if I couldn't remember my cat? But what I did forget is that if I'm away until I can magically fix everything, he's going to starve, but I've not set up the cat being part of the things I remember so if I suddenly say *hold on, I've realised I've got a cat,* he's going to twig I know more than I'm letting on." I've fucked it, haven't I? I've built this whole house of cards and it's going to come crashing down and kill my cat when it does.

"You think," Claire asks, "there's a lesson here about making up absurdly convoluted lies?"

"Claire, can you feed my fucking cat?"

"Sure, I'll just drive around Sheffield, breaking into houses until I find one with a cat in it that looks hungry."

"I'll give you the address."

"Will you give me a key? Will you ring your neighbours and say, *hi, if you see a tiny angry lesbian crawling through my front window, don't worry, she's just there for the cat.*"

"You could come and get the key. I could sneak out and..." This is getting well away from me. You'd think pretending to have amnesia would be easy on account of your not having to know anything. "Wait, no. It's fine. You can say you'd heard I'd had an accident and yez've come down from Sheffield to check on me."

"And to make sure somebody's feeding your cat."

"And to make sure somebody's feeding my cat."

She's quiet again. "So who do I put in charge of the store while I'm making the eight-hour round trip to Croydon?"

Fuck, there's nobody. Tiff's too young, New Enthusiastic Chris is too new, Amjad's great at managing himself but hates managing other people, and Brian is the living embodiment of the *before* part of a corporate training video. "Then what am I going to do?"

"Well"—I can tell in advance this isn't going to be helpful—"as I see it, you've got two options. Either you tell Jonathan Forest to his face that you lied to his face about having amnesia, or you let your cat die."

"Seems both of those end badly for one of us..." I get a sudden flash of panic that I've heard a creak except I don't know because I've got the taps running. "Shit. Got to go."

I'm so worried about getting rumbled that I hang up before she can even say goodbye. And it's a good job I do because when I turn off the water I can hear footsteps.

Then there's a knock on the door. "Are you all right?"

"I'm fine. Why?"

"You've been a while and the doctor said I was supposed to keep an eye on you."

"Yeah but"—I emerge—"not while I'm having a slash."

He gives me a stern look. "I don't think cerebral haemorrhages wait politely for people to finish going to the toilet."

I suppose he's got a point. But it's bloody typical that even when he's being caring, Jonathan Forest is kind of a dick about it. "Thanks, but I'm okay."

"And you're not feeling lightheaded or headachey?" It almost sounds like he's worried, and he probably is. Just about his bank balance rather than about my brain.

"Not so far."

"And has—I know it hasn't been long, but is anything coming back yet?" And now he sounds even more worried. Definitely a bank balance issue then.

But maybe, just maybe, this is my opportunity to get out of my dead cat problem. "Funny you should mention that," I tell him, "because while I was on the bog I was looking through my photos to see if I could jog my memory and"—I unlock the phone, hoping he doesn't ask why I remember the PIN (*not PIN number*, Amjad would have said, *because that would be Personal Identification Number Number*), and find a picture of me and Gollum, which is what the cat's called because when your mam calls you Samwise you just have to own it—"I think I've got a cat."

Jonathan recoils slightly. "That is..." Being nice doesn't come easy to Jonathan Forest, but being nice about Gollum doesn't come easy to anybody. "an interesting-looking pet," he finishes.

I'm about to say he's a stray and that his ears are like that because of an infection but then I remember I have amnesia. "Yeah, I must have took him in off the street or something on account of being an amazing person."

"Or you're a soft touch with no sense of hygiene."

"Hold on. Of the two of us"—I do a back-and-forth gesture—"which is the one who can't work a washing machine?"

He gets that angry wolf look. "I. Have. A. Housekeeper."

"And I've apparently got a cat that might starve if we don't sort it out."

"Do you not have housemates or a neighbour or—"

"How would I know? I've got amnesia."

"I'm sure"—he's trying to be patient, bless him; actually no, don't bless him, fuck him—"the cat will be fine."

Gollum is not going to be fine. Being a cat, he doesn't have a vocabulary but if he did, fine would not be in it. "What if he's not, though? What if I really care about this cat and I get my memory back and you've killed my cat?"

"I won't have killed your cat. I'm sure you made arrangements in case you were away for a long time."

I didn't. Fuck, am I a bad pet owner? In my defence, it's not like one of the things they tell you at the rescue centre is *If you're going to take this cat home, make sure he's got at least six month's food available at all times in case you get amnesia from falling into a shower*. "But what if I didn't?" I try. "My emergency contact didn't work. What if my cat's emergency contact doesn't work either?"

"That seems unli—"

"Jonathan, please." I wave the phone in his face. "Look at this picture. I clearly love this cat. That is the face of a man who loves his cat."

Jonathan's eyes flick from me to the phone back to me. "I'm not sure it's the face of a cat who loves his man."

I'd tell him Gollum always looks like that, but I'm not meant to know he does, and it wouldn't make a difference anyway. "It might help my recovery. Familiar things and all that. Get me out your hair sooner."

He thinks about it. "I'd need to arrange some things first."

"Please," I say again. "I don't want to come home to a dead cat."

He sighs. "Fine. I'll get your address from the files, and we'll drive up tomorrow. Hopefully we'll meet a friend or a neighbour who can take care of you, but if not..."—this seems to be causing him actual physical pain—"...we can bring your...animal back here for a bit."

I'm so relieved I could hug him. I don't, of course, because it'd be fucking bizarre. So I just say "thank you" and I genuinely mean it.

And Jonathan looks at me in this confused way like it's the first time he's ever done a nice thing for someone in his life. Which, honestly, it probably is.

PART TWO

GOING HOME & MEETING THE BOYFRIEND

CHAPTER 7

THE NEXT MORNING, JONATHAN RINGS Sheffield to let them know I've had an accident and won't be in work for a couple of weeks. I don't overhear much of the conversation, but I do think I hear Claire saying *oh no, but who's going to feed his cat* in a tone of pantomime concern that I think is intended to bring the distressed-cat-situation to the attention of the authorities, and Jonathan does reassure her that we're coming up to deal with exactly that issue, but that I'll be too fragile to come by the branch. Which is either nice or controlling of him depending on how you cut it.

The journey's a long, quiet one, and I spend most of it staring out the window not quite sure what to talk about with the boss who thinks I don't remember anything. "Look," I say when we get there. "You'd better wait in the car."

I'm hoping he'll let it go at that but I'm not quite that lucky. "Why?" he asks.

"Because I don't know what it'll be like in there." That's not the truth, obviously. The truth is that I don't want to have to act all disoriented and confused while I'm trying to feed Gollum and get him into his travel case. "It'd be embarrassing."

He accepts my excuse, maybe because we've been trapped in a car together for hours and he's glad to be shot of me. To be honest,

I'm quite glad to be shot of him because I've had a bigger dose of Jonathan Forest in the last twenty-four hours than any sensible person could want.

After the cat fight—I mean, the fight about the cat—we'd had a bit of an uncomfortable half hour but then settled back into pretending to be nice to each other like nothing had happened. Jonathan hadn't known how to use his oven any more than he'd known how to use the washing machine, so we'd ordered Chinese from a restaurant up the road, but I'd not really been hungry what with the concussion and the incipient risk of cat death. I'd got my own room at least, because Jonathan Forest lives alone in a five-bedroom house, but he'd kept checking on me in the night to make sure I was okay, which I would have been if he hadn't kept checking on me. I told him that what he was doing was the kind of thing you get brought up in front of the UN for doing to political prisoners and that I'd be better off if he just let me kip through 'til morning. But he seems to have got it in his head that if I'm on my own for more than half an hour together my brain'll fall out my nose and he'll have to get his housekeeper to stash my corpse under the begonias.

All of which means getting a couple of minutes alone while I went to do cat things is blessed relief.

So about my flat.

It's fine. It's completely fine. It's in a nice area and it's above a nice butcher's shop but, well, it's above a butcher's shop which is convenient but also a bit Common People, especially since I'm here now with a feller who's probably never been to a supermarket. And I haven't really done much to it, partly because I can't because it's rented and partly because… In any case, even by rented flat standards it's a bit spartan—okay very spartan, so spartan I could probably hold it against a whole army with just two hundred and ninety-nine other fellers.

As soon as Gollum hears the door open, he lies down on the floor next to his bowl and starts making how-could-it-have-come-to-this-terrible-tragedy noises. Which is bollocks because I'd left him plenty of food while I was away and, actually, he eats better than I do on account of how I got him gourmet cat food once, just to help him settle in, and now the bugger refuses to eat anything else.

I try to pat him to say hello, but he flops his tail like he's too weak to move. Mind you, his tail is pretty floppy anyway. I don't know what happened before I got him, but it's all bent into a kind of permanent question mark.

"Alright lad," I tell him. "The thing is, we've got to go to London for a little while."

He makes a sort of strangled noise which I take for agreement. And to keep him sweet I open up a new can of Wild Alaskan Salmon & Shrimp cat food. The rest I pack up into a holdall, along with some of my own clothes and other necessaries. Then I clean out his litter tray ready to bring it down to Croydon with us and, at the last possible minute, I get out the carry case.

I thought I'd been subtle. I've not been subtle.

The moment he hears it rattling, Gollum bolts. Fortunately, the nice thing about living in a tiny bedsit above a butcher's shop in Sheffield is that when your cat bolts, he's not really got anywhere to bolt to. To give him credit, though, he gives it a good go.

First, he gets behind the telly, right in the middle of all the wires, and I'm a bit anxious he's going to get electrocuted, but I flush him out okay. Then he squashes himself under the sofa like he's made out of pâté, so I shift that off him and he streaks between my legs, out the door and into the toilet, where he knocks over the toilet brush and—while I'm cleaning that up—he streaks back and hides under the bed. He curls into a tiny ball and starts crying, which would be heartbreaking if I didn't know he was putting it on.

So, I've got my arse in the air and my head under the bed, and I'm making kissy noises at a ball of fluff and claws, when I hear the door open.

"What," asks Jonathan Forest with a layer of concern hastily dropped over a deep well of contempt, "are you doing?"

"What's it look like I'm doing?"

"I dread to think."

"I'm trying to get my cat out from under the bed so I can get him in the carrier."

"And it's definitely your cat? This is the behaviour of a cat that is yours?"

I pull my head out and stare at him. "How many people do you think live here?"

"Honestly?" Jonathan contemplates my very unloved bedsit. "Zero."

This was exactly why I didn't want him up here. Well, this and not wanting him to see I still know where everything is. "I've probably just moved in or something."

"If you say so." He's not sneering, but he blatantly wishes he was allowed to.

I wish-sneer back. "What are you doing up here anyway? Didn't I ask you to wait in the car?"

"I thought you might need some help. Clearly, I was right."

"I suppose this is what I get for taking the piss out of you not knowing how to use a washing machine."

His mouth does that reluctant, out-of-practice twitch that's almost a smile. "It definitely is. Especially because I didn't make you drive for four hours so you could rescue the washing machine."

"I promise," I insist, "I do know how to operate my cat. It's just a bit more complicated than a tumble drier. This is how they are when they like you."

Gollum is still a bundle of spit and betrayal under my bed, but

I plunge both hands under and grab him anyway. He does not take well to being grabbed.

"Get the carrier," I yell to Jonathan. "Get the carrier."

Somehow, Gollum has developed at least six extra paws and he's swinging them all over the place like a lad who's had one too many bevvies on a Saturday night.

Jonathan seems genuinely alarmed. "What carrier?"

I try to point with my nose while a yowling cat does its best to headbutt me. "The one in the middle of the room."

With, if I'm in a mood to be fair, commendable alacrity Jonathan picks up the carrier and fiddles with the door. "How does this even work?"

I take a full paw to the face, and while Gollum's not a very strong cat, it's probably not great for my concussion. "There's a latch at the top."

It takes a second, but he does find it. The moment the carrier's open, I dash over and try to cram Gollum in. It mostly goes okay, apart from the help-I'm-being-murdered noises, except he manages to get one paw sticking out the end like he's in Jurassic Park and he's just been dragged into the velociraptor enclosure. Eventually, I fold him back inside and slam the door, and he looks out with huge eyes that say "I will never forgive you for this. My descendants shall haunt your descendants to the end of time and their vengeance shall be legendary."

Jonathan's white streak has come loose again, and he flops down onto my sofa. "Yesterday my life was very normal."

I flop down next to him. Gollum keeps cursing us with his eyes. "I mean, I assume mine was as well."

He tries to smooth his hair back into place. He probably shouldn't wear it so aggressively slicked because it kind of suits him now it's a bit more disarranged. "I have known you for two years and, from everything I've seen, I don't think that's true."

I shouldn't ask. I shouldn't ask. I ask. "What am I like then?"

"You live in a flat like this with a cat like that. You do the maths."

"So, I've got a slightly unfurnished bedsit with a slightly ugly cat. I think you're reading too much into it."

Folding his arms, Jonathan gazes up at the ceiling like he's not sure how much to say. "You're very stubborn and you care too much."

Somehow I'm expecting the first, but not the second. "I think I'd rather be someone who cares too much than someone who cares too little."

"Trying to care about everything is the same as not caring about anything."

I've lost track of who we're pretending to be, but I'm pretty sure the me I want to be right now is the me who calls bullshit on that. "It's not though, is it?"

"Yes," Jonathan tells me in his familiar not-used-to-being-disagreed-with tone. "it is."

I might not have amnesia, but having a concussion is no joke. By the time we've piled up Jonathan's car with my holdall and my cat and the stuff for my cat I'm fucking knackered and—which is more worrying—kind of dizzy. On the plus side, though, it does mean I drift off almost as soon as we pull out, which would've meant I could skip the next four hours of awkward small talk with my dickhead boss.

Except.

"Sam?" says the dickhead boss, leaning over me. "Sam, are you okay? If you don't respond I'm calling an ambulance."

I groan and open my eyes. We're halfway down the fucking road. "I'm responding. I'm responding. I'm just trying to have a kip."

"You need to stay conscious."

"I needed to stay conscious straight after the accident. But I have to sleep sometime."

Jonathan's frowning at me. Which, to be fair, he usually is. "Excessive drowsiness could mean there are complications."

"I'm drowsy because we've been in a car since eight and you kept me up all night."

"I did not keep you up all night. I just checked on you a couple of times."

"How is that not keeping me up?"

He frowns even harder. "Sam, you look pale. Are you all right?"

"No, I'm trying to have a kip."

"Sam." He's almost snarling.

"Okay." It takes me a second to admit it because he'll probably overreact. "I did have a moment—just a moment—of feeling the tiniest bit wobbly earlier, but I really think I'm just tired."

"And if you're not?"

I shrug. "Then I suppose I'll drop dead of an aneurism but there'll be nothing you can do about it."

Jonathan Forest is giving me a very hard stare.

"What?"

"You should take this seriously."

I know he's desperate not to be sued but I'm starting to think there might be more to it than that. "Jonathan, are you feeling guilty about what happened?"

He gives a worried little blink. "No. No. Why would I feel guilty?"

I decide to make it easy on him. "You know, because it happened in your shop and that. You don't have to be responsible for me."

"I think I do," he says, sounding almost angry about it. "The doctor as good as told me I did, and there doesn't seem to be anyone else who can."

Wow, way to stick the knife in. "Look, I'm sure I've got a thriving social life and a brilliant support network. I just can't remember them right now."

"Which is why you're stuck with me. And why I'm not going to let you pass out in the car."

I can't tell if I disliked Jonathan more back when he was trying to micromanage my work or now, when he's trying to micromanage my recovery.

As we're unloading the car, I'm still not feeling a hundred percent and I think Jonathan can tell because he orders me inside. I really want to argue with him, but I want to sit down more.

And then I lose a bit of time because the next thing I know Jonathan is standing over me with his hands on his hips.

"Clearly," he says, "that was not good for you."

"It was an eight-hour round trip on a Saturday. It's not good for anyone."

He makes a sound of frustration. "Sam, will you just accept that you've had a concussion and you're going to have to take things a little bit carefully."

I think I might hate this. I feel all pathetic and dependent, and I can't tell what's him being overbearing and what's him being nice and what's him pretending to be nice and if there's a difference. "I'm fine," I lie.

Jonathan sits down beside me. Then stands up again. Then brushes back that lock of white hair that won't behave itself. "Look," he tries. "I realise I…I realise that this isn't an ideal arrangement for either of us—"

"Yeah, I got that memo when you were asking if you could dump me at the hospital."

"Don't interrup—I mean, yes…yes that wasn't very… I'd had

a very busy week and I'm a very busy man in general and I think my point is I'm aware that makes me hard to get on with."

"Who, you?" I ask, forgetting I'm not supposed to know him. "But you're such a ball of sunshine and rainbows."

Fortunately, he's not listening. "And I'm also aware that I can be a little high-handed sometimes because I'm used to being in charge. That doesn't mean I don't want you to be comfortable here or to feel that you can't take the time you need to recover."

As apologies go, it's a D+ at best. But it's also apparently the closest thing to one that Jonathan Forest is capable of. Then again he *did* ferry me to Sheffield and back to rescue my cat and I *am* sort of on a mission here to get him to embrace his inner human being so it's probably best to be gracious about it. "All right," I say. "Thank you."

He's still struggling with basic good person talk. "And if there's anything you...need. Or...want? Then."

He runs out of steam completely. And somehow, he's managed to sneak past infuriating and into endearing. He's a bit like Gollum in that regard.

"Is it okay if I have a rest?" I ask, still kind of hating that I need to.

"Of course."

And that should be the end of it except Jonathan Forest is one of them people who doesn't think anything happens unless he makes it happen. So, while I'd be happy just being left alone on the sofa for a bit, he insists on bringing me a blanket and a pillow. And then a cup of tea and a hot water bottle. And, in between all that, he takes my stuff upstairs, lays Gollum's bowl and litter tray out in the kitchen, and starts putting together the scratching post.

It's a bit weird, really. I mean I don't need all this but there's a tiny little part of me that enjoys watching Jonathan doing things as long as the things he's doing aren't firing me or backing me into a

Nexa by MERLYN 8mm Sliding Door Shower enclosure. His idea of weekend casual is a suit without a tie, which gives everything he's up to this air of importance it really doesn't deserve. Like no scratching post in the history of the world has been constructed with this much gravity and focus.

Maybe I'm staring because he looks up and then we're looking at each other. "Is there anything we need to do in particular for the actual animal?"

Gollum has been sulking in the carrier this whole time. He's not at the vet's, though, so I'm hoping he'll be pleasantly surprised when he comes out.

"Well," I say, "we're introducing him to a new environment so we're going to have to be a bit careful with him."

Jonathan rolls his eyes. "Of course we will."

"Look, he's a cat. He's a rescue cat. Cats don't understand how cars work. We've just taken him to the other side of the country to a house he's never been in. We don't want to stress him out."

"So, what do we do?"

I try to remember what the shelter told me. "We need to close all the doors to limit the space and make sure he can see where his things are. And maybe we can put my T-shirt in front of his carrier, so he's got like a familiar smell to come out to."

After yesterday's impromptu de-shirting, Jonathan goes upstairs and grabs me a new T-shirt without being asked. This one's from Disney World and has Grumpy from *Snow White and the Seven Dwarves* on it.

"Jonathan," I ask, "why is your entire wardrobe dark suits and souvenir T-shirts?"

He glowers. "I have the suits because I buy them for work, and I have the T-shirts because other people buy them for me as a joke."

"Who's buying you joke T-shirts?"

"People with no idea what else to get me."

To be fair, I wouldn't know what to get him either. He doesn't seem to like anything except money, and he's already got a lot of that.

Once I've changed tops, Jonathan puts the one I was wearing down in front of the cat carrier and then angles it so Gollum has a nice view of the scratching post. Then he unlatches the door and, like that one act filled the non-work part of his brain past capacity, walks away to check his messages.

I crawl down the sofa in my blanket cloud to make sure Gollum can see me when he comes out. When I first brought him home, he was so traumatised he lived behind the washing machine for three days. This time, though, he sticks out his head, completely ignores my T-shirt, the scratching post, and me, and beelines straight for Jonathan, who's standing staring at his phone with the total absorption of a workaholic or a teenager.

Gollum starts rubbing himself all over Jonathan's legs.

Jonathan looks down in a bit of a panic. "What's it doing?"

"Scent marking. He owns you now."

"He does not."

"You'll have to take that up with him."

"Ow." Gollum's gone up on his hind legs and is enthusiastically climbing Jonathan's trousers. "What's it doing this time?"

"It means he likes you." I've no idea if that's true, but it seems like a reassuring thing to say.

Jonathan shakes his leg very gently but realises he probably doesn't want to punt my cat across the room. "Can you make it stop?"

"Liking you?" I ask. "Give him time. He'll work it out."

"Seriously. He's damaging my trousers. Can you move him?"

"Sorry." I hold up my hands. "You've instructed me to rest."

"Sam"—he does his best to sound forceful even though there's a cat glommed onto his shin—"you're not amusing."

"I think I am actually. I'm getting this sense that I'm a very amusing person. In general like."

"I've met you and you're not. You're just annoying. Now please move the cat."

I get up and move the cat. At least, I try to but he's not having it. The moment I pull him away from Jonathan he starts making these sad why-must-you-ruin-my-life sounds.

Jonathan glares at me over a ball of feline tragedy. "What... what's wrong with him?"

"I think you've hurt his feelings." I hold Gollum out and he hangs there like a wet dishcloth. "You see? Look at his little face."

Jonathan does, in fact, look at his little face. Then he looks at my little face and I'm not sure which of them he likes less. In fact, I can't read his expression at all. Very occasionally—when he's not haranguing yez or interfering in things that don't concern him—he's almost a good-looking man. If you like 'em sour and interesting. Which I didn't think I did.

He pulls back suddenly. "This is ridiculous. I have work to do."

Then he turns and strides off to his study and Gollum, showing a worrying lack of taste for a creature I thought I could trust, runs right after him.

CHAPTER 8

HAVING A CONCUSSION IS SHIT. Because, the thing is, I'm basically fine except I need to keep watching myself in case I suddenly get not-fine and it means I'm about to die. We've made it to Sunday afternoon, and I've managed to be all still-alive, and I've got a lot of hours of still-alive-being ahead of me before I can reasonably go to bed.

Jonathan's in his study working and Gollum's in the study with Jonathan. And that's, well, I mean, I don't really like weekends at the best of times, but at least I've got my cat. But now I'm concussed, and I'm bored and I'm alone and my fucking cat has dumped me for my fucking boss. Which really stings because he's a wanker. Plus, I'm meant to be doing this whole thing where I get him to see me as a person so he won't just fire me once I'm medically cleared, and it'll be really hard to do that if I never speak to him. Which I can't. Because he's shut up in his study. With my fucking cat.

It's coming up for three, and I'm about to queue up my fourth consecutive episode of *Homes Under the Hammer,* when I realise I have to do literally anything else. So I get up, go into the study, give Gollum—who's sitting on Jonathan's lap as happy as can be—a look of absolute betrayal and tell Jonathan I'm going for a walk.

"Jonathan," I say, "I'm going for a walk."

He doesn't even look up from his laptop. "You are not."

"I think I am. My feet are going one in front of the other and everything."

At last he deigns to swivel his chair around. With Gollum right there he looks like an actual supervillain. "What I mean," he explains, "is that I'm too busy to come with you, and you can't be walking around unaccompanied with an unhealed head injury."

The worst thing is he's not totally wrong. "So, I just have to sit in the front room watching telly until you're done being a bath and bedding magnate?"

He nods. Just fucking nods. What a prick. "I don't like it any more than you do."

"I don't think I agree with that. I'm going spare here. I'm going stir crazy."

"And I'm sorry but—" Suddenly it's like he's got an idea, and I'm beginning to wish he hadn't. "Give me your phone."

"You what?"

"Give me your phone. I'll set up location sharing and then I'll know where you are."

I'm not sure I want Jonathan Forest to always know where I am. But I'm not sure me-with-amnesia knows what a terrible idea it is. Also I really want to get out the house, so I pull out my phone, unlock it, and hand it over.

Jonathan does some stuff then gives it back to me. "There. Now I can track you and I've set up an alarm to remind you to text me every twenty minutes until you get back."

"Jonathan"—I try to sound playful, but I probably come across as deadly earnest—"do you not think this makes you sound like a little bit of a psychopath?"

"I don't care how I sound. I care that if you collapse, I'll find out before you bleed to death inside your own skull."

It's hard to argue with that. Once somebody's brung up

skull-bleeding, it has a tendency to end the conversation. So, I leave him to his work and my cat, put my coat on, and head across the road into the woods.

The afternoon is crisp and wintery, so I'm glad of my coat. It's one of them gentle, urban woods that's all wide-spaced trees and heathland, and when you've been going a bit, you forget you're in London until you get to the top of a hill and the trees clear away and you can see Croydon town centre squatting in one direction and Canary Wharf standing like a massive upright cock in the other. But even that's nice in a way, because it makes you realise that the city—no matter how big it is, no matter how much you can't get away from it—is still just buildings on a river and if you go to the right part of the right forest on the right day in December it can look small, and distant, and not important.

My alarm goes and I text Jonathan. Two words: not dead. Then I stroll back down the hill to keep up my rambling. I stop by one of those signs the council puts up. The ones with a cheery map of the woods on a green background and pictures of all the wildlife I might see if I keep an eye out. There's woodpeckers here, apparently, and Dartford warblers. Not that I'd know a Dartford warbler if I fell over one while it was warbling its distinctive warble of *I'm from Dartford*. Besides, it's winter, they've probably migrated. If they do migrate. Though from the name you'd think they stayed close to Dartford most of the time.

It's nice is what it is. The kind of place you'd want to bring your dog or your kids to, which is odd because Jonathan's got neither. He's got a cat now, of course, *my* fucking cat, but the RSPCA says walking your cat is a bad idea and even if it didn't I can't imagine Jonathan Forest walking anything. Or anywhere, really. Like obviously he can walk, I've seen him walk in an I'm-in-this-place-now-I-need-to-be-in-that-place way. And he can be a pacer. Good God can that man pace. When he's not at his desk he barely sits down because he's always doing something, or looking for something to do, or climbing the walls because he's had nothing to do for six seconds and it's messing with him.

But I can't imagine him just, like, *going for a walk*. Like thinking to himself, *I know, I shall go for a walk in the woods that are conveniently located right across the road from the very large, very expensive house I live in totally alone.*

And just like that I catch myself feeling sorry for Jonathan fucking Forest. I do not want to feel sorry for Jonathan fucking Forest. Because he's a knob. He's a prick. He's a cock. He's a total dickhead. It's just I've been as good as living with the feller for two days and I don't know how he does it. I don't know how just being him doesn't completely grind him down to nothing with the emptiness of it all. Then again maybe it has, maybe that's where the knobbishness and the prickishness and the cockishness and the dickheadishness all come from.

Or maybe that's just me making excuses for him.

I text him my not dead again, take one last look around for a Dartford warbler and, when I don't see any, I head back.

As soon as I push the front door open, I hear raised voices from inside and my first thought is that Jonathan's listening to *EastEnders* really loud. Except I've never seen him watch TV so it must actually be people.

"—is you've got all this space," an older, extremely cockney woman is saying "and there's going to be me, your dad, Nanny Barb, Granddad Del, Auntie Jack, Nana Pauline, Barbara Jane, Theo, Kayla, little Anthea and she ain't so little no more—"

Jonathan cuts right over her. "I don't need you to name every person in the family."

"I sometimes think I do. You don't see us much, do you?"

"I'm very busy," snarls Jonathan predictably, and Gollum mews in his defence.

"Since when have you got a cat?" asks another voice—this one's different, the accent is one I've got well used to in Sheffield—and I take that as my cue to stop lurking in the door like some weirdo and come in properly.

"He's mine," I tell them.

Jonathan's mid-argument with two people, both somewhere in their late fifties. There's a woman in a bright yellow cardy over a red blouse and a man in a sheepskin jacket who looks like he's about to sell you a dodgy watch.

"He's got a guest." The woman spins round and gives me the brightest smile I've seen in days. "Johnny"—she turns to the feller in the sheepskin—"he's got a guest." Then she turns back to Jonathan. "You didn't tell us you had a guest." Then, without waiting for a reply, she's back on me. "He didn't tell us he had a guest. He never has guests."

Jonathan's face is absolutely thunderous. It's like he wants to fire everyone in the room but can't because they're his family and that's not how it works. "He's not a guest. He's someone I…someone from the Sheffield branch. Sam, can you give us a moment. This is private."

"It's not private, Sam." The woman pops over to give me a hug. Which isn't something that's happened to me in a while and feels sort of intense but not terrible. "Now I'm Wendy. I'm his mum. And this here is his Uncle Johnny."

"Pleasure, lad." Uncle Johnny shakes my hand with just enough force that I think it's a test. I squeeze back slightly less hard than he does so he doesn't take it as a challenge but I don't look like a pushover.

"Mum, Johnny, stop introducing yourselves." Jonathan is not taking this well. He's taking it about the way you'd expect him to take it if he was sixteen. "Sam, go to your room."

I stare at him. "You what? You're not my fucking dad."

I'm pretty sure Jonathan Forest is incapable of contrition, but he dances round the edge of it sometimes. "I just mean, can you give us some space?"

Wendy puts her hands on her hips. "That's not it at all. He just don't want his friend to know what a bad son he's being."

"I'm not a bad son." Jonathan is this close to going full werewolf.

"It's alright," says Johnny. "Nana Pauline said I were a bad son too."

Jonathan glares at his uncle. "Please don't defend me, Johnny, we are *nothing* alike."

"We're a bit alike. You take after your dad a lot."

You wouldn't have to be, like, super special attuned to social situations to know that this is the time to leave. Politely. Jonathan's practically giving off steam. He's so on edge that even Gollum is picking up on it and keeping his distance. "Well, it was lovely to meet you both," I tell them, "but this does sound like a family matter so I'll head upstairs."

Things are tense enough that I only get quiet goodbyes from Wendy and Johnny as I scoop up Gollum and slink up to my room. Occasionally I hear loud voices from the kitchen. And usually it's Jonathan but sometimes it's Wendy and it's strange but it feels comforting somehow. Obviously people shouting in each other's faces isn't ideal like, but it's been so quiet and spooky the last couple of days I'm glad of it.

Plus, it seems to have got me my cat back.

I reach down and scratch Gollum behind the ears. "You're a fickle little bastard," I say. "But I hope you've learned your lesson."

He *murrs* at me. I don't think he has.

About twenty minutes later I get cheery *Bye Sam*s yelled up the stairs, which tells me the family are leaving.

I give it another twenty minutes and then I head back down, Gollum running behind me. Jonathan has gone straight back to work in a way that looks very much like he's trying to make a point. Probably to people who aren't here anymore.

I hover in the doorway. "You alright?"

He doesn't look up. "Why wouldn't I be?"

"Because you've just had a row with your mam and your uncle?"

"Families fight, Sam."

Gollum springs onto the desk and starts batting his head under Jonathan's hand until—to my full-on amazement—he stops typing and starts stroking him instead. He's got big hands, has Jonathan Forest, slightly too big for his bony wrists. And knotty knuckles like someone's put an Ent in a business suit.

"I know families fight," I say. "Do you want to tell me what you were fighting with yours about?"

I'm expecting him to just say "no" without even turning around. Then I'm just expecting him to say nothing. But eventually he says, "My mother wants me to host Christmas this year."

I mock-*tsk*. "What a bitch."

Now he does turn round, Gollum dive-bombing onto his lap. "I know you've got amnesia but did you just call your boss's mother a bitch?"

"I was joking. I mean, that sounds like quite a reasonable thing to ask on account of how you live in a big empty mansion."

Jonathan's dark eyes bore into mine. "Well, it's not reasonable. I'm—"

"I know, I know, you're very busy. But it's fucking Christmas and they're your fucking family."

"You work in retail, Sam. You know how important this quarter is."

I'm about to say, "It's not more important than the people you love". Except I don't because not everybody's as lucky as me and not everybody's family is the sort of family you're mad keen to spend your holidays with. And I don't want to be saying *oh you've got an obligation* if he's going to come back with *actually they threw me out when I was sixteen.*

Not that Johnny and Wendy seemed the sort. But the sort often don't.

"Look," I try, "it's not my business—"

"It really isn't," he agrees.

"—but you've worked hard and made a success of yourself—"

"Thank you for the validation."

"Can you let me fucking finish?" I'd glare at him but I've not got a face for glaring. "I'm trying to say that if you don't like your family or you've got reasons for keeping them out that I don't know about, that's fair enough. But if it really is just *the job* then...y'know...there's other things that matter in the world."

He swivels back to his laptop and makes a good go of working while Gollum makes a good go of stopping him. "I like my family," he says at last. The words come out slowly, like he's confessing some terrible sin. "But I have real demands on my time and this isn't a house for entertaining."

"This house has three reception rooms, five bedrooms, and five bathrooms. How much more made for entertaining can it get? And, anyway, you're not entertaining, you're having the family round. It's a different thing."

He flashes a dangerous glance over his shoulder. "And why should I take advice from an amnesiac who lives in an empty bedsit above a butcher's shop?"

I know Jonathan Forest's a dick and, as a dick, he sometimes—he often—says dickish things. But that was fucking personal. "Well, clearly," I say, "you're not."

And then I turn and walk away.

I DON'T SLEEP WELL THAT night. I end up thinking about things I don't want to think about. It's enough to make me wish I really did have amnesia. In any case, I look sorry enough for myself at breakfast that Jonathan—who's tucking into his customary black coffee and half a grapefruit—almost gives something vaguely like the impression that he might be beginning to feel something that might at some point move somewhere in the direction of guilty.

"About last night," he says instead of sorry. "What you have to understand is that my relationship with my family is very complicated. It's not that they've ever treated me badly. It's just that there are a lot of them and I don't have a lot of time and, over the years, we've got bad at accommodating each other's needs."

If I was in a better mood, I wouldn't push it. But I push it. "The thing about being bad at something is that you can get better at it."

"This isn't your business, Sam."

He's right. I'm not sure even sure why I give a crap. I'm not here to be Jonathan's friend, I'm here to get him to like me just enough that Tiff, Brian, and me all get to keep our jobs. Getting mixed up with family drama is exactly the kind of aggravation I don't need.

"Anyway," he goes on briskly, "I'll need to go in this afternoon. But the housekeeper will be around so..."

"So if I fall over dead there'll be someone to say *oh no, how sad*?"

He refuses to rise to this. "If you need anything, you can text."

"Thanks," I say. "Big of you."

He refuses to rise to this and all. His family must've really got to him.

I go looking for breakfast of my own, which I take as a good sign because I've not had much of an appetite the last couple of days. Only it turns out it's actually a bad sign because I'm discovering the only food Jonathan has in the house is fresh fruit and the stuff I brought for the cat. And while it's good quality and makes a big deal about how it's made with real meat and fresh fish, I'm not quite that desperate.

"Do you not," I ask, "eat? Like, at all?"

Jonathan gestures at his grapefruit. And, thinking about it, he does seem like a man who lives entirely on caffeine and citrus fruit.

"No, I mean like—there's no bread in the house."

"I eat lunch at work. If I'm hungry at home, I order something."

That was what we'd been doing the last couple of days, but I'd figured it was just because I'd disrupted his routine. "I'm not going to spend the next two weeks living on takeaway. It's bad for yez."

"It's convenient, and it's restaurant quality food."

I don't know why this bothers me so much. It's not like I've not had plenty of lonely trips to the chippy myself. Then again, maybe that's why it bothers me. "So you've got this huge state-of-the-art kitchen you just never use?"

"I have breakfast here."

"You cut a grapefruit in half. That's not cooking, that's..." I try to think of an analogy. "That's cutting a grapefruit in half."

"Sam, I know you've got a concussion, but I didn't invite you into my house to get involved with my family *or* to criticise the way I live my life."

"And I wouldn't"—again I'd have pushed back less but I was a bit ratty from lack of sleep—"except it's how I'll have to live my life too for a bit, and I don't want be eating out of cartons until I go back to Sheffield."

Jonathan gets up and leaves his plate with its empty grapefruit skin on the side for the housekeeper to deal with. "So what do you suggest?"

From how he asks it, I don't think he wants an answer, but I give him one anyway. "I'm not doing anything all day, why not let me cook?"

"You cook?"

Not well, if I'm honest. But probably better than Jonathan does. "I can make a roast."

"A roast?"

"Yeah, y'know, meat and two veg but not in a cock-and-balls way."

He looks unimpressed. "I know what a roast is, Sam. I just mean—you're going to cook me a roast dinner while I'm at work, are you? Will it be on the table when I get home?"

"Well yeah, if you text us what time you're coming in."

"I've got a housekeeper. I don't need a wife as well."

I wave a hand at him. "Okay, there's a lot to unpack there, but I'm not saying I want to fetch you a pipe and slippers while you sit by the fire, I'm saying I'd like a home-cooked meal and it looks like making it myself's the only way to get one. And obviously I could sit here and eat a roast dinner on my tod, but I'd feel like a bit of a dick."

For a moment I'd swear he's tempted. And who wouldn't be? Everybody loves a roast. "Unfortunately, as we've established, I've got no food and if we arrange a delivery, it won't get here until at least tomorrow."

I'm not letting him off that easily, especially because now I'm seeing a chance to get out and stretch my legs. "Y'know, I've heard rumours that there's these magic buildings where you go in, and you give them money, and they give you groceries."

"I'm not l—"

"And don't you dare say you're not letting me go shopping. I'm concussed, I'm not on house arrest."

There's a long silence, in which it seems like Jonathan is deciding whether it's easier for him to give me what I want or keep arguing with me until I give up. "Fine," he snaps. "But it's a workday so we'll have to be quick."

Turns out, going to a supermarket is like wiping your arse. You mostly do it alone so you assume everyone does it the same way you do, but there's actually a surprising amount of variation. I think I picked up my habits from my mam. She'd go in with a good sense of what she was after but mostly she'd wander up and down, looking for bargains and that. Jonathan seems to have got his habits from movies about people escaping from prisoner of war camps in World War II. Plan the whole thing in advance, stay close, don't talk, don't get distracted, and get out as fast as you can.

I put up with this for all of two minutes while Jonathan berates me for dithering.

"I'll know what I want when I see it," I tell him.

Jonathan looks around impatiently. "We know what we want. We want a chicken, some carrots, some peas, and that's it."

"What about gravy?"

"Okay, chicken, some carrots, some peas, and some gravy."

I scan the lavish rainbow of the vegetable section, feeling better than I have for a few days. "What are your thoughts on parsnips?"

"I thought they went downhill after their third album. What do you mean, what are my thoughts on parsnips? I don't have thoughts on parsnips. Who has thoughts on parsnips? Who has time to have thoughts on parsnips?"

I'm genuinely wondering if he's lost it. "Shall we try this again? Do you like parsnips?"

"I suppose..." He makes a bewildered gesture. "I'd eat them if they were there?"

"Good enough. I'll grab some then."

Pulling out his phone, he checks the time. "Brilliant. Can we move on?"

"How about runner beans?"

"Are you going to do this for every vegetable in the shop?"

"No, just the ones I think would be nice with a roast. Ooh"—something else catches my eye—"shall I get some mushrooms and bacon and we can have them with breakfast tomorrow?"

Jonathan unleashes the biggest sigh it is technically possible to sigh before it become a scream. "Sam, get whatever you want. I don't know how many times I have to tell you that I'm busy, it's a workday, and I don't care."

I want to say, *seriously, do you have anything in your life except your job*. But I'm pretty sure I know the answer, and I'm not really one to talk. "Alright." I try to be soothing because he seems perilously close to having a breakdown in the middle of Morrisons. "I'll be as quick as I can."

And I do try to be quick, or as quick as you can be with a concussion in a supermarket you've never been in. I get a chicken, potatoes and veg, and some bread, and some bacon and eggs for breakfasts, then I hurry back to where I left Jonathan checking his email, only he's not there. That panics me a bit, although I can't tell if it's panic like a kid who's lost his dad, or a dad who's lost his kid. A little bitter part of me wonders if he's just given up and gone home without me. But then, given how much fuss I've had to make to get him to leave me alone, that seems unlikely.

Feeling a little bit smug, I remember how he put location sharing on my phone and I figure that'll probably work both ways. And it does, but all it tells me is that he's somewhere in the same building as me. So, I run the trolley up and down the aisles looking for a miserable git in an out-of-place suit.

I find him in pets looking at cat treats. And when he spots me, he gets this expression on his face like I caught him with porn.

"I thought you'd be longer," he says.

"You told me to be quick."

"Yes, but I didn't think you'd listen."

He's holding one of those cat toys that's a stick with a mouse on a string. Teasers, I think they call them. And the idea of Jonathan Forest dangling a mouse in front of Gollum is a funny mix of endearing, bizarre, and a little bit terrifying. Clearly, he wants to buy it but doesn't want to admit he wants to buy it, so I take it out of his hand and put it in the trolley. And while he's staring at his feet, pretending he's not grateful, I throw in a bag of Felix Salmon and Trout Crispies, which I know Gollum loves, but I can't admit I know he loves, on account of faking amnesia. Thankfully, Jonathan's still too embarrassed to catch my eye.

Staying angry at anybody's a lot of effort. Staying angry at Jonathan Forest is usually less effort because he's a very angry-making person. Except sometimes I'm surprisingly not angry at him and that's beginning to get a little bit worrying.

Jonathan's housekeeper arrives about twenty minutes after Jonathan leaves.

"Hi," she says. "I'm Agnieszka."

When Jonathan said housekeeper, I was sort of expecting somebody over sixty with a blue rinse and marigolds. Not an icy blonde twenty-something who looks like a lawyer. So I feel like a bit of a prat sitting under my duvet on Jonathan's barely used sofa, watching *Pointless* until it's time to start cooking. "Sam," I tell her.

"I know."

"I've got a concussion."

"I know. And amnesia, apparently." She sounds sceptical about that last bit.

"Am I in your way?" I ask, trying to distract her from the whole amnesia question. "Do you need me to get out your way? Or, like, help with anything?"

She shakes her head. "I think Mr Forest might be a little bit upset if he asked me to keep an eye on you and I made you scrub the shower."

"Between the shower and daytime TV, I'll take the shower."

"Sounds good to me." She smirks, looking a lot less lawyerly. "You clean the bathrooms, I'll watch *Pointless*."

She's joking, and I know she's joking, and she knows I know she's joking, but I can't really back out now, or it'll seem like I wasn't really offering to help at all, which I was. I shift Gollum, who's settling for sitting on me now Jonathan is temporarily unavailable, and then, very slowly, I ease myself off the sofa in the hopes she'll tell me to stop.

She doesn't tell me to stop. She sits down and hits play—on TV Richard Osman is asking the contestants to name a US state that doesn't end with a vowel.

"Wisconsin," Agnieszka says to the telly. The bloke on the screen says Hawaii either because he's forgot how it's spelled or he doesn't remember what a vowel is, and Agnieszka winces on his behalf. "Ooh, classic *Pointless* error."

I'm about halfway across the room at this point and I keep walking slower and slower, so she has time to stop me before I have to find out where Jonathan Forest keeps his sponges.

She still doesn't stop me.

The next contestant picks New York which is at least right but it's high scoring which is bad because that's sort of the name of the game. And I'm nearly at the door.

Then I'm out the door, and I can just hear an *Arkansas* from behind me, and it's not until my foot is on the stair that I hear "Are you actually going to go through with this?" coming after it.

Counting that as a win—if a completely unnecessary win—I come back. "Were you actually going to let me?"

"Well no, I'd get fired."

That hits in a way she probably doesn't mean it to. "I'm not a grass. And I really am happy to help."

She gets up. "Seriously, there's never much to do. It's a big house, but I don't think half of it gets used." Wandering into the kitchen she sweeps up Jonathan's plate of grapefruit and separates its component parts into composting and the sink as appropriate. "I've only met Mr Forest once but from what I can tell he gets up, eats one piece of fruit, comes home, and goes immediately to bed. It's probably the easiest job I'll ever have."

"I suppose, but I'd feel like a bit of a lemon just sitting here watching yez."

"You've got a concussion. It's best to relax."

I roll my eyes. "Not you too. Did Jonathan make you say that?"

"No, it's my opinion as a medical professional."

I laugh for just long enough to realise she's not joking. "What do you mean a medical professional?"

"Fully qualified doctor. But then you lot had a referendum on *should Agnieszka and everybody like her fuck off back where they came from*, and it came out *yes*, so after that I was a bit less inclined to work myself into an early grave for the NHS."

"So you became a housekeeper instead?"

She shrugs. "It was only meant to be temporary, but I got lucky with Mr Forest, and I think I'm turning out to be more of a work-to-live person. I *do* sometimes worry that he's a serial killer, but I figure I can quit if I ever have to clean up any limbs."

"I'm pretty sure he's not a serial killer."

"How would you know?" she asks. "You've got amnesia."

Somehow, I don't think the *oh yeah, I forgot* joke would go down well. Because fooling a man who doesn't pay attention to anything except himself and doesn't care about anything except sales figures is one thing. Fooling an ex-doctor who knows how concussions work might be a lot trickier. "He runs a bed and bath superstore," I explain.

"He could *also* be a serial killer."

"I think I'd be able to tell if I was working for a serial killer."

"Again, amnesia."

This is getting far too amnesia-specific far too quickly. "I still think it's the sort of thing you'd know. Like how you can still play the piano and that."

She's midway through wiping down the kitchen surfaces now and she's right, it's not a big job because they never get used—I'm almost feeling guilty about wanting to cook on them later. "And can you?"

"Can I what?"

"Can you play the piano?"

I'm very concerned this is a trap. "I dunno. Is it not like one of those things where you don't realise but then you sit down at a piano and you're like, well look at that?"

"Not really."

"Oh. Look, I'm not sure what to tell yez because the doctor said—"

She's folded her arms now, and she's stopped looking suspicious but I'm thinking that's because she's upgraded from suspicion to certainty. "I'm willing to bet the doctor said something hurried and noncommittal because he had eight other patients waiting."

I nod, hesitantly. "I guess I see why you'd rather make beds."

"And I'm also willing to bet he didn't say *you've got the movie version of amnesia where you forget neat chunks of your past but can still form new memories perfectly well and also there's this thing with a piano*."

"He didn't say that, no."

For a long, long time she just stares at me. "You haven't got amnesia, have you?"

And for a long, long time I just stare back. Then I break. "Please, *please* don't tell him. I know how this sounds but it's not just for me, it's for my team."

"Firstly, I wasn't going to." She turns back to giving the pristine a bit of a repristining. "Secondly, when would I? I've met him once and he communicates entirely by text."

"You could text him back."

"True, I could send a message out of nowhere saying *your suit's at the dry cleaners and the man who lives in your house doesn't really have amnesia*. That would in no way make my life needlessly complicated."

"I'm not living in his house," I protest. "I'm just...sleeping here and having all my meals here and my cat's here."

"That's a cat?"

"Yeah. He's a cat. I can tell you're a doctor not a vet."

She looks at him in that medical way that medical people have. "He might *need* a vet."

"He's been to the vet. He's had all his everything. He's fine, but there's nothing they can do about the ears. Or the tail. Or his face. And, anyway, you shouldn't body shame him."

Leaving the kitchen area, she comes over to the sofa and kneels down by where Gollum has perched himself and takes him by the paws. "I'm very sorry, cat."

"His name's Gollum."

"I'm very sorry, Gollum. I'm sure you're a very good cat even if you're riddled with toxoplasmosis."

"Hey." I try to give her a warning look, but I think my essential affability ruins it. "Don't be mean. And he's not got toxoplasmosis."

"He probably does. And anyway, he's a cat, he doesn't care what you say, only how you say it." She sits down between us, and Gollum scoots off—apparently he can sense slander even if he can't understand it. "So why are you pretending to have amnesia?"

I hesitate. Partly because I don't want to drop anybody in it, partly because she does technically work for Jonathan, and partly because now I'm having to say it out loud it sounds really fucking silly. "Okay, so I'm going to start at the end, which is that if Jonathan finds out I don't have amnesia, he's going to fire me and at least two of the people who work with me, maybe more."

She looks sympathetic. Not risk-her-job sympathetic, but at least won't-screw-me-for-a-laugh sympathetic. "And why would he do that?"

"I mean, you thought he was a serial killer, so I think firing a couple of people is probably within his capabilities."

"I thought he might be a serial killer because he lives alone in a big house with far too many bathrooms and enough room for a soundproofed basement. Why do you think he's going to fire everybody you work with?"

"Because he said, *Sam, I'm going to fire everybody you work with if you don't start acting like more of a bellend.*"

"I'm guessing he didn't say that exactly."

"I'm embellishing. Makes the story more interesting. Short version is he doesn't like how I run my branch, he wants me to make cuts, making cuts means me having to fire people but not making cuts means Jonathan firing me first then getting somebody *else* to fire people, or else just shutting the whole branch and firing everybody."

Agnieszka looks like she's actually paying attention, which is something else I've not seen in a while. My team are nice but they're not great listeners, and Jonathan's the same only without the nice part. "I'm still not sure where the amnesia comes in."

"Well, we were having a bit of a barney and he yelled at me and I stepped back and through a Nexa by MERLYN 8mm Sliding Door Shower enclosure—"

"Does the exact brand of shower enclosure matter?"

"It tells you how heavy the glass is when it falls on you."

She blinks. "How heavy is the glass?"

"Eight millimetres."

"That's not a measurement of weight, it's a measurement of thickness."

I move my hands in a way that I hope conveys how big a deal eight millimetres of tempered glass crashing onto your skull is. "Okay then...bloody heavy, alright?"

"I was only asking."

This is going down a tangent that I don't think is completely relevant, but the part of me that's spent too long in showrooms can't let it go. "You've seen the Nexa, though," I tell her. "He's got a Nexa upstairs."

"I just clean them. I don't look at the brand names."

"The big expensive-looking one with very thick glass in the ensuite off his bedroom."

Agnieszka gives me a getting-it nod. "Ah, that *is* heavy glass."

"I know, that's why I told you the model."

"Which is why it was good that I asked why you told me."

She's got me there. "Anyway," I go on, "I fall into the Nexa by MERLYN 8mm Sliding Door Shower enclosure—"

"Like the one in the ensuite upstairs."

"Yes, that's right. I fall into the Nexa by MERLYN 8mm Sliding Door Shower enclosure like the one in the ensuite upstairs—you're doing this deliberately, aren't you?"

She nods. "This story is already long and very silly. I was seeing how long and silly it could get."

"It's not silly, it's very important. People's jobs are on the line here. After I fell into the Nexa by MERLYN 8mm Sliding Door Shower enclosure like the one in the ensuite upstairs, I get rushed to hospital and I'm having a bit of confusion so Jonathan jumps straight to *he's got amnesia* and the doctor who, as you say, is wanting to get shot of us pretty quick like, doesn't say I don't, so I play along because I figure it'll give me time to work out what I'm doing about these cuts that Jonathan wants to make."

Agnieszka leans forwards earnestly. "Could you not just... make the cuts?"

"Oh aye? And what's Brian going to do about his nan? What's Tiff going to do about her course? What's Claire—"

"You realise I don't know who any of these people are?"

I make another evocative gesture. "Just conjuring up a bit of human drama."

"You missed your calling as a storyteller, Sam." I get a strong sense she's being sarcastic. "But I'm afraid that this"—she waves a hand at me in an evocative gesture of her own—"isn't going to help long-term."

"I know it won't help long-term. I'm working on a plan."

She looks sceptical. "Which is?"

"I've not...I've not quite got to that bit yet."

"Well, if you think of something, you can let me know, but

otherwise..." She gets up, shaking her head sadly. "I have a Nexa by MERLYN 8mm Sliding Door Shower enclosure to clean."

I thank her for listening, flop on the sofa with Gollum, and go back to *Pointless*. Except I'm having trouble concentrating on the question of which haiku represents which classic British sitcom because Agnieszka's right, isn't she? This isn't sustainable and it isn't helping. At best, it's just delaying the inevitable. At worst it's just changing what Jonathan Forest fires me for.

And I'm stuck, because I do really need to recover from the concussion, and at the same time I have to fake getting better from the amnesia in a way that somehow ends with Jonathan changing his entire personality and all his values. And that's not completely impossible—if you spend time with someone really intensely you can get to, y'know, like them. And if he likes me, he might trust me. And if he trusts me, he won't fire me, and he might let me not fire anybody else.

Of course, there's the tiniest chance he won't trust me if he finds out I've been trying to get him to trust me by pretending to have amnesia when I don't.

Fuck. I'm fucking fucked, aren't I?

CHAPTER 10

I WARN AGNIESZKA THAT I'M going to mess up the kitchen, but I promise to fix it up after, and she tells me it's fine and it's probably nice it's getting used. And it's a nice kitchen *to* use—it's all spacious and laid out and that, and it's got a well-stocked rack of herbs and spices from which I guarantee Jonathan Forest has never used a single herb or spice. Of course, it is more difficult to keep Gollum off the countertops because there's so many that if I shoo him off one, he just goes straight to another. But eventually he gets the message and goes to sulk under a chair instead. I swear he's telling me Jonathan'd let him play on the counters. And he probably would because he's never cooked.

I soften up some butter and mix it with some lemon and thyme and I'm just rubbing it into the chicken like my dad used to—my dad didn't cook much but he made a hell of a roast—when the doorbell goes. For a moment, I think about not answering because it's someone else's house, but then I figure it might be important, so I do my best to rinse my hands and head into the primary reception room.

Jonathan's got one of them fancy glass doors so I can see, even before I get there, that there's a lot of people outside. Like, a lot of people. I briefly think I'm getting arrested or home-invaded but then I recognise Wendy and Johnny in the crowd.

"Didn't I tell you," cries Wendy the second I open the door. "He's got a boyfriend. Jonathan's got a boyfriend."

And before I can say, actually I'm not and also I've got amnesia, they're all in the front room.

A tiny old lady in huge glasses who does, in fact, have a blue rinse goes buzzing into the kitchen. "And he cooks. He's found himself a bloke what cooks."

"I'm just making a roast," I try.

"And," adds yet another feller, with a broken halo of white hair and a natty blazer, "he cooks proper food. None of this nut roast bollocks."

"Language, Dad." Wendy whacks him in the arm. "You're making us look a right bunch of wankers."

Natty Blazer Feller is peering at my chicken. "Why can you say wankers, and I can't say bollocks?"

"Bollocks is swearing, wankers ain't swearing."

"I don't think that's right, love," says the little old lady with the glasses. "If it's about your underwear bits, it's swearing."

"What about tits?" asks Johnny, who's already sitting on the sofa.

An old woman I hadn't noticed yet—though God knows how, because she's dressed like Marlene fucking Dietrich, with the cigarette holder and everything—takes a drag of her ciggy. "I think you'll find, young Johnny"—she's got a posher accent than the rest of them—"that a bra does constitute underwear. So, if we accept Barbara's terms then, yes, tits are indeed profanity."

"Well tits," says Johnny.

"Anyway"—Wendy grabs me by the arm and drags me in front of the group, which is hard because the group's fucking everywhere—"this is Sam. He's Jonathan's new boyfriend even though Jonathan's trying to pretend he ain't."

"The thing i—" I try again.

"Sam," Wendy rolls on, "you know me, you know Johnny. This is Les..." She points to a tall, gruff, crumply man who hasn't spoken yet. "He's Jonathan's dad. And that's Nanny Barb, who's my mum, and Granddad Del, who's my dad."

I'm starting to feel a bit dizzy, which might be the concussion or might be the mob. Nanny Barb is the tiny one with the glasses and Granddad Del is the one who likes to say bollocks. That just leaves her with the cigarette holder.

"And this"—Wendy brings it to a big finish—"is Auntie Jack what lives next door to Barb and Del."

Auntie Jack raises a sliver of an eyebrow. "Barbara and I have been very good friends for a very long time."

There's finally enough of a gap that I can get a word in edgeways. "Lovely to meet yez. But I should probably say that I'm really not Jonathan's boyfriend."

Everyone stares at me like I've just told them their football team's been relegated.

Auntie Jack takes another drag of her cigarette. "Let me guess, you're just staying together for a little while, for totally unrelated reasons?"

When she puts it like that, it does sound pretty dodgy. "Yes?"

Nanny Barb comes over and puts a hand on my arm. "We shouldn't pressure the boys," she says. "They'll say when they're ready."

Somehow I missed the day in school where they taught you what to do when you were living in your boss's house faking amnesia and his whole family showed up and decided you were his secret boyfriend but didn't feel comfortable admitting it to them. In the end I figure it's best not to argue. "So what are you all doing here?" I ask as friendly as I can, which is pretty friendly on account of me not being from the South and so not being genetically incapable of saying hello to a stranger.

"Funny you should ask," Uncle Johnny begins, "because me and Jonathan were talking about this business opportunity I've—"

"Johnny, not now." It's the first time I've heard Les speak. He's quiet, but firm. Sort of like I'd imagine Jonathan might be if he'd get over himself for five fucking minutes.

"Why we're here," Wendy goes on, "is because this whole thing with Jonathan not wanting to do Christmas is a load of—it's—"

"It's bollocks, is what it is," says Del. "See love, you can't wanker your way out of everything. Me and Barb do it every year—"

"Barbara does it every year," Auntie Jack corrects him.

"—and we ain't neither of us getting any younger. And it's about time he stepped up."

"Especially," Wendy picks up seamlessly, "because we've got Barbara Jane coming in from Texas and she's going to be very upset what with the divorce, and Donna will be in from Romford on the day, and we'll have Kayla and Theo and little Anthea for some of it and Les's mum'll be down from Sheffield and it's just too much, Sam."

"I'm nearly eighty," Nanny Barb explains. "You can't be humping turkeys around all day when you're eighty."

"Thing about a turkey"—Del is patting me on the back and I'm not sure why—"is it's just a big chicken." He looks pointedly at my roast-to-be.

I've got my hands in the air like I'm surrendering and I'm not sure what I'm surrendering to. "Sorry, what do you want me to…"

Now Wendy's right in front of me. "We just thought you could have a word with him, love."

"I really do just work for him."

She pats me and all. "We know, pet, we know. But the trouble is we hardly see him, do we, Les?"

"We don't," Les confirms.

"And he wouldn't listen to us anyway, would he?"

"He wouldn't."

"Time was," Wendy goes on, "he'd listen to his granddad but even you can't get through to him now, can you, Dad?"

Del gets this weird look of pride and irritation. "He's an independent man," he says, "and I respect that. He's got balls."

"Contrary to what you may believe, Derek," observes Auntie Jack from the other side of the room, "not every sentence needs to contain a reference to gonads."

I'm having a hard enough time figuring out a plan to make Jonathan not fire me. I'm really not sure I can do that while also talking him into hosting Christmas for his entire family in his empty serial killer house. "Look," I try, "I don't think—"

And then the door opens again, and Jonathan's standing there on the threshold in his black suit looking like fucking Maleficent.

"What," he demands, "are you all doing here?"

Everyone goes a bit quiet.

Then Wendy says, "I'm visiting my son. I didn't realise I needed a special reason to visit my son."

Jonathan's trying to stare everybody down at once and doing a pretty good job of it. "You visited yesterday."

"Didn't realise there was a quota neither."

"And you've brought everybody with you?"

Nanny Barb slides to the front of the group. "We wanted to meet your boyfriend," she explains.

"However"—Auntie Jack blows the kind of smoke ring you can only blow with fifty years of practice—"he has now clarified that you're just good friends and we of course believe him entirely."

I put up my hands. "Hold on, I never said we was friends. I work for him."

"Our relationship is none of your business," adds Jonathan.

"And, Jack, how many times must I tell you not to smoke in my house?"

"At least a few more times, I dare say."

Just as I'm wondering how this can possibly go wronger, Del speaks up. "Point is, we come round here to have a word with Sam about you not wanting to do Christmas, and he agrees with us."

I'm about to say that I don't feel he's representing my position in a totally accurate manner, but I only get as far as "um".

"Everybody. Out." Jonathan's doing that thing where he manages to sound like he's shouting even though he's not really shouting, and you wish he just would because it'd somehow be less scary. "You have no right to come barging in like this, and I have far too much on my mind right now to be thinking about stuffing turkeys and hanging paper chains."

For a moment people are just quiet. Then Les says, "I'd rather you didn't talk to your mother that way." And he doesn't shout either.

"He don't mean it," Wendy insists. "He's just had a long day, I bet."

"My day," Jonathan's voice is rising now, just a little, "has been just as long as yesterday was, and as tomorrow will be. That's exactly what I'm trying to say. I do *not* have time for this *nonsense*. If catering is too much for Nanny Barb to manage, then I'm happy to pay for somebody else to do it. Just not me, and not here, and not with you lot coming in and dragging"—he turns and looks at me, and it's almost like it's the first time he's seen me since he's come in—"dragging Sam into it when this has nothing whatsoever to do with him."

I don't especially want to be dragged into a stranger's Christmas family drama, but being told I can't—reminded that I don't belong—stings a bit.

"Now all of you *leave*," he finishes.

Del's the first to react. He takes his wife by the arm. "C'mon Barb, we know when we're not wanted."

The rest of them file out, and Les is the last to go. He stops in the doorway and looks back. "Jonathan," he says—but then doesn't seem to know what to say next.

And Jonathan doesn't seem to know what to say to him.

Then he's gone. And then it's just me and Jonathan Forest alone in his main reception room, a room that clearly is, whatever he may say about it, designed to have more than two people and a cat in it.

"And as for you," he says. He's jabbing his finger at me like he's Perry Mason or Elle Woods and is telling me that the defendant didn't do the murder because I did. "What makes you think you can—"

"Hey, I didn't do anything." I've got my hands in the air again. "I was just standing there making a roast chicken, and then the door goes and there's all these people there."

"Granddad said you were on their side."

I give a kind of uncomfortable shrug. "Well, I don't really know him, but I think he might be the kind of feller'd say that no matter what?"

For a moment he doesn't say anything, or rather, he looks like he's trying to say about eight different things at once. Finally he settles on, "I don't have time for this. Just stay out of my business."

And then he scoops up Gollum, who nestles against his shoulder like a smug ugly baby who's decided to abandon the person who brought it home from the baby shelter, and they both storm off into the office.

My roast chicken is sitting on the side looking all sorry for itself. And in a lot of ways, I know how it feels.

CHAPTER 11

MY MAM ALWAYS SAID YOU should never cook in a mood because then your mash'll taste of spite. But since my options are cook in a mood or not eat, I don't have much choice. I finish rubbing the chicken, stuff it with lemon and thyme, then throw some oil and garlic over it and bung the whole thing in the oven for an hour and a bit. Once I've given it a head start, load up the dishwasher and get on with the veg.

I don't get angry like Jonathan gets angry—all steaming and forceful—but I am angry with him. And it's the quiet sort of anger that sits in your gut like a mouse. The thing is, he's not tret me any different than he did when I was in the store, but at work you can't say nothing, and you've got somewhere to go afterwards. Now I'm just stuck with it and it's making me a feel a bit…not okay like.

I've always been a bit suspicious of fellers who make a big song and dance about standing up for themselves because a lot of the time they wind up, well, like Jonathan. And I know he's got his three stores and his big house and all that, but he's also the kind of person who throws his own family out of his home and bullies an employee into a Nexa by MERLYN 8mm Sliding Door Shower enclosure. And some folk think that makes you a proper man but it don't. I think it just makes you a dick.

My dad was never like that. He'd hold his ground if he had to, but he'd always try to see the other feller's point of view. Which meant he never got nasty with it and if he weren't backing down you knew he had a good reason. And I'm beginning to think I might have a good reason with Jonathan Forest. Because I *have* listened, and I *do* understand why he's upset, and I know family can be complicated, but he doesn't get to take it out on me, and the old man wouldn't want me to let him get away with it.

The timer goes on the oven, and while the chicken's resting I stick the peas on; they don't take that long and if I'd started them any earlier they'd be cold by the time I was carving up. Then I transfer everything to the island in the middle of the kitchen, lay it all out so it looks kind of rustic and yell through to Jonathan that everything's ready.

"I'll take it in here," he yells back.

Like fuck he will. I storm through to the study and I must have gone faster than he expected because he's sitting there cuddling Gollum very much not doing any work. He makes a desperate attempt to look busy but all that does is dump Gollum onto his laptop, where he steps on the Windows key and opens the calculator.

"What," I demand, "is your problem? I've roasted a chicken out there."

Jonathan's gathering Gollum off his desk. "I didn't ask you to."

"No, but you asked me to bring it through to you like I'm your fucking butler."

"I have a lot going on and I didn't want you to feel your efforts had gone to waste. If walking twenty feet with a plate is so beneath you, I'll order something."

I might kill him. I might actually kill him. "I don't want you to order something. I want you to come through and have dinner like a human being. I wouldn't mind, but you're not even working in here. You're just hiding."

"I am not hiding."

"You've shut yourself in a room alone with a cat. That's hiding."

Gollum is back on his lap, and he's stroking him absent-mindedly. "I just want some space. I don't think that's too much to ask."

"You've had plenty of space. Everything from you ordering your parents out to me whacking the chicken on the table was space."

"Sam"—Jonathan fixes me with one of his intense looks—"we're not doing this."

And there he goes again. "You don't get to tell me what we're doing. We need to have a talk and we can do it over chicken or we can do it here."

"What exactly," Jonathan asks, "do you think we need to talk about?"

"You treating me like crap."

He flinches very slightly. "I do not treat you like crap."

So I guess we're doing it here. "Look, I don't know what's going on between you and your family, but you cannot take it out on me. You also need to stop ordering me around. I know I work for yez, but I'm not your servant. I'm the manager of one of your branches and, right now, I'm your guest."

"And I'm supposed to be looking after you," Jonathan retorts, "because you've had a traumatic head injury."

Aye, that he caused. "This isn't looking after me. It's just being a dick."

"For the last time"—Jonathan stands up so abruptly that Gollum shoots off his lap and out the door—"I am not being a dick. I have a lot of demands on my time, and I'm sick of having to justify myself to you and to everybody."

It's no use, is it? I tried playing nice and it didn't work. I tried standing my ground and it didn't work. I guess I'll have to go back to Sheffield and tell Claire I've fucked everything up. "There's a simple solution to that," I say, quiet like. "I'll leave in the morning."

He starts to say something—you can't, or I won't let you, or whatever—but I'm not listening. I let the door swing shut behind me.

In the kitchen, my chicken's going cold, but I don't much fancy eating it anyway. Still, there's no sense in it going to waste so I carve it up, give a little bit to Gollum, and put the rest in the fridge with the veg.

Then I head up to bed. And maybe it's just because I gave him chicken, but this time Gollum comes with me.

I don't sleep very well again, partly because it's pretty early, partly because I'm stressed, and partly because Gollum keeps sitting on my head. Maybe I should just let Jonathan keep him. Worse, I'm getting these doubts buzzing around my brain, because while I'm glad I stood up to Jonathan, I'm starting to second-guess myself, to wonder if maybe I'm bottling it. I mean okay, he hurt my feelings, but he's my boss, not my mate. And I'm not here to be friends with him, I'm here to get to know him so as I can talk him into not firing me or breaking up my team.

Except I've said I'm going now. And if I back down he'll never take me seriously anyway. Besides, all this pretending to have amnesia is going to get tiring after a while and it's probably best to get out while I still can like.

It's a ways after midnight when I hear movement from downstairs. My first thought is that it's Gollum, but he's asleep on my foot, so it can't be him. My second thought is that it's Jonathan. And it probably *is* Jonathan—I've only been here a couple of days so I don't really know what kind of hours he keeps when he's not checking up on me every twenty minutes. But my third thought is burglars. And it's probably not burglars. In fact, it's almost certainly not burglars. But there's this little voice in my head saying *it's burglars* that won't shut up. So I shake Gollum off my foot, slip out of bed, drag on a T-shirt and some pants and try to grab something heavy. Only there isn't anything because Jonathan barely furnishes the rooms he actually lives in, never mind the ones he keeps empty for the guests he never has. In the end, I pop into the ensuite and lift the top off the toilet. It's a bit too unwieldy to get a proper swing with, but if nothing else I might be able to confuse an intruder into backing down.

I creep downstairs and Gollum creeps after me, even though I try to tell him to stay behind where he'll be safe. The noises are coming from the kitchen, and they don't sound like burglary noises, they sound like someone moving around noises, which means I feel a bit of a pillock when I show up in my pants and my bare feet, clutching the top of an Ideal Standard Concept Space close coupled toilet with soft close seat like I'm Moses with the Ten Commandments.

Because it turns out my second thought was right and it is Jonathan. He's at the fridge, unwrapping my chicken.

"Hang on," I say. "You said you didn't want any of that."

He turns around. "Why are you holding the top of an Ideal Standard Concept Space close coupled toilet with soft close seat?"

"I thought you was burglars. And you are. You're stealing my chicken."

"Isn't it our chicken?"

I gently put down the top of the Ideal Standard Concept Space close coupled toilet with soft close seat. "I'm not sure we're reached that special *our chicken* place in our relationship."

Now there's chicken in play, Gollum streaks over to Jonathan and starts rubbing against him in that *feed me, feed me, I'm dying* way. Jonathan crouches down and feeds him. "I shouldn't have... I may... I was too harsh earlier."

"You think?"

"I believe it's a possibility, yes."

"What clued you in? Was it when I said, *stop treating me like crap*? Or when I said, *I'm leaving in the morning*?"

Jonathan looks genuinely pained, though I think mostly because he doesn't know how to say anything even approaching sorry. "I've reflected."

"Big of yez."

For a while he doesn't say anything, he just lets Gollum chase every last bit of chicken from his fingers and then goes to wash his hands. After that he grabs the bread I bought earlier. "Do you want a chicken sandwich?"

"My chicken sandwich?"

"Yes, do you want me to make you a sandwich with your chicken, your bread, and your"—he looks at the spread that's already on the side—"I Can't Believe It's Not Butter."

I've not eaten and I'm not proud. "Go on then."

"Then how about I do this, and you put the lid back on the toilet and"—Jonathan clears his throat—"put some trousers on?"

In all the excitement, I've kind of forgotten I'm standing here in a pair of grey tartan boxers. "Good idea," I say. "I'll go deal with that."

When I get back, with a ratty dressing gown tossed over my pants, Jonathan's sitting at the table, already tucking into a chicken sarnie.

"How is it?" I ask, plonking myself down opposite.

"It's good," he says.

I'm about to complain that it would've been better if we'd eaten it when I made it, but the truth is, the best thing about a roast is having it cold after. Instead, I take a bite of my sandwich and I feel a bit weird that Jonathan Forest made it. Not bad weird, just weird weird. Because he's about as domestic as a timber wolf, and I'd say about as nurturing but I reckon wolves take care of each other and shit.

At first, we just eat. Which is fine on account of I'm not really sure what's going on. And maybe nothing's going on. Maybe we're just both hungry. But there's something about the way Jonathan's being right now, with the sandwich and the not having a go, that makes me feel… I'm not sure what it makes me feel. But I do know one chicken sandwich isn't enough to convince me everything'll be hunky-dory from here on in. And even now I'm not quite sure what would be.

I glance across the table, wondering how to break the silence, or if I should. Jonathan's taken his version of casual to the next level because not only is he not wearing a jacket, but he's undone his top button and rolled up his shirt sleeves. I don't think he's trying to show off or win me over with his forearms, but well. There's a decent chance he could. You'd be able to get a good grip on them like. Besides, it's nice in this day and age to see a feller who doesn't manscape.

What can I say? I like my men like I like my employment prospects: rough and hairy.

"Sam," he says, looking up abruptly.

"Aye?"

He heaves a pained sigh. "I don't want you to leave."

"If I was going to die, I'd have probably died already."

"The doctor said a couple of weeks. Is your memory even starting to come back yet?"

Fuck. "Bits and pieces," I try, hoping I can build those bits and pieces into an off-ramp sooner rather than later. "I mean, I can roast a chicken, so I can probably look after myself. Probably better than you can."

"About that." Jonathan heaves another pained sigh.

"About the chicken?"

"Not the fucking chicken." He makes a visible effort to unsnap. "About the whole situation around the chicken."

"The you treating me like crap situation."

"If you insist on putting it that way, yes."

This is going to have to be good, and I honestly don't think Jonathan Forest has it in him. I fold my elbows on the table. "Alright then?"

It takes him a long time to say anything. "I have a large family." He strokes his temples and stares at what's left of his sandwich.

"I'd noticed."

"And I do care about them. Very much. More than I probably care about anything."

"No offence," I tell him, "but you've got a funny way of showing it."

"I show it by working hard so I can support them."

This is more honesty than I've had from Jonathan since I've known him. And I have to be really careful in case I give away that I do know him. "They look quite a lot like they can support themselves. Johnny seems a chancer, mind."

"He is, and I've covered his debts more often than I should have. I'm also covering my parent's mortgage, my sister's divorce lawyer, my grandmother's residential care, and making a contribution to Anthea's school fees."

"And that's good of you, but they didn't seem like the sort of people who'd expect you to."

"They don't, but I want the best for the people I care about."

It's a lovely sentiment, and would really show Jonathan's human side, if it weren't for the way everything he says comes out kind of flat and bitter, like he's angry at something but he's not sure what. "The best doesn't always come from throwing money at stuff."

"Not always," Jonathan barely concedes. "But often enough."

I look around at Jonathan's echoing, empty kitchen which opens onto the empty, echoing reception room whose big glass-fronted doors look out over the empty, probably not that echoing garden. "I'm not saying you haven't worked hard," I try, "or that you don't deserve what you've got. But what's the point of all this"—I make a sort of all-of-this gesture—"if you've nobody to share it with."

"I do have people to share it with, I've just told you."

"Aye, but you never share it with them."

He picks at the crusts of his chicken sandwich. "I do. Sometimes. Just—it's a difficult time."

"When was it last not a difficult time?"

There's no answer.

"You don't remember, do you?"

"Ironic, really." He gives me something that's almost a smile. "Since you're the one with amnesia."

The part of me that's bad at lying worries that he's taking the piss here. That he knows I'm not. "Okay, so." I do my best to move the conversation on. "Would it really be that hard to have them all over for one day?"

"It's a—"

"Yeah yeah it's a bad time, I know. Why, though?"

He looks blank. "What do you mean *why, though*? It's Christmas and I run a chain of shops. It's our busiest time of the year."

"But is it?" I ask. "I mean, I can't really remember because"—I point to my head—"but it's not like you work in a toy shop or you sell, I don't know, jumpers or jewellery or the sorts of things people buy as gifts." I'm cheating a bit here because I know from my not-actually amnesiac experience that while we do get a bit of a seasonal bump in the bed and bath trade, it's nothing like you get in less toilet-focused industries.

"There's still a rush," Jonathan insists. "Yes, *most* people get their partners socks or earrings for Christmas, but some families do in fact invest in a new bed or bathroom suite and they call it the golden quarter for a reason." He gives another one of those sighs. "And on top of that there's the company Christmas party to organise."

Because oh yes, there is also that. Every year I take my team out to the pub to say thanks for doing your jobs, but I have to pay for it out my own pocket because Jonathan Forest insists that the company will have exactly one Christmas do, and it'll be in Croydon, and the folks from other stores can come if they want but they have to work out their own transport. Honestly, it's shit, but I usually go because I need to look like a team player. The rest of the Sheffield branch can take it or leave it, and mostly leave it, though I reckon New Enthusiastic Chris'll be driving them as wants it down this year.

All this going through my head is an unwelcome reminder that I'm meant to be working on a plan. On a way to make myself and everybody who works with me look indispensable. Or at least too useful to sack. And this might just be something resembling an opportunity. "Is there," I ask, "is there anything I can do to help?"

Jonathan snorts. He's not very attractive when he snorts. Then again, who is? "How? Do you even remember what the store looks like?"

"Not exactly. But I know what Christmas is and I know what parties are, so if you need a Christmas party organised, I don't think my memory's particularly important."

For a moment, I think I've scared him off—that the humble, chicken-sandwich-making Jonathan has gone away and the vicious bathroom shark has come back. Because he gives me this dead-eyed look. "You want me to hand over my event planning budget to a man with amnesia who doesn't even live in the city where the event is being planned? A man who, for what it's worth, wasn't very good with budgets even when he did have his memory."

That isn't true. We just had different priorities. That, and I'm not a dick. "Well," I suggest, "maybe I've forgotten all my bad habits. Besides, it's a room, some music, and some pigs in blankets. I don't think I need any special skills to pull that off. And I do technically still work for you, right?" I'm flying close to the wind but I can't quite stop myself. "I mean, unless you fired me and I can't remember it."

Jonathan mostly doesn't react, but the lines in his brow get a bit deeper. "No," he says very carefully. "But—"

"And I could help you get things set up for your family as well," I offer. "It'd give me something to do so I'm not just sitting around all day watching *Pointless* and annoying Agnieszka."

He looks blank.

"Your housekeeper?"

"Oh, yes of course."

I stare at him. "Do you—do you not know your housekeeper's name?"

At the very least, he has the decency to be embarrassed. "I don't speak to her very often and it slipped my mind."

I'm almost tempted to laugh except a man who forgets his housekeeper's name is a man who needs to take a long hard look at himself. "Because you're so busy you can't treat people like human beings?"

"I really don't believe my housekeeper cares if I know her name or not."

"She thinks you're a serial killer."

Jonathan's eyes widen just for a second. Then he goes back to pretending he's made of stone. "If she thought that, she wouldn't be working here."

"She thinks you're the kind of person who *would* be a serial killer. That suggests to me you might have a bit of an image problem."

"Serial killers can be extremely charismatic."

I don't think she thought he was that sort of serial killer. More the "oh, I should've known" sort of serial killer. But I'm not sure I want to be sitting here at midnight discussing the finer points of mass murder. "Shut up and finish your chicken."

"Excuse me, I'm your boss."

"Shut up and finish your chicken, sir."

He picks up what's left of his sandwich. Then looks like he realises he's just done something somebody else told him to so he stops on instinct and eyes me intently over the plate. "Does this mean you're staying then?"

"I think that very much depends on you."

"So you're essentially coercing me into letting you organise a party and inviting my family over for Christmas?"

"Jonathan," I say, trying not to laugh, because this is fucking ridiculous. "The fact you need to be coerced into being helped with things and seeing your family is very much the problem here."

"I don't need help." He's getting all defensive and cornered-wolf-like.

"Everybody needs help. And you keep saying you're too busy for everything. Somebody who's too busy for everything needs help by definition." I shoot him a sharp look because I can be sharp when I need to be. "Unless you're not actually that busy and this is all an excuse to not see your family."

He opens his mouth and then closes it again. Because it probably *is* an excuse. A bit. On some level. Then he sort of crumples very gently round the edges. "Fine. But if I agree to this, then you're staying until you're definitely better, and you're not suing me."

I give him my most innocent look. "What would I have to sue you for?"

"You had an accident on my property. People sue over that kind of thing all the time."

"I'm not going to sue you," I tell him, half-wishing that just once Jonathan Forest's primary concern wasn't what his lawyer would say. "But if I'm going to stay and we're going to do all this..."

The *we're* makes him shudder a bit. But he doesn't complain.

"...then," I finish, "you need to start being about ten percent less of a dick."

Now he starts complaining. "I'm not a—"

"You forgot your housekeeper's name. You keep ordering me around. You"—I'm this close to saying *threatened to sack the entire Sheffield branch* but I cut myself off just in time—"you basically told your own mam you were cancelling Christmas."

I expect him to keep arguing but he doesn't. Instead, he just crumples a tiny bit more and says, "I'm aware that I'm not a very likeable person."

"You know, that's a problem you can fix."

"I'm not sure it is." With Jonathan frowning at me over it, a kitchen table's never felt so long and so short at the same time. "I'm not the sort of man other people warm to."

"Have you ever tried?"

"No, I've been deliberately alienating everyone I know since I was six."

He doesn't make jokes very often and I'm only half sure this is one. "So, what? You've just decided not to bother?"

"I decided not to waste my time trying to please people I have nothing in common with."

I blink at him. "Like who?"

"Anyone." He shrugs impatiently. "At school, I was a gay boy from Sheffield surrounded by straight Londoners. At university,

I was a steelworker's son surrounded by the children of doctors, lawyers, and—in one particularly unusual case—rock stars."

To be fair, that did sound like it sucked. "Was there not, like, a student LGBTQ group you could join or something?"

"There was. But they were mostly artists or activists, and I was neither."

"That where you met the rock star's kid?"

"Among others. None of them really got me." There's no self-pity there. He just says it like it's a fact. Then he gets this distant look on his face—almost as if he's forgotten I'm around—and I swear his voice gets just a little more Sheffield. "I remember talking to this English Literature student—right back in my first year—and he asked why I was studying Business Management, and I told him it was because I wanted to study something I could use to make money when my course was finished and he looked at me with such *absolute* contempt. He didn't even say anything except *oh*. Then he went off on a tangent about Keats."

I'm pretty sure it's the longest I've ever heard Jonathan Forest speak. It's certainly the longest I've heard him speak without telling anyone he's going to fire them. He's finished the sandwich now and he dusts the crumbs off into the bin and puts the plate in the dishwasher before finishing the anecdote. I stay quiet to see if he'll carry on talking.

To my surprise, he does. "What struck me, even then, was that he couldn't *imagine* why financial security was something I'd have to consider." He leans back with his hips against the counter, only half paying attention to me. "And that was what most of my university experience was like. Trying not to waste my tuition fees while all the time my classmates were looking down at me from their spot just *slightly* further up Maslow's Hierarchy of Needs."

"That's rough," I tell him, because it is. "But you know not everybody is like that?"

"Maybe." He's lost in thought now, and I wonder if I've took it too far.

"What happened to the English student?" I ask. It seems like a good way to keep the conversation going.

Jonathan shrugs again. "Married a YouTuber in the end. I went to his wedding."

"Why?"

"You mean, why did he marry a YouTuber or why did I go to his wedding?"

"I suppose...both?"

"Well"—Jonathan gets that snarky expression that's the closest he comes to playful—"the YouTuber was young and hot. And, as for the wedding, it was a complicated social group. Turning up was the easiest way to show I didn't care."

I cast him a quizzical kind of glance. "You clearly cared enough to want to show you didn't."

His mouth thins. "Quite."

There's a long silence, Jonathan still resting against the kitchen counters he never uses in the fancy house no one visits. And I find myself thinking it's all a bit of a shame. Because I don't think he was born a prick. I think he had prickness thrust upon him. And, right now, he looks genuinely fucking miserable. And like he's always been fucking miserable. And like he always will be.

"Jonathan," I say.

His expression doesn't so much lift as shut down. He goes from sad to emotionless. "What?"

"C'mere a minute."

"Why?"

I push the chair next to me out with my foot. "Can you not argue about everything for once?"

"People don't normally start their own business because they like being told what to do."

Trying to comfort Jonathan Forest is already more trouble than it's worth. "I'm not telling, I'm asking. And all I'm asking is for you to sit in a chair."

"Can I not sit in the chair I was sitting in before?"

"Just sit in the fucking chair. *Please*."

He sits in the fucking chair. "What?"

"I just want to say," I begin, already wishing I hadn't, "that whatever you might think, I don't not like you."

"And I had to be sitting in this exact chair for you to tell me that?"

Somehow, I don't stab him with a fork. Partly because there isn't a fork. "Oh fuck off, man. I'm trying to do a thing here. I'm trying to be nice. And I figured it'd be, y'know, more personal like if we were sitting next to each other instead of you being on the other side of this stupid gigantic kitchen you've got for no fucking reason."

He scowls and up close it's even scarier. "How personal can it be—you've got amnesia, haven't you?"

"Which means I've got no prejudices." I fucking wish I had no prejudices. "I'm just judging on what I see in front of me."

"And you like this?" Jonathan demands, with a gesture that indicates his whole self. "Or rather, you don't not like this. Gosh, I feel so seen."

It's my turn to sigh. "I know you're being sarcastic, but I do. I do see you."

He folds his arms, leaning slightly away from me. "And what is it you think you see?"

"I see someone driven and ambitious who's been told those are bad things when they're not. I see someone who cares but doesn't know how to show it. I see someone who thinks he's got to be alone, so he pretends it's a choice." I stand up before he can object or reply or anything. "Also, you're surprisingly good with cats."

And, for once, Jonathan Forest doesn't have an answer.

CHAPTER 12

SOMEWHAT PREDICTABLY, JONATHAN'S IN HIS office with the door closed for most of the day, and my fucking cat's in there with him. Since I haven't left, I boil the chicken carcass up to make broth, and mash the leftover veg into bubble and squeak. I'm just tucking into a piece when Gollum comes through, racing to his bowl, followed by Jonathan, carrying the biggest fucking binder I've ever seen.

"What's that?" I ask.

But Jonathan's ignoring me in favour of falling for Gollum's *oh woe is me, I shall die if I do not eat at once* act. When he's fed the cat, he gives my pan a significant look. "Is that bubble and squeak?"

"Aye. It's a good way to use your spare veggies."

"I...I haven't had that in years."

This would almost be a tender, nostalgic moment except Jonathan Forest isn't a tender or nostalgic person and Gollum has his face in a bowl of Fancy Feast's natural white meat chicken and liver plus a touch of coconut milk cat food and is making a noise like when you suck up a wet cloth with a hoover.

I try to ignore the squelching cat sounds. "Do you not have it at Christmas?"

"My dad makes it on Boxing Day but I'm usually working."

"You can have a slice of this," I tell him. "But it won't be as good."

"Why?" He's already levering a wedge out with a spatula. "Are you a terrible cook?"

"No, I mean like, because of the emotions and that." Then I realise he's smirking. And that in the labyrinthine pits of Jonathan Forest's brain this is what counts as a joke. "You're not funny."

He sits down next to me. "I'm well aware."

And that makes me feel bad because I think this is him trying. And actually trying. Not just trying not to get sued. "Well maybe you're a bit funny. Sometimes."

"No," Jonathan says, "you were right the first time."

At some point we're going to have address the elephant in the room and, by elephant, I mean gigantic fucking binder. "So," I ask, "what's with the gigantic fucking binder?"

"I thought about what you said. About the Christmas party. And if you're still interested in helping organise it then... Well." He slides the improbably vast bundle of documents towards me. "Here."

While Jonathan makes a start on his "bubble and squeak", I take a look at what he's given me. It's a lot more...just generally a lot more than I would have expected for planning a work do. Honestly, it's a lot more than I'd have expected for planning the Normandy Landings.

I close the folder again. "What...is this?"

"Venue listings, costings, regulations, risk assessments, the usual."

"This is not usual," I tell him. "This is the opposite of usual. This is unusual."

Jonathan looks up from his already half-empty plate, and the look he's giving me is not an encouraging one. "I knew this was a bad idea."

He reaches out and starts to pull the binder back. I try to stop him and we sort of have the world's most bureaucratic tug o' war in the middle of the kitchen table.

"Come on." I dig in slightly harder on the folder. "I'm sorry. I didn't mean to cast nasturtiums on your...on your big book of parties."

"It's not a big book of parties," Jonathan growl, still not letting go. "I'm not six years old. It's a collection of information that's important for legal and tax purposes."

I don't let go either. "You're the real spirit of Christmas you, aren't you? I can just imagine yez as a kid running downstairs in your jammies ripping open your presents and then saying *mam, mam is it tax deductible*?"

"It's not the same thing, Samwise."

I've told him not to call me that. And I'm just joshing—at least, I started out just joshing, though if I'm honest bringing up his family was a bit low of me and I'd not have, only he was beginning to get under my skin with all his penny-pinching-branch-closing bullshit. "It's Sam," I remind him, "and I know it's not the same thing but it's still Christmas. It's meant to be fun."

Jonathan Forest stares me right in the eye. His bubble and squeak is getting cold but I don't think he cares about that. "I guarantee you that every moment of fun you've had in your entire life was made possible by somebody else's hard work."

If he'd been less of an arse about it, I might have admitted he had a point. But he wasn't, so I don't. "Okay, that's true sometimes, but it's not true all the time. Yez can be spontaneous. Have you never, I don't know, been walking along a beach and decided to run into the sea just to see what it feels like?"

"And you think the beach stays usable, safe, and not covered in raw sewage, entirely by itself?"

I sigh again. "You're being really unhelpful."

"You offered to do something for me. I tried to give you the resources you'll need to do it, and you threw them back in my face."

That's certainly *a way* to frame our most recent interaction. I don't think it is the best way, or even a fair way. "No, I just expressed mild surprise that when I said *hey, d'you want us to give you a hand with your party*, you thought that meant *hey, d'you want us to read through a stack of paperwork thicker than the Bible*."

"So what *was* your plan?" Jonathan sits back, folding his arms. "Take everyone down the pub?"

"And what'd be wrong with that?"

"Because I employ a hundred and fifty people. You can't just say, *everybody, show up at the Dog and Duck around ten. First pint's on me*."

I'm beginning to think I've bitten off more than I can chew here. It's certainly putting Jonathan's history of throwing terrible parties into perspective. I always assumed he just hated fun. "No, but you can make it feel less, y'know, corporate."

"And how would I do that? We're talking about a work event hosted by the man who owns the company."

"Look"—I sneak the binder out from his hand—"leave it with me and I'll see what I can come up with."

For a second, our fingers brush as we shift our grip on the blue plastic cover of the by now extremely overly-built-up party planning folder. And Jonathan Forest pulls his hand away like I'm a gas hob. "Very well," he says, "I'll leave it with you. But you need to take this *seriously*."

He's a dick. "I am taking it seriously."

I'm not sure what he's going to say next, but he draws in a slow, deep breath. "You won't remember this," he says at last, "but part of why you were in London in the first place is that you're…you're not always the best with budgets. I'm trusting you here, but it's important you do things properly."

He's a dick, he's a dick. "I will."

"I mean it. Your absolute maximum spend—absolute maximum—is a hundred and fifty pounds a head. You can't go a penny over."

He's a dick. He's a dick. He's a *controlling* dick. "Okay," I tell him. "I won't. Now give me the file and I'll start ringing caterers."

"Not a penny," he repeats.

"I heard you the first time. I've got it. I promise."

This, right here, is why I need to remember liking Jonathan Forest is a nonstarter. I'm trying to help him out of the goodness of my heart. Well. Out of the goodness of a desperate and poorly thought-out plan to convince him it's okay to leave the Sheffield branch alone. But the point is, I'm trying to help him, and he's treating me like a bellend who can't count. Never mind his extremely unsexy Ebenezer Scrooge impression. It's all making me strangely determined to throw the best party he's ever fucking seen. Which, in a way, means his whole terrible management style is actually motivating. And isn't that a kick in the balls?

It's one of Agnieszka's days so Jonathan gets to go into the office for the afternoon, which is probably a relief to both of us, to be honest. He's always a bit twitchy about working from home on account of being completely unable to trust anybody to do anything, but the second I take over the party project, he gets about a hundred times worse because it means he takes all that pent-up micromanagement and dumps it on yours truly. I've barely started flipping through the unnecessarily long list of venue options when he's bombarding me with suggestions that feel a lot like orders. Sit-down dinner is a must (I disagree but don't want to push it), don't book a river boat (I'm not planning to), make sure there's room for dancing (incredibly obvious), and check the DJ brings their own lighting (ditto).

It doesn't help that what I really want to do is get onto my old team and ask for their input on things, especially about how I can use my hard-won role of Christmas party planner to stop them all getting fired. And that's pretty hard to do while Jonathan's breathing down my neck and I'm pretending I've got amnesia.

So as soon as he's in the car and out the driveway, and Agnieszka's somewhere I can be pretty sure I won't bother her, I ring up the store, whack my phone on speaker, and ask Claire to get everybody in the room for a meeting. Well, by everybody I mean her, Tiff, and Amjad because Brian's a liability and New Enthusiastic Chris is too new and enthusiastic to be totally trusted with a plan that involves lying to the boss.

"You're what?" asks Claire.

"I'm organising the Christmas party," I tell her again.

"Isn't the Christmas party always shit?" This is Amjad, telling it like it is.

I gesture at my phone even though nobody can see me. "Aye, but that's why it's genius."

Claire makes the sort of noise your teacher makes in school when they're trying to be encouraging but you've just said something that's total bollocks. "Is genius really the word we're looking for here?"

"No," I protest. "Listen. The problem with the Christmas party is that Jonathan organises it his way and, because he's Jonathan, that makes it miserable and soulless. So if I organise it my way and it's great, then that means I can show him that my style of management works and he won't fire anybody."

"That seems spurious," says Amjad, telling it like it might well be if I'm honest.

"I agree," chimes in Agnieszka, who's come into the front room to dust the coffee table. "It's *extremely* spurious."

There's a moment's silence from the other end, then a confused "Who's that?" from Claire.

"It's okay, it's just Agnieszka, she's the housekeeper but she's cool. She works for Jonathan so she knows what a prick he is."

"I know no such thing," Agnieszka insists as she moves my blanket off the sofa, fluffs up a cushion, then sticks the blanket back much more neatly. "He's always been perfectly nice to me. I just suspect he may carve up hitchhikers in his spare time, that's all."

This seems to really appeal to Tiff. "He probably does, doesn't he?"

"Well, unless we can find enough evidence of his off-duty serial killing that we can get him locked up before he sacks us"—I'm doing my best to bring things back to the topic at hand—"our best bet is still the party plan."

"I still think it's spurious," Amjad tells me.

Agnieszka glances over her shoulder on her way back upstairs. "And I still agree."

"Tell you what," I suggest. "I've got my phone here and I'll set a timer for six minutes and if, when it goes off, nobody's come up with a better plan, we'll try mine."

To give them credit, they do think about it. Not for the full six minutes, which is good because I haven't really set a timer.

Then Tiff pipes up, "Do you know anything about organising parties?"

"Don't you start." I make a grumpy face at my phone. "I had enough of that from Jonathan Forest this morning."

She makes a—and I'm dating myself by saying this—a very teenage noise. "I'm not being a Jonathan. I'm just saying...you're not very fun either."

Oh, now it's on. "What do you mean I'm not fun?"

"Okay, you're not *not* fun. You're just fun in a bit of a...bit of a...dad way?"

"Tiff, I'm twenty-seven. To be your dad, I'd have had to knock your mam up when I was ten."

"Sam," says Claire. "I think we've gone somewhere we need to come back from."

She's right. The phrase "knock your mam up" is never one you want to use to an employee, even if she's making you feel old. "Look," I try, "all I'm saying is, it can't be that difficult."

"That's what my mam said," Tiff puts in, "when she wouldn't let me help her organise Auntie Rita's fiftieth. And then we ran out of booze by half past six and Uncle Colin got so aggro he threw a plate of mini quiches at Mr Pettiforth from Number Forty-Two."

"Was he all right?" asks Claire at the same time Amjad says, "That's a waste of mini quiches."

I rap on the table to try and call the meeting back to something that looks a little bit like order. "I see what you're saying, Tiff, and I'm aware that there's"—I flash back to the massive binder—"logistics and that. But the thing is, this party doesn't have to be the Royal Wedding. It just has to be better than Jonathan could do, and that is a very, very low bar."

Somehow, I hear Claire wince down the phone. "Do you remember that time he trapped us all on a boat?"

"Yeah," I say, not quite wanting to defend him but, for whatever reason, doing it anyway. "He did learn from that. Not very much like, but he did."

"The one I went to," offers Amjad, "was at a hotel where there were six other Christmas parties happening at the same time. And I had to sit next to this bloke from the Leeds branch who kept trying to convince me that Age of Sigmar was better than Warhammer Fantasy."

"I don't know what any of those words mean," says Tiff.

"So"—Amjad's launching into an explain, you can hear it coming a mile off—"Warhammer Fantasy was a classic setting with thirty years of lore and content attached to a really solid tactical war game with asymmetric gameplay if—I'll admit—quite shonky faction balance. But then they blew up the world in a way that just took an enormous dump on canon, and replaced it with a skirmish game for children and casuals."

"I don't know what any of those words mean either."

In some ways I don't want to interrupt them. I know I should, but there's something comforting about hearing Tiff and Amjad bickering like they're brother and sister. Something that feels almost like home. But I'm the boss, and this is important, so I say, "And you don't need to, because it's not relevant to the party I have to plan."

Amjad makes the huff of a man who is not appreciated in his own lifetime. "I'm just saying don't have it in a hotel and don't invite Leeds."

"I have to invite Leeds."

"He's right about the hotel, though," says Tiff. "Nothing says *I've put zero thought into this* like a hotel."

"So where'd you want me to hold it, in a disused car park in Dagenham?"

"You're in London." Tiff's sounding very slightly less respectful than I think is fair for somebody whose job I'm trying to save. "It's basically *built* out of party venues."

I grab a spare scrap of paper from the back of the binder and start scribbling notes. "Alright. No hotel. Not on a boat. We *do* have to invite Leeds—"

Amjad sighs. "Can you at least not sit us with them."

"Yeah but," Claire protests, "that means we have to sit with each other and that means we're going two hundred miles on a train to have dinner with people we work with every day."

"Better that," Amjad fires back, "than going two hundred miles on a train to have dinner with people *who suck*."

I cut them off. "Okay what I'm hearing here is that you don't want to sit with other people and you don't want to sit with each other and, if I'm honest, that's not the most helpful feedback."

There's a medium-sized pause as everyone shifts gears from carping about things they hate to actually trying to solve problems. Unfortunately, that extends the pause from medium to quite long, and I'm starting to be very aware that these people do have a real job to do that isn't this, and the more time I keep them off the shop floor the less likely they are to meet Jonathan Forest's precious fucking targets. On top of which there's always the chance he'll come back unexpectedly, because he's forgot something or decided to check up on me. At which point he'll discover that not only am I faking amnesia but that the whole team is in on it, which might just make him a little ill-disposed towards them. I glance at the tracking app on my phone and he's definitely still at the shop, but I decide to wrap things up anyway.

"I think I've got enough to be going on with," I tell them, only mostly not lying. "If you come up with anything, sit on it and wait for me to call you back. Because the last thing I need is to be having dinner with Jonathan and get a text that says *Hey, I've worked out how to use this party to trick our dickhead boss into not firing us.*"

There's another pause but not the helpful kind.

"You're having dinner with him?" Claire asks with honestly warranted incredulity.

"I'm living in his house. What am I supposed to do, eat in my room like a sulky teenager?"

"It's just the way you said it. It sounded weird."

I prickle. "It's not weird."

"It's a bit weird," says Tiff.

"It is," agrees Amjad.

"I'm trying to win him over," I remind them. "I've got to be amicable."

Claire does not sound like she approves. "You haven't forgotten what a colossal piece of shit he is?"

"Oh believe me, I'm regularly reminded. But it's...it's complicated, y'know?"

"It's not complicated," Claire snaps. "He shoved you into a shower, gave you a concussion and threatened to fire us all, not in that order."

Tiff gives a little gasp. "Shit, he's got Stockholm syndrome."

"I don't—"

"Well actually," says Amjad, "Stockholm syndrome was invented by a guy who was butthurt because one of the hostages criticised him for how he handled a negotiation. Like it's not in the DSM."

I'm getting very tempted to hang up on them. "Whether it's real or not, I don't have it."

"That's what you'd say if you did have it," Tiff points out.

"Except," Amjad points out back, "he doesn't have it because it doesn't exist."

"I don't have it," I say, not quite flipping my lid but at least tipping it up a bit, "because I'm out here faking a medical condition to save all our jobs and I don't like Jonathan Forest. And now I'm going because I have to get on with planning this party which, let's remember, is a vital part of the job saving strategy."

They're making faintly sorry noises as I hang up. And when they're gone, I just sit there stewing in this mess of frustration and affection. Because I definitely do not have Stockholm syndrome. But it's also so perfectly *Tiff* to think I might and so perfectly *Amjad* to be more concerned about whether it's a technically correct diagnosis than anything else, and so perfectly *Claire* to walk the line between the two and try to keep me focused.

Still, though, I don't have any kind of syndrome named after any kind of city anywhere in Europe. Me and Jonathan have had maybe two good conversations since I've been here. And okay, there's been times he's almost showed a human side. And okay, he gets on well with the cat, so he can't be completely terrible. And okay, he did make me a pretty decent chicken sandwich. But it'll take more than that to make me like him. Much more. Probably more than he's capable of. And I'm not sure why I even care if I like him or not because he sure as hell doesn't.

I try to stop thinking about him and turn back to the folder. Except that doesn't help at all, because just like the Stockholm syndrome debate so Tiff and so Amjad, the big old file of rules for how to enjoy yourself is just so, *so* Jonathan Forest.

SAY WHAT YOU WILL ABOUT Jonathan Forest—and you can say a lot—he's a man of his word. Which is why I'm being hugged by every woman in his family simultaneously. It's not a lads-hugging-each-other sort of crowd, but we do a round of handshakes and back-pats afterwards.

"I told you," Wendy's saying, "I told you he'd come through for us. I had a good feeling about you, Sam. Didn't I say, Les, didn't I say I had a good feeling about him?"

"You did," confirms Les.

Wendy sails past me in a purple tea dress printed with a pattern that manages to combine both leaves and polka dots. "I knew he'd be good for our Jonathan."

"Like I say"—I get the feeling I'll be repeating this a lot—"I just work for him and I'm staying here because I had an accident at the shop and he's worried I've got a concussion."

"Yes, yes." Auntie Jack is also sailing past me. "You're just friends. We understand. We understand all too well."

I'm not sure if it's helping me or hindering me that the family thinks I'm Jonathan's secret boyfriend, but I'm getting the feeling there's nothing I can do about it. And even if I wanted to press the issue I couldn't because they've started spreading out through the ground floor like schoolkids in a museum gift shop.

"We can get a massive tree in here," Wendy's yelling through from the second of the three reception rooms.

"He needs a new dining table though," Nanny Barb's replying, though at a quieter volume. Which means she has to add, "Del, tell her he needs a new dining table."

"Your mum says he needs a new dining table," bellows Del, sticking his head through the door.

"I know." Wendy's voice somehow seems to be getting louder as she's getting further away. "Les, do we still have that old one in our garage?"

Les, who isn't a shouter but who can make himself heard if he has to, goes all the way through to the other room before replying. "We have but it'll not seat thirteen."

"What was that?" asks Barb, who's still inspecting Jonathan's kitchen with the air of a woman who thinks using an electric kettle is cheating.

"He says they've got one but it'll not seat thirteen," Del relays to her.

She asks how many it does seat, and Del sends that back up the chain.

"Eight," Wendy calls through.

"It's six, love," Les corrects her.

"It's eight if you pull the flaps out."

"How many?" asks Nanny Barb again.

Del has wandered back into the middle of the first reception room by this point. "Eight," he says, "if you pull the flaps out."

And this, at last, rouses Jonathan from his study and he emerges with Gollum slinking treacherously behind him. "Can you please stop shouting about flaps while I'm trying to work." He glances at the assembled mob. "What are you even doing here?"

Wendy returns through from the third reception room like the prodigal mum. "Well, now you and Sam are hosting Christmas—"

"There's no me and Sam," snarls Jonathan.

Nanny Barb has joined us too, having completed her kitchen inventory. "Oh *what* is he *like*. You'd think it was still nineteen sixty-seven."

"We're not a couple, Nan, and even if we were I'm sure Sam has his own family he'd rather be with."

"I wouldn't know," I say quickly, "I've got amnesia."

I don't like lying to them, but I don't know what else to say.

"He's never," declares Del, looking impressed.

Wendy looks more concerned. "You don't remember anything?"

"Bits." I'm already wishing I hadn't started this. "I know who I am and how to do stuff and stuff, but there's a lot of blanks still."

They're crowding me now, and Jonathan steps forward almost protective like. "The doctors say his memory will come back on its own eventually. Until then the best we can do is give him *space*."

They back off. But not before Nanny Barb has patted me firmly in the small of the back—that being what she can reach—and told me I'm welcome to spend Christmas with them.

"It will make us thirteen, however," Auntie Jack points out. "Not that I'm personally superstitious."

"It's fine." Wendy doesn't look like she thinks it's fine at all. "One of us can just stand up all day."

"I think standing up still counts." Something tells me Auntie Jack was enjoying this a bit too much.

Growing increasingly agitated Wendy turns to Nanny Barb. "What if you brung somebody from Bingo?"

"I'll ask Mavis."

Del looks aghast. "You will not bloody ask Mavis."

"There's nothing wrong with Mavis," insists Nanny Barb.

"I think, actually"—Les is still standing in the doorway, still keeping his voice down—"there are a couple of things wrong with Mavis."

Auntie Jack has lit another cigarette. "The problem with Mavis is that the things that are wrong with her are precisely the things that make her interesting."

"You give me one good reason why I shouldn't invite Mavis." It's beginning to look like Nanny Barb's going to double down the way only people over eighty can.

"She cheats at Cluedo," says Wendy.

"She made little Anthea cry," adds Les.

"Oh be fair"—this is Auntie Jack—"those braces *did* make her look like she'd tried to perform oral sex on a shopping trolley."

"Don't make it the right thing to say to a fourteen-year-old," replies Del.

"And she gatecrashed Kayla's thirtieth," Wendy goes on, "threw up on the cake, kicked the dog, and stole Johnny's car."

"Now now"—even Nanny Barb can't quite field all of these at once—"she brought the car back eventually."

"Only after she was arrested," Del points out.

"Yes but—"

"For drink driving."

"She had—"

"In Majorca."

I can see that this might go on for a while, and although it's not really a situation that's conducive to the getting in of words, edge-or-otherwise, I don't want to be causing family strife. "It's fine," I say, "I'm sure I'll have somewhere to go."

"No." Wendy is very, very forceful on this point. "You can't not know where you're going at Christmas. You're coming here, and we'll just risk the death curse."

I'd figured they were just mildly superstitious. I hadn't realised there could be fatalities. "Death curse?"

"If thirteen sit down to dine," Nanny Barb intones, "one must die within a year."

"Are you *sure* we shouldn't invite Mavis?" asks Auntie Jack.

Del sighs. "Tell you what, I'm probably on my way out anyway, just make sure nobody gets up before me."

"Oh you morbid sod, Dad." Wendy isn't having any of it. "Anyway it don't work like that, somebody'll forget and they'll be all *ooh I need the loo* and then they'll be going through to the toilet and then *bam*."

I shouldn't ask. But I do. "Bam?"

"Massive heart attack," Wendy explains. "Or a toaster falls in the loo while you're having a slash."

For some reason, this is the step too far for Jonathan. "I do not. Keep toasters. In my bathroom. Besides," he adds with the same air of finality he used when he was firing me, "with the cat there's fourteen, so Sam can stay if he wants."

And that's that. From what I've seen, Jonathan's difficult alpha energy doesn't always work on his family, any more than it always works on me, but from time to time, when he hits it just right, he can lay down the law with the best of them. I'm honestly a bit surprised he's chosen to do that for me.

"Well then, that's settled," says Wendy cheerily. "Course we'll have to make sure we get in the turkey cat food."

"And your mum has said you can have our spare table," adds Les. "If we stick it at the end of yours it should fit everyone."

"Not quite." Del isn't the sort of man to let a nitpick slide. I wonder for a moment if he'd get on with Amjad. "If yours seats eight and his seats six, that only makes twelve."

It's bait, and I know it's bait, but I figure it's better for me to take it than anybody else. "Doesn't it make fourteen?"

"But if you put 'em together"—Del holds his hands flat and mimes two tables being shoved end-to-end—"then you lose one off each. That's twelve."

Having entirely overcome her thirteen-at-the-table worries,

Wendy waves a dismissive hand. "It's fine, we'll squeeze, it'll be cosy. I'm more worried about the tree."

The tree is news to Jonathan. "*What* tree?"

"You've got to have a tree if you're doing Christmas," Nanny Barb tells him. She's pretty matter-of-fact about it, and she's right. "Not Christmas without a tree. Where will the kids' presents go?"

"There's one kid," Jonathan points out, "and she's sixteen."

I'm beginning to worry he's regretting this. And I very much need him to not regret this so that he can be all relaxed and chilled out and not want to fire my entire staff for missing a bunch of made-up sales targets. "Tell you what," I offer, "I'll help with the tree."

And I should have realised that this wasn't shutting stuff down. It was opening it up. Way up.

"What about the decorations?" asks Nanny Barb. "They're all in a box in our attic."

Jonathan folds his arms. Jonathan folding his arms is never good. "Could we not just get new decorations?"

I don't want make too many assumptions, because everyone's family is different, but if I'd suggested to my mam and dad that we get new Christmas decorations, they'd have taken it about as well as if I'd suggested we eat Santa Claus. And apparently it's a similar dynamic here.

"No, we bloody well can't." Looking at Wendy, I'm beginning to see where Jonathan gets his temper. "Them decorations is traditional. We've been using them since you was this big." She bends down to illustrate quite how little bigness Jonathan possessed when the great Christmas decoration tradition began.

"I can help with them and all," I tell her.

"We might run a bit short, mind." Les is casting a wary eye over Jonathan's impressive square footage. "You've got a lot of halls to deck, son."

Jonathan pinches the bridge of his nose in a way that says *I've got a headache coming on* even though the headache is definitely already here. Metaphorically like. "I'm sure we can buy more decorations."

"Aye," I say, trying to keep up enthusiasm, "we can do a shop."

"There's a Christmas market up North End," Les suggests, but that seems to set something off in Del.

"Don't you dare," he says, "them things is just to rip off tourists. There's a wholesaler down Acton I know'll get you everything you want half the price."

A shadow crosses Les's face. He's had this conversation before, or one a lot like it. "Can we not—"

Before that thought can finish, the door opens and a dark-haired woman in massive sunglasses waltzes in like she owns the place. Somehow she's carrying off a smock dress and cowboy boots combo. She reminds me a lot of Jonathan; she's what he'd look like if he was girl and if his face had been put together more carefully. Like, a bit less nose and a lot less crag.

"Door was open," she says, "what have I missed?"

Jonathan just glares at her. "How did you even know to come here, BJ?"

From the expression on BJ's face, it's not an abbreviation she cares for. "Well, I got a taxi from the airport to Mum and Dad's house, and when I got there I found a note on the door saying *Jonathan's doing Xmas, we're at his.*" She makes an exaggerated *this is awkward* face. "Which means I've also dumped all of my luggage in your garden, sorrynotsorry."

Before Jonathan can say anything back there's another round of hugs—the men get in on it as well this time because the rules say it's okay when it's not a bloke—and I'm introduced to the new arrival. Her name's Barbara Jane—hence BJ—and she's Jonathan's sister just back from Texas and a messy divorce.

"Love the dress, Mum," she tells Wendy.

Wendy grins. "Thanks. Eighteen quid, Bonmarsh."

Niceties out of the way, she turns back to her brother. "You're not *really* doing Christmas, are you?"

"Why does that surprise you?" Jonathan's being remarkably defensive what with how firmly he insisted he wasn't going to.

Barbara Jane folds her arms. She and Jonathan have very similar folded-arm game. "Because you'd clearly be terrible at it. You can't cook, your house is the least welcoming place I've ever been in, and you're deeply unpleasant."

"Fuck off, BJ."

"It's alright." Nanny Barb comes to Jonathan's defence, or at least to something that looks a bit like his defence. "The new boyfriend's going to take care of it."

"New *person who just happens to be living with him*," Auntie Jack corrects her.

Pushing her sunglasses onto her forehead, Barbara Jane subjects me to a good long scrute. "You're his boyfriend? What did you do, Johnny, hypnotise him?"

"I've got a concussion," I say.

"Well"—she smirks—"that explains it."

"It does *not* explain it." Jonathan's getting so in touch with his inner werewolf he's forgotten to deny we're dating. Then again, so have I. "Now can you please just accept that Sam and I between us are capable of roasting a turkey and hanging a few paper chains. I have work to do and you have no good reason to be here."

Wendy looks aggrieved. "We come to say thank you to Sam for making you do Christmas."

I'm worried she's blown it. Jonathan is not the kind of man who likes to think that someone else thinks that someone else made him do something.

"Sam did not make me do Christmas," Jonathan doesn't half

get snarly around his family. "Sam is *helping* me do Christmas, but I'd have been happy to do it anyway."

With tremendous strength of will, I don't join in the chorus of people saying "no, you bloody wouldn't."

Jonathan throws his actual hands in the actual air. It's probably the campest thing he's ever done but it comes from the heart. "This is so typical of you lot. You harass me until I agree to do something and then you keep harassing me about the fact I've agreed to do it. And if I see a single one of you before the twenty-fifth, I am cancelling Christmas."

It's the longest I've ever seen these people be silent since I've known them. Which, admittedly, is only a couple of days.

Then BJ starts laughing. "Johnny, did you just threaten to cancel Christmas?"

"Don't call me Johnny."

"Well, don't call me BJ."

"Jonathan,"—Wendy steps between them, like it's force of habit—"we're just happy to be seeing you. But you're right. I can see we've overstayed our welcome. You go back to your job and we'll catch up with you in a bit."

"Didn't I just say—" Jonathan starts.

"Come on everybody." Wendy begins corralling the family out the door. Once they're all through, she begins pulling it closed. She pauses to give a happy little wave. "Ta-rah, love. See you soon."

"They are impossible," Jonathan says, a bit to me, mostly to himself.

"They're just showing they care."

"Then I wish they showed it in a less infuriating way."

I shrug. "Well, that's family, isn't it? You shouldn't take them for granted, especially not this time of year."

He turns fully to face me. He's slightly flushed and his hair's come loose again, so there's a stray lock hanging over one eye—I know it's just how he gets when he's annoyed, but I'm finding it increasingly tough not to imagine him looking like that for other reasons. "You will rue those words, Sam Becker."

I don't agree with Jonathan Forest on a lot. But this is the first time I can say for certain that he's flat out, straight up, dead wrong.

PART THREE

TRIMMING THE TREE & FACING THE PAST

CHAPTER 14

"WHERE ARE YOU GOING?" ASKS Jonathan a couple of days later.

"Out?" I try. I probably shouldn't be this vague but I'm hoping if I suggest loudly enough that he should mind his own business, he'll mind his own business.

"Out where?"

"Got a venue to look at. Y'know, for the party I'm organising for yez." This isn't even a lie. It's just that I was also going to look at the venue with my team on FaceTime and that'll be hard if I have to do it with Jonathan Forest hovering over my shoulder.

"And if you collapse on the way there?"

I shrug, trying to look all casual. "Then I'll be in the middle of London and even though you southerners are a pack of selfish bastards, I reckon at least one of yez'll call an ambulance."

"And if you die before the ambulance gets there?"

"Then you'd probably not have been able to save me."

Jonathan looks like he finds the idea upsetting. Apparently the man's such a control freak the idea of me dying in a way he can't micromanage messes with his head. "I'll drive you."

Fuck. That's actually pretty generous of him—it'd save me time, money, aggro, and a real risk of dropping dead with blood coming out my ears—so saying *no thanks, I'd rather go on my own because reasons* will sound incredibly sus. "I'm going to go get a Christmas tree after so it's probably not worth your while. I'm sure you've got stuff planned, and I don't want you to have to rearrange your whole day."

He checks his phone—it's one of those dead fancy ones that fold open and let you write on the screen. "Well, I'm going to have to, aren't I?"

I can't tell if he's genuinely miffed or just trying really hard to be. And that's a weird thing not to be sure about. Because if he's not miffed, that means he actually wants to come, and I don't know what to make of that. "You don't. You've got the tracking thing set up, I'll be with your dad and granddad for most of it, and if I start to feel even a little bit funny, I'll ring yez."

He's not listening. He's already sending emails and rescheduling meetings. "Wait there."

"What's the magic word?"

"Sam." He sighs. "Will you *please* wait here while I get my laptop."

Good to know the old workaholic Jonathan isn't completely gone. "What do you need your laptop for? Are you going to set up a conference call with the Christmas trees?"

"You don't need me following you around the venue. I can catch up on work while you're inside, and after that I'll take you on to—where are you meeting my family?"

The phrase *meeting my family* sort of hovers for a second. "Portobello Road."

Jonathon gives me an *it figures* look and then goes to grab his laptop. He's pretty quiet on the drive there—probably a bit twitchy about all the showers getting sold without him—but he relaxes a bit when he's able to park up out back of a Budgens and leave me to head off and see a man about a room.

"If I'm not back in half an hour," I tell him, "send the dogs."

"You're not funny."

I smile in a way I hope says *I am and you secretly know it*, then head off to check out the venue.

The manager meets me downstairs and explains the setup. They've got a bunch of rooms. Some big, some small, some pricey, some even more pricey, and honestly I'm a bit lost trying to work my way through them, but he gives me a brochure and leaves me to wander.

Pretty confident that Jonathan isn't going to just walk in on me in all my not-amnesia-having glory, I fire up FaceTime. Tiff—who seems to have appointed herself Sheffield Branch Party Officer in my absence—looks back at me with more enthusiasm than I think I've ever seen on her.

"Alright." I sweep my phone around a classy-looking room with vaulted ceilings and chandeliers fitted for the new electric lighting. "What d'you think?"

"How many's it fit?" she asks.

I check my list. "Two hundred."

"Not big enough."

I keep falling into traps like this, but I'm worried if I ever stop I'll just start falling into traps of a different sort. "How is it not big enough if we only need to take a hundred and fifty?"

"It'll be two hundred standing. People have to be able to sit down. Even if you can get Jonathan to shift on table service—"

"He won't," I tell her. "I've tried."

"Then you need half the room for tables, and if you want dancing as well—and you do—you need the other half for that. So you'll need something nearly twice as big."

It's already looking plenty big enough from where I'm standing, and the thought of going bigger makes me a bit nervous. I consult the brochure. "I think they've only *got* one bigger room."

Tiff stares at me in dead silence for much longer than a

reasonable person would consider appropriate then says, "So... take me there then?"

Turns out their biggest room is *nonsense* big. Like built-in-lighting-rigs, has an actual fucking gallery big. I pan Tiff's phone-borne image around the room and she makes approving noises.

"Yeah," she says, "this'll work."

"Is it not a bit over the top?"

"Sam, it's a Christmas party. It's a holiday where people hang lights off things that don't normally have lights on them and put giant plastic reindeer on their lawns. Over the top is the *point*."

I turn the phone around to look at her again. She's giving me you-don't-know-what-you're doing face, which is pretty normal for her and I usually chalk up to her inherent teenageriness, but today it feels more directed than usual. "Is there not—does the top not exist for a reason? I mean this place has marble walls for fuck's sake. I'm not sure I want to organise a Christmas party somewhere with marble walls. Brian's probably going to come to this. Brian is not a marble walls kind of a lad."

"You're asking people to come two hundred miles to spend time they don't have hanging out with people they don't like from a job they don't care about—"

"Hey"—I'm not having that, the actual work can be mindless but we're still a team—"I care about my job. And I hope *you* care about your job because lest we forget I'm here *faking amnesia* to protect your job so that you can keep up payments on your hair and beauty course."

"Right, but"—she bites her lip—"doesn't the fact I'm *taking* that course show I want to do other things with my life?"

It does. And she's probably right, I'm sure most people who work on the shop floor at an S&S aren't doing it out of a passionate commitment to duvets and whirlpool baths. "Okay, and that means you want to be in a room with marble walls?"

"It means if my rich boss is dragging me to London so he can show how grateful he is for my hard work, he can at least book the nice room. Besides, we don't have much choice."

She's right about that. Because apparently booking Christmas party venues in London is much harder, and much more annoying, than I'd thought. So I track down the manager and ask him how much for the big swanky room with the gallery and the marble on the walls, and he tells me it's eight hundred quid, which I reckon is pretty reasonable, and then clarifies that it's eight hundred quid an *hour* which I reckon isn't.

I haul e-Tiff into a corner. "Is that not a bit steep?" I ask her.

For the first time that day she looks as flummoxed as I feel. "Yes. But also… I don't know, it's London. You probably can't rent a toilet for less than three hundred an hour in London."

She's right about that too. London is—by the standards of any sensible right-thinking person—the absolute worst. "We're on a hundred and fifty quid a head budget. How long are we going to need the room for?"

"Since it's going to take people at least three hours to get there, probably quite a long time. Maybe seven to twelve for the party, couple of hours setup before. Eight hours maybe?"

I was never the best at maths so I minimise Tiff and stick eight times eight hundred into my calculator. Then I must pull a face, because I hear Tiff laughing at me. "That's a lot," I tell her.

"Jonathan can afford it. He must have money coming out of his arse."

He does. I mean not literally, but figuratively. His house is the exact kind of place that you only live if your arse is pretty decently cashed up. "The budget's a hundred and fifty a head."

"And if you go over"—I've switched back to Tiff just in time to catch her giving a dangerously devil-may-care shrug—"what's he going to do?"

"He's going to say *Sam, I knew you were bad with budgets, you're fired and your branch is closed.*"

"And if you go under"—Tiff has that glint of confidence in her eye that I'm sure I used to have at her age as well—"then he'll say *see, cutting corners works, now fire the chick with the wacky hair.*"

He might. It's the sort of thing he'd do. "If it helps, I'm pretty sure he wants Brian gone first."

It didn't help. And despite Tiff urging me to just take the damned room, I tell the manager I'm looking at some other options and head back out to the car.

I find Jonathan hammering away at his laptop doing—whatever it is he does when he's not in the office but feels the need to keep his nose to the grindstone anyway. "Well?"

"It's an option."

"You'll need to make a call quickly, they'll book up."

I don't *think* he's deliberately needling me, but I might have lost the ability to tell. And what with just having had Tiff in one ear and now having him in the other I really want to change the subject so I say: "Do you want to grab some lunch?"

And to my surprise, he says yes.

I'm about 70/30 on whether Jonathan's going to bring his laptop with him, but he doesn't. He just stows it under the seat, where it's out of sight, and we head up the road to look for somewhere to eat. What with us not being especially friends, and the boss/employee dynamic having been somewhat eroded by him giving me a concussion, me lying to him about amnesia, and us living together, the whole "what sort of restaurant do we go to" dance gets very awkward indeed. So we resolve that by just turning into the first place we hit that doesn't scream "obvious date venue."

As it turns out, it's a little independent pizza joint that does twenty-inch stone baked pizzas with a frankly very central London variety of toppings. So, short on pepperoni, long on rocket. Inside, it's almost rustic which would be nice except it reminds me that you can't get less rustic than Shoreditch. You're about as far from the countryside as it's possible to get in England. In any case, the "definitely not a date" atmosphere takes a bit of a hit when they bung us in a booth in the corner and I realise I'm going to have to spend a good hour staring into the eyes of Jonathan Forest over a tastefully decorated hardwood table.

He's got annoyingly nice eyes, actually. Or maybe they just stand out because the rest of him's such an acquired taste.

For a while we avoid having to interact with each other by hiding behind the floppy, freshly printed A3 menus they've given us. The selection's pretty small which, from watching *Ramsay's Kitchen Nightmares* I take as a good thing because it means they're specialised and should screw up less, but it does really cut into the amount of time I can spend pretending to read through it.

"I'm almost tempted," I tell him when it starts feeling like the silence has gone from polite to the opposite of that, "to go for the Wagyu beef, just because I don't think I'll ever get a chance to have a Wagyu beef pizza again."

Jonathan lowers his menu slightly. "Would you want one?"

The trouble with Jonathan's unrelentingly negative attitude is that it can be quite fun when it's directed at things that aren't me. He's not a man whose glass is half empty, he's a man who wants to know why you've given him a glass when he ordered the bottle. "Well no, but that's sort of why I might get it."

"I'm beginning to see why I—" He stops himself, and I'm about ninety percent sure he was going to say *why I fired you*, then remembered that I'm not supposed to know about that. Also, maybe he realised it's not an appropriate thing to say to a person in a bijou pizza restaurant in Shoreditch.

"Why you what?" I ask, because I like to torture him sometimes.

"Why," he finishes valiantly, "I was concerned about giving you control of the party budget."

"Because I'm open to trying new kinds of pizza?"

"Because"—he's leaning forward over the table now—"you'll spend thirty-two pounds on something you don't even think you'll like just for the experience."

"Sometimes, though, when you try things you don't think you'll like, they're not as bad as you thought."

"And sometimes," he says brusquely, "they're exactly as bad as you thought."

I've lost track of whether we're talking about pizza anymore, but every time I try to have a conversation with Jonathan Forest I'm reminded why not having friends is a vicious cycle. "Look, I'm getting it anyway."

"You realise these pizzas are twenty inches each. Are you really going to eat a twenty-inch pizza for lunch?"

Fuck. We're going to have to split it. We're going to have to Lady and the Tramp a twenty-inch Wagyu Beef pizza that neither of us actually want to eat. "What if we go halves?"

"I'm not having half a Wagyu Beef pizza."

"Oh come on." I do my best coaxing voice. "It'll give you something to complain about. You love complaining about things."

"Sam, you're living in my house, trying to organise Christmas for my family. Do you really think I'm short of things to complain about?"

"You see," I point out, "most people'd be grateful for that."

"No, most people would pretend to be grateful for that while secretly hating you."

A week ago this would have really pissed me off, but now I just find it slightly funny. Double fuck, maybe I do have Stockholm syndrome. "Well, you're not pretending to be grateful, so you must not hate me either."

"You're right, I don't hate you. Let's get married."

It probably says terrible things about me and Jonathan both that I can't tell if he's trying to flirt with me, trying to make me laugh, or just being really fucking insulting. Either way, before I can come up with a good counter-burnflirt, the waiter comes over and asks us if we're ready to order.

"We're having the Wagyu Beef," I tell him. "One between us, like."

"We are bloody not," says Jonathan immediately.

"Ignore him, he's having a funny turn."

Still on that weird boundary between peeved and joining in, Jonathan glares at the waiter. "Do I *look* like I'm having a funny turn?"

The waiter steps back with an apologetic half-smile. "If you were in my position, how would you answer that question?"

Jonathan sighs. "Fair point."

"What a lot of other couples do," the waiter goes on, "is get a half-and-half."

"We're not a couple," Jonathan and I say at the exact same time, which honestly isn't the best evidence of our not-a-couple-ness.

"But yes," Jonathan continues, "that's probably the best option. We'll get one half Wagyu Beef, one half margherita."

"Oh come on," I protest. "Now you're just taking the piss."

"There's nothing wrong with margherita."

"Of course there's"—I realise the waiter is still, well, waiting, probably for drinks, so I order a coke and Jonathan orders a water—"of course there's nothing wrong with a margherita," I continue when the waiter's gone. "There's also nothing *right* with a margherita because a margherita is a nothing pizza. It's just a cheese and tomato sandwich with extra steps."

"There's nothing wrong with a cheese and tomato sandwich either."

Now I'm sure he's doing it on purpose. "There is when you're paying twenty-four quid for it in a restaurant in Shoreditch."

"You're the one who picked this place."

"You're the one who lives in a town where they charge you thirty quid for a pizza."

I'm a bit startled when he flares up and not in the way I'm getting used to where it's not exactly playful but it's the closest he seems to come to it. "Can we not do the"—he lapses into a full Sheffield accent—"*ee, by gum, that London's right terrible* routine."

My eyes have gone wide. "I'm just saying things are bit expensive down here. Because they are."

"Yes, yes." He frowns extra craggily. "Everything's overpriced. People aren't friendly enough. The ground's too flat and the sky's the wrong shade of grey. I've heard it all before. And, even with all that, ten million people choose to live here."

There's genuinely a part of me that thinks ten million people are very, *very* wrong. Or at least don't know any better. But I'm getting the feeling it'll go over badly. I decide to let it go, in the name of harmony and not getting everyone fired, but after we've sat there in silence for a few good minutes, I have to admit that letting it go isn't what I'm doing. I'm more sort of wondering and maybe having one of those in-your-head-arguments you have when someone on telly says something you don't agree with.

"Hang on a second," I start. Well. Restart. "I thought this place made you feel unwelcome. You know with the rock star's kids and the English students and that."

"I'm not saying it's perfect. I'm just very tired of people from the north banging on about how much better things are in a place they left for good reasons."

"Jonathan," I say gently. "Not to go out on a limb or anything, but am I right in thinking you're not actually talking about me right now? You do remember I still live there, right? And I'll be going straight back the moment the amnesia clears up."

"I've seen where you live, Sam. I'm not entirely sure what the north is offering you."

The pisser of it is, he's got a point, and he doesn't even know how much he's got a point. "Hey, we have no idea why my flat's like that. I could be in witness protection. Or it could be temporary. Tell you what, though, if I lived in London, I couldn't afford a place as luxurious as that."

The frown's turned into a glower. Which is a frown that intends to stay for a while. "Firstly, you could. Your flat is dreadful. Secondly, in London you'd have better opportunities. At least you would if you had the initiative to take them."

"Not everybody in London's a millionaire."

The waiter comes back nervously with the pizza. I'm sure he still thinks we're a couple. Just now he also thinks we're a couple who's having a domestic.

"Thank you," says Jonathan, and all the hostility goes out of his voice immediately. And it strikes me that being able to go from bollocking one person to being polite to another without missing a beat is a highly specific skill that I'm very glad I've never felt the need to develop.

"Your pizza," the waiter tells us. "One half margherita, one half air-dried Wagyu Beef, truffle crème fraîche, cipollini onions, and salsa verde. Can I get you anything else?"

He can't, so he goes. And we're left eyeing each other over frankly too much pizza for which we're paying frankly too much money.

"I know"—I can tell from Jonathan's tone he's trying to be conciliatory and I can tell from experience he's not going to be very good at it—"that not everyone in London is a millionaire. I'm an arsehole, not an idiot. But I've thrived in this city in a way my family could never have thrived in Sheffield."

God, he's a contradictory man. No wonder he's grumpy all the time. "If Sheffield's such a worthless dump, why'd you open a shop there?"

He's silent for a long moment. "Sentiment."

Then he cuts himself a slice of very boring pizza and eats it without further comment.

CHAPTER 15

MEETING ON PORTOBELLO ROAD MADE a lot of sense when it was just going to be me coming in on my own on the tube and shanks' pony, but it makes a whole lot less sense when it's me and Jonathan and Jonathan's car that he has to stick in long-stay car park whose prices I think even he would've complained about if we'd not been fresh off a row about exactly that sort of thing.

To make matters worse—and I'm not going to admit this to him because he'll worry or at least get controlling with it—I'm getting a bit tired, and it's a level of tired I can't quite convince myself has nothing to do with the concussion I had recently. So it's probably a good thing Jonathan's with me. I don't think I'm about to collapse or anything, but people get out of his way. Even Londoners get out of his way and those people don't even stop for fucking trucks. It's embarrassing to admit but it makes me feel kind of safe like, although, since he's the reason I got the concussion in the first place, that might just be the Stockholm syndrome again. In any case, he's the reason I don't get jostled in a place that's otherwise very jostley.

Most cities, in my experience, have certain bits that you only go to if you're really *really* from there or really *really* not, and Portobello Road is one of those bits. So Jonathan's guiding us through a bustling street market whose brightly coloured stalls are populated entirely by tourists buying tat with Union Jacks on and steely-eyed locals haggling fiercely over the price of teacups. It'd be pretty overwhelming even if I didn't have a concussion because, even though neither Liverpool nor Sheffield are what you'd call small towns, London just has an intense in-your-face Londoniness that you're either about or you're not, and I think I'm definitely not.

It's not that I don't appreciate it. There's something kind of timeless here, with the fronts of the houses all painted up like a rainbow and the shops and the pubs spilling out onto the pavement in a merry chaos. The thing is it just doesn't feel like home. Then again, as Jonathan keeps pointing out, neither does home these days.

Fortunately, Jonathan knows exactly where he's going, and we weave past displays of bric-a-brac, racks of scarves, and pallets of fresh fruit and veg, until at last we spot Del in the middle of what seems to be a very serious conversation with a man at an antique stall. They're both wearing flat caps and identical navy-blue fleeces.

"Vernon," Del's saying. "Vern. Mate. When have I ever steered you wrong?"

Vernon-Vern-Mate folds his arms. "All the bloody time, mate." He's got a trace of a Jamaican accent under the thick layer of London.

"Look, I swear I never knew them carriage clocks was—Jonathan." Del turns to us, grinning. "Vern, you remember Wendy's boy, Jonathan. The one what's got them three superstores in three different cities."

"No," Vernon grins, "never heard of him because you never mention him at all." He reaches out and shakes Jonathan firmly by the hand. "Good to see you again. What have you been doing with yourself?"

Jonathan's different here—still not warm exactly, still not the kind of person you'd bring to a party and not expect to ruin it, but like he's on his best behaviour. Like when you're six and you're out visiting a family friend. "Working mostly—I'm afraid it's all administration these days. In a lot of ways I miss getting my hands dirty."

That makes Vernon laugh a loud, nostalgic laugh, then he puts an arm around Jonathan's shoulder and turns to me. "This boy," he says, pointing at Jonathan and grinning, "when he was fourteen, he used to come and help me out on the stall and I swear he could sell anything to anybody."

Jonathan almost blushes. "I was just very persistent."

From what I've seen, he still is. And maybe that's not always a bad thing.

"You hang onto him," Vernon tells me, "he's a good one."

"He's not actually—" I begin, but don't get to finish because Barbara Jane, wearing a different set of oversized sunglasses and a bright red jumper reading *Merry Christmas Ya Filthy Animal* bursts out of the crowd and starts indiscriminately hugging people.

"Vern," she cries, "it's been bloody years."

"I know, and somehow I don't look a day over twenty. Love the jumper."

"Thanks." She tugs at the collar. "Nine fifty off a stall just up the way." She points behind her. "She started at twelve but I beat her down."

Del pats her on the back. "Good girl. Though if it was Crissy she'd have done it for eight quid flat if you'd stuck to your guns. Now"—he turns back to Vernon—"about this crystal."

With an expression of great scepticism, Vernon picks up a cut glass decanter and turns it over in his hands. "If this is Victorian, Del, I'm a fucking Scotsman."

"Fair spot. It *might* be Edwardian."

Vernon peers closer at the markings on the ambiguously-antique item of glassware. "I'm pretty sure it's from Debenhams."

"So? Debenhams was around hundreds of years till it went under."

"I think they're selling them on their website *today*."

"Classic design."

I didn't notice Les showing up, but I notice him now. "Del," he says quietly, "stop trying to flog Vernon a job lot of dodgy glassware. We've got to pick up this tree you bought without telling us."

"The tree's a bargain and the glass is fine." Del's still mostly talking to Vernon. "Sleep on it, I'll catch you tomorrow."

Vernon makes some very noncommittal noises about thinking it over, and then the various members of Jonathan's family make their way across the road to a white van parked in a space that should probably have been reserved for an actual stallholder. Since Jonathan and I are very slightly slower off the mark than the others, the seats in the front go quickly and we're left bundling into the back, sitting opposite each other on low benches without seatbelts. There's things all over the floor. Boxes and boxes of *things*, all of them—I'm sure—soon to be sold for a healthy markup.

"Could you not," Les is saying as we pull out, "lay off the barrow boy routine for one day while we get Christmas sorted."

"How about you stay out of my business, and I'll stay out of yours?"

"You won't, though, will you?"

"It is *so nice*"—Barbara Jane doesn't yell, exactly, but she's got her mam's ability to make herself heard when she has to—"to have the family back together. When did we last go tree shopping together, Johnny?"

"More than a decade." Jonathan also seems to be wanting

to drown out any other bickering. "You were just finishing your A-levels."

"No, I skipped that year because I was"—she casts a sideways glance at her dad—"*revising* extremely hard."

Jonathan gives that twitch of the lips that passes for a smile. "I thought you were at one of Abigail's drug-fuelled sex parties."

"That is *slander*. Abigail did not throw drug-fuelled sex parties. She threw parties at which some people *happened* to take drugs and some people *happened* to have sex."

"Do you think," says Les, "that you could maybe talk a bit less about drug-fuelled sex parties in front of your old man and granddad?"

"*I* wasn't talking about drug-fuelled sex parties," Barbara Jane insists, "*Johnny* was talking about drug-fuelled sex parties. *I* was talking about how nice it is to have us all back together doing something as a family."

It feels a bit off to be included in the *as a family* what with me being a complete stranger and everything. But as Jonathan and Barbara Jane settle into a comfortable pattern of bickering while we make our way through London I find myself almost relaxing into it, like it's as familiar to me as it is to them. Like I belong here, even if I don't.

The place that's apparently going to sell us our Christmas tree is way out on the edge of town—a proper farm with acres and acres of the things all growing wild and proper JCBs around to haul them. And, looking around, that seems to be the range. The trees here go from *very big* through *really big* and into *absolutely fucking massive*. And as we pull to a stop at the end of a long drive, I don't think I've seen a single one that'd fit in a living room.

Del gets out and runs over to greet yet another man in a flat cap, this one with a white goatee and his hair tied back in a short ponytail. "Got a good one for us?" he asks.

"Got a great one," him with the ponytail replies. And he leads us in the direction of an already-felled, already-trussed-up-in-netting tree that's got to be twenty foot if it's an inch.

"Beautiful," Del's saying. "Perfect. Come on Jonathan, Sam, give us a hand."

The rest of us just stare. "Is that not," I try, "a little high for the ceilings?"

Barbara Jane adjusts her sunglasses, which are increasingly impractical now the light's fading. "It's a little high for the *roof*."

"Just getting us our money's worth." Either from pride or genuine inability to see the downside, Del isn't letting up on his enthusiasm for the twenty-foot Christmas tree plan.

"Nothing but the best for a mate," him with the ponytail adds.

Les, however, isn't having it. "It'll not fit in the van."

"It'll fit on the top." Del clearly has no time for Christmas tree dissent. "We'll just strap it on."

"Ah yes." Barbara Jane smirks. "An enormous strap-on, just what Christmas needs."

Jonathan heads forward. I'll say this for him, he's a hands on sort of lad. "I think it'll take all of us. Probably three at the front two at the back?"

To my complete lack of surprise, Del goes for it like he's not five foot six and seventy years old. I'm a bit reluctant to try and lift a tree with no training or supervision, but I figure if I don't he'll do himself an injury. Unfortunately all the three of us succeed in doing is rolling the thing sideways. You don't expect a Christmas tree to be this heavy, except then you realise it's an actual fucking tree.

"Les," cries Del, "Barbara J. What are you doing just standing there?"

Barbara Jane pushes her sunglasses all the way onto the top of her head. "I can't speak for Dad, but what I'm doing is watching three idiots trying to lift an entire Douglas fir onto a Ford transit van."

"Well, if you two muck in, it'll be five idiots," replies Del.

And he has, I suppose, got a point, although I think I personally would have wanted him to address the idiot question over the headcount.

"Del." Les is doing his calm thing again. And it's about now that I realise it's a calm that overlays a well of something that's not exactly scary but is deep. "Just think about this. For once."

Del lets go of the tree to argue, which means Jonathan and I have to put it down very, very fast. "I have thought about it. And what I've thought is, I might not be here next Christmas—"

"Granddad," says Jonathan matter-of-factly, "you're going to outlive all of us and you know it."

"Either way,"—Del's still not letting up—"it's the first time we've been together as a whole family in years what with Barbara J being in America and Jonathan always being too busy and Theo and Kayla spending every other Christmas with his parents, and I wanted to do something special. And you, lad..." He's wagging his finger now. It's never good when people start wagging their fingers. "You are ruining it."

Les doesn't blink. "It won't. Fit. In. The house."

"It's fine. We'll trim it down."

"So you want to celebrate," asks Les, "our special, first family Christmas in years with a headless Christmas tree?"

"It'll work," Del insists, "if we make it work. Instead of sitting around whining and making excuses."

There's a long, long silence. Long enough for me to realise quite how horrifying Christmas trees look in the dark, as if they're evil giants reaching out to strangle yez. And also long enough for me to realise that there's context to all this that I do not want to go near.

Then Jonathan says, "Come on, Dad. We can sort it out when we get home." And he sounds tired. Disappointed almost.

It takes us about half an hour of sweating and humping to get the tree onto the roof rack and get it lashed down like James Bond in *Goldfinger*. And the first time we get it up there, we have it the wrong way round so the front hangs down over the windscreen, which means we have to swivel it to put the trunk up front and leave the top dangling off the back where it goes so low it practically touches the road. Honestly, with the branches spreading all over on account of how it's too wide for the roof even with netting trying gamely to hold it in, it looks like the whole van's been eaten by an Ent. Or, as my mam would've put out, by a Huorn—them being the actual trees, rather than the tree herders.

"This is so dangerous," says Barbara Jane. "I love it."

Del bangs the side of the van confidently. "It's not dangerous if you know what you're doing."

I think he's probably wrong about that. The only question in my mind as we get in the back, fighting our way through a forest of pine needles, is whether the whole thing is going to tip over before or after we get arrested. Fortunately, the van has a low centre of gravity and over a decade of Tory underfunding means the Metropolitan police don't really have the manpower to stop us. So, by a frankly unwarranted Christmas miracle, do we arrive back at Jonathan's intact and without our tree getting impounded as a public safety hazard.

I'm a bit wobbly as I climb out and quite looking forward to crashing on the sofa and trying in vain to tempt Gollum to start giving a fuck about me again. Except we've got a gigantic tree to deal with and I don't want to let anybody down.

"You look like shit," says Jonathan, winning as ever.

"Thanks," I say back.

"No, I..." He scowls. "You look unwell. You should go inside and rest."

"What, and send the cat out to help with the tree?"

"We'll manage. Down'll be easier than up."

As usual, I have no idea if he's being nice or really patronising. "I'll be okay. I'll have a sit after we're done."

"I'm increasingly concerned we won't be done until next Christmas."

Normally when Jonathan says "we", he either means "him on his own" or "him and me going along with whatever he wants". Tonight, though, he's actually talking about a group of people with a shared goal, of which I am a part. Even if the goal in question is to fit a twenty-foot Christmas tree into a ten-foot room like we're on *Taskmaster*.

"Come on." Del gestures to us through the branches. "Gabbing won't get the baby washed."

Barbara Jane looks from the van to the house to the van again. "I don't think the baby's going to fit through the front door."

"We can open the French windows at the back," says Jonathan. "But it won't stand up once it's inside."

Del is still very much occupying his own reality. "We'll just lean it a bit."

"Lean it *how*?" asks Barbara Jane, who is at this point speaking for all of us. Except maybe Les who's giving off strong *staying out of it* vibes.

"Prop it on a wall."

More or less as one, Les, Jonathan, and Barbara Jane decide that the only thing less possible than fitting the gargantuan tree into Jonathan's middle reception room will be convincing Del that they shouldn't at least try to fit the gargantuan tree into Jonathan's middle reception room. The five of us haul it down from the roof of the van, and then at Jonathan's insistence I leave the rest of them to try to get it in the house while I go and make a round of teas.

"He's had a serious concussion," Jonathan reminds his family. "So he really shouldn't be doing this."

I try to tell them that the concussion were a week ago now and that I'll probably be fine but I don't want to push it too far, partly because I've progressed from wobbly to woozy, and partly because I don't want to be asked too many questions about why the amnesia's not clearing up. Fortunately, nobody seems to want to make a thing out of it, probably because somebody said the word "tea" and they're already throwing orders at me.

"Two sugars in mine."

"Milk, no sugar, thanks Sam."

"If you were going to make a coffee that'd be fab."

I hurry off to the kitchen and start boiling a kettle. And then I realise I've not made tea in Jonathan's kitchen yet. I sort of assumed he wouldn't have any because he doesn't seem to have any of anything else, but I root around in a cupboard and find a caddy full of ground coffee and a half empty box of Yorkshire teabags.

What with the kitchen being open-plan and looking right out onto the garden, I've got a perfect view of the tree being dragged around from the front. From inside, it looks like even more of a disaster. Del and Les are supporting the base while Jonathan and Barbara Jane are pulling from the front but Jonathan's garden has been designed for looking nice in brochures, not for having a Norwegian spruce lugged across it, and I'm pretty sure his flower-beds aren't making it through the evening alive.

I do the teas to people's specifications and to make myself extra specially useful, I open the French windows as well. It takes some wrangling for Jonathan and Barbara Jane to get in, but they do eventually. Except as they back up through the middle reception room, the tree just keeps coming, like flags out of a magician's sleeve, and before Les and Del are in with the base, the top's poking out the other side and into Jonathan's study.

"I hate to say I told you so." Les doesn't sound like he does, in fact, hate to say he told us so. He sounds, at best, neutral to saying he told us so.

"It's fine." Del has managed to squeeze through the door and is now standing on one of the relatively small areas of floor that's not completely occupied by Christmas tree. "Is that my tea? Cheers."

It is, and I hand it to him.

"This is fine," he repeats. "I got a big one because it's like I always say—what do I always say, Jonathan?"

From inside his study, Jonathan clambers over the top of the tree and comes out to inspect the damage. "You say a lot of things, Granddad, but I *think* the one that you're getting at is *you can cut a bit off but you can't cut a bit on.*"

"Exactly." Del is grinning. "All we need to do is chop it in two."

Les is looking like he thinks this is a terrible plan. Barbara Jane is looking like she thinks this is a terrible plan but she loves it anyway. And Jonathan, well, he goes to get a saw. Which isn't exactly the reaction I was expecting. I'd been expecting him to be a shade more this-is-ridiculousy, possibly edging into being get-out-my-housey. Maybe he's just too exhausted to argue. Or maybe it was the Wagyu Beef pizza.

Or maybe he's just, y'know, trying.

Which means I might be doing what I told Claire I'd be doing. Influencing him and that. Except it doesn't feel quite like I thought it'd feel. Because you don't really expect a man like Jonathan Forest to change. And if he is...sort of is...for me. Well. I'm not sure I deserve it.

CHAPTER 16

THEY'VE HAULED THE TREE BACK outside and turned the garden lights on so as they can see what they're doing, and I've retreated to the kitchen to throw together some sandwiches because it's turning into a long evening. Barbara Jane's come with me since while I get the feeling she's a hands-on sort of person, there's already three generations of her family gathered outside trying to work out how to hack up a Christmas tree in the least un-Christmassy way possible, so I reckon she feels a bit superfluous.

"Are they always like this?" I ask.

"Pretty much." She's sipping on a mug of black coffee and watching the lads out the window with strong rather-them-than-me energy. "Sometimes I think it's a toxic masculinity thing, and sometimes I think we're all just arseholes."

Outside, I see Jonathan and Del squabbling over which one is going to be doing the sawing. I sort of hope Jonathan wins because I reckon he'd look good doing manual labour. It'll give him somewhere to direct his hostility.

"So"—Barbara Jane takes a sharp left turn into a different topic—"how did you and Jonathan meet?"

"I told you, we're not dating, I just work for him."

She makes the most sceptical *mm-hmm* I've ever heard, and I've heard Claire's sceptical *mm-hmms*.

"Really," I tell her. Because there's nothing more convincing than saying "really" with a rising inflection.

"You're living in his house and he's so concerned about your well-being that he sent you inside instead of making you help with the tree. That's more consideration than he's shown half his actual boyfriends."

"I think he's just worried I'll sue him."

She *mm-hmms* me again. "Pretty sure he's got better lawyers than you."

It's only because we're about to lapse into an uncomfortable silence, and because I'm not sure what to say next, and because I've got a concussion that I follow up with, "So has he had a lot then? Boyfriends, I mean."

That makes her laugh. There's a lot about her and Jonathan that's very similar but the laughing isn't one of them. "Oh God no. A few, but he's mostly married to his work. Also, in case you haven't noticed, he's a prick."

"Hey, steady on, that's your brother you're talking about."

"Which is why I'm allowed to call him a prick."

"He's not that bad." I don't know why I'm defending him either.

"Sam"—this time she *mm-hmms* me with her eyes—"he's family and I love him. But he's exactly that bad. He's like Ebenezer Scrooge in the first two-thirds of *A Christmas Carol*. Frankly, if you're not dating him, then I'm pretty sure he's going to die alone."

"That seems very melodramatic."

Barbara Jane raises her eyebrows, and this is a much more Jonathany gesture than the laughter. "In case you haven't noticed, we're quite a melodramatic family, and I'm one of the more melodramatic members. I've been telling Johnny he's going to die in his office and be found in the morning by the janitor since he was eleven."

"That seems a bit rough." Again, I don't quite know what I'm saying because a week and a half ago I'd have agreed. "And from what I've heard, your love life isn't exactly so rosy either."

"My love life is *fine,* I assure you."

"Haven't you just got divorced?"

Now she's laughing again. "Which has been *extremely* good for my love life."

In the garden, Jonathan's taken his jacket off and started sawing. I was right, it does look good on him.

"Are you absolutely sure," asks Barbara Jane with what you might call an insinuating tone, "that you're not dating him?"

So I bung the sandwiches at her and go do the washing up.

Cutting through the tree takes a while, and getting it inside and upright takes a while more. Barbara Jane's gone to encourage-slash-annoy them, but I mainly stay in the kitchen, because I'm feeling a bit self-conscious. Eventually, though, I'm called through to the middle reception room to give my opinion.

My opinion, if I'm being totally candid, is that it looks a bit shit. And I don't really want to say that but, from the expressions on everybody else's faces, they're all thinking the same thing.

"With a bit of tinsel," Del's saying, "it'll be fine."

"I think the problem"—Barbara Jane casts a critical eye over the scene—"is that the bottom half of a Christmas tree is the least interesting half of a Christmas tree. So what we've got here is ten feet of sad pine tetrahedron and nowhere to put the star."

"You can put stars anywhere," Del claims, on the basis of no evidence.

Jonathan's standing there, full arms folded pose, looking sweaty and irate, which shouldn't be as appealing as it is. But it is. "I'm not having this in my living room. It looks ugly and ludicrous."

"Alright, alright," Del begins. "We'll—"

But Jonathan cuts him off. "No. First thing tomorrow, I'm getting someone to come round and remove this, and bring us an ordinary tree."

It's the right answer, and it's the most sensible thing to do—at least if you've got Jonathan's money—but I don't think he realises how harsh he sounds. And for a belligerent man, Del looks amazingly crushed. And I sort of get where he's coming from because, yes, this is rubbish. It's just, after going all the way out there, and bringing it all the way back, and chopping it in half with a saw, and getting it into the front room, and standing it up, and moving the furniture because the branches go out too far, it feels like our rubbish. Well, I suppose their rubbish.

No, our rubbish. I mean, I was right there with them. And, between an overpriced pizza and an oversized Christmas tree, I'm starting to think I've had a really good day. Maybe the best day I've had in a long time. And I don't want it to end with a sad old man and a team of interior decorators.

"What if," I suggest, "we take a gander at it from the outside. It might look better through the window, especially if we imagine it all lit up."

Jonathan does not seem like he's up for this—I'm worried that any minute now he's going to kick us all out of his house again—but the rest are surprisingly game. Or maybe not so surprisingly because they're pretty game people.

We troop into the mess of the garden and stand by the top of the Christmas tree, looking at the bottom of the Christmas tree through the French windows. Honestly, it doesn't look much better. It's sort of a droopy wall of green with a confused cat giving it the stink eye from across the room.

Del heaves this defeated sigh. "Okay," he says. "I see it. This might not have been the best idea."

My eyes sort of sweep up the side of the house. The bedroom

I'm staying in is right above the middle reception room, and it's got the same sort of windows.

"What if," I say, "we take the next bit and stick it in the room above and then we take the very top and stick it on the roof so it looks like the tree's going all the way up through three storeys."

Jonathan's giving me a look that's quite hard to describe. It's about 20 percent betrayal, 10 percent resignation, 30 percent resentment, and 40 percent straight up what are you talking about? "Is your solution to my house being far too full of Christmas tree to make it even more full of Christmas tree?"

"Yeah," I say. "It's sort of the festive equivalent of when a movie's so bad it gets good."

"This is the Wagyu Beef pizza all over again, isn't it?"

"Come on, what do you have to lose?"

"Time"—Jonathan's ticking things off on his fingers—"dignity and, in the likely event one of us falls off the roof, our lives."

"It's okay," Barbara Jane says. I get the feeling she isn't going to be helpful here. "We'll send Sam onto the roof and if he falls off, it'll probably just cure his amnesia."

"Fuck off, BJ."

"I think it's worth a go," Del decides. "It'll be a Christmas we'll never forget."

"Especially if one of us dies," adds Barbara Jane.

Del shrugs. "I probably won't be here next year anyway."

"Granddad," chorus Jonathan and Barbara Jane, "you say that every year."

Les seems to have been thinking this whole time. "We should go for it," he says. "We're here now."

"Fine. I'll get the ladder." Pushing his comprehensively disarranged hair back from his brow, Jonathan turns on his heel. "What's the point of having a house, if not to let your family wreck it?"

"That's the spirit," says Del.

I'd felt a bit guilty sending Jonathan and his dad up the roof, though I tried to console myself with the thought that if he did fall to his death while wrangling a Christmas tree, he at least wouldn't be able to fire us. Then again, the whole company'd probably get sold off without him so we'd just wind up getting fired by different people.

After lots of "up a bit, left a bit, it ain't lining up right", we all gather back in the garden and inspect the illusion.

"I'll admit," says Barbara Jane, "that came out a lot less shit than I expected."

I think she's understating it. I'd even go so far as to say it looks pretty good. They've arranged the bits of tree so, when you see it from outside, it looks like it's this enormous thing that starts on the ground floor, goes straight up through the guest bedroom—my bedroom, as it happens—and out through the roof like a very festive Godzilla. I reckon it'll be even better when it's decorated, although that does mean we'll have to get the ladders out again to stick the star on top.

"See." Del gestures triumphantly like it had been his plan the whole time. "I told you we'd sort it out. Isn't that better than some piddly little thing you got from John Lewis's?"

Jonathan is clearly struggling with the need to say something nice about one of my ideas. "It's very impactful. And it's impacted my entire day."

"Been a laugh, though, ain't it?" asks Del in a not-really-a-question tone of voice.

Settling her sunglasses back over her eyes, even though it's full dark, Barbara Jane grins. "Definitely a top five Christmas tree story. Almost as fun as the year we accidentally left Jonathan in the garden centre and Granddad didn't notice until we were past Watford."

"Or," Jonathan snarks back, "the year you got arrested for shoplifting from Santa's Grotto."

"I just assumed that if he had enough toys for every single child in the world he could spare a couple extra for me."

"You were seventeen."

"I was not." Barbara Jane rounds defiantly on her brother. "I was eight. You're just trying to make me look bad in front of Sam because you fancy him."

It's a bit hard to tell in the dark but I think Jonathan's gone bright red. "I do not. I don't find Sam attractive at all."

"Oh thanks," I say.

This makes Jonathan even more flustered. "I don't mean… I'm not saying you're not… You work for me, Sam. It would not be appropriate to consider you on an attractiveness level."

"Oh thanks," I say again.

The persistence that served Jonathan so well on a market stall and when starting his own business also means that he has no clue when to quit. "It's an employment law issue. I'd be creating a hostile working environment."

"Jonathan," I tell him, "you already do create a hostile working environment. You're a walking hostile working environment."

"I am not," snarls Jonathan hostilely while Barbara Jane watches in glee. "Now all of you fuck off. We've done the tree, and I need to get my car back from Notting Hill before the parking fees bankrupt me."

"I think"—Les puts his arm around Barbara Jane—"we should probably go. Your brother's getting a bit tired."

Jonathan starts gesticulating. I think he maybe is quite tired. "I am not tired. I've just put up with a lot today."

"See you later, son," says Les.

And the family leave, in a surprisingly upbeat fashion for a group of people who've just been told to fuck off by their own flesh and blood. Jonathan, meanwhile, is storming away to call a taxi. I offer to go with him but he turns me down flat and, to be honest, I'm glad. Because I am bushed. I am bushed, beat, and bloody knackered.

Avoiding the room-full-of-Christmas-tree, I head into the kitchen and make myself another cheese sandwich to keep my strength up. There's probably about three sandwiches worth of cheese left, if I'm counting, and I make a mental note to do another food run tomorrow so we don't slip back into living off takeaways. While I've got the bread out, I make a sandwich for Jonathan and all, wrapping it in cling film so it'll keep if I'm in bed before he gets back. And so he knows it's there, I send him a text saying I did you a sandwich, but he doesn't reply.

Then I flop down on the settee and stick on the first thing that gets recommended to me on iPlayer, which turns out to be a repeat of *Gavin & Stacey*. Gollum creeps in from the other room, belly to the ground and ears back, suggesting he's reluctantly conceding that round one, at least, goes to the Christmas tree, though if I know Gollum there'll be a round two. I just hope we'll make it to Boxing Day without him pulling the whole thing down on somebody's head.

He curls up on my lap with the discontented air of a cat who's wishing I was the other human, but I don't take it personal. Any more than I took Jonathan Forest going on about how not attractive I am personal. And anyway, before *Gavin & Stacey* can get to the end of the title sequence, I've fallen asleep.

I wake up I'm not sure how much later, but late enough that the BBC is asking me whether I'm still watching *Gavin & Stacey* in that judgemental way they do when you leave something on in the background. And I'm aware of a weight against my shoulder that, when I flicker my eyes open, turns out to be Jonathan. In the pale TV light, I can see he's fast asleep, with half a cheese sandwich on his lap and Gollum next to the sandwich with a *what is this shit* expression on his face.

They say people look different when they're asleep. Younger or softer or more attractive or more vulnerable or something. But not Jonathan. Sleep just makes him look like an experimental piece from a sculptor who's going through an abstract period, all strong lines and harsh angles with shadows painted across his cheeks.

And maybe it's because it's dark, and maybe it's because being unconscious substantially improves him, but I think I'm going to have to accept the fact that, visually at least, Jonathan Forest is a very interesting man.

I figure if I move I'll wake him up, and he's had a long day. Partly because of me. So I stay where I am, and let him sleep.

CHAPTER 17

THE NEXT MORNING AT BREAKFAST neither of us mention the time we spent passed out on the sofa together. Instead, I mention that we're out of cheese.

"And in just over a fortnight," I add, "you're going to have to feed your whole family with a range of socially mandated, labour-intensive foodstuffs that you do not want to be shopping for at the last minute."

Jonathan looks up from his laptop, which he's been buried in since I came down. "You realise that's the kind of thing you can pay people to do for you."

"Oh, that'll be touching. *Do you like the turkey? I bunged a stranger fifty quid to pick it out for me.*"

"I'm also intending to pay a stranger to cook it for me."

I give a bit of a yelp and Gollum looks around like he's worried we're under attack. "You can't do that. It's Christmas dinner. The rule is, you've got to spend all day making it, and then complain about how no one appreciates the fact you spent all day making it. It's part of the magic."

"It's not magic, Sam, it's an inconvenience."

"You can't call your family an inconvenience."

"I can when they're being inconvenient," he snaps.

Opening the cupboard, I grab myself a mug and boil the kettle for tea. Jonathan's a coffee in the morning person but now I know tea's an option I'm taking it. "Well," I ask the wall in front of me, "would you rather they weren't there?"

"No, of course not."

I'm still talking to the wall. "Then you need to stop acting like they're an overhead you're trying to reduce."

"That's not what I'm doing. But I'll be no use to anyone if my business collapses."

"Firstly," I say, turning back to him, "yes you will, because they're your family and they'll love you anyway. Secondly, your business isn't going to collapse because you're good at what you do, people will always need somewhere to sleep and take a dump, and you've got teams working for you that know what they're doing."

Jonathan's holding his coffee cup far more tightly than it's really healthy to be holding a coffee cup. "I still can't afford to be complacent."

"It's not complacent to take a day off. And it's definitely not complacent to cook your own fucking turkey."

"No"—he bristles his eyebrows at me—"but hiring a professional will make it better for everybody. That's how hiring professionals works."

I sigh. "If your family wanted a high-quality dining experience, they'd go to a restaurant and they probably wouldn't order the turkey because it's not the kind of thing anybody actually wants to eat. What they want is for you to share something with them. Something you haven't just paid for."

"I've worked very hard to be able to pay for things."

"And that's lovely," I tell him. "It really is. But right now you're using it as an excuse. And what's weird is, I'm not even sure what you're using it as an excuse for."

He stares into his coffee. He takes it the same colour as his eyes. "Honestly," he says finally, "I'm not sure either."

For a moment, we just hang around being faintly melancholy at each other.

"All we need to do," I say, "is head down a supermarket, fill up our trolley with meat, and stick it all in your enormous fridge you never use. And while we're there, we can get some other food because you've run out again."

"You see"—Jonathan takes his empty coffee cup over to the sink—"this is why I live on takeaways. You start buying food, you never stop."

I give him a look. "Is that a joke? You making a joke?"

He gives me a look back. "Just an observation."

"Seriously, though, we should go shopping."

Jonathan comes back to the table and sits down. He looks thoughtful, like. "How about a compromise?"

Until now, I'd have assumed that word wasn't in his vocabulary. "What kind of compromise?"

"We'll keep food in the house as long as you're staying here, and I'll roast my own damned turkey come Christmas even though I'm sure it will be a complete disaster, *but* we take advantage of the fact that it's the twenty-first century and at least get things delivered."

I'm disappointed, and it takes me a second to realise *why* I'm disappointed. "I'd been sort of looking forward to getting out the house."

"You were out the house yesterday and..." He stops short of saying *and you fell asleep on the sofa and I fell asleep on top of yez*. "And you were very tired."

"What, so you're never going to let me leave again?"

His lips go thin in that way he's got that says *I'm trying here, but you're making things difficult and I'm not appreciating it*. "I just think it would be more practical to have things delivered. I'll set us something up with Waitrose."

I resist the temptation to call him out for how la-di-da getting your deliveries from Waitrose instead of a proper supermarket is because I don't want to push my luck. And in the end, he's efficient with it—I've barely finished washing up my cereal bowl and he's got himself set up, entered his details, and is filling a basket.

He turns the laptop towards me. "Anything you think we should get—just for general supplies? You need to do Christmas deliveries separately."

I feel a bit awkward scrolling through buying groceries on Jonathan's account, but since he's living in a house without eggs, bread, or milk in the fridge I fix that for him at least. Then I throw in a couple of packs of very expensive crisps, and a meal or two's worth of everyday ingredients. "That all right?"

He runs his eyes over the cart, asks no questions, and clicks to pay. "It'll be here tomorrow. Now, what do you want to do about"—he gives a needlessly dramatic pause—"the family?"

"You mean Christmas stuff? Shouldn't be too difficult, should it?"

He clicks through a few more tabs and shows me the options. There's rather more of them than I've been expecting. "Why," I ask, "would anybody want a turkey crown stuffed with gingerbread?"

"It's a Christmassy flavour?" Jonathan doesn't look especially convinced.

"Yeah, but not with meat."

"Is it any stranger than cranberry?"

I'm not letting him get away with that. "Yes. Much. Now let's not make it complicated. You'll want a turkey, stuffing, some gammon, maybe a side of beef—" I keep scrolling. "Fucking hell it's a lot, isn't it?"

"You see why I didn't want you carting it all around a supermarket in a trolley with a wonky wheel."

He's come around to look over my shoulder, so I turn my face up to him. "That's a very specific concern."

"Trolleys always have wonky wheels. And I had a feeling this would escalate. Now should I get venison?"

I blink. "Should you what?"

"Venison." He points at the screen. "It says a rack feeds six to eight, so I should probably get two."

"It's your family," I remind him, "not Henry the fucking eighth. They'll be fine without the venison."

"But not without the gammon, the stuffing, the beef, the cheeseboard, and the three different kinds of chipolata wrapped in bacon?"

The feeling creeps up on me that he might just be taking the piss. "You know," I tell him, "you might be better off getting a professional after all."

But he's got that self-made-millionaire look in his eyes now. The look that says if the bed-and-bathware industry couldn't beat him then making roasties for thirteen definitely won't. "No, I think we can make this work."

There's that *we* again.

And he does buy the venison.

I don't quite know what's come over Jonathan the rest of the day. It's not like he's suddenly filled with the joys of the season. He's still a sullen bastard and he still spends half his time on his laptop making sure the Leeds branch is shipping enough memory foam mattress toppers and that things are still on track for the Birmingham branch to open in the new year. But he's starting to put the same obsessive attention to detail into the whole Christmas thing as well. He's been into the garden twice to check how the tree looks from outside, and around three he digs out a tape measure and starts doing some calculations in his head that I don't really get and can't follow.

"Dad was right," he announces. "We're going to be short on decorations."

I look up from *Pointless*. Fuck me, I've watched a lot of *Pointless* over the last couple of weeks. "And you couldn't tell that just by looking?"

"Measure twice, cut once."

"It's decorations you're hanging, not shelving."

"Same principle. Everybody—and I do mean *everybody*—is coming around tomorrow. So if I'm going to stop making *excuses*"—fuck, that really got in his head, didn't it—"then I have to make sure they've got everything they need."

"And you want to fix that *right now*."

Mainly I'm surprised. But Jonathan takes it the wrongest way possible. "You're the one who keeps telling me I need to do more for people."

"That's not what I said."

"It's what you implied."

"It's not what I implied, either." I take a deep breath. "You're already doing plenty. It's just...sometimes, it's a bit misdirected."

He ungrumps by maybe two percent. "Then this is me redirecting."

"To decorations?" Only Jonathan Forest would decorate his house for Christmas just to make a point.

"Yes," he says with more aggression than the subject can really bear. "We need them."

"Alright then. Where we getting them from?"

He glances down at his phone. He's apparently googled the same question. "Fortnum & Mason. And I'm getting them, you're resting."

"Jonathan, this is meant to be fun. It won't be fun if you go alone. I'm coming with yez."

He looks doubtful. "How's your head?"

I don't tell him I've had no complaints. It's not that I don't think he'd get it, I just don't think he'd appreciate it. "Not so bad it'll stop me watching you walk around a swanky department store buying tinsel."

"I don't think this will be as amusing as you're expecting."

"Maybe not, but I'll not find out by sitting on my arse at home, will I? Besides, I've never been to Fortnum & Mason before. It'll be something to tell the kids about."

Jonathan's eyes narrow. "The kids?"

"In future like. Years from now I'll be sitting around the fire saying *ooh let Grandpa Sam tell you all about the big shops they've got up London.*"

"You're being ridiculous."

I shrug. "It's Saturday, it's nearly Christmas, I'm living on cornflakes and the ghost of a cheese sandwich—of course I'm being ridiculous."

So far, Jonathan has still never actually smiled at me, but I keep thinking he's coming close. "You're going to make this into a thing, aren't you?"

"Me?" I do my best to look innocent. "No. It's just a shopping trip. Totally normal shopping trip to a place that's mostly famous for hampers."

"There's nothing wrong with hampers. They make good gifts."

"You are not at all at home to the personal touch, are you?"

He fixes me with a stare that isn't half as cold as he thinks it is. "You've got two choices, Sam. You can stand here criticising my personality or you can get your coat."

"I can probably do both," I tell him as I grab my jacket. "I'm gradually recovering my ability to multitask."

But Jonathan isn't listening. He's too busy reassuring the cat we won't be long.

I've never seen Fortnum & Mason in the flesh—or, I suppose, the brick—and I can't decide whether it looks more like a hotel or a prison. It's got the uniformity of a prison, with its regimented windows currently numbered like an advent calendar, y'know, for the Christmas theme, but it's got a fancy doorway, a big clock, and a massive royal crest. Although, thinking about it, you probably get a fair few of them in His Majesty's prisons as well. Inside, it basically looks like a shop. A nice shop, mind, with plush carpets and chandeliers and fancy displays with little Christmas trees on them.

It's quite crowded, though part of that is because everyone who goes through the doors stops and gawps for a bit. Well, everyone except Jonathan who marches right in and doesn't stop marching until he gets to the needlessly majestic spiral staircase that leads to the first floor, that being where all the festive tat is. And, my God, is there a lot of festive tat.

"Right." Jonathan whips out his phone and peers at a list he's clearly got on there. "We mostly need baubles for the tree because, and you may be surprised to learn this, the tree we had at home did not stretch across two fucking floors of quite a large house. We probably also want a wreath for the door and garlands for the surfaces."

"What's a garland?" I ask.

"I'll admit I'm not completely sure, but I think it's tinsel for the middle class."

There's something I find inherently hilarious about Jonathan Forest standing in the middle of Fortnum & Mason, dressed business casual, staring at a grand's worth of phone somehow still managing to have a chip on his shoulder about the middle classes.

He looks up suddenly. "What?"

"Nothing," I say. "You're funny, is all."

"I am not funny." From what the way Jonathan's looking at me, I can't help thinking he might want to be. A little bit. "I'm at a shop buying decorations so I can dress a tree with my family. It's a completely normal thing to be doing at Christmas."

Reaching out, I grab a single bauble from a nearby display. It's blue and sparkly, and has ballerinas painted on it. "Is this normal?" I ask him.

He stares at it, doing his best to see the normalcy. "It's a glass ball for a Christmas tree. What's un-normal about it?"

"Firstly, it's covered in painted ballerinas. Secondly, it's fifty quid."

"For a set?"

"No, for one."

For a brief moment, he gets very, very London-by-way-of-Sheffield. "You're having a laugh."

I show him the label.

"Fucking hell."

"Are you not extremely rich?" I tease him.

"Yes, but I'm not extremely stupid. Now put that down."

I crack up laughing. Because I'm starting to think my favourite thing in the world is Jonathan Forest being excessively angry about things that I am also secretly a little bit angry about. I put the ball of overpriced glass down and Jonathan's on such a mission that he grabs me by the wrist. Except the thing is, it doesn't feel controlling. In a strange way, it's more like he's letting go.

"There *must* be something here that's more reasonable." Jonathan starts browsing with a systematic efficiency that's much more entertaining to watch than he intends it to be.

"Y'know"—my arm's warm where he's still holding me—"I really don't think there must."

"Everywhere says that this is the best place to buy Christmas decorations in London."

I check a more traditional bauble—one with sort of a vintage vibe—but it's the same price. "That might be because if you're making a special trip to London to buy your decorations, you want it to be an experience. I don't think *Time Out* can say *if you want to deck out your living room, nip down the nearest Aldi.*"

In a fit of barely concealed rage, Jonathan picks up a spindly reindeer with pink shoes and candles on its antlers. "Go on," he says. "Guess."

It's bigger than the bauble, but then again, it's also uglier. "Hundred quid."

He points upwards.

"It's never more than a hundred quid."

"Hundred and forty."

From that moment it's on. We weave together amongst the shelves, each trying to pick the most pointlessly overpriced piece of crap and making the other guess what Fortnums have had the gall to charge for it.

The early rounds go to Jonathan, because the deer had been a pretty inspired opener, and while the musical piano ornament I find in response is more *expensive*, it doesn't have quite as brilliant a price-to-awfulness ratio. I pull a bit ahead later on with a purple glass fig that has much more of a genital vibe than I'd personally want on a family holiday, and he counters with a tiny fluffy guinea pig in a Santa hat that I actually think looks quite sweet.

"Okay," I say. "That's just fluffy, they can't be charging an arm and a leg for something fluffy. I'm going to say…thirty-five quid?"

Jonathan checks the label. "Twelve."

I look at him. Then I look at the guinea pig. Then I look at him again. "I think I've been here too long, because they've tricked me into thinking that's a reasonable price."

"Take it from an ex-market trader," says Jonathan, "that's *exactly* the plan. This little fellow"—he bounces the guinea pig on its decorating loop—"would never fetch more than a fiver anywhere else in the world, but stick him next to one of these"—he holds up a little glass snowman who's apparently worth thirty-eight pounds—"and he looks like a bargain."

Although he's made it pretty clear why the adorable fuzzy Santa rodent is a trap for gullible tourists, he's not putting it down.

"Are we getting him then?" I ask.

Jonathan looks ever so slightly sheepish. "He is rather cute."

He takes me by the arm again, and it feels natural, like we do this sort of thing all the time. Though we don't get far before he stops short.

"We need to get out of here," he tells me.

I mostly agree, but I want to know what specifically's set him off. He doesn't seem able to say it aloud so I just follow his gaze to a display of Christmas crackers. They're nicely laid out, if a bit basic-looking, a tasteful red colour with silver detailing. The wicker box they come in is a nice touch. But then it'd have to be.

"I *must* be reading that wrong."

"I don't think you are."

"They're never a grand."

"Back away and pretend you haven't seen anything."

I'm not sure I can. I'm frozen like an underpaid deer in overpriced headlights. "There's only six of them. What've they got inside, cocaine?"

Jonathan has his phone out again, scrolling through something while the little fluffy guinea pig hangs from one finger. "Right," he says, "new plan. We pay for this little fellow, and then we're going to B&Q."

A couple of hours later, we're back home and I'm helping Jonathan unload a carful of much more reasonably priced Christmas decorations. None of them are reindeers with pink feet or baubles with ballet dancers on but, as far as I'm concerned, that's an advantage. Also, while he's very sensibly averse to being ripped off, Jonathan isn't cheap, so we've come home with enough stuff to cover his house and garden in whatever theme you might fancy. Buckets of tinsel, miles of chains of beads, hundreds of fairy lights, and more sparkly balls than a season of *RuPaul's Drag Race*.

We leave the stuff in boxes because it's going to get used tomorrow anyway, and Gollum checks each of them to make sure it's not a replacement cat, then, when he's satisfied it's not, curls up in a pile of tinsel that I know I'll be picking out of his fur for weeks.

When we're done, and when I've cracked and let Jonathan order us a takeaway to tide us over until the supermarket delivers, he reaches into the inside pocket of his jacket and pulls out the Santa guinea pig, which he then hands me, all solemn like.

"What's this for?" I ask. "I mean, don't get me wrong, I did think he was cute, but I'm not sure I'm ready for the awesome responsibility of owning a fake rodent with festive headgear."

"It's tradition," he tells me. "Everybody in the family has one decoration that's...it's a bit silly."

"It's Christmas, the whole thing's silly. We're sticking bits of plastic on an indoor tree."

It still takes him a moment to deal with having an emotion that isn't mild irritation. "Everyone in the family has a personal decoration, either their favourite, or something someone bought for them or, occasionally, one they made when they were six." He's speaking quite rapidly now, like he's reading the disclaimer on an advert. It's sort of sweet that he's embarrassed. "And it's always the last one you hang and when they're all up, the tree is done and Christmas has started. So..." He points at the guinea pig. "This one's for you. Because you're...you're part of it this year."

My desire to take the piss has completely evaporated. And, for a while, I can't get words out. It's probably mostly shock because Jonathan Forest has done a genuinely nice thing without being prompted. And he's done it for me. "Thank you," I manage. And now *I'm* embarrassed because that feels fucking inadequate. I can't remember the last time I—

Never mind.

"Well"—Jonathan's looking increasingly uncomfortable—"you've been helpful to me. And I'm aware I…I'm not very good at… I haven't been very—"

And I don't know how it happens or what I'm thinking or what I expect to happen next, but I kiss him.

In practice, what happens next is very, very quick. I've got about half a second to think to myself that Jonathan's mouth is beautifully soft for a man who otherwise isn't. And one of his hands is on my shoulder, almost clutching me. And when he kisses me back, it's this whole body thing where he just melts into me. Except before it's started, it's over, and Jonathan's leaping away like a cat that's been sprayed with a water bottle.

"Fuck, I'm sorry," I say at the same time he says "I'm so sorry that happened." Then I say, "I didn't mean" and he says "I'm your" and it's suddenly accelerating from awkward to completely fucked.

"And you have a concussion," Jonathan concludes. "And amnesia. For all we know, you've got a boyfriend."

"Well, if I have," I throw back, "he's fucking terrible because I've been missing for a week and he's not texted."

He's turned away from me, which honestly I think is a bit over-dramatic. But I have been right all along. He looks good when he's emotional, even more so when the emotion isn't anger. "You're in a vulnerable position," he says. "And I'm taking advantage."

This is tough enough without getting into the weeds of who's responsible for what. Especially because what it comes down to is that I kissed him because I wanted to, and I still do. "You're not taking advantage. I just made a bad call in the moment."

"One you wouldn't have made," he insists, "if you hadn't recently had a sharp blow to the head."

Maybe that's the story I should go with. But it doesn't seem fair somehow. Jonathan may be a dick but he doesn't deserve to go through life thinking you have to be concussed to kiss him. "I've lost my memory, Jonathan. Not my marbles."

"I'm also your boss."

"Which is why I said it was a bad call. But, for what it's worth, I don't regret it."

He's facing me again now, all flushed and floppy haired. Maybe it's just me but people look different after you've kissed them. Or you look at them differently at least. "It would be..." He sounds kind of lost. "It would be completely impossible and inappropriate."

"I know that. But you should know"—and I can't believe I'm saying this to Jonathan Forest and I can't believe I mean it either—"for the record, like, that if I didn't work for yez and I weren't concussed and you were okay with it, I'd be doing it again."

Jonathan just stares at me, as if he's got no idea what to do or say. He's not even tried to persuade me not to sue him, which is how I know he's proper shook up. So I guess it's on me to get us out of this. Which makes sense seeing as I got us into it.

"Look," I try, "it doesn't have to be a big deal."

"Good," says Jonathan, unconvincingly.

And I don't know how to tell him I didn't mean it like that. That I just mean it doesn't have to make things difficult or whatever.

"Well," he goes on. "I should—I've got work to get back to."

And then he vanishes into the study, leaving me feeling shit and guilty. Because I should have known Jonathan isn't the sort of man to take a kiss lightly.

Then again, neither am I.

CHAPTER 18

"WHAT TIME DO YOU CALL this?" Del yells across the room as Johnny saunters in at ten to twelve the next day.

"Sunday morning," Johnny replies. He's wearing the same sheepskin jacket he was wearing the last time, and, like last time, he doesn't take it off.

Les gives his brother a look. It's not even a look of disappointment—it's gone through disappointment and out the other side. "The rest of us have been here since ten."

They had. And it was a blessing in a way because it meant Jonathan and I didn't have to spend too long Not Talking About What Happened The Previous Day. "I'll get you a cup of tea," I tell him.

"Anyway," Johnny goes on, "I'm not the last."

Nanny Barb, who had been waiting for Johnny to arrive before she'd let anybody get started, is already opening boxes. "Kayla and Theo'll be around this afternoon. They've got their own family to take care of as well."

"Whereas you, Johnny my boy," Auntie Jack observes from her perch on the arm of the sofa, "have nothing and nobody." She sighs. "Then again, neither do I. But I did bring gin."

She brought a lot of gin, in fact. Pretty much everybody brought something, but most of the rest had stuck with nibbles.

"Right." Now everybody's together, things are kicking off proper, and as always Del's the one doing the kicking. "Them boxes there is tinsel. Them ones there is stuff that hangs off the tree. That one's the stuff for the ceiling, and the one at the end is the family baubles."

"You mean like every Christmas?" Barbara Jane asks. She's wearing another ironic jumper—this one just saying *Bah Humbug*—and has already started making good use of the gin.

Nanny Barb looks pointedly at me. "He's explaining for Sam."

That doesn't seem to convince Barbara Jane. "And who was he explaining for last year?"

"Not that anybody's asking," Jonathan adds, "but these *other* boxes are decorations I bought yesterday to make sure we have enough."

Del looks at the new additions the way you might look at a mole you were sure you didn't have last time you checked. "We'll have enough."

"Well, if we don't, we've got more. You asked me to host, I'm hosting."

"And a lovely job you're doing too." Wendy's wearing a somewhat less ironic Christmas jumper. It's bright white with a massive reindeer on it. "Though I'd have brought sausage rolls if I'd known you'd not have any."

"He's been very busy, love," Les reminds her. "Now come on, let's get started."

He gets up and opens the nearest box, and once he has, things plunge very quickly into anarchy. Johnny goes straight for the fairy lights—not the new ones that we got for the windows, but a huge tangle of them ones from the '80s with the coloured shades that look a bit like flowers. Barbara Jane pounces on a set of little bells, and Jonathan is trying to remind everybody that you have to do the tinsel first or else it'll snag.

Sitting in one corner, Les is unspooling a very long, very faded paper chain made from wonkily-glued links, some of which have come undone entirely. "You got any Pritt Stick?"

"There'll be some in the office," Jonathan calls from over by the tinsel that he's still trying in vain to get people to prioritise over more interesting ornaments. "Sam, can you grab it?"

I'm about to go, but Les tells me he'll find it. Although that leaves me at a bit of a loose end because while I don't want to be standoffish, I also don't want to be inserting myself into somebody else's big family ritual. Even if I have been given a guinea pig of my very own to participate with.

"Ladder?" That's Del. He's holding a sparkly, if slightly creased, foil mobile in one hand, and looking fixedly up at the ceiling. "Or should we just pull over a table and stand on that?"

Giving up tinsel duty as a bad job, Jonathan hurries back over. "No, you should *not*. I'll get the ladder from the garage."

Johnny looks up from his tangle of lights. I'm sure they're in a worse state than they were when he started. "Get the extension cord while you're there."

"You get used to it," says a voice in my ear. I turn to see Auntie Jack. She's got a glass in one hand and a tiny plastic Santa in the other. "They'll calm down in a minute."

I look from her to the rest of the family, then back. "Will they?"

"Not by much, I admit. But you shouldn't worry about being in the way. If nothing else, it's practically impossible to *get* in the way. It's like getting in the way of a cruise ship."

Jonathan comes back in with a stepladder and an extension lead and then gets immediately into an argument with Del about which of them is going to be going up it to stick pins in the ceiling.

"So"—I lean over to Auntie Jack—"I don't want to pry but—are you with this lot every Christmas?"

"For a very long time, yes. Since before Barbara was married."

"Must be nice."

She gives a nod that manages to have a much deeper edge of melancholy than a nod should. "In a lot of ways."

"Stand back everyone." This is Johnny again. He's located the plug end of the Christmas lights and found a socket to plug it into.

Barbara Jane looks around from where she's trailing a line of artificial greenery along a windowsill. "Do we really have to? It's lightbulbs, not fireworks."

"Just giving it a sense of occasion." Johnny slams in the plug, flips a switch, and with a flash and a plink the lights go on and immediately off.

"I have bought new lights," Jonathan points out testily. "We do not need to use the old lights."

Nanny Barb shakes her head. She's holding a pinecone on which somebody, long ago, glued a very small amount of glitter. "The old lights is traditional."

"As is Johnny failing to make them work," adds Auntie Jack.

"Here, Sam, hold this ladder." I'm beginning to get a bit overwhelmed with all the voices coming at me—at least I tell myself that's what's overwhelming me—but I turn to see Del already halfway up an unsecured stepladder with a red-and-gold foil star in one hand and the faded paper chain that Les was fixing earlier in the other.

Not wanting to be even indirectly responsible for an old man breaking his neck, I dash over to help. "Are you sure you're all right up there?"

"Fine." He's not even looking at me. "Why wouldn't I be? Now pass me them drawing pins."

I glance over to Jonathan to make sure he's okay with holes getting poked in his ceiling, and it seem like he is, so I lean around and grab them for Del while also trying to keep the ladder steady.

Between the eight of us, the festive wonderland of Jonathan's house begins to take shape. It's not exactly what you'd call tasteful—it has sort of a time capsule feel, with some of the decorations being so old they must go back to when Del and Barb were first setting up home together and the family as a whole having a definite more-is-better philosophy when it comes to, well, to everything really. But there's a heart to it I find throws me more than I thought it would. Like when you don't realise your foot's gone to sleep until you try to stand up.

So I try to keep myself busy making tea while everybody else hangs things on other things and sometimes hangs third things on top of the second things. I'm making the fifth round of the day when the rest of the family shows up—and Auntie Jack does the introductions since she's the only one not neck deep in stuff that sparkles.

"So this..." She points me at a woman a bit older than Jonathan with the same dark eyes I've seen on him and Barbara Jane, "is Kayla, Johnny's daughter from his incredibly failed marriage."

"Oy," shout Johnny and Kayla simultaneously.

"Would you prefer preposterously failed?"

"I was very young," protests Johnny, like this is an old argument. "I've changed."

Auntie Jack sneers at him. "You have fucking not."

"Language," Wendy calls from the other room. "There's children present."

"I'm sixteen," says the person who, by a process of elimination, is little Anthea, though she's not especially little. Being, as she points out, sixteen and having picked up height from her mother's side. "People say fuck in front of me all the time."

"Not in my house, they don't." This is probably her dad—a thin, slightly greying man in round glasses and crisp blue shirt with the sleeves rolled up.

Anthea folds her arms. She's not sullen exactly, but she's in that kind of teenagery nonspace where you're never sure which way she'll jump, and maybe she isn't either. "We're not in your house, though. We're in Jonathan's house. And Jonathan says fuck more than anybody."

"Not around children, I don't." Jonathan barges past and grabs an armful of slightly scraggy tinsel from the box.

"I'm sixteen," Anthea repeats. "I'm not children."

Introductions having been thoroughly derailed, it falls to Kayla—who's got an air of sensibleness that must have skipped a generation—to get things back on track. "If it helps," she says to her daughter, "Barb called me children 'til you were three." Then she holds out her hand to me. "Sorry love, don't think I caught your name."

"That"—Auntie Jack is mixing herself a very large amount of G with a very small amount of T—"is because I was rudely interrupted. Sam, this is Anthea, Kayla, and Theo. Everybody, this is Sam. We're politely pretending he isn't dating Jonathan."

That joke got about six hundred percent less funny overnight. "Hi," I say.

Johnny, who's still not located the break in the lights, comes over to embrace his daughter and granddaughter, and have a manly handshake with his son-in-law.

"Anthea," Wendy yells through from the other room, "get in here and check out the tree. It's massive."

Anthea leans in the doorway. She's wearing fountain pen tips for earrings, and they swing slightly when she tilts her head. "Saw it from the garden. Just...*how*?"

"I know a bloke." It's the only answer Del seems to think matters, and he delivers it from the top of a stepladder that once again nobody's holding, so I very quietly move to steady it.

"Jonathan." Theo raises a large Tupperware box. "I brought melomakarona. Where do you want me to stick them?"

"Plenty of room in the kitchen," Jonathan calls back.

"Because he never uses it," I add.

Del, who is leaning way too far out from the stepladder for safety, looks down at me. "That's because he's waiting for you to roast him another chicken."

"Try a melomakarona, Sam." Kayla takes the box from her husband, opens it, and shoves it under my nose, the scent of honey and spices wafting up at me. "In our house it's not Christmas 'til you've had one."

So I have one. And while I'm having it, Kayla bungs the rest in the kitchen and Del finishes putting whatever he's putting on the ceiling on the ceiling and even though Auntie Jack is right that this is chaos and it'll never not be chaos, people seem to find their place in it anyway. There's Wendy in the other room on tree duty, and there's Jonathan, gone to help Johnny with the lights that they do, eventually, get working only to find that they're nowhere near long enough for a twenty-foot tree. Even Gollum's in on it, sitting proudly on Auntie Jack's lap, with that feline instinct for picking the one person the room who doesn't like cats. Meanwhile, I'm still standing around eating a melomakarona trying not to think too hard about how I got here, or when the last time was that I could say *it's not Christmas in our house until.*

My mouth's going a bit dry, for reasons that I'm sure have nothing to do with the cookie. And nobody's speaking to me right now, which is fine because I'm not *actually* part of this family however nice they're all being about it. So I sort of sidle around the edge of the kitchen and go stand in the garden for a bit.

The fresh air is welcome, though it's nippy what with it being December. I've not brought my scarf out with me and I miss it in more ways than one. For a while I just...mooch. The pisser with Christmas is that it's big. Too big. Pointlessly big. People make it into this massive thing and when you get right down to it, it's just a day. Like any day. And it's not fair on anybody to have all that pressure on it.

I can still see everyone through the windows, and for the first time Jonathan's house—his absurd more-money-than-sense house—makes, well, it makes some kind of sense. Because those reception rooms were meant to receive people, not to sit empty except for him, me, a cat, and a telly. They were meant to be alive and messy and—

It really is nippy out. There's a cold wind stinging my face and it's making me tear up. I go shelter by the tree-line, trying to get out of the worst of the weather. Despite all the chaos of Friday, the garden survived okay. A couple of begonias got their heads chopped off but that's about the end of the damage. And I say begonias, but I wouldn't know a begonia if one turned into a dog and bit me. They're probably hardy-somethings. The kind of flower that's still daft enough to be around in winter.

"So are you *actually* Jonathan's boyfriend?" asks a voice from behind me.

I turn and see it's little Anthea. Who I should probably stop calling that because she probably doesn't like it. "No."

The *no* must have sounded loaded because she looks supremely unconvinced. "Are you sure?"

"About as sure as I can be. Should you not be inside putting up tinsel?"

She glances back over her shoulder. "I'll go back in a bit. Small doses, y'know?"

I don't, as it happens. "You should appreciate them while you can."

That earns me a scornful, teenage laugh. "You sound like Great Granddad. He's been telling us he'll be dead next year for as long as I can remember."

"I suppose he'll be right eventually."

It was an unintentionally morbid comment, but she seems to be okay with that. "True."

There's a couple of seconds' silence. It's just long enough for me to reflect on how I always figured that once I was grown up like, I'd be one of them adults that's easy for young people to talk to, and apparently I'm not.

Across the garden, the tree is beginning to take shape. Though Jonathan's advice about putting the tinsel on first has been thoroughly ignored, and with the size of it, they're only about a third of the way through the first floor.

"I do have to admit," Anthea says, looking in the same direction, "the through-the-roof thing is surprisingly cool."

"It was my idea," I tell her, and then realise how pathetic it sounds to be bragging about your choices in Christmas decorations to somebody a decade younger than you.

"Great Granddad says it was his."

"The big tree was him. Call it a group effort."

Through the window, Les pulls a stepladder over to the tree and starts hanging these little vintage pompom things from the higher branches. Then Jonathan walks over to him and says something. Then Les says something back. And though I'm not an expert on body language, I think I see tension building. The atmosphere's starting to melt, slowly but inevitable as ice cream sliding off a cone, from cosy to scratchy to outright unpleasant.

They're not yelling—from what I've seen, Les never yells—but while Jonathan seems to have inherited a fair few things from his dad, calm isn't one of them. And now Wendy's stepping in, but it's not making it better. The two of them are forming the heart of this little vortex of aggro.

"I should probably get in there," I say partly to Anthea and partly to myself.

"Why? It's not your problem."

It's not. Except it is. Because if Jonathan's on edge then I'm part of that, or might be. And because it just feels—it feels a jagged tangle of sick and sharp and just straight up not okay to see things falling apart like that. For these people who, for all their bickering, clearly love each other, and were good to me when they didn't have to be.

So I go in.

"—in my own house," Jonathan's saying. Nothing good ever ends with the words *in my own house.*

"This might be your house"—Les has come down from the stepladder now and he's standing a few paces back from Jonathan, hands in his pockets, though I think he's curled them into fists out of sight—"but you're still my son, and I'll not have you talking to me like I'm a fucking child."

It's the first time I've heard Les swear.

"Leave it, both of you," Wendy is saying. "It's Christmas."

Auntie Jack looks up from the sofa with the impeccable instincts of an eighty-something drama queen. "It's the eleventh of December. Let the boys have it out."

"Nobody's asking you, Jacqueline." Les barely moves as he talks. He just casts his eyes briefly in Auntie Jack's direction.

"Nobody ever asks you," adds Del.

Les turns his head a fraction of an inch. "Not sure you're one to talk on that front."

"Leave it out, I'm on your side."

"There ain't meant to be sides." Wendy is getting increasingly flustered. "We've been having a lovely time, we've not all been together like this in a while—"

"Yes, and I'm beginning to remember why," says Jonathan.

I can't say for sure, because I'm me and he isn't, but I've got to know Jonathan Forest pretty well over the last few weeks, and I reckon he regrets it the moment it's out his mouth. But I also reckon he'd never admit it.

"Now that"—Les's attention's back on Jonathan now, and there's a weight to it, a strange weight that I only half understand—"was uncalled for."

And this brings out the other Jonathan. The one that backed me into a Nexa by MERLYN 8mm Sliding Door Shower enclosure and threatened to shut the entire Sheffield branch if I didn't shift more extended warranties. "Was it? I never asked for *any* of this. I'm doing *all* of you a *massive* favour, and you come in here like you own the fucking place, you fill my house with"—he picks up a little plastic angel with one broken wing and the glitter all rubbed off its halo—"utter tat and—"

Wendy seems more offended by this than anything else so far. "Hey, do *not* take it out on the angel. She used to belong to my grandmother."

"Oh *fucking hell*." Jonathan's losing it, he's definitely losing it. "Can you even *hear* yourself? I am *trying* here. I am really trying to do all of"—he spreads his arms wide—"*this* the way I'm apparently meant to, even if it means letting this human chimney"—that's Auntie Jack, apparently—"smoke in my reception rooms and putting up with *you*"—Del this time—"dragging me all over London because we have to do everything your way and *you*"—he's finally got around to Johnny—"why are you even *here*?"

"He's family," says Wendy firmly.

"Yes, but none of us *like* him. Even Kayla doesn't like him and she's his daughter."

Anthea raises a hand. "I like him."

"You're a child." Jonathan seems to have lost track of who or what he was angry about in the first place, so now he's just this thrashing mess of rage and venom. "And for some reason *you*"—he's back to Les at last—"choose to stay quiet about absolutely everything except for my *perfectly reasonable* suggestion that you let me handle the tree."

"Son." I've never heard quite so much baggage packed into one syllable.

"Oh, don't *son* me."

Getting involved now is probably the worst decision I could possibly make. But since I'm faking amnesia to infiltrate my boss's family Christmas in the hopes it'll save my job, I think we can accept that good decisions aren't really my thing. "Jonathan, do you not think—"

"No." He whips round to face me. "Whatever it is, no I *don't* think. Unless by some seasonal miracle what you were about to say was *do you not think that I, Samwise Becker, should shut the fuck up and mind my own fucking business for once in my fucking life.*"

This bothers Wendy even more than the angel thing. Which I suppose I should find flattering. "Jonathan, he's a guest."

"Actually, Mum, you're *all* guests and right now you're pretty *unwelcome* guests. So, thinking about it, why don't you all just listen to me for once in your fucking lives and show me some fucking respect."

Les takes half a step forward. "Now hold on, I'll not have you talking to your mother like that."

"But you will, though, won't you? That's *very* much the problem."

"Jonathan," Les has taken another half step forward. "I'm asking you to calm down."

"I am perfectly calm," says Jonathan. I don't think I've ever heard the words *I am perfectly calm* uttered by an actual calm person. "I'm just sick of—"

Whatever he's sick of, he's not quite able to articulate it, and even if he was, he doesn't get the chance.

Les looks down at his wife. "Wendy, I think we should leave."

"But it's—"

"Really." Les has this sort of dignified, resigned quality to him, but now he just seems sad. "I understand things have been difficult," he says to Jonathan. "But right now we all need a bit of space. See you around."

And they go, and the rest of the family goes with them because it'd be awkward as piss if they didn't. So about six minutes later there's just me and Gollum and Jonathan left in the partially decorated middle reception room.

He doesn't say anything. He just starts aggressively cramming things back into boxes. Except then he comes across one box in particular. The little one, the one that has everybody's special decorations in it that's meant to go last on the tree and be traditional and that. And he picks it up, and he looks at it.

And then he just starts crying.

CHAPTER 19

I DON'T SAY MUCH BECAUSE there's not much to say after someone's told you in no uncertain terms to mind your own fucking business, but I make Jonathan a cup of tea and he takes it sitting on the sofa in the middle reception room with Gollum on one knee and the box of special decorations on the other. It's open now, and I can see that on the inside it's full of a mix of all kinds of bits and bobs. There's a torn-and-taped-together snowflake made from sugar paper, a bright red bauble with a grinning red-cheeked Santa on it, a glass apple, and a lot of other random bits of stuff I can't quite make out as clearly.

"I was going to suggest you put the guinea pig in here," he tells me. "But that might not be a good idea."

It's an old cardboard box with "DECS" scrawled on the top in faded felt tip, so I'm really not sure it can take the immense symbolic weight Jonathan's putting on it. "Why not?" I ask.

He stares at his tea and doesn't answer.

"Look," I try, "about—I mean—if what happened had anything to do with what happened." Good one, Sam. Clear as mud that was.

He keeps staring and keeps not answering.

And having already brought him a cup of tea, and tried to raise the extremely awkward *did you flip your lid at your family because I kissed you that one time* question, I'm not sure where else I can go.

"I'm fucking everything up," he says, and it's touch and go whether he's talking to me, his tea, or Gollum.

"No, you're not."

"You'll forgive me if I don't consider you the best judge."

So he's going to be like that, is he? I guess kissing him that one time was part of the problem after all. "I mean, I'm pretty familiar with fucking up, so there's that."

The look he shoots at me, then, is half-betrayed and half... well. I'd almost call it longing if we were different people in different circumstances. "You're not, though, are you? Not in the same way."

"What's that supposed to mean?" I ask, because it feels like I'm being accused of something, though I'm not sure what.

"You know how to"—he makes a slightly restrained gesture on account of the tea and the cat—"do all this. People like you, even when they shouldn't."

"Shouldn't? Why shouldn't they? I'm not a serial killer or a Big Mac."

"Oh, don't be naive," Jonathan snaps.

You shouldn't roll your eyes at a man who's just been crying but I do. "Is this still because I kissed yez?"

"Yes," he says emphatically. Then, "no," equally emphatically. He slams his tea down on the coffee table, slopping it everywhere, and I'm about to go get some paper towel, before I realise that'd be one part too Stepford. "I knew from the beginning that this was a bad idea. And, believe me, if you'd had anyone else, I'd have sent you off with them and none of this would have happened."

I'm sure Jonathan doesn't realise how low that is, but that's fucking low. And while my dad would always tell me to take the high road, he's not here right now, and when it comes to Jonathan

Forest, I'm getting really sick of being the bigger man. "It would," I tell him. "Believe me, it would. If there's one thing I've seen in the last few days, it's that you need nobody's help to drive people away. Even your own family."

He's gone cold, like his tea. "And what do you know about my family?"

"I know they're not perfect, but who is? And I know they keep showing up for you, even though you're doing your best to stop them. And I know your dad didn't deserve to have you go off at him like that, because nobody does."

"My dad will be fine." There's an odd note of contempt in his voice. "He's had a lot of practice taking shit."

"Then maybe you shouldn't give him more."

He glares up at me. And Gollum glares with him, the traitorous bastard. "Remember when I said you should mind your own business? You should, because it was less than twenty minutes ago."

"Oh, I remember," I tell him. "I'm just choosing to believe you didn't mean it, just like I'm choosing to believe you didn't mean all the other terrible things you said."

I'm used to Jonathan Forest being angry, but now he's gone somewhere else entirely. Somewhere I very much don't like. "I can't decide if you're giving me too much credit or too little. I meant it, Sam. I meant all of it. But I *especially* meant that"—he waves his hands back and forth between us—"this, whatever you thought it was, it isn't. We are not friends. We are not…" he trips over his words. "We are not friends. You are a man who works for me, who is staying in my house until the doctor says he can leave. Then you will leave. That is the whole of our relationship."

I want to say it's not. I want to say I've seen a different side of him and that he doesn't need to be this way. I want to say I've been faking the amnesia and I'm sorry and I don't know how we got here. Then again, right now, I also want to tell him he's being a total piece of shit and should go fuck himself, and all those wants wind up sort of cancelling each other out. "All right," I say instead.

And I leave him to it.

The next couple of days are rough. I'd not realised at the time but I'd kind of got used to the rhythm things had settled into between Jonathan and me. I think he'd really been trying and I think we'd really been getting somewhere. I mean, he'd completely stopped barking at me and I'd mostly stopped believing he was a prick. Or, at least, started believing he was a prick with hidden depths. The sort of prick who bought you an overpriced Santa guinea pig because he didn't want you to feel left out of his family Christmas.

But now we're back to how things started, him being constantly tense, and me constantly wishing I could be anywhere else. It's been long enough since the accident that I reckon if I went to a doctor and said, oh look my memory's come back, they'd give me a clean bill of health. It's just then I don't know where I'd be with my job and where that'd leave my team. So I have to see this through, no matter how much of a pisser it is.

In a lot of ways, everybody would be better off if we could just all pretend that the whole thing had never happened. That I'd never come to London, that Jonathan'd never threatened to shut the Sheffield branch, that he'd never fired me and I'd never fallen into a Nexa by MERLYN 8mm Sliding Door Shower enclosure. And some of it, we probably can get away with never mentioning again. Because the accident, for all Jonathan's convinced I'll sue him if I ever remember it, really was an accident. But the rest—what I was doing there in the first place, which was taking a bollocking over how I run my shop—that's coming back around, one way or another.

Which leaves me in this holding pattern. And the thing about being in a holding pattern is you eventually run out of fuel and crash. Except I already have. Maybe that's what kissing him was. And now he'll probably never trust me again.

At least I've got this Christmas party to plan. Otherwise it'd be wall-to-wall *Pointless* and feeling shitty. Mostly it's come together. I've made an executive decision—and now come to think of it, I can't imagine anything Jonathan Forest would like less than an executive decision made by somebody else—to go for a buffet instead of a sit-down meal. Because Claire and them are right, being stuck at a table for half the evening, trying to make polite conversation either with people you don't know or people you see every day is flat-out rubbish. There's a top of the middle of the range DJ who we've paid enough that he's going to bring his own lighting system but not a penny more. And I've put aside some of the budget for travel and accommodation so people coming from Leeds and Sheffield don't feel completely shafted by the thing that's supposed to show the company's appreciation. As for the venue, I did have to fork out for the fancy room because nowhere that could take the number was any fucking cheaper.

As I plug the final figures into one of Jonathan's non-negotiable spreadsheets on the spare laptop he's given me for the purpose, I'm pretty pleased with myself. It comes to one hundred and sixty pounds a head in the end, which is slightly more than I was given, but that's how you've got to do it with budgets. You come in under, they give you less next year. You go too far over, you just look like you don't know what you're doing. There's a kind of an art to stretching it just the right amount and I reckon I've nailed it. Plus, there's still a little bit of me wants to make a point. Like, yes, you can spend a bit extra now and again, and it won't bankrupt you or make the roof fall in.

Jonathan's been in the office every hour Agnieszka's been around to keep an eye on me, partly because he can't stop working for ten seconds together, but also I'm pretty sure he's avoiding me. The rest of the time he's lurking in his study with Gollum, who's very much chosen his side. When I first got on the train down here, I thought the worst-case scenario was that I'd lose my job. Turns out I might lose my job and my cat.

I save the spreadsheet to the shared drive and poke my head through into the study.

"Party's as good as done," I say. "So if you approve it, I can confirm the details with everybody."

Jonathan doesn't answer. He just looks at his screen and clicks his mouse a couple of times. Then, "You're over budget."

"Not by much."

He's quiet for a while, like he's wrestling with something. And when he finally speaks, it's in that very calm way he uses at work when he's displeased. "And if I'd said the budget is a hundred and fifty pounds per head but it's okay to go over as long as it's not by much, that would be fine. What I said was, the budget is a hundred and fifty pounds a head full stop."

This is so typical of him. He just wants to make you jump through hoops for the sake of making you jump through hoops. I'd have said he gets off on it, but he doesn't and, in some ways, that's worse. It means he's just doing it because he thinks he should. "Jonathan, for fuck's sake, it's a grand. You're a millionaire. Can you not do something nice for your employees for once?"

"Sam"—his eyes flick to mine, all intense and unyielding—"I know things have been...unusual. But I am your boss, and this is a work conversation. You will not swear at me."

I sigh. He's being a dick, but he's annoyingly right. "Sorry, I'm just—you're being unreasonable."

"It's not your place to decide what's reasonable."

"You see this is the f—" I manage not to say *fucking*. "This is what you don't seem to understand. I *do* get to decide what's reasonable. You don't get to tell people how they want to be treated, they tell you. And I'm telling you right now, your employees don't want to feel like they aren't worth an extra ten quid to you once a year."

He's not backing down. He barely even blinks. "It's a tax issue."

"Fu—forget about the tax. Is that what this is all about? Never mind showing people you give a shit, just as long as you get your annual write-off?"

"If it costs more than a hundred and fifty pounds a head," —Jonathan moistens his lips, like he's about to give some major speech even though from what I can tell he's talking about tax codes—"then it constitutes a payment in kind."

"You what?"

"A payment in kind counts as part of your wages, and is taxed as part of your wages. If I throw my employees a party that costs the company a hundred and sixty pounds a head, then I'm effectively making them pay thirty-two pounds for the privilege."

I stare at him blankly.

"Then again, perhaps you're right. It's only money, after all. I'm sure somebody working part time selling loofahs in my bathroom department will be delighted to get paid thirty-two pounds less this Christmas if it means having a buffet dinner in a nice venue."

And it's at this exact point that I learn the most infuriating thing about Jonathan Forest is that he seems to make a point of being right in the wrongest possible way. "Could you not have just fucking *told* me that earlier?"

"I gave you clear instructions."

This is about to get very, very unprofessional. I turn away to face the door for a second in the hopes that I'll decide *not* to be unprofessional but it's a vain hope and was always going to be. "With respect," I begin, and he knows right away that it's an ominous beginning, "Mr Forest, Sir. What the *fucking fucking fuck*? This is—I mean—I'm not a fucking dog. I don't just sit when you tell me to sit and fetch when you tell me to fetch and get slapped on the nose when I don't give the ball back."

"In a way, you do. I'm in charge and your job is to follow my instructions, not to second-guess them."

It'd be hilarious if it wasn't so awful. "Sorry, did you just say *yes, you actually are a dog*?"

"I said yes, you actually should do what your employer tells you to do."

Why did I think I could get through to him? Why did I ever think I could get through to him? These last two weeks have been a complete waste of time. "That doesn't mean I'm not—that anybody who works for you's not—entitled to a bit of fucking consideration and some context."

"And you don't think the people who work for me owe *me* the consideration of doing their jobs the way I tell them to?" He doesn't even sound defensive. He's talking like this is the most reasonable thing in the world.

"But we can't do our jobs if you won't tell us why we're doing them. That's just—Christ, Jonathan, it's just not how human beings work. If you'd have told me why the budget mattered, I'd have come in under it. That's basic motivation."

He gives this slow blink like I'm beneath contempt. "So because you felt slighted that I didn't explain myself the way you think I should, you deliberately wasted my money?"

"Fucking hell. Your dad was fucking right." As soon as I've said it, I catch the unmistakable scent of bridges burning, and I should probably reach for a bucket of water, not a can of petrol.

"Yez treat people like children. Like less than children. Like nobody in the world is capable of anything except you."

"It's worked for me so far."

"But it's not working for you, is it?" I don't exactly yell but don't exactly not. "You live alone, you have no friends, you've as good as driven your own family away. And on top of that you're shit to work for."

I'm not sure what I'm expecting. For him to yell at me like I've seen him do with his family, or just shut me down like I've seen him do at work. But he does neither. He just looks—I don't know sad, almost—sad and stark and drained. "At one point you said you liked me."

"Yeah well, I made a fucking mistake."

There's no coming back from that. But at least it shuts him up.

"I'll fix the fucking budget for you," I tell him.

And then I go. I leave the door open a crack so Gollum can come with me if he wants to.

But he doesn't.

CHAPTER 20

HAVING TOLD JONATHAN OFF FOR treating me like a child, I go and hide in my room like a sulky teenager.

I have fucked this in so many ways. I've fucked my job, I've fucked my branch, I've fucked the fucking Christmas party, and I've fucked Jonathan. Like metaphorically. I'm pretty sure I've made him a worse boss and maybe a worse human being. I could probably have come back from dragging his dad into a work argument. I'm not sure I can come back from telling him every nice thing I've ever said about him was bollocks.

Honestly, I'm not sure I deserve to.

For a little while, I sit on the bed without a cat, feeling like shit and wondering how it all got this out of control. The plan, I will freely admit, was not exactly foolproof from the start, but I really do think it had a strong basis. And if I'd just been able to keep things between me and Jonathan relatively simple and pleasant, then maybe when all this was done he'd say to himself, "you know what, that Sam's a nice lad, maybe I'll give him and his team another chance". Except instead I got way too deep in his family drama, kissed him, then had a blazing row where I reminded him exactly why he was firing me in the first place *and* insulted him on a deeply personal level. And most of that is probably unfixable. But for the sake of the folk I work with, I need to at least un-remind him about the firing thing. Which leads me to the inevitable conclusion that even if I can't unfuck anything else, I absolutely have to unfuck the party.

Doubling down on the rebel teen energy, I sneak into the ensuite—there's advantages to staying with a man who made his money in bathrooms—lock the door and pull out my phone.

I send Claire an emergency text saying Help. Party disaster. We are all screwed. And a couple of minutes later I get a call back from the team. In an effort to be discreet, I plug in a set of headphones and keep my voice down, which leads to the conversation having a somewhat predictable start.

"You're very fuzzy," Claire tells me.

"I'm whispering," I whisper.

"It sounds like you're whispering."

"That's because I am."

"Can you hear us, Sam?" This is Amjad. "Say if you can hear us."

"I can hear you. I'm whispering."

"I think you need to adjust your settings," he says. "Put on Voice Isolation."

"I'm whispering."

He's not letting up. "What you need to do is go to the Control Centre, then hit Mic Mode—"

"I said I'm whispering," I the-opposite-of-whisper.

"Are you sure?" ask Tiff. "You sound quite loud."

"That's because I'm not whispering anymore because you couldn't hear me."

"Why were you whispering in the first place?" asks Claire.

"Because Jonathan's downstairs and I don't want him to know I remember who you are."

"Oh." Claire takes a moment to think. "You should probably keep your voice down then."

"I was trying to but—"

"Hang on"—this is Amjad again—"we'll turn you up at our end."

For a couple of minutes there's a daft little dance of no-not-that-button-that-other-button-yes-I-know-then-why-don't-you-do-it-right and finally we get to a place where I can speak quietly and still be heard in Sheffield which, when you think about it, is a miracle of modern technology.

When they're done, Claire gets us back to the point. "So why are we screwed?"

"Because I've overspent on the party by ten quid a head," I explain, perching on the edge of the Heritage Devon Double Ended Slipper Cast Iron Bath with feet. "And it turns out, Jonathan wasn't just being a tight git. We had to keep it under one fifty or else all the guests get stung for tax."

There's a brief pause. "Why didn't you tell us that?" asks Tiff.

"Because he didn't tell me that."

"Why didn't he tell you that?" asks Claire.

I make a "fuck knows" gesture up at the Silverdale Victorian high level toilet, which is one of those designs I've always found a little twee. "Because he's a dick. And now I have to fix this because otherwise, instead of treating the whole company to a lovely party, I've treated them to a thirty-two quid bill from the taxman."

"It's fine." Claire's gone all brisk, which she does when there's a problem. "We just have to cut some costs."

It'd be really useful to have the spreadsheet in front of me, but the laptop's downstairs and getting it'd be a headache. Besides, I might run into Jonathan and, right now, I'm very much feeling we'd both be better off if we never saw each other again. "I'm not sure there's anywhere to cut. If I get a cheaper DJ they won't have their own gear and then it'll just be a bloke with a Spotify playlist. If I don't reimburse people's travel expenses, then I'm costing them money again. And, worse, I'm only costing the people who don't live in London."

"Cheaper food?" suggests Amjad.

"I went with a buffet because a good buffet is both better and cheaper than a bad sit-down dinner. But if I skimp on the buffet they'll just feed us crap."

Claire makes a thoughtful noise. "Can you just get…like… everyone to give you a small discount?"

"I need to save fifteen hundred quid. That's nearly ten percent from everyone."

"Actually"—Amjad just can't stop himself—"it's six percent, which is really closer to five than ten, even if you're rounding."

"Did you just do that in your head?" I'm torn between being annoyed and impressed.

"Yeah, I've got good mental arithmetic."

"Okay,"—this one's my fault for derailing, but I do my best to re-rail it anyway—"but since we can't negotiate down other people's travel expenses, that means we've got to make it up somewhere else, so let's call it ten. And that's not happening. Not in London. At Christmas. With the weather we've been having. And talk of a tube strike." I'll admit the last two might just be me spiralling.

Tiff sighs. "Well, if you can't get lots of little savings, you need one big saving. What's the biggest expense?"

"It's the fucking room, isn't it?" This is feeling increasingly impossible. "It's six thousand four hundred pounds."

"Twenty-three-point-four percent," Amjad pipes up helpfully.

This is definitely impossible. I let myself slide slowly into the Heritage Devon Double Ended Slipper Cast Iron Bath with feet. "I'm never getting that. I could suck the guy off and not get that."

"It'd be a really expensive blowjob," says Claire. She thinks about it a bit longer. "Even with London weighting."

"It's still probably your best bet." This is Tiff again. "I mean, not the blowjob bit. The room bit."

I try some deep breathing to steady my nerves. "Okay, but—"

"No buts, Sam." The best thing about Tiff is that she's young enough to still have confidence in things you should on no account have confidence in. "You can do this."

Telling her I can't seems petty and would make me just as bad a manager as Jonathan Forest, though from a different direction. So I say *thanks* instead. And then they're quiet for a bit and I reckon they're probably keen to get back to doing their jobs for as long as they still have them, especially the ones as are on commission. So I let them go, and I lie there for a while in the bottom of the Heritage Devon Double Ended Slipper Cast Iron Bath with feet and tell myself that my team are depending on me, that at least some of them believe in me, and that I really am able to turn this around.

I don't completely convince myself. But I bluff myself for long enough to ring up the venue and tell the bloke I'm hiring it from that I'm coming in to ask him some questions.

For the first time in two weeks I leave the house without Jonathan trying to stop me. And I never thought I'd miss his overbearing insistence on taking his sort of care of me, but I do. A bit of me does. Because it's proper winter now and there's a chill in the air that cuts deeper when you're stressed and at the moment I'm very, very stressed indeed.

Without Jonathan to give me a lift it's a pisser of a journey, with a bus ride at each end and a Thameslink train in the middle, and as I stand on the platform at East Croydon station waiting for my connection, I think to myself how easy it would be to just get on a train back to Sheffield, or maybe even one back to Liverpool.

To forget about all of this and pretend that the last few weeks, or the last few years, never happened.

Except I can't, because they did.

By the time I arrive at London Bridge, the cold's settled in bone deep, and as I trudge to the bus stop, I try to think of things I'm less up for in this exact moment than going to ask a relative stranger if he'll give me a twenty three point four percent discount on a room he could easily relet that I've already paid a deposit on.

The list is very, very short and notably excludes things like *being devoured by sharks*.

And I hate sharks.

To make matters worse, though my London geography isn't great, I realise I'm only a short walk away from Fortnum & Mason and that makes me think of the guinea pig, and the box of decorations, and Jonathan.

As I make my way up the steps of the venue and tell the bloke on reception that I'm here to see the other bloke that books the rooms, I try to radiate confidence, even though right now I'm feeling about as assertive as an unusually diffident rodent.

And there's that guinea pig again.

I'm shown through to the feller's office and he's very nice and everything, but I can see from the look of him that he's got no incentive to give me an inch.

"Okay," I begin, "so here's the thing. It turns out we can't afford the room we've booked, and while I know that's not strictly your problem—"

"Glad you do"—he's still looking friendly, but no-nonsense friendly—"because it definitely isn't."

"Even so, I was hoping that since it's Christmas, maybe you'd be able to give me some options."

He gives me a cheery smile that I suspect is overselling how helpful he intends to be. "Course we can. If you want to switch to a cheaper room, we can do that and we'll happily transfer your deposit."

"Thing is," I tell him, "the cheaper rooms are too small."

"Then you're free to cancel. But honestly I don't think you'll find the same size for less. Not in this town."

"Or at this time of year," I add, which probably isn't helping my case.

The feller nods. "Or with the weather we've been having."

"And talk of a tube strike," I finish. "Trouble is we literally cannot go ahead with the current venue unless we get some kind of discount."

Del, it strikes me, would be loving this. He'd also be doing much better at it.

"Tell you what"—the man taps something into his computer and looks hard at the screen—"we'll see what we can swing. How big a discount were you hoping for?"

"Fifteenhundredquid," I say very fast in the hope that it'll bamboozle him into not noticing how unreasonable that is.

"That's"—I see him going for a calculator app and I cut him off.

"Twenty-three-point-four percent," I tell him. "I'm very good at mental arithmetic."

He gives me a sceptical look. "What's eight times seven?"

"Okay, I worked it out in advance. And I get I'm asking a lot—"

"You're asking for the fucking *moon*, pardon my French."

I am. And I know I am and he knows I know I am. "It would be really helping me out."

"It'd really help me out if you gave me fifteen hundred quid too."

"No but, like, *really*."

He's looking less friendly.

"This is going to sound very slightly absurd," I begin, knowing full well it'll be downhill from here. "But would you believe that I need to get this party planned under budget so that I can convince my boss who thinks I've got amnesia when I really don't and who's currently not talking to me because we got in a row about his dad that I know what I'm doing so he doesn't fire me and everybody who works for me?"

That makes him sit back and blink exactly once. "I'll believe it. Just not enough to give you a twenty-five percent—"

"Twenty-three-point-four percent," I correct him.

"Discount on a room I could just give somebody else for full price while also keeping your deposit."

When he puts it like that, it does seem like a bit of a silly thing to do from his end.

"Here you go." He slides a brochure across the desk to me. It's new for the new year—not the one I was looking at last time—although that probably just means they've put their prices up. "You want to switch to any other room, I can sort you out. You want a couple of quid off for good will, I can sort you out. You want a free gift of more than a grand, you can piss off."

I sigh. He's actually being pretty fair. I leaf through the brochure just in case one of the cheap rooms has magically got bigger, or the big room has magically got cheaper, and somehow they haven't. But there *is* a room that I've not seen before. And it takes a hundred and fifty with dinner and dancing, and it's half the price of the other place. Although the photos make it look…questionable. I see exposed pipes that they're doing their best to conceal and bare brickwork that's a good three steps less classy than the marble panels of the room we can't afford.

"What's this?" I ask.

"Basement," the feller explains. "Going on the list for next year, but it's not done up yet so I can't let you have it."

After the budget situation, I feel there's an important point to clarify here. "And when you say *can't*, do you mean that there's an actual reason why you can't, or is it just, like, policy?"

"I told you, it's not done up yet."

"Okay, but *done up* isn't a legally defined term, is it?" I'm sensing an opportunity here, although I'm also sensing my own desperation and I might be getting the two mixed up. "Is it unsafe?"

"Nah, done all the health and safety already."

"And is there some kind of licensing issue?"

"Nope, those cover the whole building anyway."

"So." I'm increasingly sure that *opportunity* is the right thing to be calling this. "It's just that it looks sort of shitty?"

"Yeah, that's right. Not done up properly."

"And if I don't care?"

He looks conflicted. "Got a reputation to think about."

Alright Sam, time to turn on that charm that Jonathan seems to think you have. I smile at him. "Well, I don't want to run down my own workplace like, but we're a medium-sized chain of bed and bathroom warehouses, so our ability to damage anybody's reputation is going to be extremely limited. We've got a hundred and thirty social media followers and one of them's the boss's mum."

He's still giving me *not sure* face.

"Tell you what, just let me look at it."

And he does.

To be honest, though, I'm not sure what I'm looking at. So I ring Tiff.

She answers. Which is a relief in some ways because I need her and a problem in others because she's not really meant to be answering her phone at work.

"What do you need, boss?" she asks. Over her shoulder I see a young lad in a green jumper waiting with a frankly inappropriate level of patience.

"Are you with a customer?"

"It's fine, I told him it was a Christmas emergency."

It strikes me that I shouldn't be encouraging Tiff to walk away from customers. Then again, it also strikes me that Tiff has been in work and available every time I've called, rather than taking repeated unscheduled personal days, so I count it as a net win. "Put him on."

She holds the phone out and I see the customer more clearly. To give all due credit to Tiff's judgement, he looks like the kind of feller who'd accept *Christmas emergency* as an excuse. His green jumper has reindeers all over it, and he's wearing these NHS glasses that give him a sort of wide-eyed hopeful look. "Sorry," I tell him, "I know this is really unprofessional."

"It's fine," he says, and he looks like it really is. "I'm not in a hurry."

"Are you sure? Because whatever you're after I reckon we could sort it out."

"No, no." He's giving me this little nod. "You've got me interested now. What's going on?"

"Long story."

"Still not in a hurry."

I don't really want to be telling everything to this stranger, so I give him the potted version. "I'm in London trying to organise our Christmas do, and it's wound up going over a hundred and fifty quid a head—"

"Ooh, you don't want to do that," says the customer. "It'll get taxed as a benefit in kind."

"How do you know that?" I ask him.

"I'm a tax accountant."

"And you don't just want us to tell you where the loo brushes are real quick like?"

He shakes his head.

"Anyway, I'm trying to save money, and that means swapping the expensive, swanky venue we had for"—I sweep the phone's camera around the narrow halls with their peeling paint and exposed steel—"this."

Tiff elbows the customer out the way—I really probably should talk to her about workplace conduct—and peers at the screen. She sucks in a little breath as I walk deeper into the warren of side rooms and show her row after row of dilapidated cellars with bare shelves and ruined, disused fireplaces.

"Wow," she says at last.

"I know," I reply. "It's fucking awful."

"It's fucking *amazing*."

I swing my phone around again. The room we're currently standing in has an actual girder running vertically through the middle. "Are we looking at the same room?"

"It's perfect."

"It's a *tip*."

The customer slides back into the picture. "I'm with"—he checks Tiff's name badge—"Tiffany. It's cool. It's kind of urban chic."

"Isn't that just a fancy way of saying a tip?"

"It's immersive," Tiff says, like that means something.

I'm not having that. "All rooms are immersive. You're inside the bloody thing. You can't get more immersive."

"It'll be memorable. You *wanted* this event to be memorable."

I try in vain to see what Tiff is seeing. "Yeah, for being a fun party, not for giving half the guests tetanus."

"Sam"—Tiff is looking unusually serious—"I promise you. Give me a few hundred quid for decorations and let me have the day off to get set up, and I can do something fantastic here."

I'm still missing it. But I decide to trust her. "Okay."

She gives a little squeal of delight, then with commendable

efficiency starts directing the green-jumper-NHS-glasses feller towards pocket spring mattresses. When she's gone, I head upstairs to say we'll take the basement. My phone buzzes on the way up.

The text says, Why are you in Shoreditch?

PART FOUR

KEEPING MY HEAD & KEEPING MY HEART

CHAPTER 21

JONATHAN ISN'T HAPPY THAT I ran off to Shoreditch without him, and he's not exactly convinced that downgrading from "swanky hall with marble walls" to "dark basement" is the best way to cut costs, but we're well under budget now so he can't complain too much and to his very mild credit he does thank me for getting it sorted with a kind of detached boss politeness that's its own level of crushing.

The advantage-slash-disadvantage of my having gone into town without Jonathan's say-so and come back more or less fine is that he's willing to leave to look after myself, and does as soon as he gets the opportunity. And it's not that I miss him, exactly—if nothing else I've got my cat back—it's just that for the first time since the accident I'm properly alone in Jonathan's big, empty house. It's...well, it sucks. And if I was less pissed off at him than I am, then I'd spend more time than I do reflecting on how much it must have sucked for him to live like that for, well, pretty much his whole life as far as I can tell. But I'm not less pissed off than I am, I'm exactly as pissed off as I am, so I mostly just feel sorry for myself.

And while I'm glad to have the Christmas party pretty much sorted, it does mean that I've officially expended my one source of usefulness, meaning I'm back to sitting on the sofa watching

Pointless and trying to see if Gollum will help me come up with a good example of a British Prime Minister who doesn't have an e in their name.

I'm just wrestling with this exact conundrum and trying to work out if John Major is too obvious when I hear somebody at the door. Since Agnieszka has a key and it's one of her off days anyhow, I go to investigate, reassured by the fact that burglars seldom knock.

It any case, it turns out not to be a burglar or a cleaner. It turns out to be Les.

"Jonathan in?" he asks.

"Err, no," I say. "Fraid not."

He gives me a look from under his brows. "Thought you shouldn't leave somebody alone with a concussion."

Though I'm still not in the best place as regards Jonathan, I do think it's unfair to let his dad think he's a bad concussed-person-take-care-of-er because that's one job he's done, if anything, too well. "It's been about a fortnight and I've not died yet. I'm probably fine."

"Apart from the amnesia."

"Well"—I can't tell if he's suspicious or not—"memory's a funny thing, y'know."

He's gazing at me now with a quiet concern. "Not that it's my business, but have you had a row?"

"Sort of," I say. Which isn't necessarily the best way to dispel the family's belief that we're dating but it's also true. Then I add, "Do you want a cup of tea?"

No matter which part of the country you're from, turning down a cup of tea is basically an unforgivable social taboo, although in this case I think he actually does want one. He comes inside and sits down in the first of Jonathan's three reception rooms, the one without the massive chunk of tree in it. And there's something deeply sorrowful about an old man sitting on a sofa a couple of weeks before Christmas in a room that's only half decorated because he had a barney with his son so intense that the whole family had to leave.

I bring him a tray through, set it down on the coffee table between us, and sit down in the chair opposite.

"Sorry he's not here," I say.

"Shouldn't have expected him to be." Les takes a mug, blows on it, and has a sip of tea. "Just thought he might be on account of..." He nods in my direction.

"You know we really aren't dating."

"Aye, but you've still got a concussion."

We've had this conversation, but it seems safer to have it again than to try and have a new one. "It's mostly better."

For a bit he goes back to his tea, and I leave him to it. I've got some experience with men of that generation, and they tend not to be talky unless they've got a real need for it. And I suspect Les might have on account of his having come all this way and still hanging about.

"He's a good lad," he says at last.

"Sometimes," I half-agree. "Although to be fair, other times he's a bit of a bellend."

Les takes another sip of tea. "Well, he gets that from his old man."

"No offence, but I really don't think he does."

"It's what you're supposed to say, though, isn't it?" It's warm in the house, but Les still has his coat on, almost like he's hiding. "Not very fashionable to say *oh, well he gets that from her side of the family.*"

My own mug of tea is just sitting there, hot between my hands. "I think you can if he does. It's all right to admit other people have influenced your kids. That's normal. Good even. Takes a village and all that."

"Still." And the *still* just hangs there for a long time, like he knows what to follow it up with and isn't quite able to. "Don't think I was a very good dad."

I want to tell him that's not true. I want to tell him it's not true *incredibly badly*, even though I don't have any idea what kind of dad he was. In the end, I compromise on, "I'm sure you were."

"Your son doesn't grow up that resentful if you've done your job right."

I want to tell him that's not true as well. And I'm on better ground here because I've been living with Jonathan for a while now. "I don't think he's resentful. I think he's just, y'know, bossy."

There's silence again, and Les makes good progress on his tea. I don't really fancy mine, so I plonk it on the floor and make a mental note to chuck it away before somebody trips over it or Gollum takes a liking to it.

"He were different," Les explains to the floor, "when he were younger."

"Most people are." I'm trying to be reassuring, but there's also a part of me that's curious, that wants to know how and why. "And coming south must have been tough on him," I add, thinking back to what he'd said about being the gay northern kid in a London comprehensive.

And once again, Les becomes very interested in his mug. "We'd not much choice."

"No?" I can't think of a better answer. I want to show I'm listening but not to say *please keep on talking about this thing that's clearly upsetting you and I have no right to be interested in* in case that comes across badly.

"My mam and dad couldn't take care of us, Wendy's could."

I don't ask for clarification because *also, I couldn't support my family myself which, for a man of my generation, was literally my only reason for existing* goes very much unsaid.

"What happened?" I ask. Then follow up immediately with, "not that you have to say if you don't want to."

"Credit crunch." The tea's nearly gone now but Les is still holding onto it like he's frightened it'll do a runner. "Used to work in steel. No steel in Rotherham anymore."

"You must have had transferrable skills."

"Yeah, but so did every other bugger."

There was that.

"I worked," he went on, "just not in the kind of job I'd trained for or for the kind of money I used to make. Got back on our feet eventually—sort of—but by then the damage was done and Jonathan...well, let's say he'd learned some lessons he shouldn't have had to learn."

I lean forward with my elbows on my knees. "You've got to be proud of him, though." I'm not quite sure why I go there, given what a dick he's been to me lately, but right in this moment I can't bear the idea of Les Forest thinking he's let his son down.

"Of course I am." There's something like bitterness in his voice, and something like guilt. "But it's a hard thing to know your son reached for the stars because he was determined to be as little like you as possible."

"That seems a bad way of looking at it."

He makes an imperceptibly small movement that could maybe be a shrug. "Is what it is."

Substituting business for usefulness, I pick up my tea and take Les's now-empty cup. "You were in a bad position," I tell him, though I'm sure a hundred people have told him the same thing, "and you made the best of it you could."

Gollum comes and sits on Les's knee, though I'm not totally sure he's not expecting him to be Jonathan. "Maybe, but the best I could weren't much."

"It was enough, though," I tell him, and I surprise myself with how adamant I sound.

"Was it?"

"It has to be," I say, "else what's the point?"

There's not much more to talk about after that. I let him know that Jonathan'll be back this evening and that he's welcome to wait but I can't say exactly how long it'll be, and he tells me that he needs to be getting back on account of how Wendy wants him to pick up a leg of lamb on the way.

In the doorway, as he's leaving, he puts his hand on my shoulder. "You're a good lad too, Sam."

When he's gone, I wash up the mugs and—it's funny—I don't start tearing up exactly, but I do get this sense of…I don't know. Something empty like.

"Just you and me now," I tell Gollum as I put the mugs away.

He looks up at me and *miaows*.

"Alright," I say, "I don't like it any more than you do."

Now he makes a sort of *mrrging* noise that's like a purr only antsy.

"It's not your dinnertime yet."

He *mrrgs* again.

"No."

I sit down and he sits at my feet looking up at me with an expression of pure accusation. And I'm glad he's here in a lot of ways, for all he's a selfish little bastard most of the time. It's just things keep happening to remind me of everybody else that could be here too but isn't. Like Les and Wendy. Like my mam, my dad, and my gran. Even like Jonathan fucking Forest, who's not around even when he's around these days.

My mam called me Samwise, but maybe she should've called me Frodo. Because I'm starting to feel invisible. Or like something got stuck in me and didn't heal right.

Gollum *mrrgs* one last time, and I give in. "Okay," I tell him, "you can have one of your treats. You've not earned it, mind."

I feed Gollum a couple of Felix Salmon and Trout Crispies, not that he's grateful. While he's eating them, I slump back on the sofa and flick on the telly, looking for a way to switch my brain off.

I find something to watch in the end. Though if you asked me afterwards, I wouldn't have been able to tell you what it was.

CHAPTER 22

I'M FEELING BETTER WHEN JONATHAN gets home that evening. Maybe because he's come in so late I've just sort of drifted back to normal. Gollum, of course, is delighted to see him and rubs cat hair all up Jonathan's black suit—which, despite his long stayover in Grumpsville, Jonathan doesn't seem to mind.

"There's a lasagne in the fridge," I say. "And your dad popped round."

Jonathan, who's been bending down to greet Gollum, goes very still. "Why?"

"I just fancied making a lasagne."

Time was, this would have got one of those not-quite-a-smiles. "I meant," Jonathan snaps, "why did my father come round?"

"Why'd you think?"

"Sam"—he straightens up again, Gollum fully in his arms now, purring and paws akimbo—"are you doing this on purpose?"

"No," I tell him, deciding the moral high ground looks like too much of a hike. "Words are just coming out of my mouth at random and forming sentences by pure coincidence." I sigh. "Your dad came round because you had a massive row and he felt terrible."

Jonathan's already beelining for his study. "Are you sure we're talking about the same person? My father has never displayed a strong emotion in his life."

"Neither do you mostly but you still have 'em."

He stops beelining. "I'm perfectly capable of displaying emotion."

"Only if that emotion is *narked*."

Curiously for a self-made bathroom supremo, Jonathan takes the minimum offer. "Which is still one more than you get from my father."

I shouldn't have expected Jonathan Forest to be paying attention, even to his own family, but this surprises even me. "Okay, maybe we really aren't talking about the same person."

"The man never even raises his voice."

Three weeks ago, hearing a comment like that'd have me thinking what a prick Jonathan was. A week and a half ago, it'd have me thinking he had hidden depths. Now it's got me thinking he has hidden depths but a lot of those depths are depths of prickishness. "You know there's ways to express feelings that aren't loud."

"Not in my family." Now he does give one of those not-exactly-smiles, but there's an edge to it that I don't much like.

"Yes, in your family." I'm very rapidly getting fed up here. "You just haven't noticed over all the noise. And don't get me wrong, it's good noise a lot of the time. But just because your dad isn't like that doesn't mean he's not worth listening to."

Jonathan's busy trying to open his study without dropping the cat. "Haven't we already had the conversation about you staying out of my business?"

"Yeah," I start. And then change my mind. "Actually, no. We haven't had a conversation. You just went back to barking instructions at me and reminding me I'm your employee."

"You *are* my—"

"I know. But I'm not, though, am I? I mean I am. But this is"—I make a *what the fuck* gesture—"you're holding my cat. I'm living in your house. Your family comes and talks to me and…and I care about yez."

"So you like me, then you don't like me, now you care about me." Jonathan leans his head against the door, looking, if I'm honest, a bit despairing. "And leave Gollum out of this."

"He's a cat. He's not an emotionally damaged teenager whose parents are in the middle of a messy divorce."

"Cats are sensitive," declares Jonathan with the authority of a man who's never had a cat.

He's wrong—cats are genetically programmed to be narcissists—but I let him have it. Because for some unfathomable reason the one living being in the entire world Jonathan Forest has chosen to be emotionally open with is a cat with a face that looks like other cats use it as a scratching post. "I'm sorry," I say, "that I said what I said before. I was just angry. And in my defence, so were you."

"We still can't…we shouldn't… This is for the best."

"Jonathan, this fucking sucks."

He turns his head slightly and gives me a challenging look. "Do you have an alternative?"

"Can we not just talk? About this. About us. About what happened?"

While he doesn't look enthusiastic, he at least starts heading back into the room. "About the time you kissed me, or about the fight I had with my family afterwards?"

"Either. Both. Whichever."

He sits on the sofa, where his dad sat. There's a trace of a resemblance about the eyes, but they have very different energies. Jonathan's much more tense, for a start. "How much is there to discuss?"

I'd not planned this far ahead. "I don't know exactly, but there's got to be more than nothing."

Gollum sits purring on his lap and, for a while, that's the only sound in the room. Eventually, Jonathan untenses enough to ask, "What did my dad say?"

It's probably the safest starting point. "Just that he was looking for yez, at first. I think he probably wanted to smooth things over."

"It doesn't need smoothing." Jonathan scritches Gollum behind the ears. For such a sharp man, he's got a surprisingly gentle touch. "It's just the way things are."

"What? You blowing your top if you have to spend more than twenty minutes with your family is the way things are?"

His mouth twitches. "To some extent. You can see why I prefer to keep them at a distance."

"No," I tell him. "I can't. Or rather, I can. Like I understand your reasons, I just think your reasons are shit."

"I'm so glad"—it's Jonathan's harshest, driest voice—"we made the time to have this chat."

I put my head in my hands. "Fuck, I don't mean it like that. I just mean...you can't deal with stuff you care about by pushing it away."

"That's not what I'm doing. I just—there are certain things that lead to arguments, and I try to avoid those things."

"Like your dad."

"Fine. Yes." He gives a sharp little blink. "Like my dad."

"Because," I ask, "of how he lost his job and that?"

Jonathan's expression turns wary. "What's he been telling you?"

"He didn't make out like it was a big family secret. He just mentioned he lost his job up north and it was hard for yez."

"I'm not suggesting it's a secret. It's just not something anyone needs to dwell on."

"If you're having arguments over it fifteen years later maybe a bit of a dwell would do you good."

Carefully easing a protesting Gollum from his lap, Jonathan gets up and starts pacing. "It's funny, when you submitted your CV to me, you didn't mention you were a qualified therapist."

"That's not what I—you know, you are fucking impossible to talk to."

"You can see why I prefer to keep you at a distance too then?"

He's trying to needle me now and I'm not going to let him. This is one occasion on which Jonathan Forest isn't going to be in control. "He thinks he was a bad dad, y'know."

Jonathan shrugs. "Well, he was."

"Was he?"

"Yes."

See. Impossible to talk to. "How?" I ask, much less patiently than a qualified therapist would.

"He got fired, moved us to the other end of the country, and completely failed to find meaningful work."

"Was he fired, then? Or was he made redundant like half the bloody north?"

Jonathan runs a hand through his hair. "What difference does it make?"

"There was a fucking financial crisis. The entire steel industry collapsed. Surely you can't hold him responsible for that?"

"I don't hold him responsible for getting knocked down. I hold him responsible for not getting back up again."

"He did get back up again," I point out.

Now Jonathan's doing his contempt face. I really don't like his contempt face. "What would you know about it?"

"I just see what I see. A man who did what he could for his family."

"Well, what he could wasn't enough." Fuck me, Jonathan can be icy sometimes. But there's something under it. Something kind of raw. A child who can't understand why his dad isn't protecting him. "It was bad enough being the gay one with the funny accent without the constant chants of *Johnny Forest Johnny Forest why's your dad still on the dole.*"

I stare at him. "Jonathan, are you seriously telling me that you're holding playground bullshit against your dad nearly twenty years later?"

"No, of course not," Jonathan mutters. "I just don't want to turn out like him."

And then there's this silence, Jonathan sort of shocked and wide-eyed and a bit breathless, as if he'd just spat out a chili he didn't know he'd eaten.

"Look," I say, "I know I don't know either of yez very well, but from what I've seen I reckon you could do a lot worse than to wind up like Les Forest."

"And that's what you want from me, is it?" Jonathan's gone very still. "To be a man who's content to bounce from shit job to shit job, never fighting for himself or anybody else, always playing with a losing hand, too weak to turn it into a winning one?"

I don't have a clue how to deal with any of that. So I pull a Julie Andrews and start at the very beginning. "First off, I don't want anything from you. Not in the sense of wanting you to be different like."

"You've been constantly asking me to be different."

"I've been asking to behave differently vis-à-vis being a dick. But how you act isn't who you are."

He doesn't seem convinced. "You are what you do."

"No. You do what you do. You are who you are. The fact that your dad worked shit jobs doesn't make him a shit person—"

"Of course not." It's good to know that Jonathan's opinion of Les isn't quite low enough that he'll let that slide. "But it makes him a failure."

Jonathan's pacing is doing my head in. So I get up and stand in front of him, hoping he'll stop. And he does because the alternative is either to crash into me or turn left like a woodlouse in a maze. "He's not a failure. He did what he had to do. Imagine what your life would've been like if your dad had been too proud to take help from anyone or do a job he thought was beneath him."

A shadow flickers in Jonathan's eyes as we stand there staring at each other in this half-decorated room. Gollum butts him on the shin but, for once, he's paying more attention to me. "If he'd been less willing to accept defeat, you mean?"

Sometimes I wonder why I like Jonathan Forest. But, oddly enough, this is not one of those times. Maybe I've got into the habit of arguing with him. Or maybe I keep arguing with him because I'm sure, deep down, there's someone worth reaching. "Yeah," I say. "Knowing when you're beat isn't a bad thing. Because now and again, you just *are*. And trying to hold onto stuff you've not got any more helps nobody."

"So I should be grateful my dad let the world treat him like a kicked dog."

I reach out, not really thinking about what I'm doing, and my hand fetches up against his arm. He gets even stiller, but he doesn't draw away. "Aye. You should. Because you might not respect what he did, but you wouldn't be where you are or have what you have if he'd not."

"Everything I have, I've built myself."

"Out of pieces he gave you. And that Del gave you. And the rest of your family gave you." I'm getting half-tempted to shake him now. "I'm not running you down and I'm not saying you're not a remarkable man who's achieved amazing things within the highly specific sphere of bed and bathroom retailing—"

Jonathan interrupts me with a sound I've never heard him make before. And I realise it's kind of a laugh. "How flattering."

I sigh. "It's true, though. You *are* a remarkable man. But getting to where you are's had a cost, and it's not a cost everybody wants to pay, and not everybody should."

"People who have other people depending on them should pay it." He puts a hand on my wrist, like he's going to pull my hand off him, but somehow doesn't. And it's a bit weird to be touching and having a row at the same time. Still, here we are. "I've done all of this so that I can support the people I love in the ways my father never could."

"Aye, but you've done it by letting them down in ways he never did either."

"I have not—"

"You have, Jonathan. Just look around you." I give him a moment to do just that, hoping the sad remains of the Christmas decorations would make my point for me. "Your family are doing fine. They don't need your money—"

"But what if something happens?" he asks, in this tight, urgent voice.

"It already did. It happened fifteen years ago and you all got through it. Because you had each other. And you'll always have each other unless you push everyone away. Which, to be clear, is what you're doing."

For once, Jonathan doesn't come snapping back with something dismissive or mean.

So I go on. "All they wanted was to spend time with you and you fucked that up. I mean, imagine what it's like for your dad, knowing his own son has dedicated his life to being as little like him as possible."

"It's not," Jonathan says, very quietly, "that I don't want to be like him. It's that I don't want to make the same mistakes he did."

And now I do give him a little shake, though with his hand on my arm it's more of a squeeze. "He didn't make mistakes. A bunch of bankers in Belgravia made mistakes. Your dad made choices. And his choice was to put his family ahead of his pride."

At last, Jonathan tugs himself free of me. Then he crosses to the sofa, sinks down on it and puts his head in his hands. Gollum jumps up next to him in that catty way he's got that I like to think is him being empathetic but is probably just him spotting an opportunity to sit somewhere warm and immobile.

I hover, not quite knowing what to do. I think I've finally got through to him, but I might have also broken him. Figuring he probably needs space, I'm just sneaking out the room, when he looks up at me. His eyes have that faint tinge of red they get when you're technically not crying and steering very hard into that technicality.

"Sam," he says. "Don't go."

"Alright," I say.

And we don't say much else for the rest of the evening.

CHAPTER 23

THINGS GET A BIT BETTER after that. Not right back how they were like, but better. Jonathan's still working a lot but it feels more genuinely-busy-because-holidays working, than need-to-not-be-around-you working. And I've got a fair bit on myself with party planning. Of course I have to be a bit careful with that because Jonathan still can't know I'm talking to the old team about it, but if I tell him I'm messaging "a woman about decorations", it's technically not a lie.

Though as time's gone on, I'm not sure "technically not a lie" is where I want things to be between us. It's turning into an elephant in the room. Worse, the whole house is filling up with elephants. There's the do-I-still-have-amnesia elephant, which is standing next to the am-I-still-fired elephant in front of the do-I-need-to-be-here-at-all elephant. And those three are giving the side-eye to the mostly unrelated how're-things-with-Jonathan-and-his-dad elephant, and that's one hell of an elephant, being much older, with much nastier tusks, and I don't really want to go near it again. And all those elephants are sort of sitting on top of this great big, massive elephant called also-there-was-that-one-time-I-kissed-you-and-I-liked-it. I always thought elephants were cute. But I'm going right off them.

I honestly can't tell if I got through to Jonathan or not. I mean, I don't think he's a man who changes his mind overnight or, y'know, ever. But he must be feeling some kind of way because he comes home with a chicken and starts doing something aggressive to it in the kitchen.

"Am I going to have to call the RSPB?" I ask.

Jonathan has his sleeves rolled right up to his elbows. "Well, it's already dead so they might think it's a little late."

"It's probably better off dead, the way you're treating it."

"I'm stuffing it," Jonathan informs me, in the flavour of irate that I'm beginning to think is the amused flavour.

I watch Jonathan with the chicken for a bit longer. "You're not stuffing it. You're fisting it with a lemon."

And after two years of working for him and more than two weeks of living with him, his facade finally cracks, and he laughs properly. I'm not sure if I'm more shocked or he is.

"Seriously?" I say. "I've been treating you to my wit and northern charm since the third of December and fisting a chicken is what gets yez?"

Jonathan slants a look at me, and the crinkles at the corners of his eyes are smiley instead of scowly, and that makes his whole face look different, even though he's still mostly eyebrows and jawline. "What can I say? I'm difficult to like, I use money as a substitute for affection, and I have a deeply unsophisticated sense of humour. And I'm not fisting the chicken. I'm cooking."

"That's not cooking, it's desecrating a corpse."

Jonathan reaches for something long, thin and green.

"What're you doing now?"

"Adding rosemary."

"Jonathan"—without thinking I cover his wrist with my hand, and we're standing close now and he's bending his arm to keep his raw-chicken-covered fingers off my shirt—"you cannot send this chicken to its grave with a lemon wedged halfway up it and a sprig of rosemary poking out its bumhole."

He laughs again.

"Oh, come on. You're not set off by the word bumhole?"

And again.

"You fucking are. You great bumhole."

He's laughing enough now that he's crying a bit, but he can't wipe his eyes without breaking about six different kitchen hygiene rules. So I wipe them for him, trying not to worry about how deep and dark the circles underneath them have got lately.

Jonathan clears his throat, pulling back very slightly. "Look"—his voice is still a bit soft from laughing—"this is what the recipe told me to do."

"A recipe told you to do this?" I repeat. "Where'd you find it? Chicken Haters Monthly? Serial Killer Magazine? A banned porno from the 1970s?"

"It's on my phone." Jonathan gestures with his elbow because his hand's all chickeny. "You can check if you don't believe me."

I lean over and squint at the screen. It says, "Very Easy Roast Chicken". It also says, "instructions in bold are for children". "Jonathan, is this recipe for kids?"

"I'm sure the child is optional. And besides," he adds defensively, "I'm following the adult instructions as well."

"Nowhere in this recipe does it say *violate poultry*."

He steps back, with a slightly camp flourish. "Go on then. You show me the respectful way to put a lemon into a chicken."

Upending the bird, I coax it open and gently drop the halves of lemon into it. "You see? It just goes in. You don't have to get wrist deep."

"It says *stuff*. Stuff, to me, implies vigour."

And now it's my turn to giggle into dead poultry. "Good

to know. But not in this context. Why are you trying to make a chicken anyway? We've still got that casserole from yesterday."

Jonathan rolls his eyes, but it seems to be largely at himself. "I thought I'd better practice. For when my family come round."

I'm honestly a bit surprised—not that they're still coming for Christmas because you probably couldn't stop that lot coming even if you booby trapped the driveway—but that Jonathan's preparing for it in a way that doesn't involve buying things and giving orders. "You know I'll help," I say.

"I didn't want to take you for granted. Especially after—" He runs aground.

Though, frankly, I'm not sure I'm in safer waters myself.

Then Jonathan's phone rings and I've never been so glad of a distraction. Even if part of that distraction is the two of us running round each other trying to work out how to answer a phone with chicken on our hands.

Eventually Jonathan manages to swipe it with his knuckles and stick it on speaker.

"I'm making a chicken," he says at once.

"That's nice." It's Les's voice at the other end. "Is Sam with you?"

"Yes," I say. "I'm going to go rinse my hands now so there might be a bit of a sink noise."

While I'm doing that, Les goes on. "I'm just calling to say that we've had a spot of bother at the house, so if you need any help with Christmas we won't be here."

"What happened?" asks Jonathan, wiping his fingers on a piece of kitchen towel.

I hear the loud but tinny tones of Wendy's voice at the other end of the line suggesting that we don't need to be bothered with the details. "Your mam says we shouldn't bother you," Les relays.

"Tell Mum that I'll only worry more if you don't tell me."

"He says he'll only worry more if we don't tell him."

There's more voices off in the background.

"We've had a pipe burst," Les explains. "It'll be fine. I shut off the stopcock before it could do much damage, but this close to Christmas it's hard to get anybody out, so we've no water."

More voices.

"Your mam wants me to tell you we're fine."

And more.

"She wants me to tell you that Barbara Jane's finding us a hotel."

"Get somewhere nice," Jonathan says at once. "I can cover—" Then he stops. He doesn't look at me, he looks at the chicken. "Unless—I've got spare rooms if you want to—that is, if you'd rather."

Les is quiet. Then I hear muffled conversation. "He's asking if—" followed by "don't be—" then "I think actually" before Les comes back with "Are you sure, son?"

"Why wouldn't I be?" asks Jonathan, and I have to give him points for cheek. "I'm sure we can arrange a hotel if that's easier, but since you're going to be here for Christmas anyway, and since I've got the space..."

"It'd be Barbara Jane as well," Les points out.

"That's fine." And he sounds like he means it, or he's trying very hard to sound like he means it.

Les pauses a moment. "And Johnny."

"I thought he was staying with Kayla and Theo."

"They've not got the room anymore," explains Les, "what with Anthea growing up."

It takes Jonathan a bit longer to reply this time than it did earlier. "No problem," he says. And this time he's a touch less convincing. "I'm sure I've got room for Johnny as well."

"Thanks, son." I might be imagining it, but I swear I hear surprise in Les's voice.

And it's not until they've gone—with Wendy yelling down the phone that they'll be along later—that I have a thought.

"You know," I say, "I could go have a look if you want."

"A look at what?" Jonathan's already gone back to the chicken, although he's now trying to rub it with butter that's not been left long enough out the fridge so he's just kind of stabbing it with little yellow rocks.

"The pipe."

I can almost hear the filing cabinets in Jonathan's head riffling back to Becker, comma, S from years back. "Oh yes, you were a plumber weren't you?"

"I've got none of the kit, mind," I tell him, realising that I should probably manage expectations, and hoping that admitting I remember the plumbing part of my background won't make the whole rest of the amnesia story collapse like a house of cards with a burst water main. "And if they need a new pipe, I've been out the business long enough that I don't know any suppliers. But I could at least check the damage, make sure they don't get ripped off like by whoever finally does sort it out."

He gives me a look I don't recognise, but I think is gratitude. "That'd be kind of you."

"No trouble," I tell him. And it's not. Though I try not to think too hard about the tangled-up mess of motivations clogging up the back of my head like hair in a drainpipe. Because while I want to be doing this to be nice, or because the Forests and their family have been nice to me, I'm also doing it because I feel guilty. I feel guilty as fuck. For a whole bunch things. Besides, I'm supposed to be making myself look useful so Jonathan'll remember I'm worth keeping around. At work like, for the sake of my team.

And also maybe just…generally.

"Now"—Jonathan's gazing down at the chicken with an

expression that's one part curiosity and one part pity—"what am I doing wrong this time?"

The chicken comes out all right in the end—not great, but not completely terrible. The veggies have caught a bit on top and the potatoes are a touch dry, but for Jonathan's first attempt at a mostly unaided roast following a recipe designed for six-year-olds, it could be a lot worse.

We sit at the kitchen table munching through it, and since I'm facing the windows I notice a shimmer of silver on the grass outside.

"That'll be why the pipe's burst," I say. "It's probably iced up."

Jonathan looks up from his peas. "Pardon?"

"Grass is frosting over," I tell him. "Which means it's below zero, and probably has been for a while. And if your parents' house is old, which I suspect it is because most houses round here are, then there'll be places where the insulation isn't so good and the pipes freeze. Then the water expands and they split."

"Maybe." Jonathan's turning around now to look at the garden. "Or maybe Uncle Johnny tried to flush something down the toilet he shouldn't have."

This is more like the old Jonathan, but that's okay because I don't think I want the old Jonathan to go away entirely. "Did you just imply that your uncle's a drug mule?"

"When I was thirteen, he broke my mum's favourite vase, and tried to flush *that* down the toilet to hide the evidence, so he does have form."

"Are you telling me a grown man tried to flush shards of ceramic down the bog?"

"What Johnny lacks in common sense he makes up in audacity." There's a hint of affection in Jonathan's voice. A faint hint. A hint so faint that if you served it in a cake on *Bake Off* the judges would say, "I'm sorry, it's just not coming through."

"Don't worry," I say, "we'll hide the good china before he gets here."

Then I go back to my dinner, but Jonathan's still staring out of the window which means his chicken's going cold, and that's not doing his cooking any favours.

"It's only frost," I point out. "It happens every winter."

"I know, I just"—I never thought Jonathan Forest could sound dreamy and he doesn't really but it's close—"I like this time of year. When your breath mists in the air. When I was very young I'd pretend to be a dragon."

I give him what I hope is an encouraging look. "You still can."

"I'm not six years old, Sam."

"I know. But why should kids get all the fun?"

Turning back, Jonathan spears a bit of chicken, as if the poor thing hadn't suffered enough. "I'm not playing dragons with you."

Jonathan's done such a good job of avoiding me recently that it's a bit like I'm having to learn how to be around him all over again. Because he's not the sort of man you think you'd enjoy spending time with.

Since he technically did the cooking, I do the washing up, and afterwards I find Jonathan on the sofa, with Gollum on his lap, both of them just gazing out the window, watching the setting sun sparkle off the frost-dusted grass. I sit down with them and watch it too. And it is sort of magic, in a way, if you don't think too much about how hard it is on the lawn.

It gets slightly less magic when his family blunder in, crunching over the grass in ways that really *will* be bad for the landscaping, and Barbara Jane's first words when Jonathan opens the door are, "Fuck me, why is it so cold, who's putting the kettle on?"

Jonathan greets her with a dry "good evening, BJ" that's

drowned out by everybody else coming in after her and making their own hellos, comments, and demands.

"Johnny lad." That's Uncle Johnny, who I suppose is the only one in the family who can call Jonathan Johnny without confusion. "Can I stick a couple of crates in your garage?"

"They've been in our front room for a week," adds Wendy, swanning in wearing a blouse with poppies on it under a rainbow-striped cardy that looks hand-knitted.

"And our living room," adds Les.

Jonathan stares warily at the three of them. "That sounds like more than a couple."

"Yeah, okay"—Uncle Johnny puts his hands up in the *fair cop* gesture—"there's probably closer to twelve."

"And what's in them exactly?" asks Jonathan, demonstrating the keen attention to detail that's propelled him to the top of the bed and bathroom retailing world.

With more self-satisfaction than is probably appropriate for a man in his early sixties, Uncle Johnny grins. "Halloween shit."

Now he's got me wondering. "Halloween shit?"

"Yeah." He nods. "You buy it up this time of year while it's cheap, then flog it off in October."

Les casts his brother a dark look. "Were you really planning on leaving that crap in our front room for ten months?"

Johnny shrugs. "I'd've worked something out."

"When?"

"Now." Uncle Johnny turns back to Jonathan with a expression that falls somewhere between expectant and hopeful. "What do you say?"

Jonathan's eyes narrow beneath brows that, for once, seem appropriately heavy. "And all this stuff is currently in Mum and Dad's house?"

Uncle Johnny nods.

"I'll admit"—Jonathan's sounding almost gentle, which is a new look on him—"it's not a terrible plan. At least"—and now he's sounding somewhat less gentle—"it's not a terrible plan if you can avoid paying for storage."

"Which I will," says Uncle Johnny, "because I got connections."

Barbara Jane, who long ago concluded that since nobody else was putting the kettle on she'd have to, waltzes back from the kitchen with a mug. "By *connections,* Uncle Johnny, you mean you know somebody with a garage who's just *slightly* too polite to tell you to fuck right off."

"Be fair, BJ." Jonathan looks up from the sofa with a smirk. "Nobody has *ever* accused me of being too polite."

That much, at least, Barbara Jane has to agree with.

"You can have the garage until January," Jonathan concludes. "After that you're going to damned well get yourself a storage locker."

Uncle Johnny looks crestfallen.

"If it's as good a deal as you say, you'll still make a profit. If it isn't, then *maybe* you should have picked a better investment."

"On the subject of crates"—Wendy gets back up though she's barely sat down and stretches her back out pointedly—"we should get our things moved in. Where're you putting us, Jonathan?"

"If you head upstairs"—Jonathan gets up too, pointing towards the stairs as if he's directing tourists to Marble Arch—"I thought you and Dad could take the second on the right and BJ and Johnny could take the first on the left."

"Gotcha." Wendy grabs an over-stuffed wheely case from by the door. "Come on Les, sooner we're started sooner we'll finish."

Uncle Johnny is on his feet as well, but Barbara Jane is making a very intense hold-on-a-second expression.

"You *cannot,*" she says, "seriously expect me to share with him."

"What's wrong with me?" asks Johnny in the tone of somebody who's aware there's several possible answers.

Barbara Jane just glares. "What's *right* with you? And how many thirty-two-year-old divorced women do you know who'd be happy about sharing a room with their sixty-something uncle?"

Jonathan smiles the way he only ever smiles at Barbara Jane. "I'm not sure thirty-two-year-old divorced women get to be choosy."

"Now, son." Les looks conditionally disapproving. "I'm not sure but I think that's probably sexist."

"It is," I confirm.

Barbara Jane continues to glare. "Not sure either of you are authorities. And actually, Johnny, I *do* get to be choosy because I can always book into a hotel, and if the choice is between bunking with him"—she indicates Uncle Johnny—"and going somewhere with room service, I know which I'd rather pick."

With a flourish, Jonathan pulls his phone from his breast pocket. "Then let me call you a cab."

"Works for me," says Uncle Johnny. "Means I won't have to share a bed."

Barbara Jane's eyebrows do something extremely expressive. "Excuse me, I'd assume you'd at least be sleeping on the floor."

"With my back?"

"Tell you what." Wendy has set her suitcase on end and is sitting down on it. She's probably expecting this conversation to go on a bit. "Why don't you come in with us and Johnny can have the room on his own?"

"So instead of sharing with my annoying uncle, I'm sharing with both my parents?"

"Okay then." It's looking like Wendy has a whole strategy mapped out. "Then you take a room on your own and Johnny comes in with us."

Les stirs, just slightly. "He bloody isn't."

"Alright." Uncle Johnny sounds more outraged than he looks. "I wouldn't want to be in with you either. You snore."

"I do not," says Les firmly.

Wendy gives him something that's part smile, part grimace. "You do, love."

All this while, Barbara Jane has been mulling something over. "I'm confused. Isn't this a five-bedroom house? That should be one room for you, one for me, one for the parents, one for Johnny, and one for Sam, assuming..." She flicks a suggestive look between us.

"Yes, that *would* be the situation," agrees Jonathan, "but you might remember somebody suggesting we put a third of a pine tree in Sam's old room to create a magical Christmas illusion."

"To be fair," I say, "it was me that suggested it, so maybe I should give my room up."

"You can't ask him to share," insists Wendy, aghast, "he's a guest."

"Aren't you all guests?" I point out.

Barbara Jane shakes her head. "Different rules for family. We can be as awful to each other as we like, but for *you* we have to pretend to be generous-spirited."

"You're about to move into my house, BJ," says Jonathan. "How much more generous-spirited do you want me to be?"

"You could have offered to make the tea when we came in?" The wounded tone in Barbara Jane's voice is mostly put on, but only mostly.

"And *you* could have made some for the rest of us," Johnny tells her, staring accusingly into the kitchen.

"I did."

Wendy isn't about to give false-tea-making credit to anybody, even her own daughter. "You didn't, you just left some mugs out with teabags in them."

"That way people can make their own how they like it."

"Oh, you fucking saint." I can practically hear Jonathan rolling his eyes.

I feel like the whole tea issue is distracting us, so I try to pull things back to sleeping arrangements. "It's not a problem," I say. "I've been here a while so if there's anybody should be giving their room up it's me, and I can always just go back in with the tree."

"We had to move the bed," Jonathan reminds me. "It's propped against the wall."

"So I'll sleep at an angle."

"You will not." I think Wendy knows I'm joking, but it's sort of hard to tell. "He will not. Jonathan, you're not letting him sleep at an angle. We didn't raise you to let guests sleep at an angle."

Jonathan sighs. "He's not going to sleep at an angle, Mum."

"It'll be bad for his back," she tells him. Then immediately tells me, "It'll be bad for your back."

"Okay." I spread my hands in a gesture of surrender. "I promise, I won't be trying to sleep propped up like I'm in traction. I'll probably just grab some pillows off the sofa and do myself something up on the floor."

Wendy is giving Jonathan a look.

"Really," I say, "it's fine."

She's still giving Jonathan a look.

"How about," Jonathan says at last, sounding only a little bit like he's reading from a script, "Sam takes my room and I sleep on the sofa."

"Really," I begin. "You don't hav—"

"There we are." Wendy beams. "That's all sorted. Come on Les, give's a hand with this."

I'm not sure, but I think I see Les give his son an approving look as he crosses the room to help Wendy with the suitcase. The rest of the family make similar moves to grab their things and ship them upstairs, except for Uncle Johnny, who heads off to pick up a dozen boxes of remaindered Halloween decorations.

Getting the whole family settled takes a bit, especially after they realise that one of the rooms—the one I've just moved out of as it happens—is much smaller than the others, but since Johnny has made the mistake of leaving the house for twenty minutes, he gets stuck in it by default and comes back to a very smug Barbara Jane.

When everybody's unpacked, we drift into the middle reception room and sit around the still mostly green Christmas tree.

"Shame we never got the decs up," Wendy muses, staring up at it. And the moment she says it there's a—not quite tension like, but a *something* in the air between Les and Jonathan. Because one of the elephants has just wandered in and it's hanging about under the tree like a very big present nobody wants to unwrap.

"Honestly"—Barbara Jane has given up on the tea and started on the gin that Auntie Jack left last time she was here—"it was probably a bit ambitious anyway."

But Wendy's not one to be bent off a point once she's on it. "Still seems a shame. Just leaving it there all half-naked."

"I'm not getting the stepladder out," Jonathan protests. "Not at this time of night."

Les gives a quiet nod. "It is how it is, and it looks all right to me."

"And really"—Barbara Jane waves her glass in a little circle—"what says *Christmas* more than something getting abandoned because you had a pointless row in the middle of it? I mean that's basically every game of Monopoly we've ever played."

"That's because you cheat at Monopoly." The accusation comes from Uncle Johnny, who has just come in from the garage.

"Well, it's tedious if you don't."

"No, BJ." Jonathan sighs. "It's tedious if you do, because all that happens when you steal money from the bank is that the game lasts longer."

"And also," I add, "because cheating is wrong?"

Barbara Jane puts her drink down carefully on the floor. "Not as wrong as making people play Monopoly in the first place."

"Tell you what," says Les, and I'm a bit surprised he's speaking again so soon. Normally he's a one-contribution-per-conversation feller. "How about we get the family box and do those? That's way it's officially finished."

Wendy's on her feet before anybody can say if they think it's a good idea or not, and forty-five seconds later she's poking her head back from the first reception room looking nonplussed. "What've you done with the box, Jonathan? Don't you tell me you've lost it."

Jonathan gives her a sharp glance. "Of course I haven't. It's in my room."

"What's it doing up there?" asks Wendy.

"I wanted it to be somewhere safe."

Privately, I wonder if he didn't just find it comforting to have around.

Either way he goes and gets it from upstairs, and we sit with it between us. For a moment we all just look at it, like it's something sacred. Which I suppose in a small way it is. Then Les opens it up.

"This is normally Del's job," he points out.

"Well," says Wendy firmly, "it's high time somebody took over."

"Especially since he might not be here next year," adds Barbara Jane, smirking.

With a reverence that could almost make you forget what a complete piece of tat it is, Les lifts out the sugar paper snowflake and hands it to his daughter, who pulls a face of visible disgust.

"You know eventually you're going to have to stop giving me this one."

Wendy folds her arms. "That was the first thing you brung

home from school when you was little and it's been going on the tree for nearly thirty years so it's going on it now."

Barbara Jane holds it up, inspecting it. "Fuck, I really was uncoordinated wasn't I? This is barely even a snowflake, it's just paper with holes cut out."

For all her complaining, she puts it on the tree carefully, keeping it well away from anything that might damage it.

Then it's Jonathan's turn. And his is the apple. His reaction isn't quite as performatively outraged as his sister's, but there's a certain resignation to it. "When *exactly* are you going to let me forget this?"

"Never," declares Wendy.

"Sorry," I ask, "what exactly does he want to forget?"

Jonathan looks embarrassed. Which is a pretty normal reaction to have to your parents but not one I'd usually associate with Jonathan Forest. "Let's say that we used to have one more of these, but when I was much younger I got hungry."

I look at the apple. It isn't exactly realistic. "I hope you were a *lot* younger."

"He was twenty-six," says Barbara Jane.

"I was five," Jonathan corrects her.

This'd be a good time to raise an eyebrow, but I've never had the knack. "And your parents have been reminding you of a potentially traumatic glass-eating experience ever since?"

Wendy smiles complacently at me in a way I can only describe as peak mum. "Traditions've got to start somewhere, Sam."

Meanwhile, Jonathan goes and hangs his apple, and then Les reaches back into the box of nostalgic humiliation. "Hello," he says, "this one's new."

And he pulls out the little guinea pig in the Santa hat.

CHAPTER 24

SO THIS IS WEIRD.

Good weird, I think. Not bad weird.

Maybe bad weird.

I put my guinea pig on the tree with everybody else's, and me and Jonathan both make sure not to tell anybody we paid twelve quid for the thing. And the whole evening's just...nice. Quiet, or as quiet as it can get with that lot, and everything just working and fitting and making sense in a way I'm not really used to, or I've not been used to in a while.

And now I'm in bed. In Jonathan's room while he's downstairs trying to get comfortable on a sofa that's not really long enough for him and which honestly looks like it was picked for style by an overpaid interior designer and not comfort by somebody who actually expected to sit on the thing.

And I'm not sleeping.

I'm not sure if I'm feeling guilty or just—honestly I'm not sure what the just might be. Maybe Jonathan's bed is lumpy, except of course it isn't because he owns a chain of bed and bath retailers and he'd never sell a lumpy mattress, and he'd never use a mattress he wouldn't sell. He's changed the sheets for me, but I half-imagine I can still smell him—that Radox shower gel that doubles as a shampoo for men who are too busy to take even one and a half bottles into the shower, and the clean, sharp notes of his cologne. Whatever it is, though, I can't get comfy. And in the end I get up and creep downstairs, trying not to wake anybody else.

When I get to the bottom of the stairs, I hear voices. Not family voices, though. Mostly Geordie voices. Dimly *recognisable* Geordie voices, from the TV.

Then I do hear Les. "You're going to have to set us up with this digital telly."

"You've already got one."

"Aye, but we can't work it. You'll need to come round show us how to do the"—there's a gap in which I think it's likely Les is miming his failure to engage with technology—"you know, the app thing."

"I'm very b—" But Jonathan cuts himself off. "I'll swing by after the pipes are fixed."

"Or you could send Sam if you'd rather," says Les. "I'm sure he'd not mind, he's a good lad."

"I'm not sending Sam. He isn't my—I don't get to just send him places."

"I still think he'd not mind."

Another voice comes from the television. It's unmistakably Brummie and unmistakably Timothy Spall, and I take it as my opportunity to show myself and act like I've not been very mildly spying. "Don't mean to interrupt but are you watching *Auf Wiedersehen, Pet*?"

"You can join us if you'd like," offers Les.

Now I'm in the room, I can see them. They're both on the sofa, picking at an enormous bowl of mixed nuts that Wendy brought with her and insisted on laying out. Because apparently it's not Christmas without a bowl of mixed nuts.

I dither on the threshold in my pjs like a kid up past his bedtime. "I don't want to intrude. I couldn't sleep is all."

"It's been a busy day," says Jonathan. And I peer at his face, trying to work out if he's giving me *come in* eyes or *leave me alone with my dad* eyes, but he's giving me neither. So in the end I make my own decision and, not wanting to go and lie upstairs feeling restless and messed up, I come and sit down in the free armchair.

"I've not seen this in years," I say. "I used to watch it with my nan."

"Not recently, though?" asks Les.

"She passed away," I explain. Which is true, and long enough ago that remembering it doesn't spoil my amnesia story.

Les and Jonathan both reflexively *sorry* me and I reassure them that it happened a while back and at any rate she'd had a good run. Because it's what you say, isn't it? And she had.

We settle into the episode. And even though this is the first time I've seen Les and Jonathan spend more than six minutes together without things getting difficult, it feels familiar. Perhaps it's just that sitting in front of an '80s TV show long after the '80s are over is such a dad thing that it'd feel normal no matter who I was and no matter who they were. I'm pretty sure I could be on the international space station with an actual alien and the actual alien's zyborg pod-father and as long as we were watching old episodes of *'Allo 'Allo!* it'd still be the most natural thing in the world.

Every so often I lean forwards and grab myself a nut.

"It's funny," I say in the next ad break, "watching this post-Brexit. You don't often think of Brits being migrant workers."

Les gives one of those imperceptible shrugs that's often as close as he gets to body language. "Knew a lot of lads who did, back in the day. Even more in the early '90s. Lot of demand for construction with reunification."

"You ever go yourself?" I ask.

"No. Back then I was at—well it would have been British Steel in them days. And it paid better than construction."

I'd not intended to springboard off a forty-year-old comedy-drama series from the creator of *The Likely Lads* into a detailed discussion of Les's employment history, but what's done is done and I watch Jonathan closely for his reaction. Thing is, he's not having one. Least not one he's showing.

"And I suppose you didn't have to live in a hut with six other colourful characters," I say.

"And we got you home every night," adds Jonathan unexpectedly.

For a moment that just hangs there with variously-regionally-accented actors from the TV obliviously filling the silence with wry commentary on the legacy of Thatcherism. Then finally Les offers, "Aye. I made sure of that."

We none of us say anything else afterwards. We just finish up the episode then when it's done. Les stands and stretches.

"I can put on another if you like," suggests Jonathan.

But Les seems satisfied. "No thanks, son. I'm not sure I hold with this binge watching they do these days. Means things don't last." He carefully selects one final Brazil nut, chews it, and gives us both a little nod. "I'll leave you two to it."

It's not totally clear what *it* he thinks he's leaving us to, but he leaves us to it anyway. I slant a glance at Jonathan, on the off chance he knows how to handle being abruptly left with a bloke he's sort of living with and a herd of elephants. He's wearing what I think counts for sleepwear in the Casa de Forest—soft lounge trousers and a novelty T-shirt from his stash of novelty T-shirts, this one reading "I <3 Napoli" and sporting a picture of an Italian flag and a cartoon dog who's also inexplicably serving up a pizza. Seeing Jonathan like this is a bit like running into your dentist buying milk. In that it's objectively unremarkable but, somehow, completely mind-blowing.

"What?" he asks, to the point as ever.

"Nothing," I say. "It's just very hard to take you seriously when you've Chef McPooch on your chest."

His brows dip, though not quite as ferociously as usual. "Nanny Barb had a lovely holiday in Naples and got me this as a souvenir. Besides, did you really think I go to sleep in a suit, so my pillows know who's in charge?"

"Honestly? Yeah. A bit."

"Oh shush," he says, without rancour.

I let that settle, because we're on that border now between awkward and quite nice, and I don't want to tip it the wrong way. Jonathan draws up a knee, looking more relaxed than I've ever seen him. Especially because his hair's gone fluffy now he's combed it out and that. You can't tell when he's got it all locked down with whatever product he goes for, but it's the sort you really want to run your fingers through. Or grab onto.

Not wanting to ruin the moment is one thing. But I feel I should say something. And though I couldn't quite tell you why, the something I choose to say is, "Good of you. To let your family stay."

His mouth does that thing, which I'm coming to the conclusion might just be his smile. "Letting Mum and Dad stay was good of me. Letting BJ and Uncle Johnny come with them was fucking saintly."

I think, in a roundabout way, he's being self-deprecating. Which is to say, he's being arrogant but in a sarcastic tone of voice. "You could still have packed them off to a hotel. In fact, I thought you were going to."

"And I may yet." He softens slightly, at least by his standards. "But I thought about what you—about the conversation we had and"—the words don't seem to be causing him actual physical pain but they're getting close like—"you had a point."

"Sorry, what was that? I didn't hear you."

"I said you—oh very funny."

I'm grinning. I'm not sure I *should* be grinning, but I am. "No, go on, say it again. I need to preserve this moment."

"You had a point," he says firmly. "And I resent the implication that I'm somehow unwilling to give other people credit."

"I'm sure you think that's true, but to give someone credit for something you've got to let them do it first."

"Yes, yes, I'm terrible."

It feels almost mean to still be shocked that Jonathan did a nice thing, and I'm not really. It's not that I think he's, y'know, evil or anything. But he's just so fucking stubborn. "Seriously, though," I say. "You didn't have to listen to me."

"I know. It's—you were right. Sometimes it's important to know when you're beaten."

And now I feel slightly worse. "I wasn't trying to beat yez at anything. I was just—we were just talking."

Jonathan scratches Gollum behind the ears. "That's one way of putting it. Still, you said some things that I felt I should act on."

Make that a lot worse. Whatever the plan had been, however good it was to see him just lightening the fuck up, I'd not meant to get there by being this much of a dick to him. "This isn't about the whole 'I don't like you' thing, is it?"

"A little. But I'm not a child, I'm used to people disapproving of me."

In some ways, this is flattering. In other ways, it's making my guts wince. "But you care if I do? Approve of yez?"

"Apparently."

"Why?"

That only gets a shrug. "I have no idea." He looks down. "I think I blame the cat."

I'm still feeling like I've ate a bad nut. "You know I didn't mean it. I was just angry and that."

"But you were angry because I behaved—because I treated you—you were angry for a reason." He's focusing very intently on Gollum now. "And not a reason I liked."

My guts have stepped up from wincing to squirming. "Okay, but I reckon you had reasons to be angry with me too."

From the look he's giving me, Jonathan's genuinely not sure what I mean. Either that or he's just pretending. And if he is, then maybe I should just let him pretend. Only I don't want to, because what with the shower, and the firing, and the concussion, I don't want kissing him to be one more thing that never happened. So I take a shot at the elephant. "You know, because of—what I did." And then I realise I've done a fair bit I've done. "With my lips."

"I wasn't angry about that," he admits, with something perilously close to a squirm. "I was…it was hard for me to know how to react."

"I'm sorry."

Jonathan turns towards me suddenly enough that he startles Gollum out of his ensofaed complacency and onto the floor. "You don't have to be."

"I do. I messed up."

"You're injured. And I'm in a position of authority. That makes maintaining boundaries my responsibility."

He's sort of right. But he's also sort of very not. "I'm sure that's what the HR department would say. Thing is, I think it's more complicated than that. I really did know what I was doing. And I didn't feel, like, coerced or anything. I just—I got swept up in yez."

"Which I shouldn't have allowed to happen."

There he goes again. And it probably shows how much I'm losing my grip on the situation that I'm beginning to find it sweet instead of frustrating. "It's not about *allowing*. You can't control everything, Jonathan, and you certainly don't control me."

"No," says Jonathan dryly. "Apparently I don't."

And for a while we sit there, silent like. It turns out that shooting the elephant in the room just leaves you with a dead elephant, and a dead elephant takes up as much space as a live one, and has a tendency to smell.

Finally, Jonathan comes out with, "In any case, it can't happen again."

"No," I agree, "it can't."

But Jonathan Forest, true to form, isn't taking yes for an answer. "I mean it. We have to be sensible. We can't let ourselves get carried away."

"I'm not planning to," I protest. "I don't go around kissing everybody I meet."

"I wasn't suggesting you did."

"Seriously," I protest again, increasingly aware that protesting is something you can do too much of. "I know you're all tall dark and grumpy and everything. But I can keep my hands off you." Though now I'm saying it, I will admit that there's a tiny little voice in the back of my head saying *yeah, but what if you didn't, though*?

"Sam." He runs his fingers through his lovely, ruffled hair. "This is *difficult*."

It's not the reaction I'm expecting. I'm expecting him to just keep repeating the same thing to me about nine times like he's trying to upsell me a protection and service plan. "What do you mean?" I ask.

"Don't be obtuse," he snarls, swinging back full Jonathan.

"I'm not being obtuse. You're being evasive."

"Well, what am I supposed to say? That living with you is—that you are—that I can't." He tries again. "That this is—" And promptly gives up.

I turn to stare at him, not quite incredulous but near enough you can see it on sign posts. "Jonathan, are trying to say that you're into me?"

"How can I not be?" He flops forward with his elbows on his knees and his brow against his fingertips. "You've come into my life like a beam of very annoying sunshine. You talk so much that I miss it when you're not. You try to fix things I didn't even realise were broken. You have a dreadful sense of humour to which I've somehow become habituated. You care about people so effortlessly it makes me able to put up with them. And then you kissed me and now I..." He lets his head slip further down into his hands. "...I don't know how I'm supposed to go the rest of my life without being kissed by you again."

It's so typical of Jonathan Forest that, even when he's telling me he likes me, I feel a little bit like I'm being insulted. Or maybe my brain's just gone there because I don't know how to process this. Any of this. "Well, you don't have to," I say. "I'm right here."

"I'm very aware that you're *here*," Jonathan snaps back. "I'm also very aware that you're an employee."

I'm also an employee who's lying to him about having amnesia to buy time to get him to like me. Except now it's worked and that's messed up in ways I didn't really think through even if it does save the branch. Worse still, it's worked back. Because I'm sort of on his side now as well. He's become more than my dickhead boss. He's become my dickhead boss whose baggage I've seen, whose family I know, whose laugh I've heard. And I'm not sure I want to go my whole life without kissing him again either.

"What if we just said I wasn't?" I try. "Just for a minute like."

"That isn't how it works."

"Says who?"

He looks up, his eyes all dark and shiny, like Whitby jet. "Says everyone, Sam. Says the law."

"Okay, but everyone's not here. We are. And what harm can it do really?" This is incredibly bad of me. I should not be doing this. Problem is, I can't stop myself. What with one thing and another,

I haven't had room to…to feel like this. Not for a long time. And now I do, I can't let go of it. Can't give it up. "If it's just this once," I keep trying. "Get it out of our systems."

"That's not going to work."

"It's better than the alternative."

"Of what?" he asks. "Of us behaving like sensible adults?"

"You've been a sensible adult your whole life, Jonathan. Where's it got you?"

He gives me one of his two-fifths smiles. "I suppose this is not the time to remind you that I've been very successful in the highly specific sphere of bed and bathroom retailing?"

"Yeah, but if you can't get kissed by who you want to get kissed by, what's the point?"

"Sam," he says, and it comes out a little bit of a sigh, and a little bit surrender. "This can't be what you want. Not really."

I'm pretty sure he means *he* can be what I want, but he's too proud to say it. "It is," I tell him. "You are."

There's this pause that stretches out like Blu Tack. And then Jonathan Forest's in my lap, kissing me so hard it knocks the breath from me.

"Sorry," he says. "I'm not very—"

Sliding a hand into his hair, like I've been wanting to forever, I kiss him back before he can finish. And then it's like he's trying to kiss me with every kiss he's ever had or ever will have. I suppose I should have expected Jonathan Forest would take the "get it out of our systems" thing far too seriously.

"Ow," I mumble.

And Jonathan draws back, looking flushed and abashed at the same time. "I did warn you. I…" He glances away. "I'm a little out of practice."

"Yeah, you do keep mentioning how busy you are."

He's still glancing away. It's sort of adorable actually, how he's gone from smacking into me like a truck hitting bollard to not being able to meet my eye. "The truth is, I've not had many long-term relationships, and I don't find casual sex particularly interesting, so I don't...really...that much at all."

I do get where he's coming from because I've not exactly been Mr Party Boy myself the last couple of years. But it's like riding a bike, isn't it? You do enough of it in your late teens, it sticks with you. "Well," I suggest, "how about we take it slow?"

"I said I didn't find casual sex particularly interesting"—coy Jonathan has very much left the building—"not that I'm sweet sixteen and never been kissed."

"Aye, but you don't have to go at it like you're making up for lost time, is all I'm saying."

He glares at me. "Then how do you want me to go at it?"

Not like that seems a bit harsh. It wasn't that it'd been bad. It'd just been a bit...much. Besides, if this is the only time I get to kiss Jonathan Forest, I've got to make sure it's everything it can possibly be. "How about," I suggest, "you take a breath and let me go at you for a bit."

"You make that sound so alluring."

I laugh. "Just shut up and let me kiss you."

And, to my surprise, he does. Though I don't kiss him straight away. I just get him tucked comfortably on my lap and brush my fingertips along his jaw and the bridge of his nose.

He shies very slightly. "What are you doing?"

"I'm appreciating you."

"I own a mirror. There's not much to appreciate."

"Oh, come on," I say. "I love looking at you."

Scepticism settles over Jonathan's face like frost over the lawn. "We might need to take you back to the doctors."

"I mean it. I'm not claiming you're Henry Cavill. But that doesn't mean there's nothing to like. Y'know, visually."

"Sam." He comes over all stern or tries to. I think he might be embarrassed. "This is very nice and I don't mean to be ungrateful. But we have limited time and I don't need to..." He waves a confused hand between us. "Need whatever it is you think you're doing here."

"You don't need someone to treat you nice?"

"If I did, I'd be fucked. In case you haven't noticed, there are very few volunteers."

"Well, I'm volunteering."

"Yes, but..." He closes his eyes, looking genuinely pained. "This can't last. I can't get used to this."

My heart feels like someone's jammed a corkscrew into it and started twisting, because the last thing I want to do is hurt him. I started out thinking I was being slightly selfish here but maybe I'm being very selfish. Even very, very selfish. "We can stop if you—"

"No." His hands tighten in my T-shirt.

"I don't want to make you feel—"

"I don't care."

So I kiss him again. I kiss him the way he's maybe scared to be kissed and the way I think he deserves to be kissed. I kiss him softly, then deeply, letting it flow between us, natural like, all heat and hope and tenderness, as if he's the best thing that's happened to me in a long while. And Jonathan Forest forgets, for a moment—for more than a moment—that he's a hard man who doesn't have time for anyone. Because in my arms he's as generous, as kind, as giving and as open as I need him to be.

I should have listened to him, though. We can't get used to this. Unfortunately, I think I already am. And what's waiting for me on the other side is looking very bleak indeed.

CHAPTER 25

IT'S EVEN HARDER TO SLEEP in Jonathan's bed now we've, y'know, kissed again, and in a less oh-my-God-this-was-a-mistake way than last time. Mind you, it's a better sort of sleeplessness than the one I started the evening with. I'd gone downstairs with the intention of telling him that he didn't have to the take the sofa, but we parted on the understanding that he definitely, definitely did because while we can make a one-time-kissing exception, that's as far as things can go while the employee thing and the amnesia thing and all the other things are still, well, things.

I try to shut my eyes for a couple of minutes at least, but the moment the sunlight starts creeping in the windows I decide I might as well give it up as a bad job and make a start on the day. Which turns out to be very much the path of least resistance because the Forests—and I should have predicted this—are all very much make-a-start-on-the-day type of people, and they tend to make their starts very, very loudly.

"Tell you what," Wendy is yelling from one part of downstairs to a different part of downstairs, though yelling in one part of a house is like smoking in one part of a restaurant or pissing in one part of a swimming pool, "them showers is well good in't they?"

"Like a bloody hotel," agrees Uncle Johnny.

I hear the sound of water running as the downstairs taps come on, and then Wendy's voice saying, "You don't have to do that," followed by a voice that I'm pretty sure is Agnieszka's saying something about it being her job.

"Here"—that's Uncle Johnny's voice again—"how many eggs does young Johnny want?"

"Jonathan, how many eggs do you want?" relays Wendy.

"...will be fine..." Jonathan's reply is quieter, although not so much quieter that I can't hear most of it by the time I make my way into the front room. "And can you please keep your voices down? Sam's probably still asleep."

I emerge from the stairway to find the whole family engaging in some unfathomably complex breakfast operation involving multiple frying pans, everyone swapping mugs like it's *Alice in Wonderland*, and an awful lot of shouting at people too close to need shouting at.

"See"—Wendy beams triumphantly when she sees me—"he's up like the rest of us and he'll be wanting breakfast."

"How many eggs?" asks Uncle Johnny.

"Two," I say. From the look of him it's the lowest answer he'll accept.

"Do him three," Wendy insists. "He's a growing boy."

"I'm not sure I am," I tell her.

Barbara Jane, who is clutching her coffee like it's the One Ring and seems to be the only member of her family who isn't a morning person, gives me a nod. "What you've done, Mum, is confuse Sam with Gaston from *Beauty and the Beast*."

Wendy looks affronted. "What, the candlestick?"

"That was Lumiere," says Jonathan.

"Then who was the clock?" asks Uncle Johnny.

Agnieszka looks up from the sink where she's still engaged in a small tussle with Wendy over whose job it is to clean the mugs. "Cogsworth. The teapot was Mrs Potts. I don't think any of the other furniture had names." She gets thoughtful. "Except Fifi, the feather duster with whom it's strongly implied Lumiere is in a sexual relationship."

"Well, I don't know," says Wendy, with a sad shake of her head. "I can't keep up."

"She can't keep up," echoes Les. "But I think Barbara Jane's right, love, if he wants two eggs he should have two eggs or the last'll just go to waste."

"Sausages?" asks Uncle Johnny.

Jonathan, my knight in shining pinstripes, sweeps to the rescue. "What if you just give him two of everything?"

Uncle Johnny gives a grin that on a younger man would look impish. "Right so two eggs, two sausages, two hash browns, two rashers of bacon, two slices of black pudding, and two baked beans."

"A *regular* helping of baked beans," Jonathan corrects him. "And probably two slices of toast?"

I agree because at this stage agreeing is by far the quickest option. "Where did we even get all of this?"

Jonathan heaves a sigh that's more long-suffering than he's really entitled to given he's not been suffering very long "They went out this morning."

"Well, you had nothing in," Wendy tells him. Then she immediately tells me: "He had nothing in."

That gets an in-the-know nod from Agnieszka. "He never does. I've been cleaning this kitchen for years. I don't think that refrigerator has ever been used."

"In our defence," I point out, "we weren't expecting company. And the fridge is getting used now, it's packed full of Christmas stuff."

Uncle Johnny turns briefly from the hob. "Still no excuse not to have black pudding."

From her perch at the end of the breakfast table, Barbara Jane is still looking like she's resenting every second of this. "Does anybody actually *like* black pudding?"

"Too good for black pudding, now is she?" Uncle Johnny asks the room in general.

"*Everybody* is too good for black pudding." Barbara Jane goes back to the kettle and starts making herself another coffee, though I don't think it'll help her much. "Who in their right mind makes a sausage out of blood if they've got the option to make it out of literally anything else."

"Isn't pretty much everything you put in a sausage awful?" I ask. "At least with blood you can narrow it down."

She looks genuinely nauseated. "Fair point. Just toast for me, Johnny."

"Have some bacon." Uncle Johnny pokes at the contents of the bacon pan, which are sizzling invitingly. "You need feeding up."

"Why?" The expression in Barbara Jane's face would've curdled the milk in her coffee if she didn't take it black. "Are you going to sell me at auction?"

Somehow passing up the opportunity to speculate how much his sister would fetch on the open market, Jonathan grabs a plate and heads for the condiments. "I might go the toast route as well."

"What is up with your kids, Les?" asks Uncle Johnny, apparently bemused at the state of an entire generation. "Didn't you teach them to appreciate a proper breakfast?"

Jonathan pauses mid-butter. "I can't say what's wrong with BJ—at least not in less than an hour—but I do need to get to work."

Uncle Johnny, it seems, isn't letting the slight against his breakfast craft go so lightly. "Aren't you the boss? Can't you show up when you like?"

While Jonathan is preparing his reply, I step in. "He needs to set an example. It's no good telling the staff to be on time if he doesn't get in punctual himself."

My intent is to help. I don't.

Uncle Johnny turns to his nephew with an at least appropriately avuncular look on his face. "No, no, no." He puts his hands on Jonathan's shoulders and spins him around to face him. Since Jonathan's still making toast, this means he comes very close to sticking his uncle with a butter knife. "What you want to do my lad, is say *I'm in charge and you're not, you'll do as I say not as I do.*"

With a patience that, given who we're dealing with here, borders on grace, Jonathan nods. "I'll bear that in mind."

"Sorry"—Barbara Jane has come over now, mostly to nick the jam—"how many businesses have you run, uncle?"

"A few."

"I said *run*, not *run into the ground*."

Taking advantage of the distraction, Jonathan swipes his toast and makes for the door, but Wendy stops him as he's getting his coat.

"Here," she calls after him, "when're you going to get Nana Pauline?"

"Tomorrow." And then he stops and looks at me. It's sort of the first time he has since last night—it's hard to have a what-does-what-happened-mean-and-what-happens-next moment when a man in a checkered shirt is asking you how much black pudding you want—and now there's a sort of quiet between us. A quiet that's still filled by people going on about eggs, bacon, and how Barbara Jane needs to get some baked beans down her neck, but a quiet even so. "I—Sam, I should have said, I'm going to need to go to Sheffield to pick up my grandmother and, well…"

"And he wants to know," says Les, "if you'd rather spend five hours in a car with him, or a day in the house with us."

Barbara Jane has gone back to her seat at the kitchen table.

"Oh well done, Dad. You realise that means whichever he picks he'll feel like he's insulted someone."

"Oh no, we won't be insulted," cries Wendy. "We won't be insulted, will we, Les? Whichever he picks is fine with us."

"Assuming," adds Barbara Jane, "that Jonathan trusts us to stay in his house unsupervised. Well"—she shoots Uncle Johnny a sharp look—"I say *us*."

"I resent that," Uncle Johnny replies.

"And you won't be unsupervised," adds Agnieszka. "Don't worry, Mr Forest, I'll keep an eye on them. Although I may have to ask for acting up pay."

Jonathan has his coat fully on now. "Don't push it. I'm not totally convinced you aren't on their side anyway."

"Listen to him," Wendy says to no-one in particular, "talking about sides where his own family is involved."

"He's a bad son, Mrs Forest," Agnieszka agrees.

"I *also*," Jonathan turns to me in a desperate effort to change the subject, "thought you might—it might help us to see if your memory has got any better. I was going to take the opportunity to check in on the Sheffield branch while I was there anyway and we could see if you recognise any of your co-workers."

Fuck. If I really had amnesia, that would be a fantastic idea. Such a fantastic idea that saying no sounds sus as fuck. Plus I'm not sure I *want* to say no. Even with the risk of getting rumbled, just having some time away with Jonathan to—though that's where it all falls apart. Time to *what*? To say *you know that thing we very specifically said was a onetime deal, well how about we admit that was bollocks*?

Fuck.

"Yeah," I say. "Yeah, I'll come with yez. It might help."

"*And* you'll get to meet Pauline," adds Wendy. "She's a right love is Pauline. And she'll be very pleased to meet *you*."

I've given up protesting that me and Jonathan aren't dating. For a start it's increasingly feeling like a lie. Which is ironic really, because it's one of the few things I've told them that's actually true.

Johnny does another fry-up next morning, and this time Jonathan does hang around for the full eggs, sausage, bacon, hash browns, baked beans, black pudding, fried mushrooms, grilled tomatoes combination because unlike most days, he's not headed into the Croydon branch to yell at his staff. Instead he's going to come up to Sheffield with me, so as he can yell at my staff. Something he's warned them he's planning to do because while Jonathan Forest the Boss is exactly the kind of man to pull a surprise inspection from head office, Jonathan Forest the Concussed Person Taker Care Ofer is a bit more considerate. Which bodes well for Claire and them. But not so well for me and my increasing sense of being in over my head.

Barbara Jane is still on the toast, mind, and Wendy is insisting on running the hoover around the living room.

"Should I ask why?" Jonathan asks her over the noise as we're finishing our fry-ups.

"Well, Agnieszka's coming later, and I want to make sure the place looks nice for her."

Jonathan shakes his head. "She's a housekeeper, Mum. Making the place look nice is what she's paid to do."

That's not washing with Wendy. "That don't mean you want her to think you live with grubby carpets."

Not seeing much point in pressing the issue, we say goodbye to the family, who all insist we send their best wishes to Nana Pauline even though they'll see her themselves in a couple of days, and we jump in the car around ten, hoping to reach Sheffield by three.

No sooner have we jumped than I realise what a poor idea this was. It's not the first time we've done the drive, but it's the first time since I kissed him, we got really scratchy about me kissing him, and then I kissed him again in a slightly more negotiated way. So it's not really clear how we're supposed to interact when we're trapped next to each other for five hours.

We have to go south to get north because of how driving through London is like swimming through treacle in winter, and we don't say a word to each other until we hit the M25.

"It'll be nice," I say into the silence, "to meet your other nan."

"Yes." Jonathan doesn't look at me. I mean, obviously he doesn't because he's looking at the road. But somehow he looks at the road even harder.

We drive on.

"And it'll maybe be nice to see where I work," I add. Because what I'm hoping is that once we get there, I can start remembering some more stuff and it won't look too suspicious. And then maybe I can dig myself out of this awful amnesia hole.

"Yes," agrees Jonathan.

I bite my lip. This is going to be difficult. "I'd not have—I didn't think—we sort of agreed things wouldn't be awkward."

"They're not awkward," Jonathan says while staring straight ahead of him in about the most awkward way you possibly could.

"They're a bit awkward."

"I'm just trying to stay alert because it's a long drive."

Everything goes quiet again.

"We can talk," I try. "You won't spin off the road if we talk."

Jonathan's hands tense slightly on the steering wheel. "Of course not." He flicks a cautious glance in my direction. "What would you like to talk about?"

Conversation, in my experience, doesn't really work like that. I do my best anyway. "Okay, can we start by acknowledging that we kissed, and it was great, but since we both agree it can't happen again while I work for yez, we should just try and enjoy the road trip?"

He gives a tiny nod but doesn't say anything more.

And he carries on not saying anything more for a while. In desperation I resort to remarking on things I see out the window. "Ooh look," I try, "cows."

"Yes."

"Do you reckon they're Friesians?"

At last, he risks turning his head, if only to check out the cattle. "Aren't Friesians the black and white ones?"

"Maybe. So what are the big beige ones?"

"Jerseys?"

"So what about the brown shaggy ones then?"

"Steaks," says Jonathan.

Which makes me laugh. Which makes him laugh.

"Are you really," he asks, "going to make small talk about cows for"—he checks the clock on the dashboard—"the next four hours?"

"I'll admit," I admit, "I am running low on cow banter."

"Don't worry. You might see a sheep next."

"You are not prepared," I tell him, "for my amusing sheep anecdotes."

He slants another look at me. "Go on. Amuse me with a sheep."

"Okay." I think about it for a second or two. "I might have oversold the amusingness and, indeed, quantity of my sheep stories. Because I did grow up in Liverpool where sheep are a bit thin on the ground. Not a massive urban animal, the sheep. Nor are they especially native to the Mersey."

"I'd imagine not. They'd have to learn to breathe underwater and eat kebab wrappers."

"Oi," I protest. "Don't you be having a go at the Mersey. You don't see me having a go at the Thames."

"Feel free. It's basically a giant open sewer."

"Aye, but it's *your* open sewer. You should feel proud of that sewer."

"And you're proud of the Mersey?"

"Of course I'm proud of the Mersey."

"Isn't that also a giant open sewer?" Jonathan asks.

"No," I say firmly. "It's only that shade of brown because it's got strong currents that whip up dirt from the bottom."

"That's bollocks, Sam."

"It's not. Best river in England is the Mersey. It could take the Avon in a fight."

His mouth curls up contemptuously. "Any river could take the Avon. It's a prissy southern wuss."

"Okay, but it could take the Thames too."

"Well, of course it could. The Thames is an old man. He's very tough but he's not got the stamina he used to."

This is a side of Jonathan I've not seen before. Although, to be fair, I'm not sure under what circumstances you'd ordinarily get to see the "what rivers could beat what other rivers in fights" side of a person. "I'll say this, mind, I reckon the Tyne could give it a run for its money. It'd have to cheat, but it fucking would."

"Oh, the Tyne would glass you as soon as look at you."

We fall silent again at this point, but it's a much easier silence. And that brings advantages and disadvantages. Because, on the one hand, it's less tense and that's good. But on the other it reminds me how much I like being with him. It makes me wish he could let himself be this man more often, with more people. Don't get me wrong, he's still a sour bastard. It's just sour isn't necessarily bad. That's why everybody likes sherbet lemons.

"Should I stick the radio on?" I ask.

"Go ahead."

Leaning forward, I push the button, which tunes immediately

to Heart FM. And I'm not quite prepared for the bolt of not-exactly-nostalgia that rips through me. The thing about Heart FM is that it's the country's most basic radio station—it's even more basic than Radio 1—and so it's exactly what you want when you're driving out to Rainhill on a job and the weather's living up to its name. I'm sort of surprised and not surprised that it's Jonathan's choice as well. Surprised because it's feel-good music and, until recently, I'd have said Jonathan doesn't enjoy feeling good. Not surprised because he probably grew up on it just like I did. Right now, Bruno Mars is singing about how I'm amazing just the way I am, which is very sweet of him.

Jonathan gives longest road-safe look he can. "Are you all right?"

"Yeah. No. I mean, why not?"

"You seem to be surprisingly affected by Bruno Mars."

"Well, y'know. He's a talented man."

"Sam."

I sigh. "It just reminds me of home, y'know. In a"—sometimes having amnesia is really convenient—"foggy kind of way."

"How is your memory?"

At least he's not asking for details. "Honestly, I think it is getting better. Little bits are coming back. Some family stuff, some work stuff."

There's a pause. Then Jonathan clears his throat and it dawns on me he's trying to be tactful. "I'm increasingly concerned that nobody has checked up on you."

Fuck, I don't want to have to talk about any of this. "Didn't you speak to the store since I'm on medical leave?"

"I wasn't talking about work."

I give him a grin that I hope is distractingly cheeky. "There's a first time for everything, isn't there?"

"I mean it. I'd have expected somebody to be looking for you by now. If I went missing for a fortnight, my mum would have personally visited every hospital, police station, and undertakers in the South East."

"Undertakers?"

"She likes to have her bases covered."

"Well, I suppose I just don't have that kind of—" I don't want to go here, I really don't want to go here. "You know, not everybody's close with their parents."

That shuts Jonathan up a minute. "Sorry," he says eventually. It's maybe the second time I've heard him say it, and in a funny way it's a much nicer time to hear it. "I suppose I—it's like you said, when you've got a family like mine you take it for granted. Are you—if it's something you wanted to talk about…"

"It's hard to remember," I say. It's not a lie, exactly.

"Of course."

It's odd, the different textures silences can have. This one feels—it's odd. I'm not sure I can put a name on it exactly. Caring almost. Perhaps even supportive.

Jonathan taps the touch screen of the onboard computer that I'm still thinking of as a radio. "I can pick a different station if you like?"

It's a kind offer, and one I turn over a moment before deciding if I want to take it. "No. No it's all right."

Bruno gives way to Katy Perry, who's telling us all about how she's got the eye of the tiger and that. And Jonathan Forest, in what I can only describe as a titanic breach of character, starts singing along. Not only that but he's quite good.

"Big fan, are yez?" I ask.

He casts a sidelong look at me, half smiling, half—and I'm not sure how I feel about this—still clearly wondering why I've not been looked for yet. "It gets played a lot, and the nice thing about this song is it's basically all chorus."

So I join in—though unlike Jonathan I'm *not* quite good. I'm not even almost good. But I like to think I make up for it with enthusiasm. And we just keep going. Through Katy, into Justin Bieber, David Guetta, Olly Murs, and The Script. I'm doing that in-the-car kind of singing along where you find out two lines in that you don't know the words half as well as you thought you did, and just find yourself going "murmurmur manana something" then belting out the title of the song really loudly in the hope that it'll make up for how badly you botched the rest of it.

We keep on like that for hours. Literal hours. 'Til we're both hoarse and slightly sick of relentlessly feel-good music. And Jonathan doesn't ask me any more questions about my family, or my dad, or why they haven't come trying to find me or anything. He just lets me sit with him and mime along to Rita Ora while we bomb past Nottingham on the M1. And when he lip-syncs "I Will Never Let You Down" with me, I weirdly believe him.

Because I don't think he would.

Because when we're like this, I'm happy.

CHAPTER 26

A LONG BUT EVENTUALLY PLEASANT road trip later we arrive at the Sheffield branch and Claire meets us at the door.

"Mr Forest"—she shakes his hand firmly-but-not-too-firmly—"and Sam." She gives me a look that I don't think could have been more conspiratorial if she'd done an exaggerated cartoon wink. "Do you…do you remember me?"

Right, Sam. Acting time. "Maybe," I say. "Is it—it's on the tip of my tongue."

"Claire," says Claire. "I'm extremely good at my job and you'd agreed to give me a massive raise just before you had your accident."

It's no different from the banter we'd usually have, but we're in work mode now, and that means fun Jonathan has left the building. Not just left it, burned it down behind him. "I hope not," he says. "I originally invited Sam to London because this branch has serious budgetary issues."

The thing about Claire is that although she's got no time for knobheads, bellends, or dickheads, she does have a good sense for when to stop pushing it. "Just a joke, Mr Forest. We're all falling behind inflation like the rest of the country. And while it's been a bit rough without Sam, I do think we're on track to meet our goals for the quarter."

"Glad to hear it." Jonathan nods. When he's in this mode, words like *on track* and *quarter* calm him down like a cup of hot cocoa. In fact, he's so calm that he flips straight back to his visiting boss routine. "What's going to happen now," he explains, "is that I'm going to take a tour of the shop floor, then you and I are going to have a talk about the situation going forwards." He stops and looks round at me. "Also somebody might need to look after Sam. He can get tired easily."

"Oh, *can he*?" Claire sounds unhelpfully sceptical.

"Well, you know," I tell her, "head wounds are funny things."

I join Jonathan for the first part of the shop tour, hoping that I can help steer him away from the worst parts of it and towards the bits that are at least reasonably presentable. And Claire, for all her irreverence, has a similar plan. Which is probably why the first person we meet on our seemingly random walk is New Enthusiastic Chris.

Even at this time on a Tuesday, the showroom's pretty busy what with people having a bit of time off and it being the season of living beyond your means. So there's no shortage of customers, and New Enthusiastic Chris is New Enthusiasticing up a storm right now.

"This," he's saying to the young couple he's managed to collar—him with half-rimmed glasses, her with blue hair, them both with the kind of vintage wardrobe that says they've got more money than they're letting on—"I'll admit it's not our most popular model, but while it's not for everybody, I *think* it'll be for you."

He leads them to a seldom-trod corner of the beds department, and taps the foot of the Drift Gaming Ottoman Bed Frame. A flatscreen TV rises out of a concealed panel.

"It comes in double, small double if you're tight on space, or king if you want the luxury. You can upgrade the thirty-two inch to a forty-three inch. It's an Ottoman so there's storage underneath, plus compartments for consoles, along with USB ports in both sides."

He's picked his marks right. Whatever else I might say about New Enthusiastic Chris, he's very good at his job.

"I mean," says her with the blue hair, "that *is* pretty cool."

"What worries me," says him with the glasses, "is that we'd never get out of bed."

She gives him a grin. "You say that like it's a bad thing."

"It's one seven nine nine," says New Enthusiastic Chris, glossing over the price tag to move on to other things, "and we can install it for you for a small extra charge, plus there's a matching bedside chest if you want to complete the look, and if you need a new mattress as well then we can work out a deal on the bundle, and you'll save on delivery and installation."

They talk amongst themselves a moment, but I can see they're going to go for it. And I take it as a bit of a Christmas miracle, because honestly the Sheffield branch doesn't shift very many beds with built-in smart TVs. Especially not in-store because almost by definition the people who want a dedicated gaming bed do most of their shopping online.

And with the power of his newness and enthusiasm, New Enthusiastic Chris upsells them to the king, and to the forty-three inch.

"Now," he says just as he's sealing the deal, "can I interest you in a protection and service plan?"

I risk a glance up at Jonathan to see how he's taking this, and I'm almost jealous, because he's looking at New Enthusiastic Chris like he practically wants to do him. Still, it reflects well on the store, so I can't resent it too much.

Certainly I can't resent it as much as I resent what happens next. Because Brian runs up to me shouting "Sam, Sam", and it takes me a moment to remember that I can at least respond to my name without blowing my cover.

I turn, to see him looking a mix of flustered and mortified. "Sam," he says again.

I try to look convincingly blank. "I'm sorry," I tell him, "I'm not sure who you are."

"He's got *amnesia* remember?" Claire waggles her eyebrows in a way I really think isn't helping.

"Oh," he says, "right. But the thing is, Sam. There's trouble in bathrooms."

I've said "what sort of trouble" before I can stop myself, and I hope the sheer weariness in my tone doesn't tip Jonathan off that I've been dealing with this for years.

Brian spends about eighteen seconds pulling an I'm-not-sure-I-can-say face. Then he finally explains. "Some kid's took a dump in one of the display models."

It is not, I think, Sheffield's finest hour. But it is also decidedly not the Sheffield branch's *fault*. It's just one of the unfortunate facts of selling toilets that sometimes people poo in them.

With what I almost think is chivalry, Jonathan insists that he'll deal with the dumping incident personally but that I should take the opportunity to rest on account of the long trip and my head. So while Jonathan and Brian head off to handle the faeces—not literally, like—Claire takes me for a sit down in the staff room.

It turns out there's not much space to sit down in the staff room, because it's full up with decorations that Tiff's bought for the Christmas party.

"Why are these here?" I ask.

"Well, where else are we going to put them?" Tiff's giving me that defiant look.

"Stockroom?" I suggest.

"Thing about the stockroom," says Claire, "full of stock."

"And when Jonathan comes in here and sees all of this?" I ask.

Tiff shrugs. "We'll tell him the company double-delivered for the store displays."

Briefly, I wonder whether I should be concerned at how quickly Tiff can come up with a plausible lie, but it's not the issue right now. "And when he sees the exact same decorations at the Christmas party?"

"You'll point out Christmas decorations are mass-produced in factories?" suggests Amjad, who's just finishing up his tea in the corner.

I shake my head. "Jonathan's a details guy. He'll notice, and then he'll get suspicious, and then he'll realise that I've been swindling him for the best part of a month and he'll be extremely pissed off and I won't entirely blame him."

The door opens and for a heart-stopping second I think it's Jonathan, but it's Brian. Which is almost as bad, but only almost.

"Oh hello," he says. "Sam, this is Tiff, Claire, and Amjad who you'll not remember."

"I know," I tell him. "I've not actually got amnesia."

"Have you not?" He looks bemused.

Claire sighs. "We've already explained this, Brian. Sam didn't lose his memory, he just had to pretend to so as to buy us some time before His Royal Dickishness shuts us all down."

"Oh, right." Brian looks grave. "And why's he doing that?"

Having finished his tea, Amjad rinses his mug out and leaves it on the sink to drain. "From what I've heard, Sam refused to fire any of us, so Jonathan threatened to fire all of us. It's classic brinksmanship. Like the Cuban Missile crisis but with bidets."

Slowly catching up, Brian's expression of gravity only deepens. "That doesn't seem very fair. Who did Mr Forest want to sack?"

"Me," says Tiff, "because I'm too young to have any employment rights." Technically that's not quite his reasoning; his reasoning was that she was never at bloody work, which in retrospect was at least a bit my fault. "And you." She flicks her hair vaguely in Brian's direction. "Because you're incredibly shit at your job."

He thinks about that for a moment, then nods cheerily. "Makes sense. Amjad, can I just nip past you and grab some kitchen roll and disinfectant. Poo situation."

Obligingly—or perhaps just not-wanting-to-get-into-a-poo-situation-ly—Amjad steps aside and lets Brian retrieve an armful of cleaning supplies from under the sink.

"Brian," I add when he's emerged, "we're serious about this, yeah? I know it's a big ask but Jonathan seems to have chilled out on the whole firing people front and so it's really, really important that we keep a lid on things."

I'm not particularly reassured by the way he smiles. He smiled like that when I told him the code for the alarm and explained why carrying coffee across the showroom floor was a bad idea.

"I mean it," I say. "Ixnay on the oesntday eallyray avehay amnesiaay."

This *definitely* makes it worse. He shakes his head like a confused Labrador. "Sorry, Sam, I've very much lost you."

I sigh. "Don't let Jonathan know I remember stuff. Just clean up the poo and keep your mouth shut."

"Probably good advice for cleaning up poo in general, to be honest," Amjad points out, nudging the cleaning cabinet closed with his knee.

And Brian smiles again, and I get that sinking feeling that he's going to Brian all over things somehow. If not today, then tomorrow, and if not tomorrow, then just as I'm standing at the airport with Ilsa Lund.

At last, he goes, and I turn to the others in the hope we can have at least a couple of things go right today. "Okay, that's the literal pile of shit dealt with—"

Tiff smirks. "Don't talk about Brian that way."

It feels very unfair that teenagers get to make dad jokes without looking uncool. "You know what I mean," I tell her. "But can we please focus on *this*." I wave my hands at the pile of fairy lights and tinsel. "What are we going to do with it?"

Claire looks contemplative. "Whack a blanket over the top?"

"Have you got a very large blanket just lying around?" I ask her.

This doesn't impress Claire one little bit. "Are you sure you don't really have amnesia? This is a bed and bath superstore. We've got walls full of blankets."

"So the plan is to pinch a Brentfords Super Ultra Soft Flannel Fleece from out of bedding, then hope that when Jonathan comes in he doesn't say *hey, what're you hiding underneath that Brentfords Super Ultra Soft Flannel Fleece*?"

"Don't be silly." Claire is giving me a scornful look. "The Brentfords Super Ultra Soft Flannel Fleece would be much too small."

"Yeah," agrees Amjad, "you want the Dreamscene luxury large waffle honeycomb. They go all the way up to two by two and a half meters."

Tiff adopts a doubtful face. "You'll crush the tinsel."

"Crushing the tinsel, Tiffany," I say, "is not currently my largest concern. My largest concern is Jonathan finding out we've scammed him and sacking the lot of us."

"Well, if the tinsel gets crushed," Tiff points out, "the Christmas party will suck, and he'll decide you were a bad manager this whole time. So we're sort of fucked either way."

"And to be fair," adds Amjad, "if the plan is to demonstrate how well run the Sheffield branch is, the fact that Jonathan's presently dealing with somebody having shat in a display toilet probably isn't helping matters."

"That was beyond our control," I say, hoping the new reasonable Jonathan will also see it that way.

Amjad gives a little grimace. "Still not a great look, though, is it?"

It's not. But something else is nagging at me. "Wait a minute. If this is for the Christmas party, how are you going to get it to London?"

Tiff gives the kind of shrug that inspires less confidence in others than the shrugger clearly has in themselves. "Work something out."

"What?"

"Something."

As plans go, it's not one I feel much like relying on. "Can you at least get a van?"

There's something about the enthusiasm with which Tiff says *sure* which makes me suspect I'm missing a trick. "Hold on," I say, "how old do you have to be to rent a van these days?"

"Twenty-three," Amjad tells me, and for once I'm glad he sat down one day and memorised literally every fact.

"I can do twenty-three," Tiff reassures me.

Claire pats her gently on the shoulder. "Tiffany, love, be very careful who you say that to."

"And you can't," I add. "I'm not letting you defraud a van rental company with work money. We'll have to use mine."

"Yours?" Now Claire's giving me a suspicious look. "You never told me you had a van."

I didn't. And there's reasons I didn't, but I don't want to go into them so I try to laugh it off. "How will you forgive me for keeping such a terrible secret? Anyway, I don't see we've got another option. I'll let Jonathan know that I'll not be coming back with him tomorrow, and I'll swing by here instead, drive you back to London with"—I wave a hand at the decorations—"all of *this*, and we can work out what to do from there."

Nobody seems entirely sold on this plan, and Claire seems weirdly hung up on the Great Never-Said-You-Had-A-Van betrayal, but there's no more ideas forthcoming.

"Right"—I clap my hands in a doomed effort to seem decisive—"I'm going to find Jonathan. Somebody should probably come with me so we don't have to explain how I suddenly know my way around, and we'll stop him coming in here by any means necessary."

"Ah," Claire brightens up, "we're back on operation kill him with a toilet seat."

"No," I say very firmly. Though I like to think Claire wouldn't really go to murder that quickly, I know her just well enough that I can't rule it out. "But there's still a poo situation ongoing, and the good thing about hygiene emergencies is that they sometimes take a while to sort out, so that might see us through to close of play."

"Every poo has a silver lining," says Tiff, ever in touch with her inner philosopher.

Amjad shakes his head. "If your poo has a silver lining, see a doctor."

Leaving the younger staff members to discuss the finer nuances of an unplumbed lavvy full of shit that I was too old and set in my ways to consider, I took Claire to intercept Jonathan.

To his, New Enthusiastic Chris's, and even—I have to admit—Brian's credit, they've handled the situation very effectively. The soiled area has been cordoned off with yellow cleaning-in-progress signs, shoppers are being smoothly directed to other less crapped-in models they might wish to consider purchasing, and air fresheners have been strategically deployed.

Brian has taken to cleaning with the same mild obliviousness he takes to everything else. And while that limits his usefulness as a salesman it does, now I think about it, make him one hell of a team player. There aren't many fellers who'd take the instruction to get on their knees and scrub shit as completely in their stride as Brian does. It doesn't quite give me a warm glow of affection, if anything it gives me a warm glow of maybe-I-could-have-used-this-feller's-skills-better. That maybe if I'd been less willing to just let stuff slide as *Brian being Brian*, we wouldn't be in the mess that we're in.

Jonathan is still dealing with the customer whose kid did the deed in question. "All I'm saying," she's saying, "is that there should be a notice."

He's staying professional, but having lived with him I can see he's not taking it brilliantly. "A notice saying *don't relieve yourself in these toilets*?"

"There's one on the beds," she points out.

"There's a notice telling people not to *lie* on the beds." Jonathan's trying hard to keep his voice this side of civil. "We haven't felt the need to put up a sign telling people not to, well—on the beds."

"Well, beds and toilets are different, aren't they?" The customer always being right is a rule in brick-and-mortar retail to this day but this customer is, in my view, stretching it. "You've only got yourself to blame."

The kid, who from where I'm standing looks like he makes crapping on things a point of personal pride, smiles up at Jonathan smugly.

I get a nasty sense that Jonathan's feeling the pressure here, so I step in, trying not to remember how badly that went last time. "Is everything alright?" I ask, letting my accent get just that little bit stronger.

"I was telling the manager here that these things *will happen* if they don't have clear signs saying that people should stay away from the display lavatories."

There's a second half of the customer always being right that a lot of people forget. They're always right *even when they're wrong*. So I nod and smile. "No, you're right, that's a very fair point. I will say that there is a little sign there"—I point it out, it quite clearly reads *for display purposes only*—"but perhaps it could be a bit more prominent"—it couldn't—"and at the end of the day, lads will be lads, won't they?"

The lad in question looks up at me. "You've got a stupid scarf."

"Thanks, it belonged to my mam."

"Why're you wearing a girl's scarf?" asks the obnoxious little twerp who is, unfortunately, always right.

"Keeps my neck warm," I tell him. Then I look straight to his mother. "So, what were you looking for today and how can we help you find it?"

Turns out she is, in fact, in the market for a new bathroom suite, although this one now has negative connotations for her. So I pass her over to New Enthusiastic Chris, who strikes me as the person present least liable to let a little thing like a lingering association with human excrement put him off a sale.

When she and her demon child have gone, Jonathan gives me an almost grateful look. "You handled that well," he said. Then he follows up with, "How did you know about the sign?"

Fuck. "I think things are just coming back to me, y'know, from being here. Plus it *is* actually quite prominently displayed."

To my relief, it's enough of an explanation for him. "Right," he says. "If that's dealt with, I should probably speak to the rest of the team. Can you gather everybody in the staff room?"

"No," I say far too quickly and far too insistently. "I mean—there's no sense in rushing folk, is there? And we don't want to pull people away from customers while we're busy." And we *are* busy, which helps.

"Plus," says Brian, "there's all those decorations in there."

Thankfully, Claire comes in with the save. "Oh yes, from when there was that confusion about the delivery so we got no lots and then two lots and had to bung half in the staff room because there wasn't space in stock."

"I hope we didn't get double-charged," says Jonathan, very much back in calling-his-lawyer-first mode.

"No." Claire's much quicker at this than I would have been. "It was their mistake and if they want them back they can have them. They just need to arrange the pickup."

"But—" Brian is about to say something but a matched pair of stares from me and Claire shut him down.

"How about," Claire says, taking Jonathan quite naturally by the arm, "we have another once around the floor and I show you the job our team did with putting the displays up? And then if there's anything else you want to talk about, you can run it by me and I can pass it on when things are a bit less hectic?"

Shockingly Jonathan goes for it, even though it wasn't his idea. And I am feeling a bit tired what with the trip up and the constant low-key panic, so I let Brian lead me back to the staff room where I sit down next to a box filled with tasteful sprigs of holly tied up with little red bows. Tiff and Amjad have gone back to work, so it's just the two of us, and he makes me a tea while I'm waiting.

"Well, I must say," he tells me, "I'm very confused about who's what and what's where now."

"It's all right, Brian," I reassure him. "I think things are coming together. Claire seems to know what she's doing."

"Oh yes." Brian nods like a plastic dog on a car dashboard. "She's done a bang-up job since you've been out. Better than ever really." He looks sheepish. "Not that you were bad. Just that, well, she's good too. In different ways. Also I think folks are a bit more scared of her than they were of you."

Not quite sure how to take that, I decide to just not. "I'm not sure I wanted people to be scared of me."

"Well, that's good." He looks sage. "Because we really weren't. All I mean to say is that you shouldn't worry too much about it if you need to take a bit longer because Claire's been brill."

"Oh," I say. Then I echo back: "Brill."

"She had this great idea that I shouldn't carry coffee through the show room."

"I had that idea," I protest. "Also, it's not even an idea. It's an obvious thing."

Brian tsks like he's the one who's disappointed. "I don't think you ever mentioned it."

"I'm pretty sure I did."

"Not so it sounded important, though. Anyway," he goes on cheerfully, "I just thought you'd like to know we were in safe hands."

And of course I do like knowing that. Though it also makes me feel a bit superfluous. It's not that managing a bed and bath superstore was my lifelong dream or my one true calling or anything, and...I mean...it's not that I wanted to be *essential*. Like I wanted to get back and have everybody saying *Oh Sam, we're so glad you're here, everything was falling apart without yez.* But this feels like I've been replaced. Worse, it feels like I've been replaced and everybody's better off. And that's a spiky pill to swallow.

Because the thing is—and as I sit there sipping my tea, I'm poking at this but not really wanting to poke too hard—the thing about the team, about the branch, was that I'd been part of something. And the thing about it going on without me was that I'm not so much. That worse, maybe I never was, not how I thought. And that's—well it's jobs, at the end of the day. They're bigger than you and that's nice when you're there. But every connection you make is based on cash and convenience. It's not a substitute for—

For anything.

CHAPTER 27

AFTER HIS TOUR, JONATHAN'S IN with Claire for a long time, which makes me nervous. Though not as nervous as the three texts I get about forty-five minutes later which just say:

On his way back.

Still looking for cuts.

Brian especially fucked.

Since we still can't let Jonathan see that the staff room is filled with the exact decorations that'll be populating a basement in Shoreditch three days from now, I head out with Brian to meet him and we catch up in the middle of towels.

"Go well?" I ask.

"I think so." Jonathan's looking at me even more inscrutably than usual. And though I don't want to, I start filling in blanks.

Because I know he's just been in with Claire talking about laying people off. And he doesn't know I know that. And he *also* doesn't know that I know he had the same conversation with me back when I first came down and that it was that which led to the whole shower-falling-head-bashing amnesia thing in the first place.

So now I'm feeling guilty and angry all at once. Guilty because it still doesn't feel right that I've been faking quite a serious medical condition in order to get Jonathan to reconsider his plans.

And angry because it apparently hasn't fucking worked. I've been doing my best see-me-as-a-person I-know-there-is-good-in-you act and he's still the same ruthless, bottom-dollar, grasping little shit he was three weeks ago. The worst thing is, I really thought he'd changed. But perhaps he's just changed around me.

"Oh," I tell him, swallowing hard on account of how I can't let on about a single word of this, "well that's good then. Shall we off?"

Jonathan gives a sad little nod like he's a kid whose parents are making him leave Disney World before he's had a second go on Space Mountain. It's not so much that the unique charms of the Sheffield branch have swept him off his feet. It's just that he's, y'know, a micromanaging workaholic, and the thing about my team is that, for better or worse, they dispense an awful lot of workahol.

We hop back in the car and he takes us into the centre of Sheffield where he's booked us into a Premier Inn, and if his reversion to full work mode hadn't tipped me off that this wasn't Sam and Jonathan's Romantic Getaway For Two, the choice of venue would've. Partly because he'd got us separate rooms but mostly because you would never ever take someone to a Premier Inn if you were in any way trying to pull them.

I dump my bag and then sit down on the end of the bed on top of that purple stripe thing that Premier Inn HQ has apparently decreed must be laid across every bed in the chain. After a minute or two of sitting and thinking gets me precisely nowhere, I flop backwards and stare up at the ceiling trying to put my screwed-up rubber-band-ball of thoughts, emotions, and instincts into something like an order.

I'd not been imagining it, had I? Jonathan had, in fact, been de-Jonathaning, that is to say turning into less of an unbelievable piece of shit. Pulling out my phone, I stare at Claire's texts again.

Fuck, I text back. Then, This hasn't worked, has it?

Compartmentalisation, that was the problem. Clearly from Jonathan's perspective the question of what to do about the Sheffield branch and the question of whether he should stop treating his family like a mildly inconvenient admin job were two completely different things.

Did he at least seem conflicted? I ask, and three little dots pop up to suggest Claire's texting back.

What does he look like when he's conflicted? she asks.

The funny thing is, I could probably tell her. I've been looking at Jonathan Forest a lot lately and though he seems all stoic like on the surface, he's actually got a very expressive face. Conflicted is when his eyes and his lips don't match up, when he's got that crease on his forehead he has when he's thinking, even though it's something he's pretending not to think about.

How should I know? I text back.

The next text that comes through says, I'm downstairs, do you want to get something to eat? And that one's not from Claire it's from Jonathan.

I'm tempted to say I'm too tired. It's early but we've had a long drive and a big work thing and I do still have the after-effects of that concussion, so it'd make sense. Only it feels like copping out.

He was sympathetic. It actually is Claire this time. Just not so sympathetic he could see a case for keeping Brian around.

To be fair, I text back, I'm beginning to think he has a point. Then I text Jonathan, Give me a minute.

I've been saying Brian's a liability for months and No hurry come back, so I send an I know sorry and a Where were you thinking of going?

Which means the last two texts I get that evening are It's silly but there's somewhere I usually go and If I lose my job because you made me fight for the worse salesman in England...

I think about texting Claire back. Saying *I'll sort it, I promise.* But I don't know how, or what I can do, short of murder-by-toilet-bowl. Trying not to imagine the many ways I could assassinate Jonathan Forest over chicken and chips in a Sheffield restaurant, I head down to reception to meet up with him. He's...he's not changed, I don't think he's even done his hair, but he looks different somehow. More familiar. The cold your-job's-on-the-line Jonathan who Claire was talking to twenty minutes ago has completely gone, and I'm standing by the front desk of a Premier Inn with watching-*Auf-Wiedersehen-Pet*-with-his-dad Jonathan.

"Silly how?" I ask him.

"What?" he looks confused.

"In your text you said you wanted to go somewhere silly."

He looks at the floor, then back at me. "I meant more that it was silly to go there, not that it's—we're not going to a clown restaurant."

"Oh ey," I exclaim in disappointment. "I was looking forward to a clown restaurant. We could have custard pies for dessert and everything."

He's making *let's go* motions with his head, perhaps because he doesn't want follow me down the rabbit hole of clown-themed dining, and maybe because he does but not in front of a bored receptionist in a no-frills chain hotel. As we set off, one of his hands comes to rest very naturally on the small of my back, then pulls away sharpish. And, while we're walking together up the road, with a carefully calculated ten-inch gap between us, it occurs to me that Jonathan's efforts to stop things feeling intimate are not really having the desired effect. Though if an afternoon in a bed and bath superstore followed by check-in at a Premier Inn can't kill the mood, we might be in quite serious trouble.

I've got, if I'm honest, ambivalent feelings about Sheffield. On the plus side, it's not London, but that's an advantage it shares with literally every other city in the world. And, actually, Croydon might have snuck up on me. In a funny way, I've made some good memories there, which given I made them while pretending to have amnesia probably counts as irony. I do like, though, that Sheffield feels like the north, with its red brick buildings and everything a bit more spaced out instead of crammed together like eels in a bucket. But when you get right down to it, it's just a place, isn't it?

We make our way up Ecclesall Road, past a Kwik Fit and an express car wash until we hit the bit with all the restaurants. I have to say I'm increasingly curious about where specifically he's taking me because we've been past two gastropubs and an Indian already. Then we reach the corner and Jonathan stops outside Uncle Sams Diner: a tiny little place with a white-painted facade and—always the sign of a quality eatery—its menu in a glass box on the wall outside.

I'm opening my mouth to make an amusing observation when Jonathan holds up a finger to cut me off.

"Don't start," he says, in an embarrassed monotone. "I used to come here as a child with my family as a treat. And I like their burgers."

Oh fuck. I don't know what's worse. Him being sentimental or him trying to pretend he isn't. And by worse I mean...you know. Adorable like.

"Do they do milkshakes?" I ask.

"Of course they fucking do milkshakes. It's an American diner."

He storms inside, still not at ease revisiting his childhood with a Scouse amnesiac he should have fired three weeks ago. Turns out he's got a reservation—being Jonathan, he'd never leave to luck anything he could book in advance—and we're shown to our seats by a lass in a branded T-shirt. It feels like the sort of place that should have booths, but it doesn't. Just wooden chairs at wooden tables with a menu in the middle on a little metal stand.

"It's been here since the seventies," Jonathan explains.

I can't be having him like this all evening, so I reach halfway across the table as if I'm expecting him to take my hand, though he obviously doesn't. "It's okay," I tell him. "You don't have to keep apologising. It's nice that you wanted to come here."

"It's silly," he repeats. "There's a restaurant in the hotel. We could have gone there."

"Aye, we could. But then we'd have missed out on"—I scan the menu for something that sounds nice—"the special burger with white cheese sauce, bacon, and salad."

"You joke but it's really good."

"I'm not joking. It's probably what I'll get unless you've got a recommendation."

He shakes his head. "No, no, it's a fine choice. Do you want a starter?"

"Do you want to split something?"

He gets that conflicted crease as he tries to work out if this will lead us down a dark path. Like we'll start with a combo platter of wings and mozzarella sticks and end the night fucking in an alleyway behind the Londis. Then he relents. "How do you feel about nachos?"

"Works for me."

"You don't have a problem with foreign food?"

It's possibly the weirdest thing he could have said. "No. Also it's fucking nachos. Also it's America, so technically it's all foreign."

Jonathan shakes his head like he's trying to clear out a cobweb. "Sorry, private joke. When we used to come here with Granddad John, he'd always refuse to get the nachos because they were too foreign. He felt similarly about pizza."

"But burgers are somehow inherently British?"

"In his defence, he'd usually get the steak. But either way he can't really clarify because, well, he's dead."

"Sorry."

For a moment Jonathan stares at his cutlery. "It's been a long time. I barely remember him, to be honest."

"Still sad, though."

He nods. "A bit."

"So Pauline's been on her own a while then?"

I'm just trying to make conversation, but I worry I've gone somewhere a bit too personal, because Jonathan gets all withdrawn and introspective. "I've tried to get her to come to London, but she won't have it. And the home's the best I could find."

"I'm sure you've done right by her," I say, partly to be comforting and partly because I'm sure he has.

Things have that air of being about to get awkward, but then we're saved by the arrival of the waiter. It's a pretty simple operation, nachos to share, a burger each, a strawberry milkshake for me and—after a moment's hesitation—a vanilla milkshake for Jonathan.

"A vanilla milkshake?" I ask, as the waiter departs.

Jonathan frowns in a way I've learned to recognise as the fun kind of angry. "What's wrong with vanilla milkshakes?"

"You could have had any other flavour."

"Yes, but I'm not six."

I laugh. "You're having a milkshake. Sophistication has very much left the building."

"I like vanilla," Jonathan says defensively. "It's a milkshake at its…milkshakiest."

"What does that even mean?"

"I don't know. But I feel very strongly about it."

I've still not figured out how to tell when Jonathan Forest's trying to be amusing. Mind you, I'm not sure he knows either. So I smile at him anyway because, even when he's not trying, he makes me happy. Happy in a way I'm well aware can't last but I like anyhow.

"What?" Jonathan demands.

"Nothing," I tell him. And it's not really nothing. It's a complex mix of somethings, not all of which I'm entirely able to put names on. Because, at the end of the day, he is still planning on firing Brian. Which makes it a bit hard to just sit here enjoying milkshake-themed banter. Except that's exactly what I'm doing.

And maybe Jonathan's got his own mix of somethings going on because this silence falls across the table. Finally, he tries, "I can't believe you've lived in Sheffield for two years and never come here."

I think about saying I might have but I can't remember. The problem is, though, it feels wronger and wronger to lie to him, even about stuff that doesn't matter. Not that the truth is much better. "I don't eat out much," I say.

He seems to consider this for longer than necessary. "Because of the cost? Or is it a health thing?"

He's being peculiar, even for him. "No, I just really want to see the restaurant industry collapse out of pure spite."

"Sam, I know I'm not good at small talk, but I am genuinely trying."

"Trying to what? We're just getting something to eat." Fuck, I think I might be lying to him again. But, in my defence, I'm lying to myself too. "It's no different from that time I had a Wagyu Beef pizza."

And, once again, he's quiet. "But it is, isn't it?"

"It doesn't have to be," I try to reassure him. "And if you're concerned about there being a, y'know, a dynamic..."—I gesture to the bright red walls and the room full of Sheffieldians tucking into plates of steak and chips—"then, and don't take this the wrong way, this is probably the least romantic place you could conceivably bring a feller."

"Well, in case you haven't noticed, I'm not a very romantic person."

Now *he's* the one who's lying. Admittedly, he's not a red roses and candlelight kind of bloke but, then, neither am I. And what he is, is someone who lets you use his room when his family kicks you out of yours, who buys you an overpriced guinea pig to hang on a Christmas tree, who takes you to a restaurant he remembers from his childhood, and kisses you like you're the only lad in the world. "I don't know, you have your moments."

He goes a bit red over that, and I'm worried I've accidentally taken a left turn onto Flirt Street. "I really don't. The last time I went on date, I booked a tandem skydive and he hated it."

Okay, there's a lot to unpack here. "You what?" Our nachos arrive—a proper mountain of them, cheese dripping down the side like lava down a volcano—but I don't let them distract me from what the fuck Jonathan was thinking. "No, seriously, you what?"

He shades his brow with a hand. "He was younger than me and I wanted to seem cool."

"You know"—I'm staring at him, kind of delighted—"how sometimes an answer will just give you more questions?"

"I told you, I'm not good at romance."

"And you thought flinging a guy out an airplane would make him like yez?"

Jonathan extracts a nacho with surgical precision—though, honestly, I think he's stalling. "I thought there'd be less opportunity for me to fuck it up if we had something to do and there was nothing good on at the cinema that week."

I'm trying not to laugh but I'm not succeeding. Also I'm not trying that hard. "Who was this poor bloke? And how young was he exactly?"

"His name's Coby Nightingale. He plays for Croydon FC."

"You took a professional footballer skydiving?"

"I thought he'd like to do a physical activity."

"Jonathan, the physical activity you do on dates is called sex."

I help myself to a nacho which turns out to be stuck to another nacho which is stuck to another nacho and so on until Jonathan helps me pry them apart. "Fair play to you, though, for getting with a footballer."

"Well, as established, I didn't get with a footballer. I tried to take him skydiving, he turned out to have a tremendous fear of heights, and he vomited on me in the car home."

It's got to the point where I can't tell if I'm trying to reassure him or just taking the piss. "Okay, but you at least asked him out. You were, very briefly, technically a WAG."

"Granddad Del was overjoyed. He's been a supporter since the seventies."

A thought occurs. "How did you even meet? No offence but I don't feel like you and the first eleven move in the same circles."

"I was working out a sponsorship deal. We crossed paths at a couple of lunches, he had a go at me for wearing a Sheffield Wednesday scarf but asked me out anyway."

I feel almost sorry for him. So close, and yet so far. "And your first thought was *I bet what this man really wants is to be strapped to a bloke who isn't me and dropped through the sky tied to a bedsheet*?"

"Essentially, yes."

The waiter brings us our milkshakes. And they are proper milkshakes, the ones that come in a curvy glass with two straws, even if you're not sharing them. I'm just taking a sip when another thought occurs. "Hang on a sec, does this mean you've also jumped out of a plane?"

"With a professional."

I stare at him. "Were you not scared?"

He stares back. "Given the circumstances in which I found myself jumping out of a plane, do you really think fear was my primary emotion?"

"Are you really saying that you were more bothered by a bad date than the actual ground rushing towards you at a hundred miles an hour?"

"Well, the bad date was my fault and didn't come with a parachute."

He looks like this is still haunting him. "Don't worry about it," I say. "This is a very solvable problem. Next time you're on a first date, just don't take him skydiving."

"I did work that out for myself."

We spend a few minutes wrangling with nachos. To be honest, they're a good fit for the very unusual occasion of two people who are blatantly into each other having a meal where they have to pretend they aren't. They're not so messy it's embarrassing, they require just enough cooperation that you've got to interact, but not so much it gets sexy.

Finally, Jonathan looks up from a plate of sour cream and tortillas. "I suppose you've never had a bad date in your life."

"Jonathan, everybody's had a bad date. I'll admit, the skydiving vomit professional footballer combo sets the bar very high, but I've had my share of fuckups."

"Like what?" He sounds so sceptical it's almost flattering.

And, embarrassingly, I do have to think for a moment. It's not that I'm amazing or anything. It's just there's usually something good even on a bad date. Well, unless you're Jonathan apparently. "I took a bloke to see *Gods of Egypt*."

"And?"

"And he didn't like it very much. Also he didn't like that I"—I'm not really sure how to phrase this—"didn't really care it was a terrible film? He was all, *the dialogue was awful, the plot made no sense, and Ancient Egypt was nothing like that*. And I was like, *yeah, but you got see him from* Game of Thrones *with his shirt off, what more do you want?*"

"Honestly," Jonathan tells me, "I can see why he found that annoying."

"No, you don't. If you didn't like a movie, you'd just say, *well, that wasn't very good* and if I said *I dunno, you got to see him from* Game of Thrones *with his shirt off*, you'd say *fair enough*. You wouldn't take it as a personal insult and spend the rest of the evening trying to convince me I was wrong while we were supposed to be getting chips."

"Yes, well"—Jonathan shoots me one of his intense looks that might be playful—"I've learned that trying to convince you that you're wrong is entirely futile."

I think back to the business at the store today. "No more than trying to convince you."

"Why? What are you trying to convince me of this time?"

Oh God. I can't really say, *don't fire Brian*. Partly because I'm not supposed to know he's firing Brian but mainly because he's now joined me on Flirt Street and—even though I shouldn't—I don't entirely want to show him the way back. I do, however, find another way to bottle it. "That vanilla's a waste of a milkshake."

Unfortunately, Flirt Street is much longer and twistier than I remember it being. Jonathan slides his drink towards me. "Try it."

I should probably tell him no. But not being willing to take a sip of milkshake seems like it'd be heading off Flirt Street onto Dick Move Boulevard. So I lean forward and put my lips on the straw, trying to look as un-fellatio-ey as possible—which is easy in some ways because straws are a hell of a lot thinner than cocks, but also there's just something inherently suggestive about sucking on stuff in front of someone you fancy. "Okay," I say. "It's good. But it still just tastes like a milkshake."

Jonathan lowers his brow, clearly feeling protective of the vanilla milkshake experience. "What were you expecting it to taste of? Liquid gold and angels' tears?"

"The way you were going on, aye."

"Well, forgive me if I like my milkshake to taste like milkshake and not like..." He makes a dismissive gesture with a nacho. "Generic red."

"But red's the best flavour. Everyone knows red's the best flavour."

"No," Jonathan insists. "That's just propaganda put about by Big Red."

"Are you seriously telling me that you don't think red M&Ms are the best M&Ms?"

"Peanut M&Ms are the best M&Ms."

"Okay, but within a bag of peanut M&Ms."

"Then they all taste the same because whether they've got a peanut is the salient factor about M&Ms, not the colour."

"You," I say, laughing, "have no soul."

Now Jonathan is looking at me again, with this half-confused, half-pained expression.

"What?" I ask.

"Nothing," he says. "Just...it always surprises me when you laugh."

Which as comments go leaves me substantially more than half-confused. "Why? I'm a happy person. Also most people don't take three weeks and a chicken fisting to crack a smile."

The memory of doing unspeakable things to a deceased bird sends a flicker of inappropriate amusement across Jonathan's face, but then he goes all messy-sad again. "I meant more that I'm surprised to see you laugh when you're with me."

"Jonathan"—I take quite a firm tone with him—"can you please stop this? You're not a monster in a fairy tale. You're a person. You can be funny, people will actually laugh at stuff you say, and not just in a mean way."

The nachos are mostly done, and Jonathan's picking at what's left of them without much enthusiasm. "Before you lost your memory," he tells me, and he sounds so hesitant it makes me wish I could tell him I've not, "you and Claire used to call me *His Royal Dickishness.*"

I try my best to sound like this is new information. "You're the boss," I tell him. "Everybody thinks their boss is a dick."

"You also told me I was being a dick to you just in general, after the accident."

"And you were. But you stopped. You don't have to be"—I wave my hands in little circles that are supposed to convey everything other people think about Jonathan Forest and everything he thinks about himself—"who you are at work or who people thought you were at university or whatever the opposite of your dad is all the time. You can just be you. Y'know, the *you* you are when you're with me."

The waiter comes back with our burgers and sets them down on the table with a clink. Jonathan looks down at his but doesn't touch it. He doesn't even take his knife and fork out of the napkin they've been wrapped in. "I can't, though, can I, Sam? Because—because of everything. Because you're injured. Because I'm your boss. Because—because of a hundred other things."

"Okay, but..." He's sort of right about the boss issue, and if I'd not been lying he'd have been right about the injury thing. But not about the rest of it. "You can still be that other person. You can still have the stuff the other person can have."

He's glaring now. "I don't want it."

"You do. I've seen that you do."

And now it's less a glare and more—I've not got words for what it is. He's looking at me as though if he stops he'll turn to stone, like I'm some kind of reverse medusa. "I don't want it if I can't have it with you."

Oh.

I should tell him that he's being silly. That he can find another feller and as long as he doesn't try to take him skydiving it'll work out. Except I'm not sure I want him to have this with anybody else either. For a start, I'm the one who put the bloody work in.

"Jonathan," I try, but I've got no follow-up.

He pushes his plate away and stands. "Just—whatever you're going to say, I'd rather you—" He pulls his wallet out his pocket. Perhaps it's a holdover from his market trading days but he's got a fair amount of cash in one of those clip things that nobody uses any more. "I think I'd rather we just left it here."

He throws down enough money to cover the meal and then some, and before I can work out what to say, or what it was he thought I was going to say and was so determined I shouldn't, he's out the door. Leaving me with two burgers that somebody's gone to the trouble of cooking and either of which it would feel extremely weird to eat.

I can't decide which makes me look worse: abandoning a table full of food that no-one's touched or sitting here on my tod, having a burger and chips like people regularly take me out to dinner, throw money on the table, and then bail.

I pick up a chip and pinch it between my fingers so the potato all mushes out. It hasn't got any answers for me either.

THERE WAS NEVER GOING TO be a good time for things to fall apart between me and Jonathan, but the advantage of it happening in Sheffield is that at least it's easy to go home afterwards. I mean, I say home. I mean to the flat. Which doesn't even have my fucking cat in it because he's still in London with the family of the bloke who's sort of not exactly dumped me, probably getting spoiled rotten.

I'd rented the flat because I'd just come to Sheffield and I needed somewhere to live. It wasn't the first place I looked at but it might have been the third. At the time I'd been in no mood to...well. Give a crap. About anything. And especially not about whether I got picturesque views or a cosy ambience. Unfortunately, that means coming back to it sucks very hard indeed.

There's a gentle smell of neglect in the air that, I hope, it's picked up since I've been away but which, realistically, may have always been there. Not sure exactly what else to do with myself, I clean out the fridge. Even here, I kept things fairly orderly, but three weeks out of town has done a number on my milk and my orange juice is looking sorry for itself. Frankly, I know how it feels.

When that's done, I kind of run out of steam and sit on the sofa. Technically speaking, nothing's changed. All that's happened is that my brief window of being an extremely unexpected guest in Jonathan Forest's needlessly fancy house has come to a premature end, and I'm back to being a sad bastard who manages a minor branch of a chain of bed and bath superstores and lives on his own in a flat above a butcher's shop. At least, I'm back to being that until Jonathan fires me for being shit at the job which it seems increasingly likely he will if what Claire said is anything to go by.

Of course, if he does fire me then that means he gives up his best excuse for not dating me. I mean, it'd be awkward like because then I'd be going out with a bloke who just gave me the sack. But I reckon I'd get over it. Because sitting here in my crappy, cat-less flat on my own has reminded me of all the reasons I had for being here in the first place. Which is to say, I didn't really have any. I was just looking to pay my bills and get out of Liverpool. And, thinking about it, that's literally all I did. And unless I make a serious play for something I actually want, it'll be all I ever do.

Fuck it.

I grab my coat and ring a taxi. Then I wait for the taxi, which sort of takes the edge off the romantic go-to-him-now-because-it's-your-last-chance impulse. Then again, it's quite a long way and he's in a Premier Inn. And showing up at a budget chain hotel shagged out from a long run just isn't a good way to get in touch with your inner Sandra Bullock.

"Ey up," says the driver as I get in. "You're going to that Premier Inn, then?"

"Yeah," I tell him.

Heart Radio starts up as he pulls away from the kerb. "Forget your toothbrush?"

Now he mentions it, I have. "Sort of. Also my clothes. Also my boss. Who I want to be my boyfriend."

"Eeh," he says. "You want to be careful wi' that. There's

some potentially significant implications regarding relationships in t'workplace."

"That has been a concern." I'm starting to feel like this is going to be a very long journey.

"What you want to do," explains the driver, as we hit the roundabout and start heading south on the A630, "is sit down wi't HR department."

"Actually, I was hoping he'd just fire me."

The cabbie shakes his head. "Oh no, that's no good. Then you'd be able to get him for that constructive dismissal."

"I'm not going to, though, am I? Because I'll be dating him."

"Aye, but he can't rely on that."

I squint at the back of the guy's head. "How do you know so much about employment law?"

"I was union rep at t'steelworks."

"You never were."

He looks confused. "That's a funny thing to be surprised about. They were a major local employer."

"It's not that, it's that my boss's dad used to work there too. Did you know a Les Forest?"

"Fucking hell." The cabby nods. "What's he doing these days?"

"This and that, he's in London now. But his son runs that chain of bed and bath stores, Splashes & Snuggles?"

"Not a good name," the cabby says.

"Decent shop, though. And I think Jonathan comes from the *should say what it does* school of corporate nomenclature."

"True enough. And I did go in for a loo brush t'other day."

So for the next twenty minutes we chat in a people-who-have-a-very-tenuous-connection-to-each-other sort of way. And at the end he gives me his number and asks me to pass it on to Les. Which, when I think about it, is a particularly awkward thing to happen when I'm on the way to tell Les's son that I want to, like, be with him and that. I bet this wouldn't happen to Sandra Bullock.

Nobody gives me a second glance as I head through reception and upstairs. It's easy enough to find Jonathan's room because it's the one next to mine. I bang on the door and belatedly wonder if I should have phoned first. Both to be polite and because he might not even be in.

He is, though. He opens the door, looking—and I might be using this word wrong—raddled. He's in his shirtsleeves, with a full two buttons undone, and he's hit the complimentary tea bar hard, standing there with a mug clutched in his hand. His hair's all floppy, the white streak tumbled partly over one eye.

"I quit," I tell him.

He gives a calculated non-reaction. "What?"

"With conditions," I clarify. "I quit."

"What conditions?" He sounds about ninety-eight percent suspicious and two percent hopeful.

"I had a word with Claire back at the store." It's only half a lie. And though I wish my life hadn't got to the point where I was measuring lies in fractions, it's where I am and I have to deal with it. "And she was saying you were looking for cuts. Big cuts. Only from what I've seen they get on okay without me, and so that's a saving right there." And, if I'm honest, Claire's got them in line the way I never could. The way I'd never really wanted to. "If you put Claire in charge and don't hire anybody else then you've saved a full salary and you don't have to fire anybody."

"That's very noble of you." Jonathan's suspicion level has gone to maybe a ninety-three, but that's still more than I'd like it to be.

"It's not," I tell him. "It's just—it's just the right call. For everybody. I can find another job, the store's clearly in good hands"—better hands really—"and if I don't work for you any more then..."

The *then* just sort of hangs there between us like a guinea pig in a Santa hat.

"Then?" Eighty-four percent.

"Then we can try and make it work?" I try not to let it sound like a question, but it does anyway. "If you want to like. But even if you don't, I think letting me go is the right thing to do. It gets you what you wanted and it doesn't hurt anybody who's not already been off work for nearly a month."

"Sam"—Jonathan's frown is very frowny indeed—"trying to sacrifice yourself for your team isn't noble and isn't cute. It's just—"

"I'm not trying to sacrifice myself for the team," I yell. "I'm trying sacrifice myself for—I'm not trying to sacrifice myself at all. I just...want to be with yez and I can't if I work for you."

"But—" Jonathan tries again.

But nothing. I'm not letting him *but* me so I *but* him first. "And no offence I think you'd make a better boyfriend than you do a boss."

He scowls. "Then perhaps I should date the entire branch."

"You should date *me*," I tell him real earnest like. "Because you want to. Because I want to. Because we're both allowed to have nice things even if we tell ourselves we aren't."

"It's not that si—"

"It *is*, Jonathan. It's exactly that simple. Unless you're going to tell me you're secretly an alien from the planet wanker, and you need to go report back to your people and even then, tell 'em to fuck off. It's not a good planet in the first place."

He's not scowling so much now. He's almost letting himself look amused. "Why is my home world called the planet wanker?"

"I don't know. It may come as a shock, but most times I ask a feller out he doesn't ask me to invent science fiction universes off the top of my head."

"You're still basically calling me a wanker."

"Yeah, it shows how well I know you."

"Except you don't know me." He grips his mug tighter than ever. And I remember, once again, that we're having this emotionally fraught discussion in the corridor of a Premier Inn. "You've got amnesia. If you...if you remembered what you thought of me, you wouldn't be here."

I really wish I'd never started the amnesia thing. Although I guess if I hadn't, I'd have been sacked three weeks ago along with everybody else. "Jonathan, in case you haven't noticed, you're surrounded by people who care about you, and want to spend time with you, even though they are fully aware of what a complete dick you can be sometimes."

"They're my family. They're required to."

I sigh. "They're not required to. They choose to. Just like I'm choosing to." Honestly, this is crossing the line from romantic into humiliating. If I'd realised he was going to be this stubborn, I'd have brought a PowerPoint. "Because, Jonathan, you're not the boss of me. Not anymore. On account of how I quit. And I'm staying quit whether you date me or not."

As soon as I say it aloud, I realise how true it is. This isn't just best for the team, it's best for me, Jonathan Forest or no Jonathan Forest. I'd sort of convinced myself it didn't matter what job I did. But, looking back, I think it was just a symptom of...of...stuff not mattering in general for a while.

I'm still getting nothing from Jonathan, which is the worst sort of rejection because it's like he can't even be bothered to tell me to fuck off. On the bright side, at least I've got a good bad date story out of it. It's not skydiving and vomit but in its own special way it's scary, cold, and lumpy.

"Alright," I say. Because there's not much else I can. "Bye then."

My stuff's still in my room, which is only eight feet away. Between getting a taxi down here and then just going next door afterwards it's a toss-up whether my big dramatic chasing him down moment or my big dramatic walking away was more pathetic.

In any case, it makes no difference. Because I only get about four feet before Jonathan catches me up, turns me around, and kisses me.

I wouldn't say he's calmed down exactly from the last time we kissed. More sort of honed. Which given how he runs his business doesn't surprise me. He's nothing if not efficient, is Jonathan Forest. Though at least in this he was willing to take some direction. Of course, the problem with a Jonathan Forest who's taken direction is that it's a Jonathan Forest who's pretty much unstoppable. Because once he's worked out how to do something, he does it all the way and so now he's kissing me like he's taking me apart. In the good way. In the didn't-know-how-much-I-needed-this way. In the moaning, breathless, tangle-your-hands-in-his-hair-because-your-knees-are-going-weak way.

We fetch up against the door of my room and here's me trying to swipe the key card one-handed without looking. I feel a bit like a straight bloke trying to undo a bra. From his general enthusiasm I get the impression Jonathan's fine where we are but given the last time all we had was a sofa, I'd quite like to get him on a bed. Besides, we're probably tanking the Tripadvisor score of this otherwise blameless hotel: couldn't get my suitcase through because two blokes were getting off in the doorway, one star.

Of course, the other problem with being distracted from the door you're both trying to open and leaning against is that when it does open, it catches you off guard. The door swings inwards and

I pitch back into the room with Jonathan still clinging to me. He makes a valiant attempt to catch me romantically, but while he's not exactly scrawny and I'm not exactly hefty, gravity is not to be trifled with. We end up in a heap on the floor and it seems falling over, like a fisting a chicken, is precisely the kind of sophisticated, cerebral humour that gets Jonathan going.

"Are you seriously laughing?" I ask once I get my wind back. "I've chased you across Sheffield, quit my job, poured out my heart, and gone base over apex in a Premier Inn. And that's the sort of thing you find amusing?"

Jonathan eases himself to his elbows so he's not crushing me quite as badly. Then grins down at me. "Mostly I'm just happy. Though also, as we've established, I'm kind of a wanker."

"You're happy you pushed me on my arse?"

He gets all flushed and sincere. And I like it, though I'm not used to it. "I'm just happy you're here. That we're here."

"You soft bastard."

"You were just complaining that I mocked your misfortune."

"Aye," I say. "I'm a complex man of many moods."

For a long moment he gazes down at me and it's still a bit soft bastardy—which I'm pretending very hard not to be taken by—but also sort of knowing. Which I find faintly unsettling. "That you are, Sam Becker."

I'm not quite sure how to respond to that. Maybe it's just weird to have Jonathan agreeing with me. So I pull him back down on top of me and we get back to kissing. The last time we did this we were telling ourselves it'd never happen again, which gave it a sense of urgency. And that was sort of exciting at the time, but also sort of distracting—like when you go to one of them "all you can eat for a fiver" buffets and you feel you've got to get your money's worth, which means you can't stop and savour anything.

Now, though, we're savouring. Even if there's this edge from both of us where we can't quite believe it's happening. Which is its own—and, fuck, maybe I'm turning into a soft bastard myself because I can't think of any word for it except magic. It's just nice, y'know, to be held like someone's afraid you might disappear on them. Because usually with me it's the other way around.

Magic aside I do, eventually, come to the conclusion that the Premier Inn chose their carpets to be hard-wearing, not to be comfortable for getting off on, and my elbows are getting a bit abraded like.

"How about," I say, "we take this to the bed?"

We take it to the bed, me pulling off my jumper en route. Jonathan reclines against the headboard and—figuring it's my turn since I was the one getting the carpet burns—I climb enthusiastically over him. I'm about to go in for another kiss when I realise Jonathan is looking up at me with an unexpected level of uncertainty. And it does to occur to me that between thinking we'd never be anything and discovering we were going to be something, I've probably got a bit carried away.

"You all right?" I ask.

He nods. "Very."

I tuck my palm against the sharp line of his jaw, where it's nicely rough from a day's worth of stubble. And it gives me this little shock of pleasure, just to be able to touch him. In that casual way, like he's mine. Which he is, I guess? Fuck me. "We can go back on the carpet if you like?"

To my surprise, it's almost as if he wants to. "Um. We don't have to."

"Do you have some kind of floor fetish I should know about?"

"What? No."

"It's fine if you do. I'm not judging. I'm up for most things."

"I don't have a floor fetish," he snarls, in a very Jonathan-like way. "It's just being on the bed is very... It creates an expectation."

"It doesn't have to. I know I took off my jumper pretty sharpish, but I'm not going to rush you into anything."

He gives an annoyed kind of huff. Which is also very Jonathan-like. It's very on brand for him to take my trying to respect his boundaries as a personal insult. "I'm not a—this isn't my first—I don't need to be coddled."

"Oh great," I say. "Get your keks off. I'll start lubing up the kumquats."

"Where would you even *get* kumquats at this time of night?"

"I always carry a couple, just in case. You never know when you might get lucky."

Turning his head, he bites me right on the fleshy bit under my thumb. "You're not funny, Sam."

"Did you just bite me?"

He looks sheepish. "No."

"Fair enough. My mistake."

This time, he does something that's perilously close to a nuzzle. "It's just," he says reluctantly. "It's been a while. I may be out of practice."

Frankly, it's been a while for me too. "Okay, but what would you practicing look like?"

"I think it would look..." He sounds adorably confused. "Like me having sex with someone?"

"And then you'd slap him on the leg and say, *thanks mate, that was a good practice.*"

"So what would you do?" Now he sounds adorably irate. "Drills in front of a mirror?"

Leaning in, I brush my mouth against his. "I don't think it's something you need to practice."

Fuck, I hope it's not. Otherwise I've been winging it for years.

"I just mean"—his free hand tenses up against the duvet—"you shouldn't—I might not—"

"It's going to be fine," I tell him. "Like Mariah Carey at Christmas, all I want is you."

I can tell I've caught him off guard because he goes a bit pink and awkward. "You can be very sweet." He clears his throat. "Now go get the kumquats."

"You do know I haven't actually got any."

"I was banking on that when I suggested you go get them."

"You'll just have to make do with me."

"I was banking on that too."

After that we get back to the kissing and we let that go on as long as its wants to. Long enough for Jonathan to stop worrying about whatever the fuck he's worrying about and turn all dazed and hungry beneath me. In the end, it turns out I was right. It's not the sort of thing you need to practice. If you trust it, it just sort of comes together.

We strip in stages and Jonathan looks as good under his suit as I've been imagining he would. He's not got a gym body, but I've never been particularly into that. Give me something lived in, that's real to touch, and imperfect in the best possible way. I love having him under my hands, that lovely mix of soft hair and hard muscle, and how he responds to me, holding nothing back.

There's part of me that feels I don't deserve it—not with, well, the lies and that—but I also need it. And until now I didn't realise quite how badly I needed it. How lonely I've been. The truth is, I kind of hate what the last few years have made of my life. But it also brought me to Jonathan. And I'm glad it's him. That I've come back to this with him. Because, fuck me, what a thing to deny myself. Making someone gasp and groan and clutch you tight. And letting yourself clutch them right back.

I'd assumed Jonathan would be as bossy in the bedroom as he is in the boardroom, but more fool me. Turns out he can be very easygoing. Which is exactly the right thing for me in that moment.

There's just so much I want and I've missed, and getting some of it back reminds me of everything I've lost and a bunch of other stuff I just let go of. It's kind of fucked, how much bad you have to fight through to feel something good. And then the good is so overwhelming it almost hurts again. But Jonathan's there with me the whole way. Giving me his heat and his breath and his beating heart. And the pleasure we share is everywhere between us and takes me up, up, up to better places and brighter skies.

I WAKE UP WITH JONATHAN Forest. We're neither of us snuggly people, but I've got my head on his pillow and my hand on his chest and he's angled towards me on the bed. His eyes pop open.

"Morning," he says. His voice is pretty harsh normally and sleep's made it even harsher. It's the sort of thing that when you learn it about someone feels intimate and that.

"Morning," I say back.

We lie there for a couple of minutes. I can feel we're both going to get restless in a bit but, for now, it's…I don't know. Nice?

"Are you all right?" Jonathan asks.

"Aye," I tell him.

"Last night was," he tries.

"Aye," I say again.

Because, from a certain point of view, last night was a bit embarrassing. I enjoy sex as much as the next feller but I don't normally get that, y'know, intense about it.

He gives it another go. "I'm aware I was a little…"

"Reckon I was a little and all."

"I'm not usually…"

"Me neither."

"It was good, though," he says firmly. "Really good."

"Oh yeah, definitely."

He clears his throat. "I don't suppose you want to..."

I do. But it's funny to make him say it. And, frankly, I like feeling that wanted.

He clears his throat again. "Give it another go?"

We do. And even with the cold light coming in under the blind, and us both being a bit mussy and morningy, it's not as exposing as it was last night. Or maybe it is. Just in a different way. Because, while I'm not breaking my heart open all over again, you do have to be very, very into somebody if you're up for doing them when you still smell of each other from the night before and neither of yez have brushed your teeth.

In any case, it goes well enough we nearly miss breakfast.

"It's all you can eat," Jonathan explains, as we rush downstairs.

"Yeah, I noticed."

"The breakfast," he play-snarls. And it feels good—better than good, it feels great to be getting to see so much of this side of him. The side that gives a shit about things that aren't work. The side that can be playful and sexy and generous and not just in a paying-for-the-buffet way.

And then I remember the other side. The side where I'm technically dating a bloke who thinks I've got amnesia when I've not. When the reason he thinks I've got amnesia when I've not is that it was the only way I could think to stop him firing me and everybody I work with. Only now I've quit so that doesn't apply anymore and so I should probably tell him—should probably have told him before—but I didn't and I can't and I couldn't and *fuck*.

In another world, I handled this better. Then again in that world maybe Brian and Tiff don't have jobs right now. Or maybe in that world everything is fine because I found the six magic words that would make everything okay. But I don't live in that world, I live in this one. Where things are complicated and messy and you make mistakes and compromises and stuff gets out of your control so pissing quickly.

Jonathan gives me a little nudge towards the buffet. "Come on, there'll be nothing left."

And I concentrate on piling sausages onto a plate so I don't have to think about anything else. Unfortunately, it doesn't work so it comes down to Jonathan to break the silence.

"So, did you sleep well?" he asks.

Which means, on top of anything else, I'm worried I snore. "All right I think," I say. "Then again how d'you tell?"

He gives me a suspicious look over his bacon and builder's tea. "What do you mean?"

"You're asleep, aren't you? So you might be sleeping really well but not know it. Or you might be tossing and turning and saying *ooh eck keep the badgers away from me* and you'd not realise."

"Ooh eck keep the badgers away?" He's smiling again, and it's a different sort of smile than the one I'm used to. It's still two parts grumpy and it's still got an edge of *I enjoy that you look like a knobend* but there's caring there too. Real caring that I think he's always had deep down, it's just taken me a while to see it and him a while to share it.

"Well, I don't know, do I? On account of the aforesaid *being asleep* situation. I'm just, what d'you call it? Riffing."

"Ooh eck," Jonathan repeats, totally deadpan. "The badgers."

I decide I might as well stick to my guns. "Yes. That is what dreams are like. Also badgers are scary."

He looks unconvinced. "In what way?"

"They're up to something."

"Hmm." He chews thoughtfully on a rasher. "They *do* have those stripes on their faces like they're in the SAS."

"Exactly." I don't know how we got to SAS badgers but I'm

glad of the distraction. "They're probably doing some kind of covert operation like. Don't trust 'em."

He takes a sip of his tea. "I've always found them quite comforting. I think I watched a Claymation *Wind in the Willows* when I was young and the Badger in that had a sort of"—he's looking almost embarrassed—"gentle strength to him that I found very reassuring."

"Yeah, that daddy energy is how they get you."

"I did not say *daddy energy*."

I smile at him. "No, but you were thinking it. Anyway, when're we picking up Pauline?"

"In about an hour. She's an early riser."

"Seems like the lot of yez are."

Jonathan nods. "It's a family trait. And given what a long trip it is, probably for the best."

"Soonest started soonest finished," I agree. It's the kind of nan-wisdom that seems appropriate given where we are and what we're here for. "Oh, by the way," I add trying to sound as conversational as I can, "I'm going to stick around here for a bit. I've got a van I've not used in a while that'll be helpful with party stuff, and it doesn't make sense to do two trips. Plus I thought I might see my GP while I'm up here."

"You remember who they are?" Jonathan asks. There's no suspicion in it, but for a second I fluff it anyway.

"Just googled *local doctor* then my address and figured I'd be under the nearest NHS practice," I tell him, only speaking very slightly quicker than is natural. "And once I saw the name it felt, y'know, familiar and that, which is probably a good sign."

And he buys it. And, in a way, I wish he hadn't because then I'd have to come clean, and then maybe it'd be all right. Except I'm worried it wouldn't. So I let the moment pass and we just go back to talking. And, if I didn't have the shadow of a Nexa by

MERLYN 8mm Sliding Door Shower enclosure hanging over me, it would be the most uncomplicatedly pleasant morning me and Jonathan have ever had.

Being proper grown-ups, we stop eating our all-you-can-eat breakfast when we've actually had as much as we want instead of filling our boots on principle, and then we go for a nice little wander around the middle of Sheffield, which with Jonathan in tow I'm seeing a new light. I mean, don't get me wrong, it's still just a town, and not one that austerity was especially kind to, but to Jonathan it's got that childhood home thing going for it that I get myself back in Liverpool.

Winter's painting the sky all these different colours of grey and the wind's not quite as biting as you get nearer the coast, but it's still got a definite chill to it, so I let Jonathan keep me close and it feels…it feels right. And I try not to let it feel wrong that it feels right, and to remember that I'm allowed to have this, and that things don't have to suck forever. Which is easier now than I'm used to it being.

We turn off the main street and Jonathan explains that we're a few minutes away from Pauline's, which makes sense when you think about it. I've only been in London three weeks, but I've already been lulled into that big city mindset where the other side of town is a million miles and a dedicated trek away, so it's a bit of a shock to be back in the kind of place where you can walk ten minutes and you've gone from office blocks to little stone walls and a distinctively villagey vibe.

The home where Jonathan's put his nan is this converted Victorian manor not far from the middle of town and, honestly, if my grandson had stuck me somewhere like that, I'd be pretty chuffed. Though I'd also try not to think too much about what it must be costing him because those places do not come cheap.

We're met at reception by a very smiley woman named Melissa

who's clearly expecting us, and she lets Jonathan head right on through to where Pauline's waiting for him. She's hanging out in the lounge, a pretty little room all done up in inoffensive blues with French windows opening onto the garden—least they would, only they aren't right now on account of it being winter and the last thing you want in an old people's home being a cold draught blowing over everybody's slippers.

I'm not sure what to expect from Nana Pauline. She's the only person I've met so far as came purely from Les's side of the family, and that's more jarring than I expect. She's tall, thin in that old-person way that looks brittle like porcelain. She's also wearing two cardigans and sitting by an open window.

"Jonathan." She greets her grandson with a smile and an eventual hug. I say eventual because she stands up to, y'know, embrace him like, and it takes a very, very long time. Had it been me I'd have bent down to make it easier for her, but Jonathan just stands there and lets her come to him. "Good to see you."

"You too, Nana."

There's a moment's pause. Then, "I'm not coming."

"Fantastic," replies Jonathan. "Are your bags in your—hang on, you're *what*?"

"I'm staying here." She de-embraces and goes to sit back down, which doesn't take quite as long as standing up.

Jonathan looks almost personally betrayed. "You bloody well are not."

"I bloody well am."

"You bloody well—"

This is looking like it's going to get circular. "Excuse me," I butt in, "but *why* aren't you coming?"

"Who's he?" asks Nana Pauline, "and what's he got to do with our business?"

Looking the tiniest bit like he's only just remembered I'm

there, Jonathan puts a hand on my back and does the introductions. "This is Sam, Nana. Sam, this is Nana Pauline."

"He your boyfriend?" she wants to know immediately.

"N—" I'd have been insulted by how instinctively Jonathan was about to deny it, but I'd been about to do the same. "Yes. Sort of."

I'll let the *sort of* slide as well.

"What do you mean *sort of*?" asks Nana Pauline.

"It's all a bit new," he explains.

On the whole, I'm quite keen to change the subject. "Can we get back to why you're not coming down for Christmas?"

Nana Pauline waves a dismissive hand. "Well, it's such a hassle, isn't it?"

"Yes, Nana, it is," agrees Jonathan. "For example, it was *quite* a hassle for us to drive all the way up here only for you to tell us we needn't have bothered."

"Oh, I *see*." The expression on Nana Pauline's face is a kind of gleeful outrage. And fair enough because Jonathan walked into that one like Wile E. Coyote into his own anvil trap.

Jonathan, though, isn't having any of it. "Hang on, I visit you every time I'm in Sheffield and I'm in Sheffield *quite a lot*."

My initial, porcelainy impression of Nana Pauline is getting rapidly updated. This is a woman who's never backed down from anything in her life no matter how completely pointless. "You say that, but you bunged me in here and left me languishing. *Languishing*. Do you know what it's like, Jonathan, languishing? You wake up in the morning and think to yourself *what'll I do today*, and then you think *I know, I'll have a languish*."

"Stop me if I'm out of line," I try, "but if you're upset at being left to languish then should you not *want* to come down to London for Christmas?"

I was out of line. Nana Pauline turns on me with the relish of a veteran complainer. "Oh, that's fine that is, you leave me up here, *languishing,* and then you snap your fingers and expect me to pick up everything and run the whole length of the country just because it's *Christmas.*"

"I mean…*because it's Christmas* usually is a good reason to do things," I say, then wish I hadn't.

"Now you listen here, young man." She's definitely not porcelain. More like one of them ceramic kitchen knives. "I am old enough to be your grandmother and—"

"I think he probably knows that," says Jonathan gently, "since you're *my* grandmother. But what he *doesn't* know is what you're *like.*"

"What I'm like? What am I like?"

Jonathan gives her a look. "Argumentative."

"I am *not.*"

He gives her an even lookier look. "I'm just going to leave that there. Now stop being silly."

"I'm not being silly." Leaning firmly back in her armchair, Nana Pauline folds her arms. "I'm not coming."

Hoping that Nana Pauline's love of a good row means that pushing back is making her like me more, I push back. "Okay, but what's your real reason?"

"That is my real reason," she insists. "I feel slighted. Used. Took for granted."

I don't glare at her exactly, but I move my eyes in a glarey direction. "Really, though?"

For a moment it just hangs there. Then she says: "Got a feller."

Just as I'm about to ask what sort of feller, Jonathan, with the sense of occasion and social nicety I've come to know and love cuts me off with, "No, seriously, why don't you want to come down for Christmas?"

I elbow him. And it takes him a bit to realise why I'm elbowing him, so I elbow him again.

Eventually, he gets it, and to his credit he *mostly* recovers without making a total tit of himself. "You're actually seeing someone?"

Nana Pauline's arms remain resolutely folded. "Needn't look so shocked, Jonathan."

Shocked, in my view, doesn't cut it. He looks like he's seen a ghost, and then the ghost's told him that king cobras aren't really cobras. "But you're—"

I elbow him a third time.

"I'm *what,* Jonathan?"

"Well..." I've rarely seen Jonathan Forest flustered, and he's not flustered now exactly so much as uncertain about how best to proceed. "It's not exactly *usual.*"

"I married your granddad," points out Nana Pauline. "And I had a lot of lads after me when I was young."

"Exactly. When you were *young.*" I'm getting the impression that if you pushed Jonathan into a deep pit he'd immediately yell up at you to throw him a shovel.

"But not now I'm old and ugly?"

Jonathan puts up a hand as if he's trying to protect himself. "Hold on, I *never* said ugly."

"Just old?" Nana Pauline is getting that *I've won this argument* air about her and she's not wrong.

This feels like an excellent time for me to make some kind of effort to smooth things over. "What's his name?" I ask.

"Ralph. And see, Jonathan, that wasn't so hard was it?"

Forced to concede that no, it's not that hard actually, Jonathan goes to a basic follow-up question. "And he's another resident?"

"No." I'm beginning to see where Jonathan gets his sarcastic streak. "He's a delivery lad from up the road. Twenty-six and goes like a stevedore."

"You're not helping, Nana."

I look up at Jonathan. "To be fair, neither are you."

"Whose side are you on?"

Nana Pauline smiles at me. "You know, I think I like him. You can keep this one."

"This one?" I ask.

"It's just what she calls all my boyfriends," Jonathan explains.

I'm still not completely used to hearing him say it, and it's… I like it. I think.

Nana Pauline adjusts one of her cardigans condemningly. "You are a dirty liar, Jonathan Forest."

The dirtiness or otherwise of Jonathan's lying aside, I'd been starting to feel we were getting somewhere. "So does Ralph not have his own family to go to?"

"Hah." Nana Pauline doesn't laugh exactly. She more just *says* "hah". "You think people that leave their old parents in a place like this—"

"Like this luxury assisted living facility in a converted manor house?" I clarify. "Situated in its own grounds but conveniently close to the bustling heart of Sheffield?"

"In a place like this," she repeats, "*languishing* like we are, you think they come and bring their relatives back to their place for the holidays?"

I pass a look between the other two. "Well, Jonathan does."

Which seems to put Nana Pauline in the impossible position of having to either back down or admit that Jonathan is better than other grandsons. "And Ralph's family don't. So he's stuck here, so I'm staying with him."

"He'd be welcome to join us." For a moment, I can't believe it's Jonathan talking. Like I know we've shagged and that changes things, but I didn't think my cock was the Ghost of Christmas Past. Then again, I suppose he'd been getting less uptight for a while.

"He'd be what?" asks Nana Pauline, sounding like she can't believe it either.

"Welcome to join us," Jonathan repeats. And it's not lost on me that he sounds a bit less certain this time.

Nana Pauline smiles. "I'll go tell him."

She starts to get up again very, very slowly, and this time I come forward to help her.

It doesn't go well. "Don't you mollycoddle me, young man," she snaps, "I can manage."

And she does. Eventually.

I CAN SEE WHY JONATHAN wanted to start early because once Nana Pauline has gone to tell Ralph the good news, she makes her way back up to her room to get her bags, then back down, then back up because she's forgot her coat, all without letting anybody go for her or carry anything, and that winds up being rather time consuming.

Ralph seems a nice enough feller. He calls himself *the toy boy* on account of how he's a good ten years younger than Nana Pauline, though that still puts him in his seventies. He's also only wearing one cardigan, which I'm glad of else I'd have started feeling underdressed, and I'm able to have a bit of a chat with him while we're waiting for Nana Pauline to get her things together. He managed a carpet warehouse in Rotherham for thirty years and it's left him with a deep reserve of amusing anecdotes about twist pile Fairfords.

Once everyone's ready we set off back to Jonathan's car, doing our best to enjoy the day because though it was only about fifteen minutes heading down, heading back with two older people in tow, neither of whom would hear of the possibility of us going ahead then coming back to pick them up, takes a little longer.

"Eeh, it's a lovely part of town this," Ralph observes as we wander back towards the centre. "Nothing fancy like, but we don't need anything fancy, do we Pauline?"

"We do not," Pauline agrees.

"None of that London nonsense," he continues.

"Nonsense," echoes Pauline. "You should be grateful we're coming, Jonathan. All that way, down to *London*. I ask you, who needs it?"

"Who needs it?" asks Ralph.

"I've half a mind to turn around right now and say bad job to it all," Nana Pauline goes on, which isn't exactly what we want to hear what with how we've been walking twenty minutes and are about halfway up the road.

Jonathan looks at his grandmother who, despite her protestations, is still gamely tromping away from the home and towards the car. "I'd really rather you didn't."

"Hark at the cheek on him." Nana Pauline turns to Ralph for confirmation. "Did you hear him, the cheek of him?"

"I wasn't cheeking you, Nana."

With a look of gentle disapproval, Ralph draws in a breath. "You shouldn't contradict a lady, son, it's ungentlemanly."

"Now you're just being silly." It's probably not what I'd've personally chosen to say to my nan's new boyfriend, but I'm sort of glad Jonathan said it.

Nana Pauline, though, is less glad. "Well, will you listen to that? Airs is what he's got." She turns to Jonathan. "Airs is what you've got. He's gone up that London, and it's give him airs."

Jonathan's still not standing for this, which I respect. "I do not have airs."

"You do. You're covered in airs."

"Airs aren't something you can be covered in." As I watch, Jonathan begins to slip slowly but surely from *not standing for this* to *making a bit of a tit of himself*.

Nana Pauline's eyes narrow. "What do you mean?"

"I mean airs are a thing you have."

"I know." Nana Pauline nods emphatically. "All over your 'ead for a start."

I laugh.

And Jonathan glares. "Was that a joke?"

"It was, yeah," I tell him, patting him on the back. "Come on, let's get going."

We make it back to the car without Jonathan hacking his nan off too much and without Ralph or Nana Pauline saying anything so outrageous he'd *have* to hack her off. Once we're there I quietly remind everybody of the whole stay-in-Sheffield-so-I-can-grab-the-van plan which, now me and Jonathan has become, well, me and Jonathan, I'm feeling a whole lot worse about. Partly because I'm ditching him the night after we first got together and partly because the whole van scheme is part of this tangled web of amnesia-related lies that seems like it'll never go away.

Though I'm sort of hoping it might this time. Because the GP should be able to give me a clean bill of health on the concussion and the amnesia both. Then I'll be able to head back down to London being all "yeah, it's mostly back now which explains why I'll sort of recognise folk from the Sheffield branch and that."

I kiss Jonathan goodbye. Not as much as I'd like, mind, on account of his nan being right there. And then they're gone, so it's just me again, with nowhere to go except back to my flat.

Once there, I ring Claire and tell her what's happened. Then she brings the rest in so I can tell them and all.

"You *what*?" asks Amjad.

"I quit," I explain.

"But not in a fucking us way?" asks Tiff. "Because I'll be honest, this feels a *bit* like you've quit in a fucking us way."

"I'm not fucking yez," I insist, hoping I'm right. "We made a deal."

"A deal?" asks Claire. I mean I say *asks*. I more mean *repeats in an incredulous tone*.

"Yeah. I said if I quit it'd mean he'd save my salary and you could do my job okay since you were already, and nobody'd have to get sacked."

Claire doesn't sound especially convinced. "And you're sure you did this because it was best for the team, and not because you wanted to ride Jonathan Forest's tower of throbbing man meat?"

Sometimes, Claire can be the fucking worst. "How about we make a new deal," I suggest, "where you never, ever say the words *tower of throbbing man meat* again?"

"Is it, though?" asks Tiff. "Towering?"

"Excuse me," I sputter, "you cannot ask me that. I'm your boss."

"No, you aren't," Tiff reminds me, "you quit."

"I'm still working 'til the end of the year. Which means I can still fire you."

"Won't firing Tiff defeat the purpose of you quitting in the first place?" points out Amjad with his usual infuriating logic.

This is not the love-in I've been expecting. "Look, can we not just take a moment to appreciate my incredible heroism in saving all your jobs at the expense of my own?"

With a sigh, Claire rallies the team. "Fair enough. A big round of applause for Sam, who boldly got laid on our behalf."

"You know what," I say, "I fucking hate you."

"We hate you too," they all—and I mean genuinely *all*—chorus.

After that I finalise arrangements with Tiff for Operation Secretly Move A Load of Christmas Stuff and we sort out where she's going to spend the night, and I explain that I don't care how fine she thinks it'd be, that I'm not letting her just crash in the van because she's a fucking teenager and I'm her fucking boss and there's fucking laws.

"I do it all the time when I'm festivalling," she complains.

I decide to pass it over. "Claire, can you explain?"

"He's worried you'll sue him," she explains.

If I'd been drinking coffee, I'd have spat it out. "Excuse me, I'm not."

"It does sort of sound like you are," offers Amjad.

"No," I protest. "*Jonathan* would be worried she'd sue him."

"Jonathan who you're sleeping with?" clarifies Tiff.

"Jonathan, who although he is a complex man in whom I have learned to see many fine qualities, is still in many *other* ways, a dick."

"And you don't think," says Claire, "that he's maybe rubbed off on you just a little bit?"

This is slander, this is. "Hold on, how am I suddenly the bad guy because I don't want Tiff to have to sleep in a van?"

"It's about respecting my agency," Tiff tells me. "Not respecting my agency is very patriarchal of you."

I give up. And it turns out that's all she wants, because Tiff's no fool and she'll take a free night in a Travelodge if it's offered, especially if you throw in the breakfast buffet.

Then they all go back to work and I go back to...to staring at my walls and not even having my cat for company. Catlessness aside, it's not much different from what my life was like a year ago. But it *feels* different. Emptier. In a way I almost resent.

I'm not—I hope—as extreme as Nana Pauline and Ralph in my general distaste for everything south of Coventry, but it does bother me that I've been down to London and it's made being back up north feel worse. The one thing I'm clinging to—and it's not exactly comforting, not really—is that I'm pretty sure it has nothing to do with the actual city and everything to do with the people. Sure, mostly what I did when I was at Jonathan's was plan a party, watch *Pointless,* and do the occasional bit of cooking, but I wasn't alone. Even when it was just me and Jonathan and he was still in unbelievable bellend mode, there'd been somebody around to just...I don't know, be there, I guess. Because when it's just you and the silence it's easy to feel like you don't exist, like you might as well have never existed. Like you're nothing at all.

I lie on my bed with my eyes closed and try to just sleep. But it doesn't work. The heating's on but I still feel cold deep in my chest and my arms, and sometimes I blink and I think I've been crying.

Then the phone rings.

"Umm." It's Jonathan. It's clearly Jonathan. "Hi."

"Hi."

"Sorry, are you busy?"

I look around at my copious fuck all. "No. Not really."

"I just, well, we got home safely."

"Oh. Good." I wish we weren't both shit at telephones because I really don't want this conversation to end, but if it goes on like this it'll just be *oh/yes/well/exactly* back and forth for eighteen seconds then an awkward ring off.

There's a moment's quiet when I think I hear a touch of embarrassment. "I told my family, by the way. About—I mean—not in detail—and Nana Pauline would have..."

There's a scuffling sound and then Barbara Jane's voice comes clear as a bell down the line. "He says you fucked all night and it was the most mind-blowing experience he'd ever had."

In what now sounds like the distance I hear Jonathan's voice saying *I did not* and *BJ, give me my phone back*.

"So anyway, *daaarling,* how *aaare* you?" Barbara Jane asks. "I understand that you're stuck in Sheffield overnight because Johnny is too cheap to pay for a van."

I think I catch *I am not* from one part of the distant nowhere and *nowt wrong with Sheffield* from another. "It's not that." I'd have wanted to defend Jonathan anyway, even if she hadn't been blaming him for something that was one hundred and three percent my idea. "It's just I've got a van anyway and it seems a waste, plus there's this whole thing where people get stung for income tax if we go over budg—"

"Sam, you're very close to boring me." Barbara Jane doesn't sound bored at all, though I suspect that's more because she's enjoying pissing her brother off than because I'm saying anything she actually cares about.

"Barbara Jane"—I hear Wendy's voice down the line, quieter than usual but that's a relative thing—"give your brother his phone back."

"Shan't."

I think I hear Les's voice next, but I can't make out the words.

"*Fine*," says Barbara Jane. "Here."

I have a vague sense of being passed from hand to hand, then, I hear Jonathan saying: "Sorry about that."

"No worries, I get how it can be."

"They're not usually quite this bad. I think they're overexcited."

There's commentary on that from the rest of the family. I can't quite hear it, but I can imagine it well enough. Jonathan in the kitchen trying to make a call, Wendy and Barbara Jane hovering as close as they can get away with while Les watches from the sofa. "It's fine. Good to hear from you."

"Yes, well..." He's still terrible at this. "I thought I should... you know."

There's another scuffling sound. "He means he misses you and he hopes you get back soon." That's Wendy. "Don't you, love?"

I hear a faint *yes, mother* from Jonathan, then somebody moving in the background followed by Wendy saying very loudly,

"Yeah, that'd be great, two sugars, thanks," before remembering she was on the phone and turning back to me. "Here, did you know Nana Pauline's got a boyfriend and all?"

"Of *course* he knows"—Jonathan's voice is just about audible—"he was there when we picked them up."

"I'll tell you what, though," Wendy carries on, "it ain't half got crowded now. Barbara Jane's had to come in with us to make room."

"It's a delight," Barbara Jane shouts for my benefit. "It's like I'm fucking thirteen."

Jonathan is saying something in the background, but Wendy seems to be holding me near a boiling kettle so I don't have a clue what he's saying. "Hold on," she says, "Jonathan wants to talk again so I'm putting you on speaker."

"Don't put him on speaker," Jonathan protests, entirely in vain, as I get put on speaker.

A chorus of voices *Hi Sam* at me all at once, and my mental picture of the scene adjusts to account for a much bigger crowd.

"Is everybody there?" I ask.

"They wanted to come and say hello to Nana Pauline," explains Jonathan.

"Except me," calls out Agnieszka, sounding slightly more distant than the others, "I just work here—Mrs Forest *please* stop cleaning the sideboards. If you keep doing my job, your son will fire me."

"He bloody well will not," Wendy declares.

"Is this really weird for you?" asks a voice that it takes me one moment to realise is addressing me and another to realise is Anthea.

"Yes," I admit. "Yes, it really is."

"You'll get used to it," drawls Auntie Jack. "Just give it sixty or seventy years."

"You know what?" Jonathan has finally started sounding decisive again. "I think I'm going to take this upstairs."

There's a frankly juvenile chorus of *ooooooohs* from the family, which is cut off by Anthea just saying "really?" at them in a tone of such teenage disapproval that it buys a moment's quiet.

A round of *Bye Sams* fades into the background as Jonathan turns me off speaker again and, I assume, carries me to his room.

"Sorry about that," he says again.

"No, its fine. Good to hear from everyone."

"And it really was everyone." He laughs to himself, much softer than his usual laugh. "God, I really did throw you in at the deep end with this lot, didn't I?"

In a lot of ways, I threw myself in. "I'm getting used to it."

He's quiet again. Then finally he says, "So, I'll see you tomorrow."

"Yeah."

"Good."

We both continue to be shit at telephones.

"So, I suppose..." he tries.

We both continue to be extremely shit at telephones. "Yeah," I say.

"I'm sure you've..."

"And I'm sure you've..."

"Sort of. I think Granddad Del might want to play charades in a bit and he'll get huffy if I'm not there."

"That sounds great," I say. Because it does.

"So I think I should."

"Yeah."

"Good talking to you."

"You, too."

He doesn't hang up. And neither do I.

"I'm aware," he says slowly, "that this is absurd because I only saw you this morning. But I miss you."

And then he rings off like something's caught fire. He doesn't even give me a chance to say I miss him too.

AT THE DOCTOR'S THE NEXT day, I finish up the follow-my-finger tests and wait while Dr Singh checks some notes on her computer.

"So it says here"—she sounds hesitant—"that you've been experiencing some memory difficulties."

Ah. "Yes," I say. "Sort of."

"What do you mean *sort of*?"

"Well, there might have been the tiniest of miscommunications regarding the whole, that is, memory situation."

She pushes her glasses up her nose. She's wearing very large glasses with slightly sparkly rims. Dr Singh is barely older than I am and even though I'm old enough now that I shouldn't find that surprising, I still sometimes feel like she's very young for a doctor. "How tiny?"

I put my fingers about half a centimetre apart.

"I'm not sure that's medically useful."

I inch them slightly further apart.

"Still not."

Giving up the fingers method as a bad job, I explain using my mouth words. "So, when I first fell into the shower, the doctor asked if I remembered what happened, and I said I didn't like, because it was a bit fuzzy, and Jonathan—that's my boss, well, my boyfriend, well, I mean he's my boyfriend now but he was my boss then only I suppose technically he's still my boss because I've quit but I'm still working until the end of the year and—"

"Sam, is this going somewhere?"

"Jonathan said *oh no, he's got amnesia* and I sort of didn't correct him like. And I think it must've made it into the report."

She lets her glasses slide back down her nose, just so's she can look at me over them. "Then you're *not* having problems with your memory?"

"Nope, totally fine. I really did have a concussion, though."

"I'm sure you did. But the man you're going out with who used to be your boss, and who you've been living with while you've been concussed thinks you had full-on movie amnesia?"

I nod. "Yeah."

"Maybe do something about that?"

"I am." I try to sound reassuring. "That's why I'm here. Once you've given me a clean bill of health I can be all like *it's okay, my memory's come back* and it'll be good."

"Apart from the bit where you lied to him for a month."

I put my hands up. "Okay, okay, are you a doctor or a relationship counsellor? I'm trying to make the best of a bad situation."

Not especially bothered by my displeasure, Dr Singh goes back to her notes. "Just trying to take an interest. But *medically* at least you're fine. You can go back to your boyfriend-slash-boss and tell him that the doctor says you're fit as a fiddle."

"Thanks."

"A lying fiddle."

I sigh and leave. I'd be more aggrieved if she didn't have a point.

Once I've had my all clear, the next thing on the agenda is to go and get the van. I've had it for years, but since I've been in Sheffield I've not really used it, I've just stashed it at the edge of town in this garage I rent off a bloke who lives near a chippy.

I fish the key out my pocket and open up. It's one of them private rental deals where I'm basically just borrowing a parking spot for a hundred quid a month. So I'm not exactly shocked to discover that what with my not having been back in a while the owner's filled all the space around the van with whatever crap he didn't want to keep in his house. There's a dartboard over here and a folding table over there, and a bunch of boxes labelled *Scott's Things* though I've no idea who Scott is. I feel a bit bad moving stuff, but some of it's in the way of getting the van out, so I do a bit of scrabbling and a bit of shifting and no small amount of humping until I've got everything put as carefully as I can to one side. Then I get in the van and back it out into the street.

Once the van is safely out, I go to shut the garage door, then I turn back. And I see the name on the side—*Becker and Son, Local Plumbers*—and it brings me up proper short.

I don't think it's that long, not really, though in the winter, on somebody else's driveway, in Sheffield, it feels like ages. Just standing there looking at the *and Son* and feeling—in a way I can't explain—like I've let somebody down. Pulling my jacket a little tighter, I climb in the van and try not to think too hard about, well, about anything really. Then I drive to the store.

When I get there, Tiff is waiting for me next to a massive pile of decorations. I open the back doors of the van and wait for her to get started piling them in, which she doesn't.

"Oh no," she says, "I'm bringing my *creative vision*—you didn't hire me to do heavy lifting."

"It's not heavy," I tell her, "it's bits of plastic and glass."

She looks smug. "Then you'll have no trouble shifting it."

I'm not totally convinced by her argument, but I don't especially want a debate either. So I get to loading boxes. When everything is stashed to Tiff's satisfaction, we hop in the front, I glare at her until she puts a bloody seatbelt on, and we head off.

For a while we drive in silence because while I *like* Tiff and don't think she dislikes me as much as she sometimes pretends to, we do have a bit of a gigantic age gap that makes conversation a bit tricky like.

"How's the course going?" I ask by way of an opening gambit.

She makes a noncommittal noise.

"Getting harder?" I try, increasingly suspecting that I'll be on my own at this end of the conversation.

"Just not feeling it."

"Oh." I drum my hands on the steering wheel for a moment. "Well, maybe it'll sort out once things settle a bit."

"Maybe."

We're silent again. I think about sticking the radio on, but if there's anybody who'd immediately judge me for my music preferences it's Tiff and besides, I'm not totally convinced I'm in a Heart FM mood.

It's starting to rain now, and the drumming against the windscreen at least gives us a bit of percussion to go with our no conversation.

"Actually," she says eventually, "I'm thinking of jacking it in."

"Oh yeah?" I try to sound neutral. I get you're meant to encourage people to stick with stuff, but me and Tiff aren't close—not really—so for all I know she's the worst hair and beauty technician to ever try to make somebody beautiful and hairy.

"Yeah."

We just let the raindrops do their staccato thing and I give her space to talk or not as she wants.

"Just wasn't feeling it," she repeats.

"You said," I say.

"Oh. Right."

The windscreen wipers swish through what's gradually turning into a storm. Finally I try: "Not thinking of going full time into bathrooms I hope?"

"No." She sounds shocked.

"Okay, okay, no need to sound quite that offended. There's decent money to be made in bathrooms."

"Yeah, if you own the showroom."

Some deeply uncool part of me feels compelled to tell her that she can achieve anything if she tries, even though that's not true outside Disney movies. So I follow up with a more noncommittal, "Well, y'know, work hard and maybe one day."

"Maybe one day I'll be the one threatening to sack teenagers so I can make a few extra quid?"

"Yeah," I say, only sixty percent sheepishly.

"Y'see"—now she's drumming her nails on the dashboard, tapping along with the rain—"that's the problem with modern, late-stage capitalist society. It denies people the conceptual framework to imagine an alternative, so even people who are excluded or disenfranchised by it can't imagine an alternative system, only an alternative version of the same system where they have a larger share of the wealth."

"Oh." I'm not sure what to say to that. "That's very political of you."

"Don't worry, I can't vote. And by the time I can I'll be worn down enough to settle for the second-worst option like the rest of you."

We fall quiet again.

"Actually," she says. Then stops.

"Actually what?"

"Nothing."

I let it slide for a bit, but what with this being a four-hour trip

I'm not totally sold on having an uncomfortable silence for literally all of it. "No seriously, actually what."

"I was actually maybe thinking of going into"—she waves a hand—"y'know, *this*."

"You want to be a white van woman?"

She looks at me like I'm the absolute worst. "Events."

"Oh. Right. How'll that work then?"

"There's courses you can do. It's—I don't know, it's just been interesting. More interesting than hair or bathrooms."

To be fair, it probably is. Though I'm not sure you need to work that hard to be more interesting than bathrooms. "Well, I'd hire you," I say in my best supporting-the-ambitions-of-the-youngs voice.

She's quiet again. "Funny you should say that."

"I'd hire you *if I had something needed doing*. Which I don't."

"No, but, like, I might need references. Especially because if I drop out of what I'm doing right now, I look sort of like a quitter."

"So what, you want me to write something saying, I don't know, *under my watchful eye, Tiffany has discovered her true passion for events planning and management and I believe she will be an asset to the field*."

"Forget it, I'll ask Claire."

"*Truly, never has an event been so planned as this event was planned, 'twas a revelation.*"

"Fuck off, Sam."

I flick a disapproving glance towards her for the half-second it's not totally irresponsible to take my eyes off the road. "Still your boss, remember."

"Yeah, but you weren't very good at it."

"Excuse me, I was amazing."

She squirms a little in her seat. "You were fine. But…look, banter aside you're not going to fire me or refuse to write me a reference or anything, are you?"

"No." Though I'm worried now. Which is silly because what Tiff thinks of me really shouldn't matter on account of how she's a teenager who worked for me in a job I've already quit.

"Well, you were fine, but you were always—don't get me wrong, I'm glad you weren't like New Enthusiastic Chris. I'd have *hated* it if you were one of those *hey, let's all be super jazzed to be working for the Splashes-ampersand-Snuggles family*. But you were always a bit…I don't know, checked out?"

"Checked out?"

She nods. "Yeah."

"Checked out how?"

For a moment she doesn't say anything, which feels very concerning, like she's building up to the kind of devastating burn that only a fundamentally well-intentioned teenager can deliver. "There's relaxed," she says at last, "and then there's nihilistic."

"Excuse me," I tell her, "I'm not nihilistic. I'm extremely cheerful."

"So are death row inmates."

"No, they're not."

"Yes, they are."

I risk another half-second glare. "Met a lot, have you?"

"I've seen documentaries. Point is you were always really nice, but it always felt like you were nice because you knew that deep down the whole world was a joke with death as the punch line."

"Okay, now you're making me sound like a fucking serial killer." Which I suppose, to be fair, would be one more thing me and Jonathan had in common.

"I had a bet about that. With Amjad."

"You what?"

"Before we found out you were gay, we had a bet on how many wives you had buried under your floorboards."

My hands tighten on the steering wheel. "Excuse me, gay people can be serial killers too."

"Yeah, but speculating about how many boyfriends you had buried under your floorboards felt creepy." She looks thoughtful for a second. "Strange how that works, isn't it?"

I shake my head. "I can't believe I'm hearing this."

"I'm not saying you weren't nice to work for, and I'm really grateful that you went all the way to London and did all this"—she waves her hands again—"objectively absurd shit to save our jobs. I'm just also saying that if you *had* turned out to have sixteen corpses stashed in your crawlspace, we'd have got over the shock pretty quickly."

"This is fucking slander."

"You've been better lately, mind," she adds.

"You're just saying that because you want a reference."

"No really, I think fake amnesia's been good for you."

Up ahead, we see the lights of a Welcome Break, and since I'm beginning to feel a lot like a break would be welcome, I steer into it. "Just so's you know," I tell Tiff, "I *was* going to buy yez a milkshake, but I don't think I will now."

"Good." She grins at me. "You'd probably have poisoned it anyway."

PART FIVE

COMING CLEAN & SAYING GOODBYE

CHAPTER 32

THE REST OF THE TRIP passes as well as any long road trip with somebody you only know from work can, and I get home that evening—fuck, when did I start calling Jonathan Forest's swanky millionaire pad *home*—to a house full of noise and light and chaos and it's...yeah. It's worth getting used to, and I think I'm getting used to it. Plus Jonathan's as pleased to see me as he can be without setting his family off completely, and I think that's worth getting used to as well.

Next day we have the usual fry-up in the morning and then when Jonathan heads to work, I grab Tiff from the cheap hotel I'd stuck her in and try not to feel too much like I'm having an affair with incongruously festive decor.

I drive us to the venue and, if I'm honest, I start out being—pessimistic isn't right exactly, but being at least open to the possibility that I've set myself up for a massive fall. Because as we carry the boxes down to the little warren of rooms and corridors we've decided to have our Christmas party in, I can't help but feel that this is just a dark basement in Shoreditch and that when people start rolling in from out of town, it's going to carry on being just a dark basement in Shoreditch. And then this'll be the year Jonathan decided to have the Christmas party in a dark basement in Shoreditch, which will rank just under "on a boat" on the list of places no sensible person would choose to have a Christmas party.

But as the hours—and it is hours, turning a basement into a festive wonderland is slow work—pass, I begin to see it. And to give her credit, Tiff has clearly seen it all along. With the lights up, with the decorations just incongruous *enough* and little ornaments set on all the empty shelves and strange nooks I'd seen on my first go around, it begins to look magical out of sheer bloody stubbornness. Because once you've noticed somebody's gone to all the trouble of hiding a tiny wicker reindeer between two bricks in a disused pigeonhole, you have to assume it means something.

By the time seven o'clock rolls around I'm pretty fucking knackered, and if the self-care fairy was to come up to me right and now and tell me, "it's okay, Sam, you can just go to bed and it'll be fine", I'd say *thank God* and face-plant right in front of them. But the self-care fairy isn't real. So instead I let Tiff know she's done a bang-up job and dash out to meet Jonathan, who's technically meant to be hosting.

The timings just about work. Tiff nips away up the street to hook up with the Sheffield crew, and I catch Jonathan coming the other way. What with Croydon being local, he's not had to arrange a convoy and so he can come on his own, which he has, and early, which he also has.

Since this is a work thing, I greet him in a relatively professional way, which is to say a hug but no kiss.

"I know you're worried," I tell him, "but it actually does look good."

"I believe you," he replies, and it sounds oddly sincere. Like it's a big deal. Which I suppose from him it is, because trusting other people is one of Jonathan Forest's twelve least favourite things.

Of course the impact of his big, sincere, I-have-faith-in-you moment is slightly undercut when I lead him in and down to the venue and he looks around at the way Tiff has done it up—soft lighting in a variety of colours, decorations strung just dense enough that you forget you're in a basement until you remember in a cool way—and gives the biggest sigh in the history of inhalation and says, "Oh thank fuck."

"I thought you said you believed me."

"I did," he lies. "I really did. I just—you have to admit, given the budget situation, it was a bit touch and go."

I give him a coy little nod. "Yeah, I suppose so."

We take a tour of the rest of the setup—one room for the buffet, the room where the DJ is for dancing, with overspill rooms nearby wired for sound and other rooms wired for *less* sound so's you've got somewhere to have a talk if you want to. It's big enough and complex enough that by the time we're done taking it all in, the Leeds branch have started showing up and Jonathan has to switch into his highly specific "boss trying to be relaxed" mode, which is painful for everyone involved. So painful, in fact, I leave him to it.

I must have done something right because the party begins to fill out quickly. The Leeds crowd are soon joined by the first of the Croydon lot—the ones who were either afraid of being late or were determined to impress the boss, so their local equivalents of New Enthusiastic Chris. Then we get Sheffield, en masse, then the rest of Croydon trickling in fashionably late like the people who live closest always do at this kind of thing.

For a while I just circulate, trying to take some satisfaction in a job eventually well done. I say hello to a few folks but there's an odd sort of in-betweeny feeling, knowing that I won't be here next year or, if I am, it'll be as Jonathan's plus one. Which is a thought I don't quite know what to do with. Across the room, I catch a glimpse of him making visibly excruciating small talk with someone from another branch. That should not be the sort of thing that makes you want to go and stand next to someone, or hold their hand, or anything like that, but it does. Unfortunately being half-fired, full-quit, and less far from fake amnesia than I'd like to be, I don't quite have the balls.

In the next room, I find Tall Earnest Pam, the manager of Leeds, congratulating Claire on finally replacing me, which doesn't seem like a conversation I'd be an asset to. Over in the corner, Amjad's having a very, very lengthy debate with some feller I don't recognise. And that doesn't seem like a conversation that'd be an asset to me, but I get sucked into it anyway.

"—so fucking basic," concludes a lad with a slight Leeds accent.

"I'm not being basic," Amjad is insisting. "Just because everybody worth listening to agrees with me doesn't make me *basic,* it makes me *right*—here, Sam, back me up on this will you?"

I approach reluctantly. "I'm not going to know what I'm backing you up on, am I?"

"Just repeat after me," he says with a deadly serious look on his face. "*Malekith turning out to be the true Phoenix King was fucking bullshit.*"

Having understood zero of those words, I do my best. "Why are you arguing about the villain from that *Thor* movie?"

Amjad and the feller from Leeds he's been arguing with glare at me like I've spat in their faces and called their mums slappers.

"Not what you're arguing about?" I ask.

"No," they both say at once.

"See what I put up with," Amjad says.

"It's awful." The Feller From Leeds sighs. "I was talking to Pam about *Lord of the Rings* the other day, and you know what she said?"

Amjad gives him a look of deep shared suffering. "They should have just got the eagles to fly them to Mordor?"

While they're commiserating over that, I back away and go back to circulating. It's nice and all to see everybody, and they do seem to be having a genuinely good time—or at least a better time than they had the last couple of years—but my in-betweeny feeling has settled into knowing I don't belong here. Of course, it's too soon to say I belong with Jonathan either, only I'd rather be there than here. And by there I mean on his uncomfortable sofa, watching him trying to pretend he's not spent the last hour making Gollum chase after a mouse on a string.

It's a comforting thought, and I let myself be comforted. I let myself so much that I manage to spend about twenty minutes just swiping through my mental photo album of warm-making Jonathan images. And it turns out I've got a lot, even if he's scowling in most of them. Except, as I run to the end of the folder, I sort of become aware that a lot of people are...looking at me, and not just in a "why is that berk standing in the corner with a soupy expression on his face" way. And probably it's nothing, probably they're just saying, "oh, that's the feller what organised this, he seems like a good bloke". And then the lass from Croydon gives me an actual fucking thumbs-up, which feels far worse than any thumbs-up has a right to feel because you don't thumbs-up someone to say "well done putting together this slightly above average office Christmas party."

Oh fuck me. I hope this isn't what I think it is.

"Sorry," I say. "But can I ask what you're thumbs upping me for?"

"Just, y'know," she unexplains, "good on you."

Her conspiratorial tone reinforces my suspicion that she's not congratulating me on my expert choice of decorations. "Good on me for what?"

She nudges me with her elbow. "For getting one over on the Prince of Pricksylvania."

Bollocks. Very probable bollocks. "Getting one over *how*?"

"Well, what I heard," she tells me, though at this stage she's very much explaining it for the cheap seats, "is that Jonathan was threatening to fire your whole team, so you pretended to have amnesia and—"

Confirmed bollocks. "Who told you?"

"It's fine." She's smiling in a way that I really wish she wasn't smiling. "None of us'll tell *him*."

This is not reassuring. Reassurance is not occurring. I am distinctly unreassured. "Who's *us*?"

She thinks about this for far, far too long. "Well, I got it from Agnes, who got it from Jim, who got it from Mickey, who got it from Liam—"

I don't let her finish. I just take off and start running around like a whippet. I'm not sure what I'm trying to achieve really, but I think if I stand still I'll have a complete fucking breakdown. Because there is no way this is not getting back to Jonathan and when it does—

I can't even think about that.

Out of either desperation or a masochistic need to remind myself how screwed I am, I start stopping randoms and checking if they've heard, which not only makes me terrible at a party but is also probably making things worse, because it means the ones who *don't* know, and there's a couple though not many, now know there's something *to* know and so there's a good chance they'll find out later.

I spot Liam, the Croydon lad what'd been there when I fell through the Nexa by MERLYN 8mm Sliding Door Shower enclosure and breathlessly, and slightly incoherently, ask where he heard what he heard.

To my immense frustration, he shrugs like it's not a big deal. "It's just going around," he says. "But don't worry. Everybody thinks you're cool."

If my chief concern was *will the Croydon and Leeds branches think I'm cool*, that would be very helpful. But it's not. I pinball off Liam and—across an artfully dingy party-space lit only by fairy lights—I catch sight of Brian. He's wandering over to the buffet table and I hoy after him.

"Brian." I'm trying not to sound angry and fortunately I'm panicked enough that I mostly just sound terrified. "What did you say and who did you say it to?"

"Well, I had a lovely talk with Jill from Leeds about this new powder she's got for her feet and—"

That was on me. Should've been more specific. "About the amnesia."

He beams. "Don't worry, Sam. I remembered not to say a word to Jonathan."

Ah. Right. Should have been more specific about that too. "Or to anybody else?" I ask in my most hopeful voice.

"Oh, I've been very discreet," he reassures me. "I've only mentioned it to one or two people, and I've told them they're not to say anything to Mr Forest."

So it's over then. I mean, I knew it was over. But now it's over in this axe-coming-down kind of way. Because either somebody will forget and tell Jonathan. Or they'll decide that the boss has the right to know he's been played and tell Jonathan. And if it's the second, I'm not sure I'd blame them. I should have come clean weeks ago. I'd just been scared of losing everything all over again. And now I'm going to lose it anyway. Him. I'm going to lose him.

I'm sweating that cold dread sweat through my suit as I search for Jonathan. At this stage I don't think getting to him first is going to make a blind bit of difference, but what else can I do?

So here I am, running around that beautifully decorated, surprisingly Christmassy, increasingly claustrophobic and disorienting basement in Shoreditch like I'm in some kind of festive nightmare with all my work colleagues doing guest spots.

After I don't know how long, I come out into one of the little side rooms and at last I see Jonathan. He's talking to Tall Earnest Pam. And if there is anybody who would decide, for perfectly earnest reasons, that Jonathan Forest has a right to know that I don't have amnesia, it'll be Tall Earnest Pam.

And she's looking really earnest.

I don't quite go into slow motion, but I do become very, very aware of everything that's happening around me. The DJ is playing Slade and from across the dancefloor I watch Jonathan's expression go from that polite engagement bosses get talking to staff to a kind of say-that-again uncertainty. Then Pam says whatever it is she was saying again, and he looks—not how I'd expected. I'd been expecting angry. I'd been expecting him to flip his lid like he did back when I told him he didn't take criticism well. But he just looks...nothing.

Over the speakers, Noddy Holder is yelling *Iiiiiiiiiiits Chriiiiiiiiiiistmaaaaaaaas* at everyone and on the other side of the room Jonathan Forest turns away from Tall Earnest Pam, and he looks right at me. Looks right at me but doesn't see me or doesn't seem to.

And suddenly I'm feeling very detached like. As if I'm not really here. As if he's not really here. I can't say for sure but I think I reach out to him.

But he's already walking away.

Though I know Jonathan Forest can throw a hell of a strop when he wants to, I also know that there's nothing he takes more seriously than his work, so there's no way he's gone far. I gamble on him not having made it further than the pavement outside the venue, and sure enough there he is. He's got his hands stuffed into his pockets and he's staring up into the sky like he's trying to count the stars.

"I've got to hand it to you, Sam," he says, not looking at me. "It worked."

There is no possible answer I can give to that.

"You wanted to keep your job, and you kept it. At least until you left on your own terms. You wanted to save your branch and your team, and you saved them. And, of course, most importantly you wanted to take His Royal Dickishness down a peg or two."

I don't know what's worse: that he thinks that, or he's sort of right. "I didn't mean—"

"You did."

"I di—"

"Please, Sam, don't."

Turns out, I'm not very used to Jonathan Forest saying *please.* Turns out I like it less than I thought I might. There's so much that I want—that I need—to say to him. But trying after he's just told me not to would be selfish. And I've done enough of that. Unfortunately, what this means in practice is we stand there in silence outside an overpriced party venue in Shoreditch.

At last, Jonathan says, "The local branch call me the Prince of Pricksylvania."

"I know," I admit.

"Leeds just goes with *Wankerthon Forest.*" He shrugs. "Which I think lacks creativity."

It's very late in the day for empathy, but I try anyway. "I'm sorry. That must actually suck for you."

He's still not moved. He looks like a statue entitled *Sam, you totally fucked it.* "I'm the boss. It goes with the territory. All that's changed is that I never used to care."

I'm not strictly sure that's true. Because he used to get quite angry about Claire calling him His Royal Dickishness. Then again, I suppose caring like pissed off isn't the same as caring like hurt. "They're just people who work for yez," I try, very, very sensible of the irony that I'm the one saying this. "It doesn't matter what they think."

He scowls into a space a moment. Then finally looks at me, with this careful expressionlessness that's its own kind of devastating. "It matters what you think."

I should have been braced for that but I'm not. And it kicks the wind out of me. Makes me feel like a total piece of shit. "What I think is...is what I've spent the last month working out, I think. Which is that who you are as a boss and who you are as a person are different things."

"If that was true, you'd have told me what was going on." He gives one of those tight blinks you do when you're trying to stop yourself crying. "If that was true, you'd have trusted me."

"I should have," I say, a bit desperate like. "But I was scared and confused and...and I know this is probably the wrong thing to bring up right now, but I really did have a concussion."

"But you did remember me?"

A passing Londoner makes a frustrated noise as he weaves between us. "Yeah," I say. "And I didn't mean to...to...lie to yez. I just got caught up. And I wasn't trying to get one over on yez either. I just needed time to—I don't know. Fix things." I risk taking a few steps closer to Jonathan. He doesn't exactly pull back but he holds himself very rigid. I never realised a couple of paving slabs could feel so fucking far. "But then I got to know you more and—" God, I'm making a hash of this. "And," I press on, already knowing it's probably useless, "I really did—do—like yez. That wasn't part of...the other stuff. That was—that was real."

You can't really have silence in London. But there's silence between us and it's big enough to swallow the city. Then Jonathan just says, "I know."

Which should be a good thing to hear. But he's not saying it in a good thing way. The bit of me that's grasping at straws, though, grasps anyway. "Then what's the problem? I like you, you like me, I don't work for you anymore. I made a mistake and I'm sorry, but it's not a mistake I'm ever going to make again."

"You like me," Jonathan repeats like a death sentence, "but not enough." He pushes a hand through his hair, his white streak falling over his fingers the way, a few nights back, it fell over mine. "You're the person who's thought best of me...who's come the closest to understanding me...who made me feel I wasn't—wasn't impossible to... Wasn't impossible. But all that time, deep down, when it mattered, all you saw was your arsehole boss."

"That's not who I see," I tell him. Because it's not. It hasn't been for a while.

"Then why are we here, Sam?" He still doesn't sound angry. In some ways, I wish he did. I wish he'd just shout at me and I could back into another Nexa by MERLYN 8mm Sliding Door Shower enclosure and we could take another run at this. "All you had to do was be honest with me. Instead, you played me for a fool."

"Aye, but I played myself as well." I'm beginning to hate those two paving stones. "You're the best thing that's happened to me for years."

He gives one of his least pleasant snorts. "My condolences."

He's just being a bastard—and he's got reason to—but it still catches me somewhere tender like. "Don't say that. I can't handle it right now."

"And I'm supposed to handle"—he makes an "everything all at once" gesture—"this."

"I'm just trying to say sorry and that I care about yez. And I hate the thought I've fucked it up over...over nothing."

"So do I. But you did."

Well, that feels fucking final. "Please don't let this"—I'm

begging and who cares—"I don't know. Just please don't. I just need—"

"Time?" Jonathan asks. And he just sounds so fucking sad.

"A chance?" I try.

"Sam," he says. "You'll be fine. Give it a week and you'll forget all about me."

I flinch. "I won't. I couldn't."

But Jonathan just shakes his head. "This would never have worked. I'm too—you're too—this was too much."

And that's when I know it's proper over. Because you don't kiss a man like Jonathan Forest lightly. And you don't hurt him lightly either.

CHAPTER 33

IT STARTS RAINING AS I walk away and I'm halfway to the bus stop before I remember I brought a van and I'm halfway to the van before I realise I've been crying and my face isn't just wet from the weather. Fortunately—well, fortunately relative to how things have gone recently rather than relative to a world where Brian didn't completely drop me in it—while I've managed to leave my jacket behind, everything I'll need to pack up and go back to the empty something I call my life is in my trouser pockets. And by *everything*, I mean *my keys and my phone.*

And thinking about it, even the phone's optional.

I've stashed the van in a long-stay car park not far from the venue, though the stay is turning out to be a lot less long than I'd intended. And I'm so cut up from the Jonathan thing that I don't even stop to get double-cut-up about the *Becker and Son* sign. Which I suppose is one of those small blessings you're meant to be thankful for.

I open the door, swing myself inside, and start driving.

The first thing I realise is how cold, damp, and miserable I am. The thing about being in the rain is you're sort of at one with the elements, so even if it's a bit nippy out it's bearable. But the moment you're not being pelted with sky-water and you get somewhere that's less warm and cosy than it could be, you start to really feel all the ways you're shivering, and how your clothes are clinging places they shouldn't cling and climbing up cracks they shouldn't climb.

The second thing I realise is that I haven't got a clue where I'm going.

I mean, I do. Obviously. Long-term I need to get back to Croydon to get my clothes and my cat—though maybe not on that last one, maybe I should just let Jonathan keep the little bastard—and once that's done I need to fuck off back to Sheffield where I belong.

Where I just quit my job.

Where I wasn't much cop at the job I quit anyway.

Where I never really belonged in the first place.

I'm driving in circles now, going around and around Finsbury Circus staring up at all those huge, intimidating, archetypally London houses looming five or six storeys high above me.

Well, Samwise Eoin Becker, you've made some terrible choices.

Hoping to feel at the very, very least like I'm going somewhere instead of nowhere, I start driving in a direction I think is south. Though it's well past rush hour, London doesn't care and the traffic's still so backed-up that it takes well over an hour to get to Croydon. Then once I'm there it takes me another twenty minutes to build up the courage to go in the house. Confronting Jonathan was bad enough—confronting his whole fucking family is going to be carnage. I mean, what am I going to say to them? "Hi, Jonathan's dumped me on account of how I don't actually have amnesia and didn't have the bollocks to talk to him like a sensible human being."

I park the van and creep towards Jonathan's front door, hoping I've dithered for long enough that everyone'll be in bed. And it nearly works, except I find Wendy in the kitchen wearing a blue dressing gown printed with white roses and a pair of novelty slippers that turn up at the end into tiny leopard seals.

"Hello, love," she greets me, much as I wish she wouldn't. "I wasn't expecting you back yet."

"No," I say.

Though I've not given her much to go on, Wendy is putting twos together into fours very quickly. "Where's Jonathan?"

"Still at the party. I—we—look, there's no easy way to say this but I've not got amnesia."

"Oh." She sticks her hands in the pockets of her dressing gown. "Do you want a cup of tea?"

"Did you not hear me?"

She's already got the kettle on. "Well," she says, "I won't say I'm not confused, but the way I see it, what you remember's up to you, and we've all got things we'd rather forget." She drops two teabags into two mugs, pours hot water and milk over each and then plonks them both, teabags still in, onto the kitchen table. Then she grabs a side plate and a teaspoon so I can stop brewing when I'm ready.

I take the tea like it's a reflex, like it doesn't occur to me that I could, y'know, not. "Aye, but I really hurt Jonathan."

"Well." The *well* hangs there a while, then she adds, "That's between you and him, isn't it? He's always been a sensitive sort."

I'm about to say that I'm not sure we're talking about the same Jonathan, but then I realise that we completely are. If he wasn't sensitive, he wouldn't be half so much of a prick and I wouldn't have fucked this up half so badly. "I probably shouldn't be here when he gets back."

"You reckon?" This is a mam tactic. She means "you're wrong", but she knows saying it outright will just make me dig in.

"I reckon it's what he'd want. I tried to say sorry but it didn't take."

She nods, sort of reassuring. "Doesn't surprise me. Angry's easier than sad, especially for blokes."

"He wasn't angry, though. Just sad."

"See." Wendy pokes me in the arm. "You've been good for him."

"If I'd been good for him, he wouldn't be angry or sad."

She gives me a look that's just a "you reckon" in visual form. "That's not how it works, Sam. If you go through life expecting other people to feel the feelings you feel like they should be feeling, you're going to make things very hard on yourself."

That takes me a second to parse, so I just say "s'pose" to fill the gap.

"You don't have to leave." She scootches her chair around towards me, sliding it across the kitchen floor with a *burrdurr* of rubber feet on tiles. "Jonathan'll come round."

"I don't think he's the coming round type."

"He weren't the having the whole family over for Christmas type neither but look how that went."

I try not to listen to that with my hopeful ears on. Because whatever time of year it might be, I'm past expecting miracles. "It don't feel right to stay. Not after...what I did."

"I'm sure you know best." She clearly isn't and I clearly don't. "But you really don't want to be driving back to Sheffield this time of night."

Fuck, I really don't. For so many reasons. "I'll work something out."

"I'm sure you know best," says Wendy again, sipping her tea.

I look at her across the table. "You know I'm wise to this trick."

"What trick?"

"You telling me you support my decisions so's I'll all second-guess myself and think maybe I'm wrong."

"Oh." With a ceramic clink, she sets her mug down slightly to the left of the nearest coaster. "That trick."

Swallowing hard, I try to psych myself up to say some things I'm not sure I want to say. "I know you think he'll be fine," I begin, "but the thing is—I think I won't. Like I don't know how to face him."

That gets through to her. She gives me this quiet, understanding look that I've not really had from anybody since my own nan went and it sort of makes my mouth go dry in ways I'm not prepared for. "Fair enough," she says. "Let's see about getting you sorted out."

Getting me sorted out, it seems, means making sure Gollum's in his travel case, then trying to work out where the hell I can find a pet-friendly hotel room at basically no notice the wrong side of midnight. Both of which take longer than they have any right to.

"Well," Wendy says, with that over-eager expression mams get when they know they're going to offer you exactly what you need exactly when you need it. "If you're okay going without water you can stay at ours."

"I couldn't," I tell her and then immediately follow it up with, "I mean, I might have to, but I'll feel bad about it."

"Don't be silly," she reassures me. Beside her, Gollum makes grumpy noises in his carry case. "Best for everybody. Besides, means there's somebody to turn the lights on so burglars don't know we're out."

"My mam used to think about that too," I tell her. "If I'm honest, I sometimes wonder if burglars spend as much time watching hall lights as we think they do."

She shrugs. "Well, all I can say is I always leave me lights on, and I've never been burgled. So I must be doing something right."

My tea's still hot so I can't really drain it, but I take a big swallow, then push the mug away. "I should—y'know."

"Yeah," she says, "alright, love." She hands me my bag, and my case of irate house pet, and that's it. I'm going. Standing in the doorway taking one last look back at Jonathan's huge, pointless, nowhere-near-as-empty-as-it-used-to-be detached residence in the nice part of Croydon.

Wendy gives me a hug. "You stay in touch, you hear?"

"Will that not be a bit odd?"

She doesn't look like she cares if it is. "You're a nice boy, Sam, which is more than I can say for most of Jonathan's exes. More than I can say for Jonathan sometimes."

"Still it—"

She shushes me, then kisses me on the cheek. "You know where we are if you need us. Have a safe trip."

And then I go. Just me, my cat, and my dad's van, off to spend the night in my briefly-boyfriend's mum and dad's house.

It was sweet of Wendy to offer but, good God, does it feel shit in practice.

Les and Wendy's place is only about thirteen minutes away from Jonathan's, but it's a very different style of house. A two-up-two-down terrace job that was probably originally built for factory workers in Victorian times or something. I let myself in, go to get a glass of water, then remember there won't be any. I think about turning in—to my immense relief they've got a spare room which means I'm not going to have to sleep in Jonathan's mum and dad's bed—but I'm still too agitated to really sleep at all. So I let Gollum out and watch him run around like he's looking for lost pirate treasure while I flop down in their living-room-slash-dining-area and try not to think about anything.

I fail.

So I get up, head to the van, and come back with a pipe cutter, a junior hacksaw, a half-round file, some steel wool and—well, in the end I say fuck it and just grab the whole toolbox.

Tracking down the burst pipe is simple enough—and it's under the sink right by the stopcock which makes it nice and easy to work with. I drain what's left of the water out the system, then

I lie down, cut through the bit that's burst, sand off the edges on what's left and attach a bit of pipe coupling. Once that's done I tighten everything up, give it a polish, turn the water back on and job's a good 'un.

In the eight seconds after I'm done, I go through this weird, plumbing-related emotional wringer, where I start off feeling all satisfied and that because I've done something useful and I've got a lot of good memories associated with plumbing. Except good memories can be really hard sometimes, which is sort of why I've not done much of this kind of work in a while. Only they're... they're not. Not now. And that's great until I remember how badly I fucked things up with Jonathan. And then I'm right back to lying on somebody else's lino with the one person whose opinion I give a fuck about thinking I'm a lying piece of shit.

Worse, Gollum's apparently decided that he likes Jonathan more than me and that Jonathan's parents smell more like Jonathan than I do, so he's gone to sleep in Les and Wendy's room.

Making a mental note to give the bed a once-over with the lint roller before I go, I leave him to it.

But I don't have a very good night.

CHAPTER 34

ON CHRISTMAS EVE I GET up early, wrangle Gollum back into his case, and head out into the cold, grey, really fucking windy as it happens, Croydon dawn. And I drive.

Leaving London is always hard. Not emotionally—emotionally London can get fucked. But practically. I'm in the south and I want to get north, but I still have to drive south for about twenty minutes to get on the M25, then *around* the M25 for the best part of an hour before I can even begin to get away from the fucking city.

I'd like to say that when I do I feel something like release. That the part of my life that had Jonathan and the Christmas party and the whole complicated business with actually having a concussion and not actually having amnesia and wanting to do right by everyone and not doing right by anyone and it all going to total, absolute shit right at the last possible minute fades into the distance as I speed past Watford Gap. But it doesn't. Everything just continues to suck.

Since I've left early—too early probably, because I've not slept well and am probably only borderline safe to drive—I get back to Sheffield only slightly after noon and find myself in the middle of town on Christmas Eve with no idea where to go or what I'm meant to be doing.

I go home first, to get Gollum settled in, though he's been away so long it's like getting him used to a new place all over again. Thinking about it, maybe I should have swiped one of Jonathan's T-shirts to calm him down with.

"I'm sorry," I tell him as he makes a very determined effort to squeeze himself into the gap behind the fridge. "I know you liked him better, but you're stuck with me now."

He looks back at me, uncomprehending, or possibly just peeved—it's hard to tell with any cat, but especially one with a face like Gollum's.

What with him being so antsy, I feel a bit bad leaving him, but it gets to where I can't not. Being shut up in an empty-but-for-cat flat from now until—I don't know, until I get a job, die, or have to go to the shops I suppose—feels like a particularly cold, damp flavour of hell. Besides, cats aren't pack animals; he'll only notice I'm gone if he wants something.

Not being what my mum would call a fashion plate, I've only got one jacket, and that jacket is currently in a basement in Shoreditch, or maybe in a lost-and-found box at a venue in Shoreditch, or if I'm very, very lucky being transported back to Sheffield by one of my team members who might have recognised it and forgotten that they don't really have any way to get it back to me on account of my not working with them anymore. Either way, it makes my walk through the town centre incredibly fucking bitter, which I find bleakly appropriate. For a while I just put up with it out of a misplaced sense of penance, but in the end I say fuck it and grab myself an olive colour block padded jacket from George at Asda.

Between the cold, the sad, and the nothing, the whole day slips away, until I get to the point I realise I've not eaten since last night and I should probably do something about that. I'm not sure what fit of masochistic despair sends me back to Uncle Sams. I think on the way I tell myself that I just really want a burger, then when I'm there I tell myself that it's too late to go anywhere else even though there's at least three other restaurants I've gone past on the way.

Finally I admit I'm being pathetic.

I get myself seated and order a burger.

"I like your jacket," says the waitress when she's brought my order. "Is it new?"

"Aye," I say, and then immediately add, "twenty-three quid, Asda George."

If it wasn't for the whole bit where it tastes of ash and misery, it'd be a pretty decent burger. But it does. Still, I tip generous-ish and then finally mooch my way home.

Since I've got nothing to do with the rest of my evening or, for that matter, the rest of my life, I whack on the TV, and I'm just navigating by instinct to *Pointless* when I realise that *even that* is going to remind me of Jonathan now.

But fuck it, I'm in a wallowing mood. So I set myself up for a good long wallow. I turn off *Pointless*, download UKTV Play and stick on *Auf Wiedersehen, Pet*.

I'm all of two episodes in before I start crying for no fucking reason.

It's Christmas day, and I've got nothing to do and nobody to do it with, so I go visit the family.

One of the tricky things about the north, especially when you've let yourself get all Londonified by a scowly man with hairy arms and heavy eyebrows, is that you start thinking of it like it's all one place like, when it's actually fucking enormous. Well, enormous by England standards—I understand Americans see it differently.

Either way, the trip from my cold, empty, miserable flat to the cold, empty, slightly less miserable place my parents are at is a bit over two hours in good traffic.

And there they are. Right where I left them.

Allerton's a nice cemetery, all told. Green and well maintained, and I like to think it's where they'd have wanted to be if they'd been remotely at an age where they thought it was worth making plans for that kind of thing. Which of course they weren't. Mostly they'd been making plans for their silver wedding, which should have happened about two weeks after they got run down by some prick in a Bugatti on the way home from their regular Friday dinner out.

"If it's good enough for Ken Dodd and Cilla Black," I can imagine my dad saying, "it's good enough for me."

Not that he ever got the chance.

They're actually pretty close to Ken Dodd. Not that he was really either of their sort of comedian. My granddad was a fan, though he went a while back, and so was my nan, who I lived with after. It was her going that set me running to Sheffield in the first place.

So, there they all are in a row. Six of the buggers, my mum and dad in the middle and their parents on either side like the bride and groom's family at a wedding. Which is sort of...how it's meant to work in a way. There's a reason that Hugh Grant movie had a funeral in it as well as a clunky line about the Partridge family and some very silly hats.

William Becker. Mary Becker. Thomas Becker. Louise Becker—she was a modern woman, my mam, but it was still pretty rare for a lass to keep her own name back when she got married. Then after that Bridget O'Brien—last to go, right next to her daughter—and Samuel O'Brien, who used to tell his friends I was named after him even though I technically wasn't.

It's snowing.

It never fucking snows on Christmas. Not even this far north. But it's snowing now. I don't really believe in God, but if I did I'd think he was trying to mess with my head. That or he just wanted to teach me a lesson for being too proud to bring my Olive Block Colour Padded Jacket.

"Well," I say to my mum, and my dad, and all four of my grandparents, "this is where I am now. It's been a bit of an odd month, to be honest."

It's not just God. I don't think I believe in much of anything, really. But times like this I fucking wish I did. I wish I did so badly it makes me want to have stern words with whichever prick made up the rules about blokes crying.

"See I met this lad," I go on. "I mean, I say met. I'd been working for him for a couple of years and, well, honestly I don't think you'd have got on." I give Granddad William a look. "Okay, you might. But then from what I remember you were a bit of a prick yourself when you were with us."

The wind's picking up, and I pull the coat I'm not wearing tighter around myself. At least I've got Mam's scarf, though she picked it for how it looked not how well it kept off the breeze. She was never a practical woman, our mam.

"The thing is," I tell the Becker-O'Brien clan, "I messed up. I don't quite know what I was thinking at the time, but I'm also not quite sure what I should have done differently other than—well—look I blame you for this, Dad, because we had that fucking Goldie Hawn movie on DVD and it was one of your favourites, but I told him I had amnesia."

I tuck my fingers into my sleeves. I should've brought gloves. I've *got* gloves. I just didn't think ahead, which given how things shook out might be more like the story of my life than I've been willing to admit.

"You must be freezing," says a voice from behind me. And

even though I don't believe in ghosts any more than I believe in God, I jump out my fucking skin because while it's a very nice graveyard and it's the early morning and everything's very un-scary, I *am* still surrounded by dead people.

When I turn around I see Jonathan Forest. He's looking wary and I don't think I've ever seen him look wary before. But that's the only thing that's unfamiliar about him. The rest I could have filled in without even turning round. The way his lips turn down like he's scowling when he's really not. Those heavy brows that, if he was a different sort of man, he'd have done something about. The streak in his hair that looks even whiter in the snow. I'm a bit afraid to be glad to see him, but I can't stop myself.

"You forgot your coat," he says, holding out my jacket.

"'Bout the only thing I did actually forget." I really, really hope it's not too soon to be making jokes about it.

"So I gather." He comes forward and drapes the jacket over my shoulders. And it's like—you know when you come in from the cold and you don't take your coat off exactly that second, and then your mam or your granddad says you need to get it off right now or you'll not feel the benefit when you go out again? It's that, only backwards. I feel the benefit more than I've ever felt anything.

I look at him, then I look at the jacket, then I look around at the cemetery in a town which, to my knowledge, Jonathan has never even been to. "What are you doing here?"

His ears go a bit pink. "I told you. You forgot your coat."

"And that made you come randomly to a graveyard in Liverpool?"

"No. It made me go to Sheffield. Realise you weren't there. And then..." His ears go even pinker. "Well, I did put a tracker on your phone."

Oh, he had, hadn't he? Of all the high-handed, controlling, actually kind of sweet things he'd done, that was probably the most high-handed, controlling, and actually kind of sweet. "Yeah, remind me to turn that off."

"You agreed to it at the time."

"I did but I've made a lot of very bad choices recently."

He glances away. "Was I one of those bad choices?"

"No," I reply, faster than any human being has ever replied to anything. "Fuck no. I meant, I made bad choices that made things go wrong with you and I wish I hadn't. And I wish I could—but I can't."

"And so you left?"

He doesn't sound accusing. He doesn't sound anything. Which is sort of something all by itself. "You didn't want anything to do with me, Jonathan. You wouldn't even let me say sorry."

"I didn't want you to leave, though." He turns back to me. The snow's still coming down and it's beginning to settle, turning the ground the same colour as the sky, and making Jonathan look like he's the only real thing in the whole place. "I was surprised. And at a work event. And not prepared for you to…to…"

"Be faking amnesia?" I asked. "To be fair, that's not the sort of thing people are prepared for in general."

His gaze is dark and unwavering. "To hurt me. To be able to hurt me."

It's kind of the worst thing someone can say to you. Because you can't hurt someone unless they care. And you shouldn't if they do. "I really am," I say, "beyond fucking sorry."

"I know."

"And I wasn't faking liking yez."

"I know that too." He swallows with a dry little click. "After all, you clearly have terrible taste."

"Oi. I do not."

"I've met your cat."

"You love my cat."

Jonathan clears his throat. "I suppose I do. And I suppose part of the reason I'm here is that, well, maybe I'd like your cat back in my life. Because I never meant to make your cat feel he had to leave."

This is another one of them Jonathan Forest closest he can get deals. And you know what? I'm fine with it. "The cat was just really cut up about letting you down like," I say. "And he'll do a better job of trusting you in future."

"I really do understand why he..." Jonathan blinks, as if he's only just realised what he's participating in. "This is silly. Why you acted the way you did. And while I'm not...thrilled about it, I don't think I want to lose you over it."

The fact he'd driven for six hours on Christmas morning should have probably tipped me off to the possibility that he might be willing to give me a second chance. But hearing him say it—especially when I was so convinced it was over—messes me up a bit. "Really?"

"Yes, Sam, really. And it's very cold and I'm quite nervous and I've missed you more than I should in thirty-seven hours, so if I could have an answer that would be good."

My answer is obviously yes. But my head's all over the place and I'm scared of saying the word in case it breaks. So I kiss him instead. And straightaway he puts his arms around me, and it's snowing, and it's Christmas, and we're in a fucking graveyard and I'm wearing a jacket that isn't properly on because it's just over my shoulders and my fingers are still freezing and—when we break apart I realise I'm crying, like, loads.

"Sorry," I say. With, let's be honest, very little clarity and absolutely no dignity. "I'm just a bit. It's a lot."

"Thinking about it, I should probably have waited until..." Jonathan brushes a small minority of the tears from my cheeks. I wonder if the day'll come when I stop being surprised by how gentle he can be. "Until you weren't in a cemetery?"

I shake my head. "No. I'm...glad you're here." And because there isn't really a good way to introduce someone to your dead family, I take his hand and lead him over to the graves. "These are...I mean...part of why I...I know I should've been straight with you, but it wasn't just the job, you know. It was...it was this. Like when you were asking what I had waiting for me, where my family were and that, it was so much easier to say I didn't remember. Because then I didn't have to."

He doesn't say anything. He just nods. His hand in mine is this little ball of warmth when all the world is cold.

"Car accident," I explain. "A few years ago."

We're side by side now, standing in front of them, watching snow gathering on the headstones. "Do you want to tell me about them?" he asks.

And it turns out, at last, I do.

EPILOGUE

IT'S CHRISTMAS AGAIN.

"Why didn't you cut crosses in them sprouts?" Nanny Barb is asking.

"Because you don't have to," Jonathan's telling her. "BJ, for once in your life back me up on something. You don't need to cut crosses in sprouts."

"It disgusts me," she says, "but he's right."

Things have been okay for the past year. It did, in the end, take us a bit to get completely past the whole faking amnesia thing—

"Who finished the gravy?" Granddad Del is staring at an empty gravy boat with a look of frankly disproportionate outrage. "I've not had mine yet."

"Yes, you have." Auntie Jack points at his plate with her fork. "You can see it right there. It's just the potatoes absorbed a lot of it."

—but we got there in the end. And we can laugh about it now. Just like we laugh about the time Jonathan threatened to fire me and my whole team a few weeks before Christmas. I think it helps that we're both quite awful people.

Across the table, Ralph is reading a joke from a cracker. "What's Santa's wife's name?"

"M—" Barbara Jane begins, but Nana Pauline points a warning finger at her.

"No guessing. Barb, tell her she's not to be guessing."

"You're not to be guessing," Nanny Barb agrees. "I don't know what it is with young people today."

"Think they know everything." Nana Pauline turns to Ralph. "They do, don't they, they think they know everything."

"They do," echoes Ralph and, for that matter, everybody in the room over the age of sixty.

Barbara Jane rolls her eyes. "I don't think I know *everything*. I just think I know the punch line to a very old Christmas cracker joke."

Since I've been with Jonathan, I've got very used to this dynamic. I'm still not quite as part of it as everybody else, but then some of them have had a fifty-year head start, and I'm definitely getting there.

"Just let him read it out," Auntie Jack tells us. "It'll be quicker in the long run."

I've got a sinking feeling it won't be.

"Mary," says Ralph.

"Is that it?" I ask.

He looks down at the scrap of paper he's holding pinched between thumb and forefinger. "Yes."

"Are you *absolutely* sure?" I'm doing my best to nudge him without sounding too much like a back-seat joke-teller.

Nanny Barb is shaking her head. "Jokes have got very strange these days."

"Is it"—Anthea raises a hand from the other end of the table—"is it possibly *Mary Christmas*?" I've only known her a year but I'm amazed how much she's changed between sixteen and seventeen. She's not much taller but she's cut her hair short and got really into nail art and '70s psychedelia.

Ralph looks down again. "Oh hang on, I had my thumb over half of it." He moves the obscuring digit. "Yeah, that's right."

"Well, I still don't get it," grumbles Nanny Barb.

"What's not to get?" I ask. "It's *Mary Christmas.*"

"Is it because of the Bible?" Les wonders aloud. "Y'know, because she was Jesus's mum."

"No," I try, "it's because it sounds like *Merry Christmas.*"

Les looks contemplative, which to be fair is very much his resting look. "It don't, though, does it?"

"I will admit," I admit, "it doesn't work perfectly in my accent. Like I think you have to really imagine stretching out the e in *Merry*. Like, y'know, *Meeeery Christmas.*"

"You see when Quincey told this joke," Barbara Jane cuts in—Quincey was her ex, the Texan oil feller—"it worked perfectly. *What's Santa's wife's name?*" she asks in what I assume is an okay Texas accent. "*Mary Christmas.*"

"Bloody liberty that is," Nana Pauline tells the whole room, "charging us good money for jokes as only work in a foreign accent."

Jonathan gets up from the table. "And on that note, I'm going to get Granddad some more gravy. Does anybody else want anything from the kitchen?"

"Tell you what, I'll come help you carry." I don't think he'll need it, but it'll be nice to get a moment to ourselves a whole six feet away from the family. As we're slipping back into the kitchen, Jonathan's hand still on the small of my back like it lives there, my work phone goes. "Fuck," I say, "sorry, I'll tell 'em to piss off."

"It's fine." Jonathan grins at me. "I can take the weight of a jug of Bisto."

"Hello," I say in my best clipped, professional tone, "Becker and Son plumbing." I'd not normally be taking a call during Christmas, but I'm trying to get the business off the ground in a new town and that means building a reputation for being obliging.

Jonathan brings the gravy back to the table while I'm explaining to the caller that this had better be a real fucking emergency (I use more polite words) because I'm having my bleeding Christmas dinner (I use more polite words than that too) and if it turns out he's just got a leaky tap, I'll be telling every other tradesman in Croydon that they're more trouble than they're worth (once again, politer in the moment).

"I'm really sorry," I tell the crowd, "there's a feller had his water go out, the whole family's round and, well, they need to be able to use their loos. It's just on Sandrock Place and I'm hoping it'll be a quick one."

Jonathan kisses me goodbye and tells me to hurry back, I tell him I will and ask the family to take care of him while I'm gone. It's sort of a ritual, but it's one we all like.

"Took care of him his whole life," Wendy says, "I can manage another hour. Be safe and wrap up warm."

As I'm grabbing my coat I hear a crash, and turn to see Gollum sitting on the floor, next to the remains of the just-refilled gravy boat.

"It's fine," Ralph is saying, "if the carpet needs replacing, I've still got contacts."

And it is. Fine, I mean. I head out to the van and though I'd rather not be taking a call out I'm not bothered. Because I know when I get back I'll have everybody waiting for me.

The cat. The family.

And Jonathan fucking Forest.

GLITTERLAND

In the past, the universe is a glitterball I hold in the palm of my hand.

In the past, I am brilliant and I am happy and my every tomorrow is madness.

In the past, I am soaring, and falling, and breaking, and lost.

And now, there is only this.

Once the golden boy of the English literary scene, now a clinically depressed writer of pulp crime fiction, Ash Winters has given up on hope, happiness, and—most of all—himself. He lives his life between the cycles of his illness, haunted by the ghosts of other people's expectations.

Then a chance encounter throws him into the path of Essex-born Darian Taylor. Flashy and loud, radiant and full of life, Darian couldn't be more different...and yet he makes Ash laugh, reminding him of what it's like to step beyond the boundaries of his anxiety. But Ash has been living in his own shadow for so long that he can no longer see a way out. Can a man who doesn't trust himself ever trust in happiness? And how can someone who doesn't believe in happiness ever fight for his own?

1

Now

MY HEART IS BEATING SO fast it's going to trip over itself and stop. Everything is hot and dark. I've been buried alive. I'm already dead.

I have just enough grip on reality to discard these notions, but it doesn't quell my horror. My mouth is dry, strange and sour, my tongue as thick as carpet. Alcohol-heavy breath drags itself out of my throat, the scent of it churning my stomach. I'm pickled in sweat. And there's an arm across my chest, a leg across my legs. I am manacled in flesh.

god, god, fuck, god, fuck

My body is far too loud. Blood roaring, heart thundering, breath screaming, stomach raging, head pounding.

I'm going to have a full-blown panic attack.

The first in a long time. Except that's not much consolation.

Where am I? What have I…

out, fuck, have to get out

I twist away from the arm and the leg, rolling off a bare mattress onto bare floorboards. Maybe my first instinct was right. I am dead and this is hell. The darkness scrapes against my eyes. Where are the rest of my clothes?

And breathe, I need to breathe more. Or breathe less. Stop the light show in my head. My vision sheets red and black, like a roulette wheel spinning too fast, never stopping.

god, fuck, clothes

Scattered somewhere in the void. Trousers, shirt, waistcoat, jacket, a single sock. My fingers close over my phone. A cool, calming talisman.

Half-dressed, everything else bundled in my arms, I ease open the door, dark spilling into dark and, like Orpheus, I'm looking back. The shadows move across his face, but he doesn't stir. He sleeps the perfect, heedless sleep of children, drunkards, and fools.

My footsteps creak along a narrow hallway of peeling paintwork and I let myself out onto a wholly unfamiliar street.

NEXT

Breathe, just keep breathing. Keep breathing, and get away.

I stumbled down the pavement, the awfulness of this—this and everything—hanging off my shoulders like a rucksack full of rocks.

Still no idea where I was. Suburbia spiralling away in all directions. And, at the horizon, a haze of pale light where the distant sea met the distant sky. I fumbled for my phone. 3:41.

god, fuck, god

There was a single blip of battery left. I called Niall. He didn't answer. So I called again. And this time he did. I didn't wait for him to speak.

"I don't know where I am." My voice rang too high even in my own ears.

"Ash?" Niall sounded strange. "What do you mean? Where are you?"

"I just said. I don't know. I... I've been stupid. I need to get home."

I couldn't control my breathing. The most basic of human functions and even that was beyond me.

"Can't you call a cab?"

"Yes...no... I don't know. I don't know. I don't know the number. What if it doesn't come? I don't know." Anxieties were swimming around inside me like jellyfish, but I was usually better at not confessing them aloud.

It hadn't occurred to me to get a taxi, but even the idea of it seemed overwhelming in its magnitude. A quagmire of potential disaster that was utterly terrifying.

"Can you come and get me?" I asked.

Later I would see how pathetic it was, my desperate pleading, the weasel thread of manipulative weakness running through my words. Later, I would remember that calling for a taxi was an everyday event, not an ordeal beyond reckoning. Later, yes, later I would drown in shame and hate myself.

Niall's hollow sigh gusted over the line. "Oh God, Ash, can't you—"

"No, no, I can't. Please, I need to go home."

A pause. Then the inevitable, "Okay, okay, I'm coming. Can you at least find a street sign? Give me some idea where you are?"

Phone clutched in my sweat-slick hand, I ran haphazard along the houses. The curtains were shut as tight as eyes.

"Marlborough Street," I said. "Marlborough Street."

"All right. I'll be there. Just... I'll be there."

I sat down on a wall to wait, irrational panic eventually giving way to a dull pounding weariness. There was a packet of cigarettes in my jacket pocket. I wasn't supposed to have cigarettes, but I was already so fucked that I lit one, grey smoke curling lazily into the grey night.

Don't drink, don't smoke, don't forget to take your medication, don't break your routine. Nobody had ever explicitly said, "Don't have casual sex with strange men in unfamiliar cities," but it was probably covered in the "Don't have any fun ever" clause. The truth was, casual sex was about the only sex I could stand these days. On my own terms, when I could control everything. And myself.

But tonight I'd broken all the rules and I was going to pay the price. I could feel it, the slow beat of water against the crumbling cliffs of my sanity. I was going to crash. I was going to crash so hard and deep it would feel as though there was nothing inside me but despair. The cigarette, at least, might hold it off until I got home.

I lost track of time, my nerves deadened with nicotine and my skin shivering with cold. But, eventually, Niall pulled up, and leaned across the seats to thrust open the passenger door.

"Come on," he said.

He was shirtless and tousled, a pattern of dark red bruise-kisses running from elbow to shoulder.

"I'm sorry." I stamped out my cigarette (how many had I smoked?) and climbed in.

He didn't reply, just shifted gears abruptly and drove off. I rested my head against the window, watching the streets of Brighton blurring at the corners of my eyes. The motorway, when we came to it, was nothing but a streak of moving darkness.

Niall's fingers were tapping a tense rhythm against the steering wheel. He'd known me since university, back when I was different. We'd been friends, lovers, partners, and now this. Pilgrim and burden.

"I'm sorry," I tried again.

Silence filled up the car, mingling with the darkness.

ABOUT THE AUTHOR

Alexis Hall writes books in the southeast of England, where he lives entirely on a diet of tea and Jaffa Cakes. You can find him at:

Website: quicunquevult.com
Instagram: @quicunquevult
Twitter: @quicunquevult